Games & Players

Manna Francis

CASPERIAN
BOOKS

The author wishes to dedicate this book to everyone on the FC list. If she'd never found you, none of this would have been written.

www.casperianbooks.com

Cover illustration by Orit "Shin" Heifets.

Cover photograph "CrissCross" by Tabassum Fakier.

ISBN-10: 1-934081-10-8
ISBN-13: 978-1-934081-10-5

Table of Contents

Game, Set

Chapter One

❖

No one had told *her,* which had a surprise factor of minus several million. Why would anyone bother to tell her anything? All she had to do was reorganize Toreth's caseload, arrange facilities for the visitor, and generally turn her life upside down. But, of course, she wasn't *important* enough to be told.

The first Sara knew about it was on Monday, when a second desk arrived for Toreth's office. When she politely inquired what the hell was going on, she didn't get any sensible reply, beyond the information that the orders were from somewhere nonspecifically "higher up." Toreth himself had been called in to a meeting with Tillotson first thing, and he hadn't reappeared.

So she went to work on the comm, but the only story of note circulating was that there was a socioanalyst in the building, assignment unknown. That was old news. Toreth had met him late on Friday afternoon, when he'd spoken to senior paras from several sections, but she'd gone home before the meeting had ended. Hopefully there was no connection to the new desk, because she didn't fancy the idea of a spook in the office. She'd never met one, but she'd heard they were extremely creepy.

By the time Toreth came back from Tillotson's office, she was nearly biting her nails with impatience. From his air of restrained fury, she guessed the news wasn't good. Before she could say anything, he stormed past her into his office. She followed him in and almost ran into him. He'd stopped inside the doorway to survey the new arrangement. "What's going on?" she asked.

"I'm resigning, that's what's going on." He stalked over to his own desk and started sweeping up bits and pieces. "I'm going to clear my desk, and go back to tell Tillotson exactly where he can shove his fucking job, with illustrations, and then I'm going out to get hammered enough to forget the whole fucking morning."

She stared at him, horrified by the sincerity in his voice. All she could manage to say was, "Really?"

A long silence followed, then he dropped everything back on the desk. "No, of course not really. But I was this fucking close." He threw himself into his chair, just catching the edge of the desk as he nearly went over backwards. "*This* fucking close."

"What's wrong?"

"What isn't wrong? I've been—" And he stopped, lost for words, which was something worth seeing. "I've been given to this fucking spook as some kind of bloody errand boy. Like a . . . a . . . like a *pet*. His own personal . . . it's outrageous. I'm a bloody senior. Tillotson stood there and as good as told me that if I don't give the smarmy fucker—"

"Should I come back later?" asked a velvet-smooth voice from behind her.

Sara turned and found herself looking up into the widest, bluest, deepest, most come-hither eyes she had ever seen on a man. Long, fine lashes swept down and up as he blinked slowly. When she managed to tear her gaze away from his, she unconsciously braced herself for disappointment, but the rest of the tall, blond, elegant package standing in the office doorway wasn't half bad either. Far too old, unfortunately—even older than Toreth. But still, God in heaven . . .

It took her several seconds before she could even try to frame a reply. Then she found she couldn't remember what he'd said. "I beg your pardon?"

"Am I interrupting? I can go away and come back, if I'm being a terrible nuisance." He smiled, nearly causing her to lose track of the conversation again. "Although I would like to start work some time this morning, if that's not *too* much of an imposition."

"Oh! You're the sp—" She caught herself barely in time, although what she'd meant to say was still blindingly obvious. Great first impression she was making here.

"Socioanalyst, yes. Jean-Baptiste Carnac." He offered his hand. "You must be Ms. Lovelady."

His hand enveloped hers, warm and dry, his grasp neither aggressively tight nor unappealingly limp. Perfect. "Mm. Yes. That's me." When he released her hand, she added faintly, "Call me Sara."

She thought she was prepared for it, but his smile dazzled her again. "Delighted to meet you, Sara, although I doubt you'd say the same about me, since I'm afraid I'll be making extra work for you."

"It'll be a pleasure." Behind her she heard something snap—hopefully nothing more exciting than the pencil Toreth had been holding. Time for a diversion before he started snapping anything else. "Look, why don't I show you where the section coffee room is, and generally do the tour and Toreth can," convince himself that killing a socioanalyst will look bad on his record, "get the office sorted out?"

Carnac glanced up over her shoulder. Toreth didn't say anything, but he must have managed a nod, because Carnac looked back into her eyes and said, "That would be tremendously kind of you, Sara."

8

So she took Carnac for coffee, thinking as she did that, old or not—and spook or not—she really wouldn't mind taking him for something else as well.

Chapter Two

❖

The surprise wasn't that Carnac wasn't particularly good at blowjobs, it was that he was willing to give them at all. They broke two rules which Toreth had come to see as central to the socioanalyst's entire existence: they stopped him from talking, and they interrupted the illusion that the world, solar system, and probably entire galaxy revolved solely around him.

Even Toreth could appreciate the irony of the complaint. But in a self-centered egotist competition, he was more than prepared to yield first place to the man currently on his knees in front of him. Not that he wasn't grateful, especially for the part where Carnac shut the fuck up for ten minutes. Even a not-terribly-good blowjob was better than none at all, and about a thousand times more enjoyable than listening to him talk.

It was a tough call, but he'd eventually decided that the theme "it's not easy being a socioanalyst, surrounded as one is by mundane minds who sabotage one's otherwise invariable success" was marginally more annoying than his diatribes on the deficiencies of I&I's systems and processes, or the lovingly detailed accounts of old cases. But more or less everything he said was irritating to a degree.

Sharing an office with the man was driving Toreth mad. He'd suggested to Carnac that Sara would be able to find him a room of his own, but Carnac had said he preferred to maximize interaction with the organization. Meaning that he didn't want to be sidelined in some cupboard at the far end of the building. Which, by a coincidence, was exactly what Toreth had been thinking of when he'd suggested it. So here they still were, together all day.

There had to be some kind of plea-in-mitigation that would allow him to get away with throttling Carnac. Self-defense of his sanity, perhaps.

The worst part wasn't the day-to-day irritation, or even the disruption to his current cases—Jesus, teeth were *not* what he wanted to feel at this point, but at least the sharp scrape dampened down his arousal and bought him another couple of minutes' silence. No, the worst part was that it was all his own bloody fault. If he'd just ignored Carnac when he arrived, some other poor bastard would be the recipient of his ever-open mouth. But a socioanalyst was a rare sight at I&I, and experience of working with one was a valuable career booster. Besides, the man could flirt at championship level. Toreth had never fucked a spook before—and wouldn't be fucking one again, without references—so he'd responded in kind. Curiosity killed the cat. Lucky fucking cat was all he could say, because the next thing he knew, Tillotson had called him into his office and handed him over to Carnac as his "personal liaison." Hah. He'd have to remember *that* one next time Sara asked him what Warrick was.

Sara was another source of annoyance because she thought Carnac was God's bloody gift. It was the only time he could recall her looking actively envious of him fucking anyone. Carnac had infinite reservoirs of charm for dealing with the admins and he had the whole section full of them eating out of the palm of his hand in a couple of days. So now there wasn't even anyone willing to hear Toreth's complaints. Probably for the best, because Sara would have ruptured something laughing.

It was, technically, sexual harassment, and he was almost tempted to make a complaint, if he could have stomached the utter humiliation. But Carnac got whatever he wanted from management, and since the fucking was the most bearable part of the whole experience, he probably ought not to tempt fate. At least the man had been quiet now for what?—he managed to check his watch discreetly—for ten blessed minutes.

This was the one kind of fucking which *did* shut him up. He'd never met anyone else who could talk so much during sex. It was frankly off-putting, trying to fuck someone to the accompaniment of musings on proximal and distal causation. Warrick was hardly a model of reticence, but at least when he managed anything more coherent than "Christ, yes, fuck me harder," it was still closely connected *to* fucking. He didn't start reanalyzing the hierarchical structure of I&I.

Now he'd started thinking about fucking Warrick—Warrick begging for him, Warrick pulling on chains and calling his name, Warrick's hair smelling of fresh sweat—and that was sending quite the wrong kind of signals to his cock. Desperately, he tried to force his mind back onto something dull, to buy a few more minutes' peace and quiet. Too late. He managed to hold back for just a few seconds, clenching his fists against the wall. Then he was coming, closing his eyes and saying Warrick's name, in the vain hope that Carnac would care enough to take offense and get a new senior para assigned.

He didn't, of course. He just stood up, wiping his mouth fastidiously and smiling, as Toreth tried to get his breathing back under control and refasten his clothes. There were moments, like now, when he was sure Carnac knew exactly how much Toreth detested him and was merely conducting a twisted experiment into how much he was willing to take for the sake of his CV before he told Carnac to go fuck himself. Toreth closed his eyes again, imagining how very satisfying that

11

would be. Especially if he added a succinct evaluation of Carnac's sexual prowess, or lack of it.

A delicate cough interrupted the happy fantasy. Opening his eyes, he found Carnac regarding him through a veil of yard-long lashes, which had once, very briefly, been attractive. As usual, he had the unnerving feeling that Carnac knew exactly what Toreth was thinking. "Shall we get back to work?" Carnac said. No— purred. The man actually purred.

Never, in his entire life, had Toreth wanted to finish an assignment as badly as he did this one.

Carnac loathed the assignment. He'd known that he would even before he'd been told what it was. It had been no more than the expected punishment for turning in the report he had been asked to make on his previous job, rather than the one they had wanted to read. Some things he wouldn't stoop to, though, and falsifying his conclusions was one of them. He might, as he often told himself, be prostituting his talents for the unappreciative Administration, but at least he wasn't faking the orgasms. Scant comfort at the moment when he was here, at the Investigation and Interrogation Division, assessing the probabilities of the employees becoming infected by the anti-Administration sentiments they heard during their working day. He hated the place, he hated the people, and most of all he hated the vindictive wasting of his time.

Forcing him to come here was the beginning of the persecution. He could have compiled the report without ever leaving Strasbourg. Predictive analyses of the social and psychological dynamics of large organizations were his bread and butter. From long-term group behaviors down to shorter-term individual futures, he could have dissected I&I no less effectively from the comfort of his office at the Socio-analysis Division.

There was little to no chance of any problems at I&I, because the staff, at least those who lay within his remit, were either functional sociopaths or one of a variety of other charming psychological aberrations that the Administration in its boundless wisdom had carefully channeled into the division. None of them were ever likely to be stricken by a sudden fit of conscience over the work they did; anyone who might actually possess the requisite emotional development had been weeded out during the rigorous training. The real danger of subversion lay with the admins and other support staff, who were somewhat closer to normal human beings. However, they had been excluded from his investigation, a move which, he suspected, had been designed purely to layer the icing of pointlessness thickly onto the cake of boredom. The only entertainment he could expect here was whatever he could make for himself.

When Carnac began an assignment that mandated actual contact with the subjects—always a bad start in his experience—he made it one of his first tasks to have a personal liaison assigned to him. Someone with a reasonable degree of seniority, who would be a direct link into the people under study. If the assignment mattered or was, God forbid, challenging, he would take care to choose a liaison who would provide the greatest amount of information and insight, and be most useful in smoothing the course of the investigation. If, like this current task, it was a piece of time-wasting nonsense dictated by internal politics, he picked them on looks and orientation. If he had to be bored, his reasoning went, he might as well at least enjoy some nonintellectual stimulation.

Carnac flirted with even-handed enthusiasm, but he fucked, and was fucked by, men. For preference, by attractive, well-built men with no desire to attempt any kind of intellectual relationship with him, which would only be profoundly unsatisfying for both parties. Val Toreth had been a natural choice on those grounds, and had proved more or less amenable to the physical requirements of his temporary role. He had also proved surprisingly interesting, or at least mildly unusual.

On assignments like this one, Carnac was used to being treated as something made up of five parts CV points, four parts freak and, if he was especially lucky, one part human being. It didn't bother him any more, except when people made painfully inept attempts to cover it up and pretend that they liked him. He knew that he wasn't naturally likeable—physically attractive, perhaps, but not likeable—and he'd long ago given up attempting to pretend to be anything other than what he was, unless being liked was required. That kind of game-playing interfered with his work, and it took up energy better used elsewhere.

Toreth didn't like him, and he didn't pretend to. He had been willing enough to return his interest at first meeting, probably out of curiosity, and to take up Carnac's offer of a drink, a meal and, subsequently, an hour or two in his hotel room. The next day, though, when Tillotson had accepted without question the request for Toreth's more official assignation, the para-investigator had been thoroughly disgusted by the turn of events and hadn't even attempted to hide it.

That was partly Tillotson's fault, of course. It had been painful to watch him antagonizing Toreth further with every word. Whatever his administrative talents, staff management did not number among them. Eventually, he'd asked Carnac to leave them alone, but Carnac could easily imagine the rest of the conversation, complete with heavy-handed threats as to what would happen if the unwelcome visitor wasn't kept happy. By the time he'd seen Toreth again, the man had been positively incandescent.

Fortunately, the change of general attitude hadn't affected Toreth's willingness to participate in the less official parts of his assignment; the air of sullen resentment with which he complied with Carnac's requests had its own subtle charm. And as a liaison, Toreth had additional redeeming qualities.

13

For one thing, he generally stayed silent unless spoken to. When addressed directly, he gave a direct and useful response, and shut up again. This allowed Carnac to continue his own train of thought with minimum interruptions—most other people's idea of conversation bored him terribly. For another thing, he couldn't recall Toreth asking him a single personal question, or even a question about his job as a socioanalyst. On the occasions when he said anything spontaneously, it was work-related, intelligent, and relevant. Years of answering moronic inquiries for the thousandth time made this a novel and restful experience.

In another division, his first thought would have been to put his silence down to the man's general dislike of him. However, here in I&I, the explanation was obvious: Toreth simply didn't care. He had no interest in other people's lives, unless he was torturing the information out of them, or hunting for clues, or had some other practical use for the data. His psych file described excellent observational skills and memory for details, both material and psychological, and Carnac duly noted the man's need to categorize and gain control over his environment. People as people, though, didn't matter to Toreth. In fact, they barely even existed as anything other than problems or toys. He appeared at first glance to be a classic, and therefore rather dull, result of I&I's policy of recruitment from the tail end of the human bell curve.

Carnac had held that opinion for a day or so until he had, quite by chance, overheard Toreth and Sara talking. It had only been for a few minutes, but it had demonstrated to his satisfaction that to Toreth, Sara was, for want of a better word, "real." To a trained observer, the subtle differences in their interaction stood out starkly. In another situation, Carnac wouldn't even have consciously noted the existence of a commonplace friendship. Here it had broken his model of Toreth, and that was enough to pique his interest. His first thought had been, "Why her?" Sara herself was nothing special, no more nor less than what she appeared to be. Indeed, whatever interest she held came from the fact that she was so straightforward, a trait he rarely encountered, especially within Administration departments. He marked it as a possible contributing factor to Toreth's attitude towards her.

Suitably charmed, Sara had proved to be a bountiful source of information about Toreth. Carnac had been intrigued to discover the existence of someone referred to by Sara as Toreth's "regular fuck" (did that make Carnac himself an irregular fuck?), whom he noted as a second potentially real person in Toreth's life. When he discovered this person had held the position for approximately eighteen months, his interest had been sharpened again. Not that the man was exactly a scintillating web of complexity, but he was a mildly intriguing aberration. So, to occupy his copious free time in this mind-numbing assignment, Carnac had decided to see what it took to make oneself real to a personality-disordered para-investigator. Or at least more real than the general masses.

His own job was, in some aspects, not so very different from the interrogation part of Toreth's, distasteful as the thought was. He sat in his spacious office and wrote his reports, while Toreth worked here, in this awful place with its windowless rooms and hospital smell. They were both manipulators, though, persuading people to do things they may not want to, but couldn't help, Carnac directing organizations with his delicate, subtle alterations of environments and psychological pressures, Toreth focusing on the individual, using his drugs and nerve-induction equipment.

It gave them something in common, even if Toreth was unlikely to see the similarities, and it would be interesting to see if the parallels might be turned into an emotional connection of some kind. Considering the time available, he had set himself the modest goal of three or more personal conversations, or an invitation to the man's flat. He would award himself a bonus prize for an offer of an introduction to the regular fuck, who sounded rather interesting in his own right.

Doctor Keir Warrick. He'd met someone of that name years ago at the Data Division Encryption Unit, during one of his first assignments. At the time, the man had been a humble Administration researcher, although even then he had impressed Carnac as someone with *potential*. It was rare enough to meet an original mind, or at least a mind capable of the occasional original thought. If his old acquaintance was indeed Toreth's regular fuck, it would be a coincidence, but coincidences happened all the time. Only the general mass of humanity, pathetically incapable of dealing with even the simplest probabilistic concepts, would read anything into it. The odds were very high that it was the same man, given the details he had obtained from Sara.

It would be interesting to see how Keir's potential had unfolded, or if, like so many other people Carnac had met, it had been eradicated by the grind of daily life. In this case, the latter seemed unlikely, given his achievements. The concept of computer-simulated realities was intriguing, and also a field Carnac knew delightfully little about. There were few enough of those left.

Toreth hadn't told him anything about Warrick, of course, and it would be a violation of his self-imposed rules for this project to broach the subject without some lead-in. But from the details Sara had disclosed, it was obvious that Toreth's affections, such as they were, were thoroughly engaged. That regrettably decreased the number of available approaches towards him. Carnac had no illusions that mere sex would be enough to generate any meaningful connection. For the time being, he settled for maintaining Toreth's awareness of him as more than part of the furniture by annoying him. It had the advantage of requiring very little more than Carnac's normal, unmoderated behavior.

It wouldn't be enough, but it would do for the time being. Something else would come along, Carnac felt sure.

15

Chapter Three

❖

On Thursday morning, the fourth day of Carnac's unwelcome occupation of his office, Sara came in with an expression suggesting that she thought she had interesting gossip. "He knows Warrick," she announced.

"Who knows Warrick?" Toreth asked, knowing perfectly well whom she meant, but hoping in vain it would be someone else. Carnac was out of his hair this morning, bothering the psych assessors about their profiling techniques, and he'd rather not have to think about the man more than necessary.

"Carnac knows him. From years ago, I think, but he definitely knows him. Isn't that a weird coincidence?"

"Not really." And not that he cared if it was. She looked disappointed, but before she could say anything else an unpleasant idea struck him. "Why was he talking about Warrick at all?"

Sara stared at him for a moment, and he could see the lies racing behind her eyes. Luckily for his fragile temper, she didn't use any of them. "I, um, think I mentioned him first. He, er, asked about you. Whether you, um..."

"Whether I, um, *what*?"

"Whether you had a regular thing going on."

He felt his anger poised, balanced on a knife-edge between Sara and Carnac. Then it tipped decisively. *Bastard.* What the fuck was he playing at? "And you just told him?" he asked.

She shook her head, but it wasn't a denial. "I—yes. Yes, I did. God, I'm sorry." She did sound it, which was slightly mollifying. "I don't know why...I didn't think."

"No, you didn't." He was angry enough for some to spill over. "You were too busy gazing into his bright blue fuck-me eyes, weren't you? Well, you're wasting your time. Unless you're planning on having the operation, you don't have a prayer."

"Really?" She actually looked a little crestfallen, and his jaw clenched. He

16

took a deep breath. Not her fault, he told himself firmly. Carnac had been fishing, obviously, and he could hardly be expected not to land her. When would the man finish here, fuck off, and stop disordering Toreth's nice, quiet life?

He ought to ask what else she'd said, but he didn't want to hear it. "Just go away," he said. "Go away, and try not to tell him anything more. If there *is* anything you haven't told him already."

He watched her go, then called up the list of prisoners with currently active high-level damage waivers. Time to see if he couldn't find something to encourage Carnac on his way.

At the end of the first week, Carnac sat in his hotel room, listening to music and reading interrogation transcripts that he wished he had in hard-copy form so that he could tear every page into tiny pieces and flush them down the toilet. He had arrived at I&I with a conviction that interrogation was crude, wasteful, and barbaric, and nothing he had learned since had shaken that. However, he had added revolting and grotesque to the collection of adjectives.

Despite the futility of the investigation, he had conscientiously created a project outline that required, among other things, numerous initial interviews with interrogators, investigators, and their hybrid cousins, the para-investigators. Job titles had made little difference to his findings.

His subjects had varied in attitude from bored to hostile. Questions about aspects of the job they found unpleasant had elicited a range of baffled expressions, and an impressive list of management, procedural, and paperwork grievances. Faced with prisoner and interrogation scenarios which could be expected to provoke sympathy and outrage in actual human beings, they had given answers that might have been lifted verbatim from the I&I training manual. Except that, of course, they hadn't been. The replies were spontaneous and they had genuinely believed every word. The last faint hopes that he might discover something unexpected (that, say, the Administration's carefully trained monstrosities were all secret bleeding hearts who faked their interrogation transcripts) were quickly dashed.

Even with his self-created hobby project, it was still simultaneously one of the dullest and the most distasteful assignments Carnac had ever experienced.

On the fourth day of his sentence (as he was beginning to think of it), at the end of an afternoon spent going over some of the theoretical aspects of interrogation, Toreth had said to him, "You know, you ought to see this stuff firsthand. I could arrange something for tomorrow, if you've got the time." In other words, "You've come to poke your nose into our work, so can you handle seeing it?" A pointless, irritating test of machismo. Regrettably, it was also absolutely necessary that he go through with it if he was to expect any cooperation within the division.

It would be worth putting up with anything, he had thought, to make the stay there shorter.

On reflection, he could almost count that as one of his rare misjudgments. He would give a great deal not to have the memory of today, ready to spring to mind in the future whenever he casually included "send for interrogation" in a strategy outline.

Toreth had actually enjoyed it. Not the interrogation per se (which was, after all, merely a day's work for him), but the opportunity to demonstrate his profession to an outsider who might appreciate it. He had, in essence, been showing off, making it a textbook job for Carnac's benefit. That it was also clearly intended to traumatize the unwanted spook was quite a separate issue.

From a purely technical viewpoint, Toreth was very good at it. Horrendously, stomach-turningly good. He'd even managed to work in a running commentary, with only a small reduction in the efficiency of the interrogation. It had added, perhaps, an extra twenty minutes of suffering for the prisoner and for Carnac.

Empathy was a requirement for a socioanalyst. He knew how other people thought, what they felt. What they wanted, what made them too afraid to try to obtain it, what would tip them over one edge or another. It was an instinctive skill that he could no longer switch off. Usually, though, the knowledge was applied at a distance. He worked through the filter of security files, psych profiles, and the compiled results of research and thousands of case studies. He proposed and others disposed. This had been a new experience for him.

Minds, personalities, psyches—these were Carnac's stock in trade. Tedious as he found most people in the flesh, he'd never realized how ghastly it would be to see someone being destroyed in front of him. To watch Toreth find every crack, every emerging weakness, and to exploit them mercilessly to strip away another layer of resistance. Turning the prisoner into the thing Toreth required, not the person he had been before he entered this hell.

When one thoroughly understood how people in general behaved, people in the particular became dismally predictable. Sitting in that room, trying not to listen to what was being said and done, he'd known exactly what would happen from the moment they'd brought in the prisoner. He'd read the man's file and it had been nothing if not profoundly ordinary. Mildly surprising, in fact, that someone so average had found the determination to rebel against Administration rule. In a way, the worst part had been knowing that the man would break in the end, and that all the pain and degradation his resistance generated was ultimately futile. Knowing, indeed, when he would break and that it wouldn't be yet. After an hour or two he'd had to fight back the urge to plead with the prisoner to give it up, for both their sakes.

There had been one positive outcome from the interrogation: he had always been curious about the phrase, "the stench of fear." Emotions seemed to be an unlikely source of an olfactory experience. Well, now he understood.

18

"He'll crack tomorrow," Toreth had said with casual, uncaring confidence, after the guards had finally taken the man back to his cell. "Of course, there's no real need to do it—the woman we arrested with him has already talked. She didn't have the same quality of interrogation resistance treatments he'd had. But he came in with a level eight waiver, so I thought he'd make a good example. Do you want to finish it off in the morning? I know it's Saturday, but I can come in if you'd like to see it."

He'd managed a polite refusal, although by that time he could cheerfully have murdered Toreth, and every other interrogator in the building, so that what he had just witnessed would never happen to another human being again. For a few irrational minutes he had wanted nothing more than to get away from the interrogation building, throw up, and resign from the Socioanalysis Division, even if it meant he had to sleep on the streets for the rest of his natural life. It had passed, of course—his training carried him through moments like that. Then, as they had walked through the endless security doors, back up to the relative sanity of the investigation levels, Toreth had turned to him and asked, "So, do you want to fuck?" It had been the only time since they'd met that he had directly initiated the sex.

Once they were back in the office, Carnac had let him fuck him, because the distraction of having Toreth inside him was better than dwelling on the memory of what he'd watched the man do. They had to work together for the remainder of the assignment, after all. It was the first time they had got as far as penetration, but there wasn't a great deal of discussion involved, merely a gesture inquiring whether he preferred the wall or desk. He'd decided the desk would be easier on his calves. Neither was there any question about who would be doing what to whom.

Toreth was a talented partner, when he made the effort to be. That time he had been calculating and controlled. Minimal foreplay, and then Toreth's weight above him, deliberately applied. He'd hurt him—not much, just enough to make a point—and he'd made sure that Carnac came first. After that he had held him down on the desk as he finished, fucking him hard, not making any sound at all as he came. Then he'd pulled out and walked off, leaving Carnac flat on the desk, sticky and breathless.

On reflection, an entertainingly stereotypical display of dominance and territoriality, pressing home, so to speak, his physical superiority and training. Carnac hadn't cared. In fact, he'd rather enjoyed it, apart from a forgetful moment later on when, sitting down on a too-hard chair, his eyes had crossed so far that he'd briefly stared down his own optic nerves.

Toreth, of course, had been hoping that the brutal sex and the interrogation would in combination encourage him to ask for a new departmental liaison. Far from it. Carnac had encountered enough apprehension and cringing respect in the course of his career that Toreth's attitude was, at least, refreshing. If he'd cared about the job in hand, it would have been different. As it was, it simply let him know that he had succeeded in making Toreth take notice of him.

19

He might try Sara again on Monday. She had become unexpectedly reticent over the last couple of days, which probably meant that she had let slip to Toreth that Carnac had been asking questions about him. Annoying, but there had been no practical way to keep her quiet. In any case, he suspected he had already got most of the useful information out of her, and what she had held back would be inconveniently difficult to extract. He put down the transcripts and considered his progress so far. What *had* he learned from Sara?

Reading between the lines—not a challenge with the woman—Toreth seemed to have had an uninterestingly unpleasant childhood, which held some explanations, but no immediately useful leverage. It had been impressive that she knew anything about it at all (further unrequired evidence that Toreth had a genuine relationship with his admin), and mildly interesting that she had actually met his parents. Unfortunately, the details of the encounter had fallen under "information held back."

She had also slept with him, as Carnac had suspected she must have. Just once, and there had been no explanation offered as to why, although according to her, one or two encounters seemed to be a modal length relationship for Toreth.

That was an interesting fact in itself—an interesting pathology. Perhaps he had been mistaken in his earlier assessment, and continued sexual contact might yield results through sheer repetition: familiarity breeding intimacy, rather than contempt. It was worth a try, as well as being what he had planned to do anyway. Now that he had made his impression, it might be time to see if he could moderate Toreth's view of him from dislike to something more suitable for his project.

Chapter Four

❖

They returned to Warrick's flat after a morning at the gym that had, unusually, failed to put Toreth in a better mood. That was a shame, because he'd only recently managed to chivvy Warrick along to the gym at all. Swimming was about the only thing that he would find time for, although Toreth suspected (immodestly) that it had more to do with seeing him wet and mostly naked than any enthusiasm for exercise. Although he didn't know why that should be such a draw, when Warrick could see him wet and entirely naked any time he wanted to.

Arriving back at the flat, they'd drifted automatically to the bedroom. But instead of a warm post-exercise buzz, Toreth felt irritable and restless and, worst of all, he couldn't stop thinking about Carnac. Not anything very specific, just the general awareness of his presence in the city; the fact that the man would be in I&I when he got in tomorrow morning; and that unless he'd had a personality transplant over the weekend, he'd be as much of a fucking nuisance as ever.

Toreth took his shirt off and stared moodily into the mirror. How long did it take to work up to permanent frown lines? Fuck that—he'd end up with gray hairs if he didn't get his office back to himself soon. And right *now*, even when he wasn't present, Carnac was still annoying him. Worse, he was cutting into his time with Warrick.

"Toreth?"

He looked around to find Warrick lying on his stomach on the bed, with his feet resting against the headboard, watching him. His expression was more or less neutral, but judging by the way his clothes were scattered on the floor rather than folded on a chair, he was keen for company. Toreth discovered, rather to his surprise, that he wasn't in the mood. "I think I might go home."

"Oh. All right." Flattering disappointment, but not flattering enough to make him change his mind. "But before you go, are you going to tell me what's wrong?"

"Why the fuck should anything be wrong?"

Warrick gave him one of his particularly patient looks, which were an inspi-

21

ration to homicide even under normal circumstances. As an alternative to strangling him, Toreth decided to tell him about Carnac. "Work."

If Warrick didn't want to hear about I&I, he shouldn't ask, but Toreth thought he'd give him a chance to object. When Warrick didn't say anything, Toreth sat down on the small sofa under the window and continued. "We've been saddled with a socioanalyst who's checking us for subversive tendencies. I'd rather have Internal Audit for six months. It's all bollocks, anyway. The last time anyone got arrested for anti-Administration activities was years ago. And that was a bunch of admins down on level three—it was nothing to do with *us*."

He could hear a petulant edge creeping into his voice. Warrick was listening with sympathy, though, or at least what passed at a glance as a working imitation, and Toreth was enjoying the chance to vent his irritation too much to look more closely. "Mind you, if he stays much longer, *everyone* will be turning political. I'm surprised no one's thumped him yet. I swear Mike Belkin was getting close, but even he knows better than to fuck with a socioanalyst." Unlike Toreth himself, unfortunately. "But do you know what he's been asking people? Trained paras? 'Have you ever experienced a feeling of admiration for the willingness of political prisoners to suffer for their beliefs?' Jesus Christ. Socioanalysis must be staffed by morons. No one who gives a shit about that sort of thing makes it through the first week of training at I&I."

He noticed that Warrick's gaze had shifted away to a point about a meter left of his shoulder, so he decided to drop that line of complaint. "The real pisser is that *I've* been stuck with the job of nannying the bastard until he finally writes his report and fucks off. 'Personal liaison,' which means I have to hand most of my cases over to someone else and follow him around, doing sod all useful."

Or sod quite a lot, actually. Too much, which wasn't something he said very often. He was beginning to feel as if a layer of Carnac was sticking to his skin, contaminating him. Stupid idea. He dismissed it. "I've had a wonderful week of it. The rest of the paras clam up if I get within three meters of them, because they're worried about what I'll pass on to him. And Sara's following him around, practically drooling on the floor, just because he's a world-class fucking flirt and he gave her the full blue-eyes-and-killer-smile treatment when he first showed up."

And not that I fell for it as well. Oh, no.

"What's his name?" Warrick asked, which was an unexpected question since Toreth hadn't even mentioned yet that they were fucking.

"Carnac. Actually, he told Sara he knew you."

"Well, well." Warrick was smiling, and Toreth had the feeling that he hadn't needed to be told the name. "Talks a lot, does he? At inopportune moments?"

"Yes, he does. You have met him, then?"

But now Warrick had started to laugh. "Yes, I've met him. Rather more than 'met,' in fact."

Toreth stared. "He *fucked* you?"

Warrick raised his eyebrows. "Is it really *that* improbable that he might have been interested in me?"

"No. No, of course not. I meant—" He groped for words, and settled for Sara's. "It's a weird coincidence."

"Yes, I suppose it is. Anyway, it was years back, when I was working for the Administration. I'm surprised he even remembers me. He was studying the psychology of security systems. Very good work, as I recall. I haven't met many socioanalysts, but he was the best I've seen."

Oh, God. He wasn't sure if he could bear to hear Warrick singing Carnac's praises. "If he's so good, why is he pissing his time away at I&I?"

"I have no idea. Of course, if he's still contracted to the Administration, then he'll have to do whatever projects they give him. I do know he had some moral objection to working for corporates."

"*Moral* objection?" Not an easy word to connect with the Carnac he knew and loathed. "What kind of moral objection?"

"You'll have to ask him. I never did."

"Was he as bloody annoying then as he is now?"

"Well..." Warrick considered for a moment. "Not to me. I admit it helps if you get to know him, though, and many people would probably say it wasn't worth the effort. I thought he was...an interesting person. But I can't imagine ever considering him as a close friend."

"I know him well enough to know that he's a waste of office space." That wasn't entirely true, but it was a relief to find one person who wasn't a committed member of the Carnac fan club. "And that he certainly didn't learn much from *you* about sucking cocks."

A moment's stillness, then Warrick grinned. "You say the sweetest things."

"Fuck off." He looked at Warrick closely, feeling mildly aggrieved that he was discussing the situation so calmly. This wasn't Toreth's usual one-night thing and he felt, somehow, that it ought to get more of a reaction. "Do you mind?"

"Mind what?"

"That he's...that I'm fucking him?"

Warrick shrugged, relaxed and blatantly unconcerned. Or was that "ostentatiously unconcerned?" "Well now, that would entirely depend on whether you were enjoying it. And if so, how much."

"The actual fucking isn't bad. It's just the rest of the time that I want to kill him."

"Then no, I don't mind." Warrick cocked his head, half smiling. "Or would you prefer that I did? Should I declare a proprietorial interest? Perhaps get you labeled?" He drew a little rectangle in the air. "'This para-investigator belongs to...'"

He wasn't putting up with *that*. "Get up."

Warrick looked at him for a moment, unmoving, smile still in place. "So you *would* prefer it?"

Oh, yes. Provocation, and Warrick knew he'd have to pay for it.

"You'll know if I want you to do anything, because I'll *tell* you to do it. Right now I'm telling you to come here." He paused, Warrick lying still and watching him. "Come here," he repeated.

"No, I don't think so."

Toreth had quite forgotten that he'd been leaving and that he wasn't in the mood. Warrick wasn't keen on keeping much gear here in his own flat, but that didn't matter. Props were fun, but unnecessary, and he could always improvise. He got off the sofa and stood over the bed, looking down at Warrick. "You don't bloody learn, do you? How complicated is it?"

Warrick made a move to get off the bed, quick, but nowhere near quick enough. Brief struggle, then Toreth was pinning him down easily as he twisted. Holding him tight, but not hurting him. Not yet. Soon, he'd want it, although he'd still complain about the bruises afterwards. Toreth could tune it so finely, so easily, these days, giving Warrick exactly what he needed. That was the satisfying part of this . . . regular thing.

He lowered his head and bit, hard, turning the uneven breaths into moans. Swimming-pool-clean body, beginning to take on a tang of sweat. Pulling away a little, he watched the marks turning red against Warrick's pale skin. "Now, are you going to keep still?"

Warrick didn't say anything—maybe couldn't—but he didn't stop struggling, which Toreth was delighted to interpret as a "no." Reaching down onto the floor, he swept his hand around until he found Warrick's discarded trousers, and pulled the belt free. A loop around Warrick's wrists, and he buckled it tight. Then he rolled away and sat up, arms around his knees, looking down at Warrick. He always enjoyed watching him like this, when he was so caught up in the game. Warrick twisted against the leather strap, his shoulders flexing, his chest heaving. Probably more exercise than he'd got at the gym.

Eyes closed, dark hair disarrayed and starting to curl with sweat. Pale skin, marked by Toreth's mouth. Panting through parted lips, mouth twisting as he writhed. Toreth had done this to him, and the idea held a kick like a drug. He wanted to fuck him now, and he wanted to wait, to watch, to make it last. And if it didn't last this time, it didn't matter, because they could do it again later. Tomorrow. Some time. Many times.

Wonderful regular thing.

Finally, Warrick opened his eyes. Dark, dark eyes, asking for it before his mouth did. "Fuck me."

Chapter Five

❖

Carnac worked as Toreth watched him, appearing oblivious to the scrutiny. He was also quiet, which improved Toreth's mood considerably. In fact, for whatever reason, Carnac had been astonishingly tolerable so far this week. That was mildly annoying in itself, since it meant he'd wasted all that irritated apprehension over the weekend. Admittedly, it was only Tuesday afternoon, which gave the bastard more than half the week to return to aggravating form, but if Carnac could manage to keep it up until he finished his pointless investigation, Toreth might even not have to kill him. That made him think of the conversation he'd had with Warrick. "Carnac?"

He looked up, eyebrows lifting with surprise at the interruption. "Yes?"

"Are you Administration or corporate?"

Carnac leaned back in his chair, steepling his fingers. "Is that a personal question?"

Toreth blinked. "Well, yeah, I suppose so. Forget I asked."

"No, no, I don't object to answering, I merely wished to clarify the context." He smiled, looking distinctly self-satisfied. "I'm neither. I freelance."

"So what the hell are you doing here?"

"Ah. I do not, alas, freelance all the time. I'm still paying off my training obligation to the Administration. At the moment I'm thirty-four point six percent freelance, which works out to one hundred and twenty-six point two nine days a year when I can do as I please, and two hundred and thirty-eight point seven one during which," he reached out and tapped a pile of papers, "I have to plow through tedious shit like this."

Toreth might have been offended, if he hadn't had exactly the same opinion of the enterprise. "You can't find a corporation to pay it off for you?"

"Easily. However, that would merely result in transforming an onerous debt to the Administration into a far more onerous debt to a corporation."

"No free payoffs available?"

Carnac shook his head. "The training cost for a fully qualified socioanalyst is approximately three orders of magnitude greater than that of a para-investigator. Corporations are understandably reluctant to offer any deal that does not guarantee a fair return on their investment. Most of the corporate definitions of 'a fair return' I've seen included the rest of my life, and the lives of my hypothetical unborn children, even unto the seventh generation. I don't find slavery to my tastes, so I prefer to buy my own freedom."

"Three orders of...?" Toreth whistled. "And you've got it down to under seventy percent? What the fuck do you charge?"

"What the laws of market forces dictate—not as much as I would like, but as much as people can afford. Why are *you* still working for the Administration? I'm certain that you could find a corporation willing to offer more generous terms."

"I like my life the way it is. Anyway, like you said, would it make any difference? I don't fall for 'the grass is greener.'"

Carnac nodded slowly. "No, of course not. May I ask a personal question?"

Something about his manner put Toreth's hackles up, but that was hardly unusual. "All right."

"I'm given to understand that you have a more long-term personal arrangement of some kind, outside I&I. I hope I won't be the cause of any difficulties?"

No point asking Carnac where he got his information. "No. No problem at all. He doesn't care."

Carnac's analytical talents seemed to be well up to the task of spotting a "fuck off and die" tone of voice, because he merely nodded again and returned to his work.

In his hotel room that evening, Carnac reviewed the progress of his official investigation (as uninspiringly good as could be expected) and his private study (also good, and more interesting).

His new approach seemed to be working out very well. One personal conversation, initiated by Toreth, was a significant payoff for two days of careful pleasantness. A third of the way to his first goal and, unfortunately, plenty more time to complete the project. At this rate he would be finished with Toreth long before his time at I&I expired. Sometimes winning was no fun.

The comm interrupted his thoughts. He was—delightfully—astonished to recognize the caller. "Keir Warrick! What a surprise, and I do mean that."

Keir smiled, and Carnac was delighted again to see that he understood why that was noteworthy. "I heard that you were in the area and I thought you might be at something of a loose end."

"Oh, you have no idea—never looser, regrettably. I take it that you're getting your information from an I&I employee?"

"Toreth seemed to think that the project was largely pointless."

"I don't mean any insult to him when I say that any idiot would notice that. The chance of finding anything intellectually rewarding in the assignment is—how does the fairy tale go? The king set the miller's daughter the impossible task of spinning straw into gold. That is a reasonable analogy, although I might pick a less fragrant substance than straw as a metaphor for that place. You have no idea how much I would give to move to something even half as interesting as the study at the DDEU."

"I can offer you dinner on Thursday, if that would do instead."

Carnac hesitated. Accepting the invitation would invalidate his aim of persuading Toreth to introduce him to Keir. On the other hand, refusing would deprive him of what would probably be an enjoyable evening. Moreover, he might be able to uncover some fresh information on his subject from a new source, now that Sara's shallow seam had been mined out—a consideration which tipped the balance in favor of accepting. He found himself smiling; that had been nicely rationalized. "A perfectly adequate substitute, yes," he told Warrick.

Anticipation of the evening to come had made the next two days at I&I the least unpleasant Carnac had suffered through since his arrival. The restaurant was the most neutral of neutral territories. Exclusively corporate, it wasn't, Carnac noted, cheap, but price mattered little to either of them. Keir remembered the past at least well enough to choose Oriental, Carnac's favorite. However, the lighting was bright, the service brisk, and the décor expensive but severe—not an ambience to encourage the renewal of old intimacies.

They perused the menu and ordered. As they waited for the food to arrive, Carnac tolerated a stretch of social conversation regarding work and the time that had passed since their last meeting. It wasn't too dull, because it gave him a brief overview of the sim, which sounded every bit as interesting as he had hoped. Probing the effect of hard-earned corporate status on the man he'd known as a scientist was almost as engaging. "Did you remember to vote today?" Carnac asked.

Warrick looked at him blankly. "I'm sorry?"

"Weren't the Parliament of the Regions elections today? I thought that the New London representative was on the list this year."

"Then I'm sure I did." Warrick smiled, the same neat, controlled expression Carnac remembered so fondly. "Corporate perks—I'm registered to submit my votes automatically."

"Arranged in what is no doubt the most socially correct manner."

"Truthfully? I don't remember the exact details." Warrick gave a small shrug. "I asked Gerry to set it up for me."

"You know, I've always admired your refreshing mix of idealism and pragmatism."

A tiny flicker of alarm creased Warrick's friendly demeanor. "Idealism?"

"In an intellectual sense, purely." Carnac held up his hand in apology. "Forgive me, I intended no unfortunate implication. All I meant was, you pursue truth at the expense of personal comfort. You could have taken your pick of Administration or corporate posts, and instead you chose to take a tremendous gamble in order to realize your dream, to put it rather tritely. And it has paid off handsomely, so I understand."

"I have no criticism of the Administration's voting system," Warrick said with emphasis, as though the latter comments hadn't even registered.

"I'm sure." Carnac couldn't resist. For someone like himself, in a place such as this, risk was negligible and could result in nothing worse than a reminder to remember the good name of Socioanalysis. "I admit that there's a Platonic beauty to the idea that we have finally achieved the pure distilled essence of universal democracy: providing the inept masses with the illusion of an influence over the state which they are utterly unqualified to exercise in actuality. Meanwhile, the Council rules in name, and the heads of departments rule in fact, and all is right in the Administration."

This time, Warrick remained silent. Carnac sighed to himself. Of course, he couldn't expect Keir to forget to whom he was speaking, and no doubt Toreth had informed him of the nature of Carnac's project at I&I. In the old days, though, Warrick might have answered. Somewhere along the roads they had traveled apart, he had learned more caution. Or Carnac himself had come to represent more of a threat.

"But then I suppose none of that is of much interest to you," Carnac said lightly. "Why should it be? The system suits both of us very well, and a corporate such as yourself has the opportunity for far more direct and personal contact with the arbiters of political power than mere votes can provide."

Warrick looked at him rather more sharply than Carnac felt the comment merited. Had Warrick been politicking heavily on behalf of SimTech? It seemed somewhat unlikely, from Carnac's knowledge of him, but not impossible. In the first instance, though, he felt an obligation to pursue his self-appointed inquiries into Toreth. The sim would wait until later.

After they had finished their first pass through the selection of dishes set out for them on the table, Carnac asked, "How is your lovely wife?"

"She's my lovely ex-wife."

"Ah. I thought she would be, by now. It was a mistake to marry her."

Keir paused, midselection, and looked at him thoughtfully. "Actually, I didn't think I had, when I saw you last."

"No, but you were going to. Still, all's well that ends well, and similar platitudes."

After a moment Keir said, "Don't you ever get bored of asking questions when you already know the answers?"

That offered a nice entry point. "Yes, but people seem to prefer it to my simply telling them what they think. However, here's a genuine question I *don't* know the answer to: how do you cope with Toreth?"

The switch clearly caught Keir off-guard. "With what about him?"

"The things he does in the course of his working day." Carnac cocked his head, ostentatiously considering. "You couldn't, of course. Which means you don't know, which means you haven't asked. And you most certainly haven't seen. I do believe I'm disappointed in you, Keir. I never thought you were the ostrich type."

He bridled slightly. "Not that it is any of your business, but I have seen."

Interesting. When? On reflection, it made sense that Keir would have made some effort to see with what he was getting involved. Carnac had always admired his intellectual honesty. "In that case, I apologize and withdraw the remark. And I return to my earlier question: how can you stand it?"

"You tell me. You're fucking him as well. How do you manage it?"

The unexpected crudity of the verb, or perhaps the crisp delivery, discomforted Carnac for a moment. He realized he had placed too much weight on Toreth's conviction that Keir wouldn't care about their temporary liaison. This might present a problem for his plans for Toreth. He reordered his approach and continued. "Irrelevant. I'm trying to get through a boring assignment without entirely losing my sanity. You, on the other hand, are in love with him."

Keir went pale. "Don't be ridiculous."

He realized in passing that he was willing to forgive Keir the occasional burst of stupidity such as this, because most of the time he managed to be almost rational. "Please, do remember who I am. Do you really want me to explain how obvious it is?" Rhetorical question, fortunately. Warrick wouldn't say yes, so he wouldn't have to confess that he was primarily relying on Sara's opinion. "I've been studying Toreth. He fascinates me."

"Really."

"Yes." Time to test the strength of Warrick's detachment. "He destroys people's lives, their minds, and their self-worth. He perpetrates acts which most people would find impossible. He listens to people in pain, begging for their lives, for the lives of their loved ones. And none of it touches him because he doesn't perceive other people as real. Would you agree with that?"

"It's an opinion I've heard expressed before." Unreadable expressions and coldness can give away as much as anything else.

"Yet, somehow, he manages to accept your love and to love you in return, insofar as he is capable, although I'm sure the word has never occurred to him. Indeed, he *trusts* you, which is actually more significant. I imagine that you still tolerate a measure of thoughtlessness and indeed cruelty on his part, but your in-

29

evitable dissatisfaction must be outweighed by the rewards of pleasure and affection. A relationship is maintained, against all probability. It's really terribly interesting."

Keir groaned. "Please tell me you haven't said any of that to him."

"Good Lord, of course not. He'd kill me, somewhere around the middle of the first sentence, and the extent of his self-deception is another fascinating aspect to the situation. Now, will you answer my question?"

After a long silence Keir said, "You're right. I don't think about it. My self-deception, if you like." When he didn't comment on that, Keir looked at him expectantly. "Well?"

"Well, nothing. I don't give relationship advice." Especially when, as in this case, the only advice he could give would be: he's dangerous, leave him.

"Not even if it's asked for?"

"I'm not cheap, and in this case I couldn't honestly recommend the expense, since you wouldn't follow it."

Keir nodded. Maybe he guessed what the advice would be. "So why ask the question in the first place?"

"I was curious, that's all—it's an unusual psychological situation of which I have few examples. I presume that you're satisfied with it, and with him. I'll admit that I can see his attractive qualities for someone who enjoys being dominated in a sexual context."

It was unfortunate, on reflection, that Keir was in mid-drink when he said that. As he mopped tea from his trousers and the table, he said, "Jean-Baptiste, that is an extremely obnoxious habit."

"Yes, I'm rather afraid it is. However, that doesn't make the observation any less true."

"How do you *know*?"

"It's obvious, from your choice of partners if nothing else. Actually, if ever the subject had arisen, I could have told you before. Melissa, the dear—" He shook his head, suppressing a smile at the memory of Keir's last-ditch and sadly misguided attempt to satisfy his relationship requirements in a more socially acceptable format. He had sincerely loved the woman, and laughter would offend. "However, you wouldn't have been ready to hear it back then."

Warrick looked up. "I'm surprised that you'd worry about that."

"Oh, I'm not saying that I wouldn't have said it, had the topic been broached, just that it would've been a potentially damaging thing for you to hear."

"And you say Toreth doesn't treat people as real."

It would do no good to explain that it was more a question of people being so pitifully unaware of their own fears and desires that there was little point making the effort to spare them pain. They suffered anyway, as they thrashed blindly in the incomprehensible quicksand of their meaningless lives. On the other hand, the parallels had occurred to him as well, so it would be dishonest to deny the accusation entirely.

"I will concede a certain similarity in some aspects. However, that is part of why he's so intriguing." Something he hadn't seen before occurred to him. "He's emotionally immature and, indeed, potentially dangerous, and yet he has his 'regular fuck' and I don't. Does that strike you as unfair?"

Keir laughed, although without sounding terribly amused. "Actually, no, it doesn't. But anyway, would you want one?"

That kind of thought-provoking question was the reason he didn't mind spending an evening with Keir. "Do you know, I have absolutely no idea. And you cannot imagine how much the novelty of that appeals to me."

"Then, if you'll *take* some advice, you'd be better off looking at Socioanalysis than I&I."

Touch of defensiveness, quite unnecessary—Carnac didn't have the right suicidal tendencies to go after Toreth as a serious partner, or any of the rest of the I&I menagerie. It was probably as far as Keir would permit himself to go in laying claim to Toreth, though, so a little reassurance was only fair. "Neither, I would say. I don't see much potential for long-term contentment with either sociopaths or egomaniacs."

Keir smiled slightly. "Well, then, good luck in finding someone who does."

Touché.

As they continued the meal, and the conversation turned to the sim, Carnac found himself using some of his attention to measure his companion up to the role of partner. Considering the starting point that no one would ever be suitable, Keir wasn't a bad fit. Interesting, intelligent, independent, rich enough to function as an equal. Tolerant, as his liaison with Toreth amply demonstrated. Carnac knew full well that tolerance would be a major requirement.

Considered in that light, Toreth really didn't deserve Keir—not that merit played much part in such matters. More frustratingly, he realized that choosing Toreth as his personal liaison had irretrievably ruined whatever small chance might have existed of engaging Keir's interest. Yet, without that choice, Keir would never have contacted him. One of life's supremely annoying paradoxes.

Eventually, after they had gone through dessert, coffee, and quite revolting authentic Eastern liqueurs, Carnac looked at his watch. "I should go. I have another scintillating day at I&I ahead of me tomorrow." Then he waited, making the silence an invitation. Just in case he was, for once, wrong.

He wasn't, of course. Keir smiled, shook his head. "Thanks for the offer, but no."

"Oh?"

"I'd hate to spoil old memories."

Carnac understood at once, but he made the comment for form's sake. "As I recall, *you* terminated the proceedings back then, in short order."

Keir rose, folding his damp napkin neatly before setting it down. "Precisely."

They shared a car as far as Carnac's hotel and he permitted himself to keep hoping for the length of the journey that Keir might change his mind. Which, naturally, he didn't. As he prepared for bed, Carnac gave their conversation some serious consideration. Perhaps it would be worth investing some time in refreshing his understanding of indices of attractiveness and drawing up a profile for a partner. After all, if an individual as damaged as Toreth could find his regular fuck, there had to be a chance for himself. Not, of course, that they were so similar that the comparison meant a great deal.

In the end, he decided that it had been an interesting fantasy, for an evening, but he didn't think he'd pursue it. The likelihood of the search yielding a candidate who was both suitable and available was far too small to justify the expenditure of effort. Barring an event of miraculous improbability, he would have to continue to content himself with his personal liaisons. Still, when the investigation was over, perhaps he would contact Warrick again and ask if it would be possible to try out the sim. No ulterior motives were required for that. Or perhaps he could see if Toreth could arrange it. That might make an informative test of his progress.

All in all, he'd had an enjoyable evening.

Chapter Six

❖

The next day, Warrick sat on the virtual beach, skipping virtual stones across the calm sea, and trying to enjoy the heat of the virtual sun. He wasn't, much. This was the first personal sim time he'd taken on his own for a while, and he knew what he was doing—hiding. Taking some time to think, in his safe, beautiful sim that had been a refuge from the real world for a long time.

He'd chosen the beach because he liked it, and because Toreth didn't. Or didn't now. At first he'd claimed to love it, but then Warrick had tried to demo underwater breathing to him. Toreth had tried it once, failed miserably, and then announced that it wasn't his sort of thing, and that he wasn't doing it again. End of discussion. After that, he'd always preferred one of the other rooms.

Warrick had wondered about it, but he hadn't asked. There was no point. There was a particular kind of conversational shutdown, signaling that any further probing would provoke trouble. Like the time when, quite without expecting any problems, he'd asked about Toreth's family. Missing the signs, he'd pressed too hard; he hadn't seen Toreth for a week after that. A week Toreth had no doubt spent working his way through enough strangers that he could eventually forget what had happened and come back.

Dilly had asked how he could tolerate it, and sometimes he wondered the same thing. Ultimately, the reason was that the strangers didn't matter; he'd grown used to ignoring them. Not that it wasn't ... unpleasant, now and then, and he wasn't going to lie to himself about that. It was a balance between living with Toreth's infidelity and not trying to fool himself that he didn't care at all. Inevitable dissatisfaction outweighed by the rewards of pleasure and affection.

The reason he was here, sulking in the sim as Dilly would say, was because of Carnac. He'd met Toreth's casual partners before—on occasion, they were hard to avoid. Sometimes Toreth lied about them, sometimes he didn't bother, and sometimes he went out of his way to make damn sure Warrick knew about them. That was usually another sign that Warrick had, by Toreth's standards, done something wrong. Then there would be an argument which would at some point transmute seamlessly into sex, and then everything would be all right once more. Or at least back to normal.

The casual partners, though, however deliberately flaunted, didn't usually want to sit down to dinner and *discuss* the situation. That was partly his own fault for not thinking things through. He'd felt curious to see Carnac again, to find out what he was doing and if he had changed. He should have known Carnac would expect him to demonstrate an interesting opinion on Toreth. Also on I&I, which had led to the stupid slip-up of mentioning Marian. Dangerous, however oblique it had been. Thank God Carnac hadn't pursued that mistake.

Carnac was, annoyingly, right about I&I. It would make things intolerable to think too often about how Toreth knew what he did about pain and how to use it. Seeing the recording of Marian's interrogation had been bad enough. Watching her die had been worse, not only because of her death but also because of Toreth's reaction to it. While he himself had been appalled by what he'd helped to do, Toreth hadn't cared. It had meant nothing to him, except that he was out of trouble and safe from Psychoprogramming.

Another point to Carnac.

When Toreth had come back up to his office...well, it hadn't been Warrick's most shining performance of composure under stress. He didn't kill people every day, though, or even help arrange for them to die. Seeing it in the sim hadn't prepared him for it. He'd wanted nothing more than to leave, to hear it was over and done with and to get away from I&I forever. Toreth had stopped him, physically stopped him, and kept him in the office long enough to complete the charade they had devised.

Toreth had been angry. Maybe, in retrospect, also frightened by the cost of it going wrong. "Do you *want* to fuck everything up? Do you want to end up down on level C, where she was, spilling everything for one of the others? You'll stay in here long enough to make it look good, whatever it takes. I'm not going to risk ending up dead as well, just because you're too fucking gutless to stick it out. It was your fucking idea—live with it."

And, God help him, even then, even right *then*, he'd wanted Toreth. It hadn't hurt—or hadn't helped—that Toreth had been holding him against the wall while he delivered his little speech. The controlled anger in his voice, his hands on him...it had combined irresistibly with the adrenaline generated by their desperate plan. Being brutally honest—which he might as well be since he was here inside his own mind with no one else to hear him—it had gone straight to his cock, and Toreth had realized that straight away, too.

He'd managed to resist Toreth for all of twenty seconds. Maybe even thirty. Mm. Something to be proud of there. Then he'd let Toreth fuck him, against the desk, by the screen where he'd watched Marian die, and he'd enjoyed every moment of it. The best sex they'd had, up until then—close and hot and urgent. They'd come together, perfectly together, and he'd drawn blood biting his lip to keep quiet.

Afterwards, he'd managed to get himself back under control, and the sex had, strangely, helped that. Endorphins, probably. He'd still hesitated on his way out, before he'd opened the door. Toreth had put his hands on his shoulders from behind, and he'd braced himself for another blast of contempt. Instead it had been calm instructions and a reassurance that everything was going to be fine. Then, finally, he'd said, "I'll be in touch."

Even while he was still sickened by what had happened, Warrick hadn't thought for a moment that it might be the end of things between them. They were bound together by what they'd done for each other. Or was it really just the sex? He smiled wryly. It might not be that entirely but, God, it would almost be enough on its own to stop him from thinking about the other things. Incredible then, and even better since. He rubbed his wrists, thinking about the previous Saturday morning at his flat. Would it always be that good? Could it possibly be?

He lay back in the warm sand, tempted to stop trying to think about the difficult, unpleasant things and instead to concentrate on the rewards of pleasure. He tried to imagine them both in some vague number of years, still doing it, still playing the game. To his surprise, he could, easily. In fact, he couldn't imagine ever stopping wanting it. He would never, he knew, find anyone else who could do that to him.

Then there were the other encounters, rarer and so more individually memorable. Sunday morning sex, when they had plenty of time and Toreth might briefly let his defenses down. Not often, or for long, but the fact that it happened at all showed that Carnac and Marian were wrong—Toreth was more than his job at I&I and his psych file. Warrick didn't need to read psychology textbooks to know that. Slow, passionate, after-breakfast sex provided all the evidence required.

There were additional things he wouldn't mind trying, too. Fucking Toreth, for one. He'd done it here in the sim, during SMS runs, which, in fairness, you could say didn't count since Toreth was in sensory deprivation at the time. Toreth hadn't complained about it afterwards, though. In the real world it would probably be different, something else he'd learned from Toreth. Sometimes, when Warrick was pulling on the chains, desperately close to coming, he would get a sudden flash of their positions reversed: Toreth bound, while *he* fucked him. Just the thought of it, of being inside him, of how it would feel, was almost enough to make him resolve to go around to Toreth's flat tonight and ask him. I want you. Let me, please. A little give and take isn't an unreasonable request, is it?

He wouldn't go, though, even though normally he had no problem asking for what he wanted. It was just that he'd never been able to think of a way of wording it that didn't leave him with the fear that Toreth might refuse without thinking about it. Once he had said no, he wouldn't let himself change his mind.

35

In truth, Warrick had no concrete reason even to suspect that Toreth would turn him down. Toreth's hedonism was generally all-encompassing and enthusiastically experimental. However, this was something that required trust and a certain relinquishing of control and he hadn't needed Carnac to tell him that Toreth's trust was a far rarer commodity than his sexual attention. So he'd decided to wait until, eventually, Toreth might suggest it himself. It was all the more irksome because he knew that Toreth sometimes took it from his one-night, no-consequence partners. Them and not him—perhaps because the limited surrender the act required was easier with someone Toreth would never see again.

Warrick smiled wryly. An evening with Carnac had made him excessively analytical.

What Toreth did with his casual partners wasn't something Warrick had ever wanted to know about in detail, but he'd caught comments, let slip accidentally or deliberately. Like this time, when it had been the fact that Carnac had sucked him off. In Toreth's office, possibly. Despite himself, Warrick played with the image. Easy to create the scene. He knew how Toreth would sound, how he would move, how he would respond. What he liked. Except, presumably, that he hadn't been saying Warrick's name when he came. Or had he? He should have asked Carnac.

No, he shouldn't have. What he should do was stop thinking about it, get out of the sim, and get back to work. Why was he letting this get to him so much? It was Carnac. Or, more accurately, what Carnac had told him. "You, on the other hand, are in love with him."

He'd also said Toreth loved him in return. Of course, he knew Carnac well enough not to believe every word he said, especially when he was fishing for a reaction. And they *were* just words. Putting a label on whatever feelings either of them might have didn't change them, or make them any more significant. There had been plenty of labels and "I love you"s with Lissa, and that hadn't turned out to be the lasting romance of the century.

It wasn't just sex between them any more (at least not on his part), and he'd known that for a while. He'd wanted it, in fact. That knowledge didn't tell him what it was, though. Dilly had asked him about it at New Year. A direct "do you love him?" which he'd weaseled out of answering. She'd let him get away with it, too, which implied she didn't want to hear the answer. Maybe she thought she knew.

He wondered for a moment what Sara thought. Then he decided that if he was reduced to taking a poll on the question, then that in itself probably gave him the answer. If he wasn't sure, he couldn't be, could he? He stuck by his nonanswer to Dilly: it would be an incredibly stupid thing to do.

Even if it were true, would that change anything? Was that why he was still thinking about Carnac? No, it wouldn't, and it wasn't. Even without Toreth's track record, bizarrely reassuring in this context, Carnac wasn't a serious threat, for all

36

his "I find him fascinating" routine. Toreth disliked Carnac, while Carnac's opinion of Toreth didn't seem to leave much room to worry about his showing a long-term interest.

So why hadn't he asked Carnac, politely or otherwise, to stop fucking his... whatever? Because—back to this again—he had to put up with it whether he liked it or not, because Toreth wasn't about to stop. Besides, Toreth would be furious if he heard he'd warned Carnac off, and Warrick certainly didn't trust Carnac to keep his mouth shut about it.

A light touch against his leg made him look down. There was no visible clock in the beach room, and he'd always meant to do something about that—now some-one had beaten him to it. On the sand beside him sat a large crab, with a clock face set into its violet shell. Its eyestalks goggled at him briefly, then it clicked its claws. "Time's up, Doctor Warrick," it said in a voice he recognized as one of the staff's from the Artificial Life lab, and then it sidled down to the water.

Warrick stood up, automatically brushing the sand from his clothes without using his hands, and called up the control panel. He hesitated for a while, though, staring out over the glittering, unreal ocean. Half an hour of useful sim time wasted in self-indulgent self-absorption. After that investment, he must have solved the problem.

Carnac didn't matter that much, that was his conclusion. If he let himself get obsessed by this one, then the next one would only be worse. Time to get back into the real world and get on with real things. If he ever caught them fucking on a Sunday, then he'd worry.

Chapter Seven

❖

Life at I&I had settled into a routine; it was still dull and unpleasant, but it allowed Carnac to work more effectively. Coffee breaks, primarily taken in the coffee rooms, were an interruption, but apparently a cultural requirement. In the interests of completeness, he'd asked Toreth to take him to coffee rooms in various sections. He'd discovered a few things—for one, that General Criminal was by no means the worst place in the building to have coffee. That honor went to the Interrogation levels and the interrogators, who were very like para-investigators, only with fewer inter-personal skills. From a distance, the social dynamics of the freak show might have been of mild interest. While actually sitting in the same room as people discussing difficult prisoners, they made his fingers itch for a heavy blunt object.

As would be expected in a job that was bound to engender a degree of para-noia, I&I employees seemed to conduct an inordinate amount of their business via unofficial interactions. While unsurprising, the observation would fill a space in the report. Whereupon, no doubt, I&I senior management would seize on the fact and try to mandate some kind of reduction in the practice, thereby damaging morale and efficiency. The usual effect of writing an intelligent report and handing it to morons. He would find the prospect quite depressing, if he didn't so thor-oughly despise the lot of them.

They were drinking coffee again when Toreth surprised him with another spon-taneous question. "How long have you been doing this?"

Carnac tipped his head. "That's rather open-ended."

"I meant your job. Socioanalysis."

Interesting question. An oblique approach to discovering his age, or a genuine inquiry? "Counting training, or since I qualified?"

"Either."

"Since I was fully licensed—the end of my first independent case—thirteen years less a few weeks. Since I entered the official training scheme, a little over thirty-seven years."

Toreth blinked. "Fuck, they do start you young."

"Historically, the division took recruits as old as twelve, but the end results were less satisfactory. I was picked out as having potential by postnatal neural screening. All the initial training and testing was carried out locally." He left the location unspecified, and added a pause, but Toreth didn't ask for details. "Then, after my four-year assessments proved acceptable, I was transferred to the central Socioanalysis training facility and officially enrolled."

"You didn't see your family much, then." He sounded as if he thought that was no bad thing. Not surprising, in view of Sara's indiscretions.

"Controlled visits are permitted—it isn't a prison." Time to try something a little more ambitious. "The arrangements were perfectly satisfactory. I occasionally felt sorry for my siblings, though, overshadowed as they were by my success. My parents were inordinately proud of me."

Silence. Then, "That must have been nice for you." He'd never heard Toreth's voice so dispassionate, not even when he'd been laying out the terms of the damage waiver to his prisoner. He decided not to push that further.

"Feel free to ask anything else," Carnac said.

He thought Toreth might close the conversation, but after a moment he asked, "Is there much of a dropout rate?"

"No. As you can imagine, with the per-head investment, the entry screening is rigorous. Neural changes during adolescence account for the greatest number of losses, but these days development is more effectively managed. I benefited from some of the early trials."

Toreth smiled, not very pleasantly. "Sounds like you were quite a lab rat."

"I thought everyone had heard the stories about our training. I've encountered some quite lurid rumors from time to time."

"I don't believe everything I hear. People talk a lot of crap about para training, too. So—" His eyes narrowed. "You're forty-one."

"Yes." Gratifying to have his guess confirmed. "And?"

"And nothing." Toreth shrugged. "You don't look it."

"Thank you."

Another shrug. "Just an observation." He checked his watch and stood up. "I have to get down to interrogation. I won't be long, but one of my junior's cases is wrapping up and I need to sign it off."

"Before you leave, I have a question."

Toreth stopped in the doorway. "What?"

A touch defensive. Good—that would make him more likely to agree to an apparently innocuous request. "I have some free time on Sunday, and I hoped you might be available to help me fill it."

"Oh. Yes, I suppose so. Is that it?"

"Yes. I'll see you later."

Carnac watched him go. Second personal conversation, which hadn't yielded anything that wasn't classic, unsurprising, and absolutely in agreement with his psych file. Still, it was always mildly interesting to see how profound and destructive an effect a childhood could have. He was grateful, at times like this, that his own had been so carefully controlled.

"I want to see my wife."

"As your Justice rep explained to you, that's not possible."

[pause 3 sec]

One of the things that made Sara such a good admin was her talent for multitasking. While proofreading transcripts ready to send off to Justice and painting her nails in preparation for a Friday night out, she had enough attention left over to worry about Toreth. Or to be more accurate, to worry about Carnac and whatever he was planning. Thinking about Carnac at all made her furious, mostly with herself. How could she have told him those things about Toreth? Tactical gossip was her specialty. She should have known better, been more careful, but she'd felt flattered by his attention, and told him far too much. She wouldn't have blamed Toreth if he'd never spoken to her again. The fact that he'd taken it so well only made her feel worse.

Then, this week, the atmosphere had changed. Carnac was as ingratiating to Toreth as he always had been to the admins. More so, in fact. She didn't like to think there was anything dangerous behind it—even now that she knew what the man was capable of she couldn't help responding a little to him when he was deliberately charming. But in her heart she knew he was Up To No Good.

"You'll remain in custody until we've had a chance to question your daughter."

...[signal inadequate]...

Hell. Abrupt reduction in volume. The microphones needed checking, because they should have compensated. After making a note for maintenance, she manually adjusted the volume, listened, and watched the system add in:

[pause 4 sec] "No. You can't."

She authorized the manual intervention and the transcript started up again.

"I'm afraid we have no choice. We have to have the information."

"She's underage. She—"

"Will be fifteen in three days. We are confident that in this case Justice will give us a waiver for retrospective interrogation. The application is already being processed."

[pause 8 sec]

"Please. She doesn't *know* anything."

"Unfortunate for her, if true. Nevertheless, we will proceed, if we have no alternative."

[pause 10 sec]

"If you cooperate now, there is a possibility of a deal. That possibility stays open for only so long. Three days."

[pause 25 sec]

She allowed her conscious attention to tune out the recording again and watched the transcript. After a while, names, dates, and places, all nicely articulated and accurately recorded, began to flow smoothly up the screen. She'd be able to get away early after all if it ran like this to the end.

Really, she shouldn't get involved. The memory of her last foray into helping with Toreth's personal life was still sharp, particularly the part where he'd called her a lying cunt in front of the rest of the office. He was old enough to make his own mistakes and live with the consequences. On the other hand, if he screwed things up with Warrick, the consequences would be unbearable for her to live with. Looked at like that, it was pre-emptive self-defense.

She didn't doubt that he was more than capable of screwing things up. Or, rather, Carnac was more than capable of making him do it, for whatever reason. The unfortunate part was that she simply couldn't think of a way of broaching it with Toreth, not even via her usually reliable method of getting him pissed enough to handle reality. What could she say to him? Her guess about Carnac's strategy was only a guess, although she felt the evidence analysis system would give it a high confidence. Having been on the receiving end, she recognized the deliberate application of charm, the pleasant and perfectly measured focus of friendly attention. And with Toreth, it had the element she hadn't at the time noticed missing from Carnac's attack on her defenses—seduction. Worse, she'd seen Toreth's response, the slackening of dislike and suspicion, and the growing ease. How could she possibly find the words to warn him?

He's trying to get you involved with him. He's going to string you along until he's finished whatever mind-fuck game he's playing and then he's going to drop you cold and go back to Socioanalysis.

He wouldn't believe her. And, Christ, if he did believe her, he'd kill Carnac. He'd have to. She might not be a spook or even a para, but she knew how Toreth's mind worked. He wouldn't be able to bear the humiliation.

The transcript finished, and she authorized it, filed and submitted. Done for the day—or at least officially done. She tapped on Toreth's door, got no reply, and went in. God, the place *stank* of sex. At their age you'd think they'd have a bit more restraint. Or a bit less stamina. Toreth was at his desk, alone, folding paper. Half a dozen crumpled origami birds littered the desk. She thought she'd seen Carnac leave, but she'd better check before she started this. "Is he still here?"

Toreth shook his head. "Come and gone."

41

"I can tell. You should get some air-freshener." He just nodded. Not his usual sparkling self, which was worrying. He looked preoccupied, in the way she'd only ever seen him look with Warrick. Please don't let that mean what she thought it meant. "I was wondering..." How should she phrase this?

He looked up. "What?"

"He asked me to arrange some things for Sunday. A taxi booking and lunch. For two."

He grinned briefly. "Yeah. So what? Jealous?"

She shook her head. "Aren't you going somewhere with Warrick on Sunday? Some SimTech thing?"

She braced herself, expecting him to bite her head off for interfering, but there was only silence. Eventually, he said, "How do *you* know?"

"'Cause *you* told me, a few weeks ago. I remember stuff like that, remember?"

"Then you ought to remember it's in the evening." He paused. "I can make both. No problem." He'd forgotten. Totally and utterly forgotten.

She gave him a deliberately bright smile. "That's okay, then. Sorry to bother you. I'm off, now. See you Monday—have a good weekend."

He didn't even reply.

Back at her desk she gathered her things together and wondered what the hell she was going to do. This was more serious than she'd thought. Two-timing his boyfriends, almost like a normal person. Except that when you thought about who he was, and who the boyfriends were, it was like watching a slow-motion recording of a train accident, the inevitable carnage approaching with plenty of time to appreciate it.

She could call Warrick. Call Warrick, warn him that Carnac was up to something, and let him handle it. She didn't like to think how pissed off Toreth would be if he found out she'd done *that*. Still, it would be worth being called a cunt again, if it stopped Carnac from hurting him. Or should she wait and see how things went on Sunday, and then call?

Chapter Eight

❖

Sunday lunch had been nice: long, expensive, and well lubricated. Then they'd gone to a gallery, of all places, which had something to do with someone Carnac knew. Toreth hadn't been paying that much attention, but it had only been two-thirds as boring as he'd expected. The hotel afterwards had been much more fun— better than Carnac's usual standard of self-absorbed fuck, anyway. Warrick was right; the man was bearable, when you got to know him. Now Toreth was horren-dously late. He'd barely had time to dash home, change into something smart, and get around to Warrick's before "late" became so late it turned into "didn't show." He thought up excuses in the lift up to the flat. For some reason, mentioning Carnac felt like a bad idea, so he settled on something simple and easy to remem-ber. He'd half expected, and half hoped, that Warrick might have gone without him, but he was still waiting. Not to mention looking thoroughly fucked off.

"You're late," Warrick said unnecessarily, as he let him into the flat.

"I know. I'm sorry. I was at the gym and I lost track of time." He smiled with all the apologetic charm he could muster. "I'll make up for it, I promise."

It might have worked, except that he tried to follow it up with a kiss. Warrick pulled back, turning his head away sharply.

"What?"

"You weren't . . . you weren't at the gym."

"Yes, I was." Even as he said it, he knew it was a mistake.

"Please, at least don't lie about it. I can smell him on you." His voice was tight with anger. "Carnac. At least I assume it's him, unless you're fucking someone else as well."

Toreth blinked, surprised at the sudden venom. "All right. Yes, you're right. I'll have a shower. It won't take a minute."

"You do that." Warrick took a deep breath. "Go home, have a shower and don't come back here."

"What?"

43

"Go away. Don't come back. I don't think I can make it any simpler unless I draw pictures."

The icy words brought a touch of real fear—stupid, because Warrick didn't mean it like that. Couldn't. "Why, for fuck's sake?"

Warrick laughed without any humor at all. "Quite. I suddenly find that I don't have the patience for this any more. Not on a Sunday."

Understanding, he was simultaneously angry and unsettled. "That's not what you said before. What happened to 'I don't own you, I don't want to own you'?" No mention of any days of the week, as far as he could remember.

Warrick sighed with exaggerated patience. "Toreth, I'm not saying 'don't fuck anyone else.' I'm not even saying 'don't fuck Carnac.' I'm saying . . ." He frowned, as if he wasn't entirely sure himself. "What I'm saying is that as long as you are fucking him, I will be busy doing other things. I don't think that's an unreasonable position to take, and if you think otherwise, then it has just become your problem, not mine."

"He'll be gone in a couple of weeks." No response. He gave it one more try. "I don't see why it's such a big deal."

"Yes, I'm quite aware of that. Now, please leave." Warrick opened the door, held it open.

So he left.

On Monday, Toreth came in in a foul mood. Sara gave him until lunchtime in the slim hope that it might be a hangover. Then she waited until he'd gone out for lunch—with Carnac—and called SimTech. "I'd like to speak to Doctor Warrick, please. Tell him it's the inestimable Sara." One day she'd have to look the word up. She'd always vaguely worried that it would turn out to be something unflattering.

The screen changed to show Warrick, doing "mild surprise and polite interest." "Hello, Sara."

"Hi." Get to the point. "I need to see you. About Toreth."

All expression vanished. "I'm afraid I'm busy."

She knew what that meant. "It won't take long, I promise."

"If he wishes to leave me a message, he can call me himself."

Oh oh. Flying debris from a row that must have been a good one. No further explanation for Toreth's bad mood was required, anyway. The question was, had they argued about Carnac? "*I* want to talk to you. Toreth has no idea I'm calling. Please, Warrick." Then she held her breath while he thought it over.

"Very well. Public or private?"

She briefly imagined Toreth accidentally seeing them together. Unlikely, but she daren't risk it. "Private, please."

44

He nodded once. "My flat, eight o'clock." After giving her the address, he canceled the connection without saying goodbye.

When he let her into the flat his expression was for once perfectly readable. If it hadn't been, his opening words were a bit of a clue. After he had shown her through to the living room—and distracted as she was she still noticed that it was a *nice* flat—he offered her a seat, sat down opposite her, and said, "If you've come all this way to let me know that their relationship is rather more than professional, then I'm afraid you've had a wasted journey."

At least he knew, which she had been worried about. The bad temper she could excuse. "It's not that. It's Carnac. He gives me the creeps. He's fucking with Toreth in more ways than the usual."

Warrick frowned. "Explain."

"He's got some game going, only I'm not sure what. I think he's trying to hook Toreth and then he's going to do something . . . Jesus, I wish I knew what."

"Mm." Thoughtful pause. "Would you like a drink? Coffee? Tea? Something alcoholic?"

"Coffee would be great, thanks."

She didn't mind the change of subject—he was still thinking about what she'd said. She followed him through into the kitchen (huge and full, as Toreth had told her, of a bewildering array of cooking equipment) and watched as he made expensive coffee in an expensive antique brewer, some weird-looking type of thing she'd never seen before. She'd forgotten how loaded he was. Loaded *and* domesticated. If Toreth ever decided he didn't want Warrick any more, she might be tempted herself.

Once the coffee had been made, they sat down in the kitchen, which she guessed to be a step up in intimacy from the living room. He watched as she added milk and sugar to her coffee, then asked the question she'd been dreading. "What makes you think Carnac has any particular plans?"

"I'm . . . well, it's hard to say, as such." She shrugged. "It's the way he is. He was God's own bastard to start with—to Toreth, anyway. He drove him mad and it had to be deliberate because he can be so bloody smooth you could skate on him. Not that that stopped Toreth screwing him, of course. It never does."

Warrick closed his eyes very briefly.

"Sorry," she said.

"That's quite all right." Liquid nitrogen politeness. "Carry on."

"Anyway, then he did a real number on me." She looked down at her cup. "He got me to tell him all kinds of stuff about Toreth."

"Oh?"

"Yeah." She looked up and smiled, despite the situation. "All kinds of stuff I'm

45

not going to tell you. After that he started being, well...nicer. Nothing you could point out specifically as wrong, but just... Toreth's getting less and less annoyed with having him around. And he's still screwing him. I mean, *still*. I don't like it."

Warrick smiled wryly. "You think his displaying interest in someone for any length of time is a bad thing?"

"You know what I mean."

"Yes, of course." He sat for a while, turning his coffee cup slowly around in the saucer, expression closed. "I spoke to him," he said eventually.

"Toreth?"

"Carnac. We had dinner."

She stared, far too stunned to say anything.

Her expression triggered a fleeting smile. "Nothing very exciting happened. We chatted about various things, primarily the sim, and he made a not terribly serious pass at me. However, he did mention Toreth and, adding what he said together with what you've said, I think your guess as to his motives is substantially correct."

"Does Toreth know you saw him?"

"The occasion to mention it never arose. Needless to say..."

"I won't say a word. Warrick, what's 'substantially correct' supposed to mean? What's he doing? Why is he doing it?"

Warrick looked past her for a moment, frowning, then said, "Have you ever... seen Toreth's psych file?"

Meaning he *had*? "No. But he's a para. They're all the same, aren't they? More or less. He's—" She hesitated, but if he'd seen the bloody file he must know. Still, she didn't want to say it out loud. Toreth would hate the idea of them talking about him like this. It sounded better in the generic and nonspecific. "They're not normal, basically. That's how they get selected for training in the first place."

"Right. So how many people would you say Toreth trusts? *Really* trusts?"

It took her a moment to make sense of the question, before understanding triggered a memory. "Oh, God. Carnac asked me that." She smacked her forehead. "And I *told* him: me and you. I'm an idiot. Could I have screwed it up any more?"

"Probably not. He thought it was 'terribly interesting.' And also that..."

"What?"

He shook his head. "That he, ah, maintains a relationship with us. That we're real people to him."

She never thought of it in quite those terms before, and it was weirdly flattering to think that out of everyone, it was her. Warrick as well, of course, but her first. Flattering and horrible, because it made her betrayal that much more awful.

Warrick was still speaking. "The point is that, I suspect, Carnac's curious as to how and why Toreth does trust us, because his file suggests it's something rather improbable. I expect he's testing a theory."

Her stomach sank—it sounded nastily plausible. Spooky mind-fuck games.

"A theory? Getting Toreth to trust him is testing a theory? Because he's fucking *curious?*"

"That's only what I think he's doing. I can't be sure."

He sounded pretty bloody sure. "And then Carnac's going to turn around and tell him he was just fucking with him? In the mind-fucking sense."

"That I don't know. I don't know why he would want to, or what it would add to the hypothesis. But you're at I&I and I'm not, so perhaps you're right."

"Oh." Her stomach seemed to have taken up gymnastics. "It'd kill him." Her earlier fear returned. "And then he'd kill Carnac."

Warrick didn't comment.

"Aren't you going to say anything to him? About what Carnac's doing?"

"No."

"*No?*"

"He can work it out for himself. He's a grown man, Sara, and he's not stupid."

She tried to think of a tactful way of saying, "Yes, but emotionally he's about ten. On a good day."

"Maybe he could . . . do with a hint?" she suggested.

"It's not that simple." He fell silent, looking lost for words, and, for the first time she could recall, she felt sorry for him. Much as she liked Toreth, he would be the world's worst nightmare to try anything serious with.

"Carnac is his problem," Warrick said eventually. "As I've already made clear to him."

A sudden chill, real enough to give her goose bumps. "Already?"

"Toreth was here yesterday. Briefly. I told him that unless and until he was finished with Carnac, I would be unavailable. Looking at it in this light, that may have been something of a mistake."

Oh, Christ. He wasn't wrong there. She understood why he'd done it—she even agreed with it—but still, oh, Christ. Lousy, rotten timing, hers and his. If only she'd called him on Friday. Still, regrets butter no parsnips, as her mother said. Whatever the hell that meant.

Warrick was pouring more coffee for them both.

"What are you going to do?" she asked when he'd finished.

"Nothing." Flat and final.

"Can't you talk to Carnac?"

"Why suggest I do it? You're working with him."

"He wouldn't listen to me."

"Nor to me." He added a quarter of a teaspoon of sugar to his cup and stirred it. Three left, three right, three left again, before he tapped the spoon against the edge of the cup and set it in the saucer. Then he pushed the cup away. "One thing I do know for certain about Carnac is that if he has a set goal he will carry it through. He would deny there was any ulterior motive to his treatment of Toreth, and then carry on."

"Warrick, please, you can't let him—"

"Sara." He stood up and took a few paces away across the kitchen. When he turned, his expression gave away no emotion. "What exactly would you propose that I do?"

That's what she'd wanted him to tell her. "I don't know."

"Quite. I have to stand by what I told him. I can't unsay it, still less can I go back on it. Frankly, I don't want to, however unpleasant the consequences. Beyond that, I have no idea how to tell him, without doing exactly the same damage as Carnac would. But I'll bear what you've said in mind."

Bear it in mind. He was worse than Toreth sometimes. Pair of bloody control freaks—they deserved each other. There was one last question she had to ask. "Will you take him back? When Carnac's...finished with him?"

He hesitated for so long she didn't think he would reply, and she hadn't really expected him to, but in the end he answered with a question. "Do you think he'd want to come back?"

She didn't say anything. She didn't need to. Of course he wouldn't, not if he realized what Carnac had done to him. Most especially if he thought Warrick might know. Fine. If Warrick couldn't, or wouldn't, do anything, she'd just have to make sure by herself that it didn't come to that.

Eavesdropping was a bad habit Sara couldn't get rid of. She'd stopped biting her nails years ago, she'd given up sugar in tea (but not coffee), and she even ate a moderately well-balanced diet (if you counted vitamin supplements as a food group), but she couldn't give up listening to conversations she wasn't supposed to. For one thing, at I&I it was a required survival trait. So much went on unofficially that the only way to stay ahead of the game was to be plugged into the network and to have enough juicy tidbits to buy the good stuff in return.

On Tuesday morning she'd got in very early and performed a small readjustment to the comms unit on Toreth's desk. She'd felt slightly guilty, but not much. It was for his own good, after all. She'd listened on and off all yesterday without hearing anything either useful or too alarming. Now it was getting towards late afternoon on Wednesday. She'd had the comm switched off for a couple of hours while she ate a late lunch at her desk and dealt with stupid queries regarding Toreth's offloaded cases. Some people couldn't manage to follow instructions, even written in words of no more than two syllables.

The last one complete, it occurred to her that it was long past time to offer them a coffee. Not for the first time, she wondered how she'd ever got into the routine with Toreth, since refreshments appeared nowhere in her job description. A bad habit she'd picked up from the other seniors' admins, probably. She didn't actually mind, not when it *was* Toreth, but she objected to having to make coffee for Carnac as well. Maybe she should just poison it.

She tapped the official link and after a few moments Toreth answered. "Yes?"

"Does anyone want a drink?"

Brief pause. "No. No thanks, we'll go along to the coffee room in a bit."

He sounded breathless, and she only needed one guess to work out what was going on. "Okay."

She canceled the connection, listened while her conscience explained that this would be a bad thing to do, and then commenced spying.

After a couple of minutes, she began to wish she'd taken the extra risk of setting up the visual link as well. She'd only have got line-of-sight from the desk, but from the sound of it they were quite close to it and the curiosity was beginning to feel potentially fatal. The only one she could hear was Toreth, which meant that Carnac either had his mouth full or was naturally very quiet. What she could hear from Toreth backed up her first guess.

It was strange, listening to them screwing, able to glance up and see the other admins working away at their desks. It would be a fairly safe bet that none of them were listening to anything half as interesting. She wondered briefly what she could charge for broadcasting the audio.

Toreth was getting close to coming, and it surprised her that she could tell so easily. It was the change in pitch of his voice more than the words. She'd only heard it once at very close range, as he'd held her close on top of him during their one and only fuck, and then a few times since when she'd overheard him under more conventional circumstances. She shifted in her chair, getting a little uncomfortable now, but unable to bring herself to switch it off. As a compromise, she lowered the volume, Toreth's voice fading to a faint whisper.

"Deeper. Take it deeper. Yes. That's it, that's, uh..."

There he goes, she thought, catching herself in an oddly affectionate smile.

Suddenly she heard Carnac coughing, quite violently, and then after a while Toreth speaking over it, sounding almost concerned. "Fuck, I'm sorry. Are you okay?"

"No...lasting harm inflicted." More coughing, then, "I'll take it as a compliment."

Toreth laughed. "If you like. I don't have any serious complaints anyway."

"No. It didn't feel as if you did."

The voices stopped, so she turned the volume back up to catch the sound of chairs moving, a zip fastening. "Do you fancy coffee now, or do you want to finish things here?" Toreth said at length.

"Finish off, I think." The movements settled down, a distance from the comm. They must be at Carnac's desk. She turned up the volume again, wondering whether she should set up his desk as well. Probably too much of a risk.

"What are you doing tomorrow?" Toreth asked.

"Ah…the remaining interrogation specialists' interviews. Provided they go according to plan, and there are no more 'unavoidable absences,' that should be the last day of those."

"Do you need me for them? Only I have some things I ought to do on my remaining case."

"Please feel free to take the morning, but I would appreciate your attendance in the afternoon."

"That's fine. Have you got the transcripts?"

"Yes. Sara has arranged it all, with her usual efficiency."

"I hope you're going to say something nice about her in your report." Well, at least he hadn't entirely forgotten *her.*

"Alas, she lies outside my area of inquiry. But I shall make sure I mention to the powers that be that she's been most helpful."

"Thanks."

"There is nothing to thank me for—I would've done it in any case. Working with her has been a pleasure. I've visited a lot of divisions, and she is undoubtedly one of the most effective administrative assistants I have encountered. In fact, I'm tempted to offer her a job at Socioanalysis."

Disgusted with herself, she still felt a little glow of pleasure at the compliments. Eavesdropping wasn't all bad.

Toreth laughed. "I'm afraid I can't let you do that. She's mine."

"Are you quite sure that she isn't open to offers? We pay very generously."

"You won't get anywhere. People have tried to poach her before."

"Really? Yes, I imagine that they would have. And she's been here for nine years? You're very good at this, left-handed."

For a moment, she didn't understand the comment, delivered in exactly the same tone as the preceding ones. Then Toreth said, "I'm ambidextrous, for all the important things. But I'm still better right-handed."

A squeak, as a chair swiveled, and Carnac said. "Oh, yes. So you are. A little tighter. Yes, that's good. Really…*very* good." Then silence for a while, broken only by a sharp, cut-off gasp. Eventually, slightly breathless, Carnac said, "It must be gratifying that she's so loyal."

Oh, Jesus. Oh, God, no. Carnac had been talking about her, and at the *same time* he'd been… She felt sick. Really, genuinely sick, so that she missed a section of the conversation while she concentrated on keeping her lunch down. When she caught up with them again, Carnac was saying, "Sara mentioned that she volunteers for testing in the sim."

"Yeah, she does. I don't mind giving her the time off. I think she had some holiday booked this week. Though she might have canceled it."

Of course she'd canceled it, because she was doing a ton of extra work for the oversexed prick sharing his office.

50

"The sim sounds fascinating," Carnac said. "I imagine the waiting list for volunteers is quite long."

"Yes, I think so. Months, at least. Sara jumped the queue, mind you." There was a brief hesitation, then he added, "Warrick arranged it."

"I see. As a favor to a friend? Perhaps you might ask him if I could try it some time?"

Sara smiled with twisted satisfaction. Oh, no Toreth wouldn't, and he wouldn't say why, either.

"Sorry, I can't. I'm not seeing him at the moment."

She actually yelped out loud in sheer horror. Looking up, she was relieved to see that most of the rest of the section had gone for coffee, and that the couple of people left seemed not to have registered the noise. For a moment, her hand hovered over the comm, not wanting to hear the rest.

"Ah." Delicate exclamation from Carnac, followed by a delicate pause. "Nothing to do with us, I hope?"

Us? Where the fuck did Carnac get "us" from?

"In a way," Toreth said.

"When I said that—"

"Forget it, Carnac. It's . . . well, it's no big deal. He'll get over it."

"I'm glad to hear I shall cause no lasting damage."

Don't say any more, she begged silently, but Toreth didn't hear her.

"No damage at all. We don't see each other all the time anyway—it's not a serious thing."

She wished that his voice wasn't so transparent when he talked about Warrick. "Not a serious thing." Oh, God. She'd like to think she only noticed because she knew Toreth so well, but surely Carnac could hear it, too?

"That's good," Carnac said, and she knew that he had. Hearing the smug smile in Carnac's voice, she felt tempted to fix the problem then and there by going in and braining the spook with a chair.

After a moment, Toreth said, "Coffee?"

By the time they came out she was industriously reorganizing interrogation schedules, seething fury hidden under her best professional shield. She would fix this, somehow. She'd make up for her stupid, careless blabbing. Carnac wouldn't get what he wanted, even if Toreth did kill her for it.

Carnac didn't drink, as a rule. He enjoyed clarity of thought too much, and organic solvents were not healthful companions for the human nervous system. If the occasion merited celebration, though, he would allow himself a glass or two of wine. It was good for the heart, after all, and his family had a tendency towards mild heart problems on the distaff side. All genetically audited and perfectly adequately monitored for, but he found the small excuse amusing.

This evening, he was celebrating the conclusion of his first set of objectives with Toreth—three conversations of a personal nature. He suspected that he had continued to underestimate the depth of Toreth's attachment to Warrick. Certainly what he had read from Toreth today suggested as much. Luckily for his current project, the man seemed perfectly oblivious as to the strength of his feelings or, possibly more accurately, to be capable of deceiving himself to a remarkable degree.

Carnac sipped the wine, paying close attention to the cool slide of liquid over his tongue. Rare treats were to be savored, or they became commonplace and pointless.

He and Toreth had an evening appointment on the coming Saturday. Carnac had decided that this would be the time to press for his next goal of a visit to Toreth's flat. He felt confident of success, given his progress so far. The only disappointment was that it would leave four more days at I&I until he could legitimately return to Socioanalysis, hand in his report, and get on to some real work before his brain atrophied entirely from disuse.

He was too good, sometimes. Or Toreth had proved an easier target than he'd anticipated. As he rarely made mistakes, Carnac's first instinct was always to attribute errors to faults in the original data supplied. Perhaps he should suggest a review of Toreth's psych file, with some more extensive assessments with higher discriminatory power. Not part of his remit, though, and he had no particular inclination to help I&I refine its recruitment and staff management criteria. Instead, he wondered about adjusting his sights upwards. Changing the scoring system after the game began wasn't really in the spirit of self-appointed challenges, but he was bored enough to waive the rule in this case.

What further intimacy could one reasonably aim for with Toreth, assuming the upcoming evening went as planned? He still seemed, in Carnac's judgment, reluctant to initiate sex, or to suggest activities outside working hours. Passive resistance, proving that there was still more to take from him. What would serve as a demonstration that Carnac had completely broken through? The obvious thing was a request to see Carnac again after his assignment had ended. Was that too ambitious? Perhaps. On the other hand, one didn't learn unless one was prepared to stretch oneself.

A request, then, for a continuation of the liaison. A request that Carnac would refuse in no uncertain terms, with a full and detailed explanation as to why. Toreth would be left in no doubt as to how expertly and easily he'd been played, although naturally he'd do that part by comm. There was no point risking life and limb and he'd still be able to see Toreth's face.

Really, a para-investigator ought to appreciate the elegance of the scheme and the depth of pain inflicted using nothing but words and a little patience for the setup. The sophistication of the approach was probably outside his reach, though. Even if it were within his grasp under normal circumstances, he would be in no condition to admire it. With his profoundly limited resources, Toreth was not emotionally equipped to handle a shock of this kind without serious consequences. One of those consequences would be that Toreth's relationship with Keir would be damaged or, more likely, destroyed completely. His trust was so fragile a thing that to have it so comprehensively violated by one person would very probably render him unable to maintain his limited affections towards the only other two people with whom he had connected.

Carnac was in two minds as to whether this was a minus or a plus. Taking the broader view, it did Keir no good to be tied to someone so manifestly unsuitable. One might even construe it as doing him a favor. A little short-term pain for a greater long-term gain.

He smiled thinly and poured a second glass of wine. Looking beyond the levels of rationalization, he foresaw a highly pleasing result: it would be a most satisfying recompense for the unpleasantness of the demonstration interrogation.

Despite her resolution, Sara let the rest of the week go past in worrying and formulating dead-end plans. She had at least, via a friend of a friend of a friend on the admin network, discovered that Carnac was expected back at Socioanalysis sometime next week. Unfortunately, the pressure of a looming deadline didn't cause any great ideas to spring to mind. It didn't help that the atmosphere in the office was so... pleasant. Friendly. It was only occasionally that she caught Toreth looking, if not unhappy, then at least a little preoccupied. Not that she got to speak to him much. Carnac was monopolizing his coffee breaks, and she wondered if he was deliberately keeping Toreth away from her.

It was Friday again before she found something that might count as inspiration. There was one sure-fire way to get Toreth to sit up and take notice. One thing that could snap him out of this awful downwards spiral of intimacy. She really ought to have thought of it before. Maybe the idea of using his feelings as a lever felt too much like what Carnac was doing to him. But she was doing it to help, not to play mind-fuck games. That wouldn't make him any less pissed off if he found out.

Productivity suffered in the afternoon as she considered the plan from as many angles as she could, finally deciding it was acceptable. Although right now so would be pretty much anything that seemed to have even half a chance of working. Still, she had an approach. And, even better, she had the perfect tool to exploit it.

The next question was, when should she try? Should she leave it until next week? The idea of letting Carnac have free rein to screw with Toreth for any longer made her grind her teeth, but on the other hand, if everything went horribly wrong, it would be a disaster to have the two of them in the same office for any longer than was necessary.

Chapter Nine

❖

It had taken Carnac longer than he had anticipated to work Toreth around to the invitation. It was late on Saturday evening when he finally achieved his goal and stepped through the doorway. He had had to manipulate more than he'd really wanted to, but he didn't feel that he had broken any rules. If Toreth gave it any thought he would be certain that the invitation was his own idea, even if he might have trouble explaining to himself why he'd wanted to extend it.

The flat was a mess, which had been one of the two possibilities—this, or obsessive tidiness. If he could have found anyone willing to take such a sure bet, he would happily place a large sum on Toreth's parents' home being show-house perfect. If he recalled correctly, Warrick's home had been extremely tidy. An interesting parallel there which he might point out to Toreth later.

"Do you want a drink?" Toreth asked.

"Coffee, thanks." That would, at least, involve boiling water and so might not actually constitute a health hazard.

"Bedroom's through there."

Carnac could take a hint, and besides, he was curious. The bedroom proved to be less of a mess than the small living room, and to have some unusual fixtures. Bolts had been set in the wall, although without the chains they were plainly designed to anchor. Presumably those were kept somewhere out of sight. Leather straps hung from the bed head and foot. All rather uncomfortable-looking, and not really Carnac's thing.

Opening a wardrobe, he found the contents neat and well ordered. On reflection, the brief surprise lessened. Smart clothing was a necessary part of the façade Toreth presented to the outside world, his unimpeachable physical and sartorial shield. Plenty of worn clothes lay scattered on the floor where they had been discarded. Snake skins, his mind supplied whimsically. Carnac recalled a psychology tutor who had maintained that a person's home was a direct reflection of their state of mind; he would have been absolutely enthralled by Toreth's flat.

Carnac looked around the room, at the positioning of the furniture, and took a guess as to where the rest of the bondage equipage might be found. When he opened the drawer, he discovered a box that contained a rather expensive-looking set of chains, metal wristbands, and a metal collar that looked positively painful. There were also more leather straps, blindfolds, a gag or two, and two pairs of handcuffs that had probably made an unauthorized escape from I&I. Warrick must find the arrangement quite satisfactory indeed.

"See anything you like the look of?"

He hadn't heard Toreth come in. He closed the drawer and turned around. "Not really."

Toreth smiled, handing him a coffee. "No? I thought you might have."

Just for a moment, Carnac wondered what it would be like. It would be an excellent opportunity to try the experience, because he was certain Toreth would be very good at it. Then he dismissed the idea. Fucking or being fucked by I&I's finest was one thing. Allowing them to immobilize one first required an entirely different level of trust, and one he couldn't manufacture. "No," he said, more firmly.

Toreth merely nodded. He stood for a moment, looking at the bolts in the wall, blowing on his coffee. Then he turned back to Carnac and smiled. "So, do you want to fuck?"

Toreth couldn't sleep, which considering what a night they'd made of it was fairly astonishing. He lay in bed and listened to Carnac breathing next to him (snoring, actually, which he really should've expected), and stared sightlessly at the ceiling until he had to accept that he was awake, and going to stay that way.

Getting up, he located a pair of trousers and went to hunt through the fridge for something to drink. He found and threw out a couple of containers of no longer fresh juice that Warrick had left behind last time he'd been there. In the end he had to settle for something processed that might, at one time in its long life, have been somewhere near a grapefruit.

He also discovered a carton of takeaway noodles of uncertain ancestry, still with a fork in it. That sort of thing drove Warrick mad, but as far as Toreth was concerned, it just meant that the cutlery was already with the food when he needed it. Like now. Sitting on the floor by the fridge, he picked through the noodles and tried to work out what was wrong.

He felt strange, as though the ground was shifting under his feet. Lots of little things felt wrong, and somehow they added up to this formless worry stopping him from sleeping. It felt wrong that Carnac was here, in his flat. He couldn't even remember how or why he'd invited him back. It didn't really matter, in an absolute sense. It was out of place and disturbing, though, all the more so since Carnac was here and Warrick wasn't.

Then there was a constant niggle of annoyance that he couldn't go to Warrick's. Normally he didn't worry about not seeing him for a day or two. Or even longer, although they'd been seeing a lot of each other lately. Maybe that was the problem—the regular thing turning into a habit. It might be no bad thing not to see him for a while. It would serve Warrick right, because he'd been completely unreasonable about the whole thing. Then the memory of last Sunday came back, making him feel even more unsteady and off-balance. Warrick so cold, really angry—it hadn't bothered him until now, but...

Something else wrong: Carnac in the office yesterday. Reading the screen from behind him, one hand kneading Toreth's shoulder, the other reaching down to rub his cock through his trousers. Bizarrely, he almost hadn't noticed what Carnac was doing until it had felt so good that it triggered some instinct, something like his current disquiet, and he'd tried to pull away. But Carnac had slid his hand around his shoulder to hold him back and murmured, "Don't move. I know you like it."

So he hadn't moved. Instead he'd closed his eyes and enjoyed the moment, until he'd come into Carnac's hand, arching against the arm across his chest and saying...Carnac's name? But that was too bizarre. He couldn't have done it—his memory was playing tricks.

Besides, whatever he'd said, it was stupid to feel uneasy about it. He should be grateful that the man had turned out to be less annoying than he'd seemed at first, as well as a rather better fuck. He was even becoming tolerable to talk to. Earlier in the week they'd discussed Sara—nothing he specifically remembered, but Carnac seemed to like her, or at least appreciate her efficiency, which was always good to hear. Toreth valued his reputation as someone who could attract the best to his team.

Carnac would be gone soon, anyway. He'd mentioned next week as the end of the investigation. After that Toreth would have his office back to himself. He couldn't remember if Carnac had ever said where he was based. The Socioanalysis Division Center at Strasbourg, he'd always assumed, insofar as he'd ever thought about it. The Administration could send Carnac anywhere they liked, of course, or he could be on to his freelance time after this job. Either way, he might well be in New London. And available.

It wouldn't be entirely a bad thing to see him again. Sometime. There wouldn't be any need to mention it to Warrick. Maybe he'd ask during the week sometime where Carnac was going next. Still, he couldn't shake the feeling.

I know you like it.

Carnac had no business knowing something like that.

Sara stood around the corner from the entrance to Toreth's flat, drinking out of a quarter bottle of vodka and hating every mouthful. God, it was revolting stuff neat, but she didn't have the leisure for mixers. The problem with Toreth was that there was no point pretending about something like being drunk. He'd see through it in a minute. So she had to *be* drunk, but still capable of following the plan. The other problem was that she would have to lie, quite a lot, about what she knew and how she knew it. She had everything prepared and corroborated, ready in the unlikely event that he'd check, but he was too damn good at spotting lies to make it a comfortable idea. And if he worked out what she was doing...no. Don't think about that.

It was for his own good.

It would have a been a lot easier and far more pleasant to have done this in stages over the evening, in the normal way. Except that that would've been too much like admitting she was going through with it. Besides, she'd spent most of the evening sorting out her alibis and getting the story straight. So, here she was, downing spirits on an empty stomach. At least that would mean she'd need to drink less of the stuff.

When she'd had a quarter of the bottle, she used the next mouthful to wash down a couple of tablets she'd wangled from Daedra Kincaidy in the pharmacy. She'd feel like seventeen kinds of shit in the morning, but some things had to be done. As she kept drinking, the alcohol settled into her limbs and tongue, but the focus of her thoughts sharpened. Drunk around the edges and sober in the middle. Daedra had come through on this one.

When she felt convincingly plastered, she dropped the bottle into a waste re-cycler and let herself into the building. She could have let herself into his flat as well, but she didn't like to, when he was there. There was no answer on the comm, for such a long time that she began to worry that he wasn't even in. Why hadn't she checked? God, it was horrible being sober enough to feel yourself being drunk.

Just when she was about to resort to banging on the door, he opened it. "Sara? Are you all right?"

She caught herself thinking, "how sweet," and had to fight down an urge to gig-gle. Concentrate. "I changed my code," she said. "For home. And now I've forgot-ten it. Can't get in."

He looked over his shoulder, and she realized straight away what that meant. The shock nearly sobered her completely. Carnac was here, in his flat. In his *flat.* Toreth never, ever invited his fucks back home. Unless you counted Warrick, which of course you didn't. What if she was too late again and he'd said or done something really stupid? Please, please, please God, let Carnac be asleep.

"'M really sorry." She leaned against the doorframe, half an act and half need-ing the support. "Can I crash, an' I'll sort it out in the morning?"

"Yeah, of course you can."

He took her through to the living room, cleared junk from the sofa and disap-peared in search of bedding. Moving very quietly, she noticed. She wondered if he could be embarrassed by Carnac's being here. It seemed unlikely. It hadn't bothered him the couple of times she'd slept—or rather not slept—here, with Warrick doing his well-screwed cat impersonation in the bedroom, and she somehow couldn't imagine Carnac as very vocal. Or...if he was embarrassed it was for another reason. Maybe the fact that Carnac was here at all. That was a cheering idea.

He came back with blankets and a pillow. Sweet, she thought again.

"Looks like you had a good evening," he said. "Where've you been?"

This was the tricky bit. "With Daedra. She can really put it away, you know?"

He grinned. "Probably had chemical help. Never get into a drinking competition with a pharmacist."

Too sharp for comfort. "Yeah, I should've remembered. It was just me and her—oh, 'cept we ran into Dillian. Small world, huh?"

That was an out-and-out lie, but he'd never call Dillian to check, not when asking Daedra would be so much easier. Dillian didn't like him and, if you excluded his compulsion to fuck her, the feeling was probably mutual. Still, the name definitely caught his attention.

"Yeah? How is she?" Hesitation, which she kept quiet for. "Did she say anything about Warrick?"

"Warrick? Not really." He'd asked. Thank God, he'd asked. She let the giggle escape. "Oh, 'cept he was chatting him up."

"Who was chatting who up?"

"Carnac. Chatting Warrick up."

His eyes narrowed. "What? Where?"

"Dunno. Dillian said they had dinner. Didn't he say?"

"No...he didn't. When?"

He hadn't known. Better still, he wasn't questioning whether it had happened, just when. Good. "Not sure." She lay down on the sofa. "Dillian reckons he was dead keen on him, way back when. Carnac on Warrick." She blinked, trying to fake a belated realization. "Warrick wouldn't, though. Screw Carnac." She pulled the cover over herself and curled up, yawning. "I mean, he's got you fucking him cross-eyed. Why'd he want Carnac? One-man whatsit. Man."

Toreth didn't answer. Final bit of the plan, and she was done—he could tie it all together for himself. "Anyway, they were talking about the sim, Dillian said so. That's Carnac's kind of thing, isn't it? Mind-fucking. I bet he'd go mad for it."

"Yes. Yes, I bet he would." Soft and dangerous. Oh yes, that was what she wanted to hear—the Toreth she knew and had the odd nightmare about. She closed her eyes and let her breathing drift off. She could feel him standing by the sofa, and she counted seconds, willing him to leave.

He wouldn't go to talk to Carnac. He'd go see Warrick. He had to. Go see Warrick. Don't let me have put myself through this for nothing. Go on. Go to Warrick. Go *on*.

58

Eventually, he left, and she held her breath until she heard, of all things, the shower running. It went on for a long time, and every second she expected to hear Carnac's voice. Then it stopped, and a few minutes after that she heard the outer door open and close.

She gave him a good twenty minutes head start, then weaved her way unsteadily out of the flat and caught a taxi home. Tempting as it was to stay until the morning and see Carnac, it wouldn't be a good idea, because she really didn't like the thought of him connecting her to Toreth's disappearance. She could always tell Toreth she'd remembered her code after all.

She felt extraordinarily pleased with herself. It had been a pretty good plan, if she did say so herself. Toreth wouldn't say a word about what she'd told him because it would make him look jealous, and he hated that. Warrick wouldn't say he'd spoken to her, because then Toreth would know they'd been talking about him. Shame she couldn't have told Warrick what she was planning, but it wouldn't have been fair. He'd have been left having to lie to Toreth, and that would've knackered the plan for certain. As it was, all he had to do was let Toreth in, screw him, and not ask too many questions. He must be getting good at that by now.

59

Chapter Ten

❖

As he stepped out onto the street, it occurred to Toreth how very satisfying it would have been to have thrown Carnac out of the flat. Preferably through the window. But he'd been afraid that if Carnac had woken up and said anything, just one fucking word about Warrick, he would've hit him. It had taken him ten minutes, and a long shower, even to be able to go back into the bedroom to get his clothes without giving in to the urge anyway.

Bastard. Planning his next fuck already. Which Toreth didn't care about—of course he didn't, why the hell would he?—except that he seemed to think it might be Warrick. Fuck that. Warrick was *his,* and no one else's. "This SimTech director belongs to . . ." him, not Carnac. Definitely not Carnac. That was never going to happen.

In the shower, his mind had veered towards the idea once or twice—Carnac fucking Warrick, in the sim or in the real world. Carnac telling him, "I know you like it." And then . . . then he'd wanted to strangle him. Not a good career move.

Lately, he'd somehow ended up thinking about Carnac too much and let Warrick slip out of his mind. That was a testament to how incredibly annoying Carnac was. He ought to buy Sara another bunch of flowers for making him notice that, as well as inadvertently passing on Carnac's plans. On the other hand she mightn't remember doing either. Best to forget it, and to concentrate on sorting things out with Warrick. Toreth had to make absolutely sure that when Carnac was done at I&I he didn't find a welcome elsewhere.

Interested in the sim. Nice line, and Toreth should know.

So he stood in the street, and wondered where to go for the rest of the night. A hotel or Warrick's? The hotel was the logical choice. It was so logical that, in the end, he had to admit that he was trying to talk himself into going to Warrick's. Why else had he had the shower?

There was the small problem of what Warrick had said the last time he'd seen him. Much as he hated the idea, he'd still have to think of his career and fuck

60

Carnac in the office, on demand, until he finally went, and then he could forget the man. Easiest just to tell Warrick it was over—only another week and it would be true. If it wasn't finished in the technical sense, it was in the...whatever. No more fucking outside working hours, anyway. No more Sundays, which was what had annoyed Warrick. That would be enough. Maybe Warrick wouldn't even ask. It had been a few days, and he was bound to have got over his sulk by now.

That theory didn't mesh well with reality when he activated the comm for the flat. It took a while for Warrick to answer (not surprising, when Toreth looked at his watch) and when he did, he didn't sound delighted to see his visitor. "What the hell are you doing here?"

No picture, just a voice. Déjà vu. At least this time he wasn't going to throw up anywhere, and he could manage the words. "I just want to talk to you."

"Perhaps I didn't make myself clear before."

"That's all finished," he said, trying not to think about Carnac asleep in his flat.

A short silence followed, then Warrick said, "All right. Come up."

He wondered if Warrick would have dressed by the time he got upstairs, but he hadn't. He opened the door in his dressing gown, looking sleepy and irritable. And fuckable. God, he looked good. How could he have forgotten in just a few days how much he could want him? Especially when there was a bad temper to coax him out of.

"Do you know what *time* it is?" Warrick said.

"Half past two."

"Oh, good. I had wondered if you bother to check before you wake me up. Well, come in, then." Warrick closed the door behind him, but didn't reset the security. "What do you want to talk about?"

Toreth hesitated. Now that he was here, he had no idea, since he hadn't thought beyond the conviction that Warrick would be happy to hear he was done with Carnac and...things would be all right. Everything would be fine and they'd fuck, or they'd fuck and everything would be fine.

Warrick sighed. "If you don't have anything to say, do you think I could get back to sleep?"

"I had a shower."

Warrick looked at him blankly for a moment, then said, "I see." Toreth thought—hoped—that he caught sight of a brief smile as Warrick turned away to reset the alarm. "And?"

"And...I didn't want to talk." He hooked his fingers through the belt of Warrick's dressing gown. "I'd much rather fuck."

"What a surprise." Warrick resisted the pull. "You disappear for a week—"

Unfair, for once. "The fuck I did. You threw me out."

"You disappear for a week, and then you expect to walk back in here and find

61

me ready for you?" If he was smiling, it didn't show in his voice. "Grateful for your attention?"

Toreth blinked. What the hell else should he expect?

Warrick turned around, the belt sliding through Toreth's fingers. He kept his grip, but Warrick ignored it. He was pale with anger, which didn't help Toreth's concentration in the least. Having Warrick so close was making him achingly hard. The last fuck with Carnac seemed like a distant memory. He itched to touch Warrick, strip him, fuck him right here in the hall. He'd need another shower in a minute, a very cold one.

"Do you imagine that I don't have anything better to do with my life than to wait around for you to turn up unannounced at some godforsaken hour of the night and fuck me?" Warrick asked.

Well, yes. "No, of course not."

"Very convincing."

He fell back on formula. "Warrick, I'm sorry."

Raised eyebrow. "About what, exactly?"

Bastard. "I'm sorry I woke you up, and . . ." And whatever. Whatever it was that would put it right. Why was he making it more difficult than usual?

"Mm." Warrick turned and walked off, getting free by the simple expedient of unfastening the belt so that it pulled through the loops of the gown.

Still holding the belt, he followed Warrick into the bedroom, fighting down the first stirrings of doubt. Dinner. Sara said they'd had dinner. What if Carnac had already said something to Warrick? What if they'd already . . . Doubt edged into fear, with anger not far behind.

He caught Warrick's arm, harder than he'd meant to. Warrick stopped dead and turned, looking down at Toreth's hand until he released him. Then he walked away again, not far, and stood staring into the mirror without seeming to focus on it. Toreth didn't try to touch him again. "Warrick, listen, I'm sorry about last weekend. But it's finished." He felt desperate enough to repeat the lie and risk drawing more attention to it. "That's what you said, wasn't it? What you wanted?"

He had déjà vu again, although he couldn't imagine why; he found himself beginning to wish he'd gone to a hotel instead, or anywhere else but here. It had been stupid to come back. He should've waited and sorted it all out later, when Carnac was gone for good. Better just to leave. At least try to get out of here with some dignity. "If you want me to go away again, I'll go. But—" What had Warrick said, before? "Will you tell me what's wrong first?"

"If it were anyone else—" Warrick shook his head. "But you have no idea, do you?"

Not when you're being so fucking cryptic. "If you'll just fucking *tell* me, then I will."

After a long moment of silence, Warrick shook his head. "It's nothing I want to talk about at half past two in the morning. And...no, I have no particular wish for you to leave." He smiled slightly, reflected. "You do pick your moments, don't you?"

For what? He went over and rested his hands on Warrick's shoulders, wanting everything to be all right again. Wanting to feel safe, solid ground. "So *do* you want to fuck?" Warrick didn't say no, not yet, so he added, "Anything. Anything you want."

That got his attention. Warrick looked up, catching his eyes in the mirror. "Anything?"

"Yes." He dipped his head, lowered his voice, watching Warrick's face. "Anything at all. Just ask me, I'll do it for you."

Warrick turned around to face him. "Even...let me fuck you?"

"Yes, of course, if that's what you want. I said anything." He grinned with sheer relief. "Hell, you can tie me up and fuck me if you'd like to."

"I don't know." Warrick tilted his head, considering. "I might. Would you?"

"What?" The offer hadn't been meant seriously, and the reply unbalanced him all over again. Warrick didn't ask again. He simply stood there, expression neutral, waiting for a reply. Toreth didn't have one, not straight away. Did he want to? Did it matter what he wanted? He'd promised, so he couldn't back out. Before he could change his mind, he offered the belt to Warrick, who smiled brilliantly.

"Really?" Warrick asked.

"I said anything, didn't I?" He shook the silk slightly. "Go on."

When Warrick took the belt, Toreth held his hands out. "No," Warrick said. "Behind your back."

Yes, of course. He stepped past Warrick, facing the mirror, and put his arms behind him, crossing his wrists. He could see Warrick, behind him, his face and shoulders and glimpses of the rest of him as he moved, touching him. Fastening the belt around his wrists. Unfastening clothes. He watched, fascinated. When had anyone last undressed him (at least when he was conscious)? He always enjoyed fucking in front of mirrors, or windows, or anywhere else where he could see Warrick's face reflected. Never before with himself in front and Warrick behind, though.

The reversal was weirdly disorienting. Unexpectedly arousing. He was going to let Warrick fuck him. Let him, hell—he wanted it. Not in the sim, but for the first time here in the real world. He tried to get the anticipation under some kind of control. No reason to think it would be anything that special. It wasn't as if he'd never been fucked before. Just never by Warrick.

And like this, never by anyone. He twisted his wrists, feeling the fabric give a little as the knot tightened. To his surprise, he felt his pulse pick up speed, and trusting his voice seemed like a bad idea. They did it in the sim, or something like it—Warrick stripping his movements and senses away one by one until there was only touch left. This wasn't anything like as extreme a surrender...but it was real.

Once Warrick had removed all the clothes that could be removed under the circumstances, he pulled Toreth's shirt back over his shoulders, pinning his arms more effectively than the belt. Toreth focused on Warrick's face in the mirror, his lips moving as he spoke. "Close your eyes."

It seemed a pity to lose the picture, but he did it. Playing the game. He felt Warrick's hands on his bare shoulders, thumbs stroking. "I should bite you, don't you think?"

He cleared his throat. "Whatever you want."

Toreth felt Warrick's weight shift, then a touch of soft lips on the back of his neck. Kisses, not a bite, until he relaxed. Then he gasped as teeth sank in. Hard mouth, sucking hard, as his spine tried to curl into a ball to escape. He gasped again when it stopped. God, was *that* one going to bruise.

Warrick was silent for a moment, surveying his handiwork—mouth work—then Toreth heard him mutter, "*That* won't wash off."

Labeling him. His stomach tightened at the idea, with a prickle of hot and cold. Not wanting to think about that, he licked his lips and whispered, "Fuck me." Trying the words.

Behind him, Warrick went quite still.

"Fuck me." It sounded good. Tasted good. He had no idea why he wanted it so much right now, but when he added, "Please," he meant it.

The hands on his shoulders tightened. "Say that again." Warrick playing the role, and meaning it, too.

In return, Toreth decided to try the whole thing. "I want you to fuck me."

Warrick. Not Carnac. Not a hundred other nameless fucks. He wanted Warrick, right now. Because he couldn't say any of that, he pressed back against Warrick, bound fingers finding his cock and making him gasp.

"Fuck me. I need it." I need *you*.

Warrick's fingers dug into his shoulders. "Then maybe we should go to bed."

He opened his eyes. "No." The refusal was out of character, but he didn't care. "Do it here, in front of the mirror."

"That—" Warrick stopped, coughed, started again. "That might be tricky. It would be a lot easier with your hands free."

Which was a good point, although it brought an unexpected twinge of disappointment. "Okay."

The belt pinched his skin briefly, then loosened. He quickly stripped off his shirt and, before Warrick could discard the belt, he turned around and offered his wrists again.

Warrick raised an eyebrow, surprised by the acquiescence. "You don't have to—"

"No, I don't." If Warrick wanted it, that was a good enough reason for tonight.

Without further comment, Warrick bound his wrists again, and turned him back to face the mirror. He reached out, touching his own hands in the glass.

Warrick crouched beside him, resting his cheek against his hip, and stroked his hand up the back of his thighs, making Toreth think of the first virtual fuck in the sim. Despite the fact that he wanted this—he really did—he could feel the muscles tensing under Warrick's touch, however much he willed them to relax. The hand slid over his buttocks, down between them, and the muscles clenched again, a shiver running down his back.

Warrick paused. "Are you—"

"Oh, for fuck's sake, yes, I am."

"I didn't even finish."

"I'm fine, I'm sure, I'm whatever."

"I was going to ask, are you cold?"

"Oh." He thought about it, trying to isolate the information from a nervous system occupied by other things. "Yes, a bit."

"I thought you might be. Housekeeping: temperature up four degrees in the bedroom."

Warrick ran his other hand up over Toreth's stomach, tracing the muscles. "The problem being, of course, that you lack any sort of insulation." He turned his head and kissed Toreth's hip, lips moving against him as he spoke. "Not that I'm complaining, you understand. Quite the opposite. I could sit and admire the lack for hours, despite what it would do to your already monstrously overinflated ego. Or even kneel and admire. Anyway, I usually turn the heating up before you get here, or set the system to do it if we've gone out."

"All right, all right. Next time I'll call."

"Better all around. Not that it takes long to kick in."

It didn't. Or possibly the excuse wasn't needed any more, because Warrick hadn't stopped touching him, and while he wasn't paying attention the tension had quietly slipped away. Now Warrick looked around, then checked his dressing gown pockets and produced a tube.

"That's not where you usually keep it."

"No, I—" Warrick laughed. "I picked it up off the side when I heard the comm. Reflex, I suppose. I knew it was you—who the hell else would it be at this time?"

He felt safe enough to risk teasing. "So I can expect to walk in here and find you ready for me?"

"Apparently, yes, you can."

"Well, then, in future I'll—oh!" Cool gel, firmly applied. He started, forgetting his hands were tied. He'd been watching Warrick's face, not his hands.

"Serves you right," Warrick said.

"That wasn't nice."

"Sorry." Even less convincing than his own apology earlier. "How about that?"

Warrick's finger slipped easily inside him, and Toreth let his shoulders roll back. "Mmm. Yes."

Looking between Warrick beside him and their reflection in the mirror was excitingly strange. He had nothing to do except watch—being done to, not doing. Warrick watched him in return, intent on his reactions. It wasn't really the optimum position for relaxed, thorough foreplay, but the bed would have felt too claustrophobic, too...submissive. Although that was a pretty stupid thing to think, when he was standing here with his hands tied up and his head bowed, aching for more than just fingers inside him.

He was thinking about this far too much. So don't, he told himself. Just enjoy.

Warrick was incredibly good at this. He wondered where he learned it. With whom. It couldn't be Carnac, of course. That thought triggered another, the memory of the fuck in the office. He'd said Carnac's name as he came. He knew he had. What if, for some stupid reason, he did it again? Warrick would throw a fit, or maybe even throw him out again. Toreth felt himself tensing up again. He was—

Thinking again.

Warrick moved around to kneel in front of him, giving a thoroughly appreciated view of his back and arse, from midthigh upwards. He couldn't see, in the mirror, what Warrick was doing, but he didn't need to, because he felt a hand on his cock and then a brief, hot breath before Warrick's mouth closed around his cock. Tonguing him, light and shallow. Not enough to push him too far, but enough to distract him from whatever the hell he'd been thinking about.

Don't think. Just enjoy it going on.

On and on, until he'd forgotten where it was leading, or even that his wrists were tied. Toreth's eyes drifted closed without his noticing. His hands rested lightly on Warrick's head, stroking absently through his thick, soft hair.

Then Warrick's fingers and mouth were gone, leaving him cold again. Someone was breathing loudly, very close by. He was trying to frame a protest, when he realized that Warrick had said something. He looked down, meeting Warrick's hot gaze. "What?" Toreth asked.

"I said, ready?"

Oh, God, yes. He nodded, then, bracing his hands against the glass, he closed his eyes again. Not because he was expecting it to hurt, but because he wanted to remember the feeling.

Warrick stood up, moved around behind him and put an arm around his waist. Slight height adjustment. Then...nothing. "You have to ask for it," Warrick said after a moment.

Of course. He managed to gather enough breath to speak. "Fuck me."

"Again."

"I want you—" and a pause before he remembered to add, "—to fuck me."

He could feel Warrick's cock against him, so tormentingly close to where he needed it. He could see why Warrick got such a kick out of this part of the game—the anticipation was killing him.

"Now?"

"Yes, *now*. Please."

Pressure, stretching him, starting to fill him. Warrick's hands on his hip and shoulder. He clenched his fists against the glass, biting back a moan, not wanting to give away how very, very much he wanted this. Warrick stopped, halfway, and he could feel the effort it took. Did Warrick think he hadn't done this before? Take a breath. "Go on. I'm okay."

"You...you might be. But I'm not." Warrick drew his breath in sharply as Toreth pushed back towards him. "God, don't. I need a minute. Or this will be the highest ratio of foreplay to fuck on record. I haven't...done this for a while." He took another breath, let it out slowly. "And it really *isn't* like the sim. So strange, because there's no reason why it should be different. The modeling is relatively simple and very accurate." He eased deeper and sighed. "No. Not at all the same."

Toreth smiled, watching himself, and Warrick behind him, face hidden as he breathed raggedly into his shoulder. That felt better, somehow, knowing that Warrick wanted it so badly. "I'm not going anywhere."

"I should think not, after dragging me out of bed." Warrick pushed forwards, all the way, and his hands tightened on him. "Mmh. Dragging me out of bed, demanding sex, and—"

"Warrick."

"Mm?"

"Shut up." Too many conversational fucks with Carnac he didn't want to remember, and thinking about Carnac was dangerous. "Shut up and fuck me."

Saying the words gave him the same weird thrill, and from the way Warrick pressed against him, shuddering, he wasn't getting bored with hearing them yet. "Toreth, if you keep...saying that..."

"Fuck me." Himself in the mirror, and Warrick behind him. "Fuck me. I want to feel it. Do it. Now. Fuck me. I want—"

Whatever self-control Warrick had managed to gather wasn't up to that, and he pulled back, thrust in hard. Then again, a little clumsy—out of practice as he'd said, or nearly out of control. Toreth shifted his feet, angled his hips to meet each stroke until—yes—that was it. Oh, yes. Every movement building the pleasure. He moaned out loud, not caring now because Warrick was already making more than enough noise to cover it.

"Yes, oh God yes, so good..." Warrick's voice muffled against him, showing precisely how close he was. Even though they'd never fucked quite like this before, Toreth could read him as easily as ever. It wouldn't last long, but it didn't matter because whatever had been wrong before, everything was all right. He wasn't so close, yet, but he was desperate to be touched, needing it *now*. If he'd been able to get a hand free, he would have done it himself, but the knots had tightened hopelessly and he couldn't slip a hand through. "Warrick."

Warrick didn't hear him—probably couldn't even hear himself by now, words blurring into harsh sobs.

He struggled for a moment, panting, almost panicking if he hadn't been so aroused. He couldn't bear the idea that Warrick might come without him, leaving him like this. From now on he was tying, not being tied. He raised his voice. "Please. Warrick, please."

Nothing so coherent as a reply, but he got a response, which was much better. A hand sliding down to take hold of his cock, just exactly, perfectly how he needed it. How he liked it. Bracing himself against the mirror, he pushed back hard.

He forgot about the belt around his wrists. Everything he wanted was elsewhere: Warrick against him, skin on skin, inside him, his arms around him, hand stroking him faster, hot breath against his neck, all wonderful, all making a lie out of the idea that it was nothing special. He gave himself up completely to the overwhelming sensations, gasping Warrick's name without having to think about it at all.

Toreth awoke to the sharp burn of pins and needles in his hands and a pillow wedged uncomfortably under one shoulder. Then he realized that Warrick still had his arms around him and that his face was pressed into Warrick's chest, hair tickling as he breathed. He could taste salted skin again.

As well as his hands, his calves were aching and he could feel the bites on his neck, both the first one and some more he didn't remember getting. He was sticky, and slightly, pleasantly, sore. Just enough to know that he'd been having fun.

At least they had made it as far as the bed before they fell asleep. It felt good, lying there. It felt better than the fuck itself. Almost. He gave it a minute, a long minute (probably nearer five, but who was counting?), then shrugged his way free and sat up. Warrick opened his eyes and looked up inquiringly.

"Get this stupid belt off me," Toreth said.

Warrick laughed. "Do you ever wake up in a *good* mood?"

He had been in the shower for about thirty seconds when Toreth joined him. It was a little disconcerting, because Warrick had more than half expected to get back to the bedroom to find Toreth gone. That would have been a pity, but he wouldn't have minded a little time alone to sort out his thoughts. Still, he wasn't complaining. Not after that. It had been more than worth waiting for, and the belt had been an unexpected bonus, although in the end he'd actually enjoyed that part of it a lot less that he'd expected, and he wondered how it would have been in the sim.

Sex is strange, he thought whimsically, as Toreth stepped under the spray, nudging him aside. An illustration of the difference between theory and practice, fantasy and reality—sim and reality. Endless scope for entertaining investigations and comparisons. He really needed to set up a focused research program to explore the purely psychological limitations of the sim experience.

Warrick raised the temperature of the water, before Toreth asked him to. Toreth found something else to complain about, anyway. "Have you seen the state of my neck?" he said, turning his back towards him.

Impressive suck marks, hints of teeth here and there. More impressive than he'd intended or remembered, but Toreth didn't sound genuinely annoyed. "Indeed I have. I had an excellent view."

"Couldn't you have done it a bit lower down?"

"I'm afraid not." He worked the soap into a lather between his hands and smoothed it over the offending bites, then down over Toreth's back. "Although to be quite fair, I seem to have bitten your shoulders as well. Sorry."

"What the hell is Sara going to think tomorrow?"

"She's going to think—" The soap escaped, but there was enough on Toreth now that it didn't matter for the moment. Warrick pressed up against him, enjoying the view all over again. "She's going to think that I fucked you senseless."

Toreth turned around in his arms. "You should've noticed by now that I usually fall asleep afterwards. That says nothing at all about the quality of the fuck."

"I see." He bent down to find the soap, surprising Toreth on the way back up with a quick—slightly soapy—suck. More of a lick, but it made him jump. Not a good thing in a shower. Warrick steadied him, then asked, "It wasn't up to standard?"

He continued washing them both while Toreth pretended to think about it. It would've been more convincing without the smirk. "It wasn't bad," he said eventually. "I wouldn't mind doing it again some time—without the belt, though. You?"

"Mm."

His expression must have said the rest, in highly flattering terms, because Toreth laughed. "You could have asked, you know, if you wanted it that much."

And Toreth could have said no, couldn't he? Warrick didn't want to know the answer to that, though, because kicking himself at this point would be risky. Too much soap around. Anyway, the feel of hard muscles, also slippery with soap, was giving him ideas he'd like to follow up later. Tomorrow morning—this morning rather—which was Sunday. "Are you staying for the rest of the night? Insofar as there is any."

"If that's okay?"

"Perfectly."

"Thanks." Toreth pushed wet hair back from his face. "Actually, I don't have anywhere else to go. My bed's full of snoring spook."

Warrick stared at him, wanting so badly to have heard that wrong. All he could think was that he'd been crassly, unbelievably stupid, and that everything Toreth had said earlier, and worse, everything he'd done since, had been a lie. The moment passed, but it left Carnac's words behind. *A measure of thoughtlessness and indeed cruelty on his part...*

He didn't think that, right now, he could bear to hear any more. Toreth seemed to be expecting a comment of some kind, though. "That's why you came here?" Warrick asked.

"Yeah." Toreth smiled brightly. "I didn't want to wake him up, because if he'd opened his fucking mouth, I would've put my fist through it and out the back of his head."

"Oh." It was the only thing he could think of to follow that up. That, and assorted questions, none of which Toreth would answer. At least the unspoken message was clear—Carnac had, for whatever reasons, seriously outstayed his welcome. However he'd ended up at Toreth's flat tonight, he wouldn't be there again. Still, the worry and doubt lingered. He couldn't ignore it, and his self-respect wouldn't let him. He stepped back, and the water washed the soap away from where their bodies had been pressed too close together for it to reach. "Just to get one thing absolutely clear, you do remember our prior conversation? You won't be seeing Carnac again?"

"Of course I'll be seeing him. He's still squatting in my office."

"That's not what I meant." Where had the unaccustomed euphemism come from?

There was a long silence, so long that he was half expecting the answer when it came. "Warrick, be reasonable. Please. I can't *not* fuck him while he's at I&I. That's what he volunteered me for. Even Tillotson realized that, and he didn't like it but he made it pretty bloody clear I had to do what I was told."

For a moment, between outrage and disbelief, he genuinely couldn't breathe, never mind speak. Then, before he said anything, the sense of the words fought its way through to his consciousness. Did Toreth really mean that? *Could* he mean that?

"You're saying that you don't want to?" It sounded so ridiculous he expected Toreth to laugh.

Instead, Toreth reddened, obvious even through the flush of the hot water. "No, I don't. Look, if you're that interested, I didn't particularly want to fuck him in the first place, and now it's getting..." He shrugged. "You know me. Twice is once too many."

"Then...don't do it?" He wondered if the idea had never occurred to Toreth—his initial expression suggested that might be the case. But after a few seconds, he shook his head, scattering water.

"It's not that simple. He'll shaft me in the report instead, and his opinion means a lot. I don't need that kind of thing in my file. If I piss him off, I can kiss my career goodbye."

"He won't do that. He'll write an honest report. If you've been doing your job well, then that's what he'll say." Never mind what "doing your job well" meant. That wasn't the issue right now.

Toreth mulled the suggestion over, his expression serious this time. "Are you sure?"

"It's what he did for me at the Data Division."

He frowned, dubious. "You told him you didn't want to fuck any more, and he just said 'okay'?"

"Yes. Precisely so. And he put a very favorable mention of my work in his report."

"Oh. Right. Then I'll tell him tomorrow." He grinned happily, a minor but irritating problem solved. "See? I told you it was no big deal."

Warrick could have hit him. "Thank you."

That was almost that. As they were drying off, Warrick remembered something. Something he ought to mention. Maybe now wasn't the time, but there wouldn't be a better time, either. "I had dinner with him," he said. "With Carnac."

Toreth looked up. "I... You didn't tell me." His voice held a hint of accusation.

"I'm telling you now. It was a few days ago. He told me—"

"Forget it," Toreth said sharply, then shrugged. "Who gives a fuck about him, anyway?"

Chapter Eleven

❖

Carnac arrived at the I&I offices early on Monday. Waking up yesterday to find Toreth gone had been a slight surprise. He didn't have many of those in his life, so he was keen to discover the explanation. He had a good idea of where he had gone, since Toreth's personal comm had refused his calls all yesterday, and so had Warrick's. His hard work was undone and Warrick had once again resumed his position as the central massif of Toreth's barren emotional landscape. Yet he was perfectly confident that it was impossible for Warrick to have called Toreth, or vice versa, as things had stood when he'd fallen asleep on Saturday night. Something unexpected had, most irritatingly, interfered with his plans.

Toreth arrived exactly on time and came straight over to sit on the edge of Carnac's desk. He picked up a piece of paper and started folding it. "You had dinner with Warrick," he said.

It was most definitely a statement, not a question. Carnac realized at once that he'd made a very serious mistake in not following through all the possible consequences of his impromptu acceptance of Keir's invitation. He should have told Toreth about it before. Honesty was the key to gaining his trust. "Yes, I did," he said.

Toreth nodded. "Did you fuck him?" he asked in the same measured tones.

"No."

"Did you try to?"

With his plan ruined anyway there was no real point in deception, but with Toreth in such close proximity it seemed wise. "No."

Toreth glanced up from the paper, finger stilling on a folded edge. "For a socioanalyst, you're a fucking awful liar." Nevertheless, Toreth seemed to like the answer. Of course—it demonstrated that Carnac was afraid of him, which he was, to a certain extent. He was also curious as to how and when Toreth had found out about the dinner, since that confidence hadn't come from a guess. Had this triggered the new turn of events?

"Lying isn't an official part of our training," Carnac said evenly. "As regards the other matter, I asked him, and he said no."

"Piece of free advice: don't ask him again. He's not available."

Possessiveness rang in every syllable—potentially dangerous possessiveness, if Carnac was any judge. "I don't waste my time chasing reluctant partners when I have a willing one."

Toreth smiled pleasantly. "Not any more you haven't. Find yourself another liaison."

"Oh?" That was another surprise; he'd thought Toreth's ambition would keep him in line for the duration.

"Yes." Toreth set a completed paper bird down on the desk, not badly made. "I'm bored with it, and besides, it's long past time someone told you that you're a lousy fuck. I have better sex on my own."

That hurt. Pathetically mundane as the insult had been, and primitive and irrational as the feeling was, it still hurt. Enough that he spoke without thinking. "You're not bored—you're frightened."

A moment of absolute silence and stillness followed, long enough for Carnac to begin to wonder how quickly he could make it to the door. Almost certainly not quickly enough. Then Toreth spoke, slowly and coldly. "You don't know the *first fucking thing* about me."

He could have said so much. Toreth was so vulnerable to his own unexamined emotions, so deeply in denial of his needs and motivations, that it would be trivially easy to come up with a response that would devastate him. An interconnected cascade of pain to demonstrate how very wrong he was.

I know that your parents resented your existence, and never gave you a second's love or approval that didn't carry with it a reminder of your failure to live up to their impossible demands.

I know that you trust exactly two people in your life, and that the only way you are capable of understanding that feeling is by trying to own them.

I know that you want Keir, more than you have wanted anything in your adult life, and that that uncontrollable need makes you sick with fear.

I know that, in the end, the pathetically little you have to offer him will no longer be enough, and he will leave you. And I know that there will be nothing you will be able to do to make him stay.

On the other hand, having his testicles torn off and stuffed down his throat didn't appeal half as much as, say, not. Destroying Toreth's future with Warrick wasn't worth major surgery. Carnac stood up. "Of course not. I apologize. Consider your assignment concluded. And don't worry—I'll write a glowing report for your file."

He wasn't expecting a reciprocal apology, and he didn't get one. "Shut the door on your way out," Toreth said.

73

Then Toreth sat down at his own desk and ignored him. As Carnac gathered his belongings, he watched Toreth surreptitiously. He could see the tension draining out of him. This experience wouldn't last long for Toreth. By the time Carnac's report was finished, he would be background noise again in Toreth's life. Something that had come and gone and perhaps been mildly unpleasant, but had barely touched the important parts. So. He could, he supposed, call it a technical victory on points, but there was no point cheating at solitaire. Chalk this one up as a failure.

After a brief hesitation, he took the paper bird and added it to the top of the pile. Memento. As he left, he paused in the doorway to look back. Toreth didn't look up.

On his way past her desk, he smiled at Sara. She smiled back, faux sympathetically. He judged her to be pleased by his departure, but unsurprised. So that was where the information regarding his dinner with Warrick had originated. It must have been very cleverly phrased to get the reaction it had. The woman was clearly capable of more subtlety than he had anticipated—careless of him to discount her. Really, he hadn't been on form. Perhaps the toxic atmosphere of I&I had unsettled him more than he'd realized.

"Do you need any help with that?" Sara asked, her courteous admin manner perfectly in place.

"No, thank you. And thank you for all your time."

She smiled again. "Try Senior Para Chevril, if you're looking for a new personal liaison."

Since the senior para's profile had indicated that he was as straight as a die, Carnac took her suggestion in the spirit it was offered, and went to inform I&I upper echelons that he'd finished his study and was returning to Socioanalysis. He could write the report as well there as anywhere, and, quite frankly, fuck his bosses if they wanted him to serve out his full time here.

He knew where he wasn't welcome. He should, by now.

As Long as It Lasted

(Five years before Mind Fuck)

There had been drinks at the bar, and with the meal, and at the club. Toreth had also borrowed a handful of assorted fun from a friend in the pharmacy and that had mixed very pleasantly into the course of the evening.

On the way back to his flat, he'd stopped off to buy a bottle of something bubbly and expensive. Sara deserved it. Exceeding the limits of a damage waiver was a serious charge, about the most serious that only resulted in dismissal from I&I and not anything more penal. It had been all the more serious because the complainant had been rich enough to afford a whole circus of trained attack lawyers.

Sara had fixed it for him. When he'd asked her how she'd found out that Justice was backing the complainant, she'd just shushed him, and said, "We admins have our little secrets as well, you know."

I&I higher-ups, who'd been quite happy to hand feed him to the dogs when it looked like a quick route out of the situation, had jumped smartly when their own empires were threatened. The help he'd been desperate for had rolled out overnight and the complaint withdrawn within a few days. All thanks to Sara and, strangest of all, she hadn't wanted anything in return. She hadn't even told him she was behind it. Chevril had found out from *his* admin and congratulated Toreth. Sara had shrugged off Toreth's thanks and said she'd do it for any of her friends.

For once in his life someone had done him a favor without even a hint of strings attached, and it was a strange feeling.

Now he lay on the sofa in the flat that he never invited anyone back to, wishing he'd tidied up, and listening to her talking. She was out of sight, by the window. "'S a nice flat," she said.

"It's a tip."

"Yeah, but it's cozy. Anyway, it's no more of a tip than mine. Maybe a bit more. Yeah. A bit. But it's nice. Near work. Mine's miles away. You can practic—prac-

75

tically fall out of bed and into the office." She leaned over the back of the sofa, then further over, and then she slid down onto him. Luckily, her glass was empty. He caught her automatically, and she ended up on top of him, her thighs astride his. She leaned on his chest and gazed into his face with drunken friendliness. Her stomach pressed down warmly on his cock, which responded enthusiastically.

He took the glass from her and put it on the table. "Hello," he said.

"Hello. Mmm...you're comfy." She wriggled into him and looked at him again, expectantly.

He should have taken the opportunity to kiss her, but he found himself hesitating. She'd worked for him for two years, now, and she'd never showed any desire to do this before. In fact, over the first few months she'd turned down his advances firmly and consistently until he'd given up. He strongly suspected this U-turn was due more to the particular combination of drugs and alcohol than to any new appreciation of his charms. He should have made a better note of what he'd given her.

Still, he felt an uncharacteristic need to clarify the situation. Simple and direct was best. "Are you sure you want to do this?"

"Do this?" She blinked at him. "'M not doing *anything*. Know why? 'Cause you're my boss. And I don't screw at work. It's messy." She giggled. "Well, 's always messy. Different mess. Though not with you. Wouldn't be a mess, 'cause I love you."

Why did she have to go and spoil it? "Don't be silly."

"It's not *silly*." She inched closer, her eyes crossing slightly. "It's why I saved your arse with Tillotson and everyone. 'Cause you're my friend and I love you."

He could have thrown her off easily, of course. But he didn't. Her breath, sweet with alcohol, smelled of something distantly remembered. Pomegranates, part of his brain supplied, while the rest of it wondered what the hell he was going to do. Left to its own devices, his body was getting on with business as usual and somehow he had ended up with his arms around her, pulling her down against him. Small, soft breasts against his chest, and her hips moving gently against him. "Sara—"

"Shh," she said, and kissed him, wetly, wonderfully.

She might not even remember, whispered a treacherous but distinctly convincing voice. Even if she does, where's the harm? Fuck her. She wants it. You want it. What the hell's the problem?

The problem was...the problem was that it was Sara. Even though he was far from sober himself, he still knew full well that she didn't really want to do it. She'd hate him in the morning, if she did remember, and while that was no novelty in general, he discovered suddenly and quite unexpectedly that he didn't want Sara to hate him under any circumstances. Especially not now, when she'd put herself on the line for him. Suppose she applied for a transfer? Or left I&I entirely?

He couldn't do it. *Shouldn't* do it, rather, because he most definitely could and if he didn't stop himself in the next minute or two, he was going to. "Sara, don't." Another mild objection, which wouldn't be any more use than the last one. So tempting to let her stay there.

"Shush." She kissed him again, one hand cupping his face—elbow wedged uncomfortably in his ribs—and the other hand sliding down him. Then she was groping him, the kiss fading away as she concentrated fiercely on the fastening of his trousers. Pissed as she was, she'd manage it before long.

He really ought to...move. Soon.

Then she succeeded, and her hand slipped inside. He had a nasty moment, imagining her fingernails as he'd last seen them, long and blood red. Then her fingers closed gently around his cock and he forgot about sharp nails, and about the ridiculous idea that he wasn't going to do this. Let instinct and long practice take over. He ran his fingers through her hair, tilting her head for a more careful, thorough kiss. She kissed him back, still stroking his cock, gentle caresses making him want a firmer grip.

He slid his other hand up her thigh, stopped at the top and slipped his fingers around the scanty fabric of her knickers. Tracing their edge around her hip, he discovered that they seemed to consist entirely of lace. He'd always wondered, but before now he'd never fucked anyone he'd felt like asking...

"Are those comfortable?"

She lifted her head. "Comfortable?"

"There's not much to them."

"Yeah, they are. Not cheap, but comfy. Because they're not cheap. Soft lace. See?" She took her hand away from his cock, put it over his and guided him further around, further down.

"I see," he said seriously. "Very nice."

She giggled, then drew her breath in sharply as he stroked his fingers along between her legs, exploring the territory.

"*Very* nice," he said. Not to mention very wet. Wetter than was justified by a few minutes' groping and a couple of kisses.

"How long have you been thinking about this?" he murmured into her ear. One finger slipped into her, stroking, as he began to rub her with his palm, small circles—gently to start with, gauging her reaction.

She let out a long breath and, on the end of it, said, "All evening."

"You've been thinking about me fucking you all evening?"

She nodded, her hair brushing his face. "Yes."

"Before that?"

She giggled again, a brief, cut-off hiccup. "Sometimes."

He slipped another finger into her, pressing harder with the heel of his hand. No complaints so far. "Tell me about it."

"No."

77

He started to take his hand away, and she grabbed his wrist with gratifying speed, pushing him back down into her. "Tell you what," he said. "I'll keep going if you tell me what you were thinking about me. And when."

She hesitated for a moment longer, then let go of his wrist. "'kay. Remember when you took me to play squash and I was rubbish?"

"Yes." He shifted his arm, getting more comfortable, and settled into a rhythm.

"Mmm. Up a bit. Harder. Yes—that's right."

"And?"

"And, okay, anyway, apart from the fact that I'm just *so* pathetic at sport, I kept missing the ball 'cause I was looking at you in those incredible shorts."

He smiled, flattered. "Go on."

"That's it. Just you in shorts. Nice body." She ran her hand down his chest. "Very nice body."

"Do you really want me to stop?"

"No, I . . . oh, all right, no. That wasn't it." She hesitated again, long pauses between the sentences, but he let her take her time because he knew she wouldn't stop. "By the time we finished I was so hot. God, I wanted you. And I don't screw at work, told you that already. But if you'd asked . . . just then I'd have let you do me right there on the court. With the whole division watching if they'd been there. Glass box. I'd have done it. I wanted you that much. *That much.*"

She squeezed around him, his fingers suddenly gliding slick against tight muscle.

"And?" he prompted when she relaxed.

"And, anyway, it was late so there was no one else there. In the changing rooms. Empty. Just me. Being so fucking hot for you. So I had a shower, hot shower. And I did what you're doing right now."

She fell silent again, her breath coming in whimpers. He sped up, feeling an ache starting in his arm but knowing it wouldn't matter now. He kissed her ear lightly, felt her shiver. "Come on. Tell me the end."

"No. Yes. All right. Yes. I mas . . . I masturbated in the shower, thinking about you. And I came, thinking about you screwing me. Against the tiles. Under the water." She drew in a deep breath as he kept kissing, breathing into her ear. "And that's all there was, that's everything, I promise. I came, thinking about you. Like I'm going to . . . please, keep it going . . . keep it, oh . . ."

That had done it. She went over the edge, words trailing off into a long, soft moan into his neck. He pushed his fingers into her, relishing the strong muscles spasming. Oh, but that was going to feel good around his cock, if she let him fuck her.

When she stilled, he slipped his fingers out of her and wiped them on the nearest bit of fabric—they were so close together he couldn't really tell to whom it belonged. "Sara?"

"Mmm." She lifted her head, and even though her face was shadowed he could see how wide her pupils were. If he was counting favors, then he owed the I&I pharmacy a large one. Lucky that they'd never find out. "What?"

"Better than the shower?"

She laughed throatily. "Oh, yes." She kissed him a few times, running her hand through his hair. "*Definitely* better." She kissed her way away from his mouth, down to his shoulder, and nibbled gently, unfastening his shirt to get at his chest.

He was wondering how to phrase a polite request for her to skip the preliminaries and move on to something more active when she nudged his thigh with her knee, pushing him sideways. He eased his hip away from the back of the sofa so that she could move further up his body, her soaking knickers brushing up along his cock. He reached down, but she pushed his hands away. "I'll do it."

It would've been a great deal easier if she'd taken her knickers off. But he didn't want to risk them getting too far apart and giving her a chance to remember properly that she didn't fuck at work.

The idea made him uneasy. So, not really wanting to, he gave it one more try— more insurance for the morning than anything. "Sara, are you sure—"

She leaned down, kissed him, and knelt up again. "'Course I'm sure." Her hand enclosed his cock again, positioning him, and then she stopped, looking down at him, abruptly serious. "Are *you* sure?"

He blinked at her. "God, yes. *Quite* sure."

In some strange way, he wasn't. But the tiny whisper of doubt lasted barely another three seconds, until she came down onto him slowly, and he groaned out loud.

Wet heat engulfed him, and he only realized he'd closed his eyes when he opened them to find her looking down at him, still wide-eyed and solemn. She tilted her head. "Good?"

"Not...at all bad."

She rocked against him, pressing down. "Know what I want?"

He shook his head.

"I want to come again. With you inside me."

"I was inside you before."

"Not like that." She squeezed tight around him. "Like this. Filling me."

No complaints from down here. "If you like."

"I like. 'S different. Feels different. You wouldn't...oh, of course you would. Or you might. Is it different?"

He smiled up at her. "Is what different?"

"Coming." She was starting to breathe faster again, rubbing against him harder. "Coming with a man screwing you, instead of coming without."

"Yes, it is."

She nodded, her eyes closing. "Thought it would be."

79

Normally talking during sex bored him, but with Sara it was ... sweet. Charming. A variant on her usual funny, dirty, undemanding conversation, with the delightful addition of fucking her. Or, as it happened, her fucking him.

He unfastened her blouse, then slipped it back over her shoulders. Coordinating underwear, of course. He'd always loved her skin color, and now the beautiful honey tones set off the white lace. He'd heard the opinion expressed at I&I, always well out of Sara's hearing, that she'd be more attractive with bigger tits. Obviously expressed by people who hadn't enjoyed this angle, he thought smugly. He stroked his palms over the soft lace and softer skin, cupping her breasts as she pressed forwards.

It wasn't getting anywhere productive from his point of view, but he didn't mind. It felt very nice, and he had an incredible view of her above him. Sara the perfect admin, flushed, her eyes closed, her lips parted, her breathing turning into the whimpers he'd heard before.

He reached up, brushing her lips with his fingers and she opened her mouth wider, closing her lips around them, sucking hard. The sensation ran like wildfire down his arm and spine, straight into his groin, making him moan. She ran her tongue across his fingertips, back and forth. God, that was good. If she didn't get on with it, he wouldn't be able to stop himself from rolling her over on the sofa and fucking her, very hard and not for very long.

Then he had to pull his fingers away quickly as he felt her start to bite down. Her hands dug into his shoulders and her head fell forwards, and she moaned again as she began to contract around his cock, still pressing down hard onto him. He meant to wait for her to finish, but his remaining self-control abruptly evaporated. Grabbing her hips, he lifted her and then pulled her down, thrusting up to meet her. "Move, Sara. Now. Fuck me."

She did, bracing herself on the back of the sofa and his shoulder. She wasn't very well coordinated—neither of them were—but it didn't matter. The sofa wasn't terribly comfortable, they still had all their clothes on, and her knickers were stretched against the side of his cock, but those things didn't matter either.

It felt like something stolen, and it was. Perfect admin, perfect fuck. He was taking something she hadn't meant to give him, letting her do something that her mind hadn't wanted and her body had been gagging for. The idea of that had him almost there, and the feel of her tight around him, still twitching from her own orgasm, was enough to carry him the rest of the way.

Then he was coming, coming into her. Sara. He pulled her down, pressing her close and kissing her hard for as long as it lasted.

When he woke up, he found her chin dug into his shoulder and what felt like about six elbows jammed into other bits of him. For someone so petite, she felt like a hell of a weight. He had a terrible crick in his neck and he was extremely messy.

Taking hold of her wrists, he eased her up and slid out from underneath her, leaving her lying on the sofa, blinking at him with drunken bemusement as he sat on the floor beside her. "Where're you going?" she asked.

"To bed."

"Oh. Okay." She rolled onto her side and curled up. "Night, then. Love you. D'you know I love you?"

"You told me before."

She smiled, her eyes closing. "Good. Love you. Don't forget." And she fell asleep again.

Not fucking likely. He'd meant to go at once, but he sat for a while, watching her, stroking her hair away from her forehead. Asleep she looked so . . . young. So vulnerable, so un-Sara. All the passion and animation drained from her expressive face. He licked his lips, still tasting the last kiss. Not something he usually did, kissing as he came. Maybe he should take it up, because it had felt great. Her breath going into him as he squeezed her against him. Pomegranates.

He dug out a duvet to cover her. Then he had a quick shower and went to bed, wondering what she'd have to say about it all tomorrow. Wondering, too, if she'd want to do it again, which wasn't something he found himself thinking very often. On the very brink of sleep, he had a thought that he didn't remember in the morning.

Love you.

So that was what it sounded like when someone knew you, and they still meant it.

They'd left the windows clear last night, so the living room had been light for a few hours by the time he came back from his trip out. Even so, Sara was only just beginning to stir, probably woken by his return. Completely hidden by the blanket, the first sign of life was a heartfelt complaint. "Oh . . . Christ in heaven. Oh, God, my *head*."

There was a short silence, broken only by soft moans, reminding him of last night, even though this was hangover induced rather than anything more fun. Then her nose poked out, and she said, "What can I smell?"

He began to empty the shopping bag onto the table. "Real coffee and . . . bacon sandwiches."

That produced a surprisingly lively reaction. "Bacon? You are an *angel*." She pushed the cover aside and looked up at him. "Well, maybe not an actual angel."

He sat down on the floor by the sofa, the same place he'd sat last night. She struggled upright, shook her head, then winced. She sat, eyes closed, combing her hair straight with her fingers.

"How do you feel?" he asked.

"Absolutely fucking *awful*. I'm never touching another drop of alcohol as long as I live."

"A week?"

"Maybe even two." She opened her eyes and reached carefully for a sandwich. "You?"

"Oh, I'm fine. Years of practice." He took the lids off the coffees.

"Is this your flat?" she asked through a mouthful of sandwich. "I don't remember ending up here. In fact, I don't remember a single thing after we left the club. Did I do anything horrendously embarrassing?"

"Nothing at all," he said automatically. Then he took a sip of coffee, thought about it, and added, "Well, not unless you'd be horrendously embarrassed by crawling all over me and offering to fuck me."

She stared at him, her mouth falling open. Then she licked crumbs from her lips and said, "Jesus. Tell me I didn't."

"I'm pretty sure you did. It was fairly memorable."

"Oh, God. I'm really sorry. I don't—" Then she stopped dead, suspicion dawning on her face. "You . . . we didn't?"

Either she'd forgotten everything, or she was a very good actor. For a moment he thought about telling the truth just to find out which. Then he shook his head. "You fell asleep before there was any serious damage done. Even I have a minimum consciousness level requirement for a fuck, however fuckable the woman is who's passed out on top of me."

She looked at him for a long moment, then nodded. "Thanks. Because, you know, I'd have to apply for a transfer. If we had."

He took a sandwich. "I don't see why."

She had a mouthful of coffee. "Ah, that's hot. Because it's a disaster. Screwing, not the coffee. Coffee's fine. The whole fundamental idea, nothing personal to you. You're my boss, I work for you, that's the way it is. It's not equal—you can't base a relationship on that."

That left an opening. "And what about just fucking?"

She shrugged. "I don't do 'just fucking.'"

She had last night, and very nicely. "Maybe you should try it."

She took a second, more cautious, sip of the coffee. "No, thanks. And even if I did, it wouldn't be with you. It wouldn't stay that simple. I've seen it happen before. It screws up both people's jobs, because neither of them knows what they're supposed to be any more."

"No danger of that."

"No?"

"No. I know perfectly well who's in charge."

She grinned. "I won't ask."

82

He concentrated on the food, wondering if she really didn't remember, or if she was pretending. She must know—he'd come inside her and she'd been dripping wet anyway. Admittedly, most of it had ended up on him, but even so. Maybe she'd gone to the toilet in the night, still completely hammered, dealt with the remaining evidence and forgotten that, too. He had no idea if that was possible (how would he know?), but it didn't sound absolutely impossible.

Whatever, he wasn't going to tell her if she didn't want to know. She'd been pretty firm about the transfer; there was no point losing the best admin in the section over something so trivial. He'd still have liked to do it again, but at the same time there was an odd relief that they wouldn't.

For a few seconds he wondered why. Then he took another sandwich and decided not to dwell on it.

The door of the flat closed behind Sara and, when she was sure he wasn't going to come out after her, she stopped and leaned against the wall. Of all the stupid things she'd done in the nineteen years of her life so far, this was probably among the top three.

She'd screwed him. She'd told him she loved him, which she obviously didn't mean. Or as a friend, that was all. It had been the high from the end of the investigation, the knowledge that he was safe and the bastards in management weren't going to leave him to twist. Although some of the exact wording was mercifully hazy from the alcohol and whatever pills he'd been handing out, she'd told him a lot more than that. Fantasies. She hated telling fantasies anyway, and here it was a disaster. How the hell would she manage to face him in the office on Monday? She'd never play bloody squash again, that was for sure.

They'd been getting on so well until now, professionally. She knew that she did a good job, and that he appreciated that she did. She'd let herself start to like him; he was a great boss, and she'd thought he was turning into a good friend. Now she'd fucked it all up. Literally.

She tried asking herself why, once, then decided she was too hung over for lying to herself. Why was easy. She been pissed enough, and high enough, to forget all the reasons it would be a disaster, and remember all the reasons it would be great. Which were, in reverse order, that he was blond, tall, handsome, incredibly fit, and that she'd fancied him something wicked since the first day she'd been assigned to him. However, when it came down to it, he was still a para, and they were all, in essence, fucked. Dangerous people.

She'd meant every word she'd said to him about not sleeping with her boss. It was only sensible, wherever you worked. Working at I&I, with para-investigators and interrogators, it had another dimension. When she'd started the training, among all the computer courses, interrogation habituation, and other practical things, one of the senior admins teaching the course had taken her aside and explained it.

He'd started off with questions. Do you know what personality disordered means? Do you know what a sociopath is, clinically speaking? When Sara has said no, he'd explained. And when she'd asked, "*All* of them?" he'd smiled, obviously used to the reaction.

"To some extent. And every para you meet will seem like the golden exception to the rule, if they're any good at what they do. You're free to ignore this, but don't come crying to anyone if you play with fire and find out it's hotter than you wanted."

She'd made the first big mistake—she'd thought Toreth was different. Even now, sober and chagrined, she could almost see why. Last night she'd felt something with him, surely? A connection. Something between them that wasn't just sex. She shook her head to clear the idea, then clutched her temples and moaned. This God-awful hangover was the consequence of the "connection." Drugs and booze, that was all it had been. Toreth was as broken as any of them.

Partly that was what had led to this mistake. Now and then she felt weirdly sorry for him. Maybe that was why she'd said she loved him, because he seemed to need it so much. There was something lonely about him, even though as far as she could ever tell he was perfectly content with his life of work, the gym, drinking, and screwing an endless procession of strangers. It would make *her* feel lonely.

Well, now she'd joined the procession, and he'd lied to her. He'd lied about screwing her, which somehow felt horrible, even though she'd wanted him to do it. She'd started the lie rolling, when she told him she didn't remember anything. Maybe he was just being polite, or more likely he didn't want to cope with her getting hysterical if he told her that she'd come like a train, twice, and fucked him with every sign of keen enjoyment. Or maybe it was because he was hoping to do it again next time she was too far gone to resist? Or because he'd been pissed too and hadn't particularly wanted her, she'd just been available? Or because she'd been such an awful fuck?

She grinned. At least that hadn't seemed to be a problem. Her lips still felt imprinted with the kiss he'd given her; she'd thought he was going to break her back, he'd held on to her so tightly as he came. She doubted there were any complaints on the physical score. She felt a warm flush, just from thinking about it, so she terminated the reminiscence sharply. She wasn't getting into this.

Whatever the reason, he was willing to pretend he'd forgotten what she'd done, and what she'd said. He hadn't said anything about "love," only that she'd offered to fuck him. Well, that was a good start. She'd meant it when she said she didn't do casual screwing. She knew her limits; she couldn't keep it casual. Toreth, dangerous, incapable of love and chronically unfaithful, was so far from being a potential partner for anyone that she caught herself feeling sorry for him again.

84

It was pointless. He wasn't unhappy with what he was. She'd have to learn to accept it, too. So she would realign her expectations and feelings towards him. She didn't want to stop thinking of him as a friend, or at least as more than simply her boss, but she'd be more careful to remember what he was, what *his* limits were. If his attitude changed towards her at work because of last night, then she could always apply for a transfer. Most importantly, she would never, ever, fuck him again. It hadn't happened—all she had to do now was make sure it didn't happen again.

Rules of Engagement

❖

"What do you think about Rick?" Sara asked as she sat down beside him in the coffee room.

When it came to the subject of tall, attractive blonds with enough arrogance to keep a corporate board supplied for a year, Toreth considered that he knew what he was talking about. On the other hand, given how well Sara usually took advice about her sex life, he thought he'd also better be tactful.

"I think he's a prick."

Her face fell. "You only met him once, for five minutes."

"We were in the same room for at least an hour. And anyway, so what? I've done courses in rapid character assessment. Got distinctions in them, too. Do you want to see my career development record?"

She frowned. "That's about prisoners and witnesses, not my boyfriends."

"Prisoners and witnesses are human, too. Okay, maybe that isn't a popular theory down on level D, but I'd say it's a transferable skill. And I'd also say that he's a prick."

"But you don't *know* him. People can be so unfair. Rick has a lot of very good qualities."

"Rich?" Toreth guessed.

Sara waved her hand, and Toreth watched the light sparkle on her collection of rings. "His family is loaded. But he's very independent. He wants to make his own way in life, without them."

"I thought you said last week he was moving in with you?"

Sara nodded, and sipped her coffee. "Right. The real world, not his parents' place, which practically needs its own post code. He showed me some pictures."

"So your flat's a bit of a comedown for him."

"Well...it isn't perfect," she admitted. "Bastard doesn't like him, to start with."

Toreth's normal position was that the cat hated all forms of life and so his individual dislikes weren't a surprise to anyone other than Sara. In this case, he had to agree the evil little fucker was showing some taste. "So what's he doing? Wearing full body armor in bed?"

Sara narrowed her eyes. "No. I just have to shut Bastard out when Rick's around. Which is fine now that the weather's nice, but I don't know what I'm going to do when it gets cold. Maybe they'll be getting on better by then."

Maybe, assuming that Rick had had Bastard shot, stuffed, and mounted. "I hope he's a great fuck, anyway, if I'm going to have to put up with this crap on a regular basis."

Her slight frown melted away into a reminiscent smile. "Oh, you have no idea. *No* idea. Usually guys that good-looking are rubbish in bed, because they never need to try, but—" She closed her eyes and sighed blissfully. "Oh, my *God*. His *hands*. He can just make me—mmm." She opened her eyes again. "See, I think you're judging him because he's so pretty."

The conversation stood poised on the brink of a slide down into a very long coffee break indeed. "Is this why you've been wandering around like someone spiked your drinks?" Toreth asked.

"What?"

"The Justice submissions you misfiled last week?"

"I already sorted—"

"And today I'm missing three junior investigators for the new forgery case, because apparently you didn't apply to the pool."

"Oh no!" Her eyes widened in what his distinction-graded assessment skills suggested was genuine dismay. "You're right. I'm so sorry. I'll do it now. I can ask Tiz to sub me a couple until I send her the application."

She picked up her mug and left the coffee room before he could say anything more. Toreth stared after her, wondering what he'd missed. Sara didn't usually give a shit what anyone else thought about her boyfriends, and particularly not Toreth. Most of the ones he'd met were exactly the kind of corporate tossers Toreth loathed, and Sara knew him better than to expect a genuine stamp of approval.

Clearly, something must be very wrong with the current one, despite his magical hands. Sara didn't fuck up admin work just because of a good screw. He hoped she worked out what the fuck the problem with him was and fixed it or ditched him before she seriously messed up a case.

Sara wasn't the only one with sex-induced trouble at work that week. When she announced his visitor, Toreth wondered briefly if she was winding him up. Warrick hadn't been to I&I since Marian Tanit's death. "What can I do for you?" Toreth asked, as Sara reluctantly closed the door behind her.

Warrick seemed to weigh up a couple of different openings, then simply said, "Where were you last night?"

Fortunately, he'd set the story up that morning. "I went out with Sara and a few other people from work."

"No, you didn't."

Toreth shrugged and gestured to the door. "Ask Sara if you don't believe me."

"And listen to her lying on your behalf? I don't think so."

"What?"

"I saw you. Not with Sara." Warrick crossed to the desk, movements stiff with anger. "If you're going to go to the trouble of lying to me—and frankly I don't understand why you bother—you could at least go to the additional trouble of taking your fuck of the day somewhere a little further away from the AERC."

At that point he should have given up, but he felt unexpectedly defensive. "If you see me with someone, that doesn't mean I'm fucking them. I do *talk* to people sometimes."

"Oh, please." Warrick looked as disgusted as he sounded. "Don't insult my intelligence. I saw you walking out of the bar with her. I can recognize conversation when I see it and that was not it."

"She's—"

"I know perfectly well who she is. Ellin works for the university at the AERC. And her husband works for SimTech. And, incidentally, thank you so very much for putting me in such an uncomfortable position at work. I assume you met her at the dinner last week?"

"Yes." Toreth decided to skip through this as fast as possible. Relentless honesty until Warrick got bored and went away.

"I should've know better than to take you," Warrick said. "I *do* know better. Have you ever actually turned down an opportunity for sex in your life? Or even thought for a moment that you ought to?"

Toreth could recognize a rhetorical question when he heard one. Even if he'd heard wrong, that wasn't a topic he was touching with a two-foot shock stick.

"Yesterday wasn't the first time you had sex with her, was it?" Warrick continued.

"No."

"No. I could tell." His voice changed, became more measured. "An interesting choice for you, I thought. Because, since she works in the building and since her husband works for me, I happen to know that they're separated."

That was news to Toreth. "What?"

"Didn't she mention? I thought she might not have. She's a good judge of character. She was using you," Warrick continued with satisfaction, still acid-tinged with anger. "I'd arranged to take visitors from P-Leisure for a drink to the bar you were walking out of. If we hadn't changed the plans, her almost-ex-husband would have been there with me. I doubt his reaction would have impressed my guests, which was presumably her intention."

The devious bitch. Maybe he should've failed his character assessment after all. Toreth stared at Warrick open-mouthed, then laughed. "All right, no, I admit it—I had no idea. No wonder she kept looking at her watch. Well...don't worry, I won't see her again." Not that he'd been planning to, but the concession sounded good. "And I'm sorry about nearly fucking things up with the sponsors. But no harm done, anyway."

"No harm done?" Now his inflection could've etched glass. "Asher was also with us, who of course you know. And she knows you. So I was treated to her valiant attempts to pretend she hadn't seen the two of you. Strangely enough, my definition of fun, broad as it is, doesn't extend to having my friends witness someone very publicly touching up my, my—"

Warrick stopped dead, took a deep breath, and walked away, over to the window. Toreth saw his face reflected faintly in the glass, eyes closed as he struggled for calm. He looked so fuckably good, pale and furious and on the edge of losing control, that Toreth could barely resist pinning him against the wall there and then. With an effort, he limited himself to going over to stand behind him and resting his hands on Warrick's shoulders.

"Touching up your what?" he asked. When Warrick didn't answer, Toreth ran his hands down his arms, down to his hips, and murmured, "Want to fuck?"

Warrick stood absolutely still for a long moment, then shook his head. "Yes. God help me, yes, I do," he said despairingly.

Toreth leaned forward, his mouth right against Warrick's ear. "Now?"

"Yes."

"Here?" Long, hot breath, and a brush of lips that made Warrick twitch against him.

"*Yes.*"

He let his hands roam, pulling Warrick close as his body relaxed and surrendered to his touch. Really, it was too easy, but somehow that didn't make it any less exciting, or Warrick any less desirable. He wondered briefly when he was going to get bored with this, with Warrick. There was no sign of it happening yet. Thank God great sex didn't wreck *his* concentration at work.

"Like to fuck me?" he whispered, suddenly wanting it, and knowing that Warrick would.

"Mmh...oh, yes."

Yes. Here in his office, over his desk—something to remember when the paperwork got too boring. Toreth disentangled himself and activated the comm. "Sara, no calls and no visitors. Absolutely no visitors."

He heard her snigger as he broke off the connection, so he voice-locked the door, just in case she was feeling vindictive about his dismissal of Rick.

And that was the end of the argument.

89

The Int-Sec gym was always pleasantly quiet on Friday lunchtimes. Toreth was into the second set of repetitions when he caught sight of a flash of pale skin to the left. He locked the weight bar into place and looked around. Daedra Kincaidy stood waiting, arms folded. In her skintight vest and shorts she looked like an interestingly tattooed famine victim. "Yes?" he asked.

She leaned on the end of the weights and peered down at him, thin bleached braids cascading forwards around her face. "Sara's boyfriend," she said in a low voice, and stopped.

"Rick the Prick, right?"

Daedra nodded approvingly. "Thought you might be interested to know that Sara mentioned things have been going missing from her flat since he moved in."

Toreth sat up. "Really missing? Or she just can't find them under all the crap?"

Daedra grinned. "Missing. Little stuff, though—stuff you *could* lose."

"Did she claim on the insurance?"

"No." Daedra gave him a significant look. "The Int-Sec housing cover requires a Justice report."

"So she does think it's him."

"She says she asked him about it a couple of weeks ago, whether he'd picked anything up 'by accident.' He denied everything, and said that he'd invited some friends around and maybe one of them had done it. He made all sorts of promises about it not happening again. Then this morning there were fifty euros missing from her emergency pot."

"And she finally kicked him into touch?" Toreth asked with more hope than genuine expectation. If she had, Daedra wouldn't be here.

"No." Daedra sat beside him, looking frustrated. "He weaseled his way out of it again, somehow. I reckon he's blowing the money on illegal pharmaceuticals. His parents are supposedly stinking, but from what I've heard they've cut him off without a euro, and I bet that's why."

"Got any evidence you'd file in an IIP?"

"Well, given that I don't have to file any IIPs down in the pharmacy." Daedra shrugged. "I just know that when I met him he was definitely high on something, and very interested in my job. He's subtle, I'll give him that, but I know what I'm looking for."

Toreth hadn't noticed it himself, but he trusted Daedra's opinion as one of I&I's more creative pharmacists, both on and off duty.

"And I know he's spectacularly good-looking, too," Daedra continued. "If you like that kind of thing. But I'd really have thought Sara would be more...I spent fifteen minutes in the coffee room with her, and twelve of 'em were her making up reasons why it couldn't be him."

And that part was hard to believe of Sara, with her ruthless dating policies and high relationship standards. "She didn't tell me any of that. She just said he was a great fuck."

"Well, maybe that's why. Can't say I understand it myself."

"Did she say anything else about him?"

"Not much. And at the end she suddenly made me promise not to tell you either. I expect she thought you'd hunt him down and slap the fuck out him, then dangle him out of a window until he comes up with the money to pay her back. And then maybe slap him again and warn him that if he doesn't clear out and leave her alone, you'll break his arms and legs and drop him off a handy bridge." She smiled thinly. "That's probably the kind of thing she was worried about."

He nodded. "How much has he taken?"

"She was pretty vague about the details. But you know what a magpie she is." Daedra shook her head, braids swaying. "I could sweep once around that flat and pick up enough bits to keep me in illegal pharma for a long time."

Well, no way could he ask Sara for the amount. "Guess for me."

"Maybe a thousand euros' worth, give or take? I think she was fudging downwards in a big way."

"So if I tried for two, that would cover it?"

"I should think so, with plenty to spare. Some compensation wouldn't hurt."

"Thanks." He turned to lie down again and Daedra patted his thigh and stood.

"Say hi to him from me," she said, and strolled away.

Toreth spent the weekend mending fences with Warrick. Carnac had proved that there was only so far he could be pushed before the side effect wasn't great make-up sex but a chilly silence. The weekend left Warrick intricately bruised, and both of them exhausted.

Sara was at work before Toreth on Monday morning, unusual enough that he stopped to ask why.

"I didn't finish the trainees' assessment drafts last week, and I forgot HCT wants them back today. I started them on Friday afternoon but—well, I was late for a thing and I had to go. I'm sorry. I'll have them done by coffee time."

Late for a thing. Presumably Rick and his amazing hands, after which she'd spent the weekend doing much the same thing as Toreth. At least this time, Toreth didn't really care whether Human Capital and Training got their forms or not. And, technically, assessments of the trainee investigators gaining casework experience weren't part of Sara's job anyway. They were supposed to be written entirely by him, but Toreth didn't see why he should waste his time when Sara had excellent judgment of her own, and knew exactly what he thought of them. Which wasn't much. So he said, "No rush," and went to fetch himself a coffee.

He brought one back for Sara, too, since her mug had been empty. She stared at it with astonishment. "What's that for?"

"To drink. Don't worry, I didn't poison it. I just don't want you falling asleep while you're filling in the assessments. They always knock me out."

"Thanks," she said, still looking bemused.

Bemused, but not suspicious. Good, when he'd brought the coffee to remove the main reason for her to disturb him in the next hour or so.

In his office, Toreth used a spare access code to pull up an assortment of information on Rick the Prick without leaving traces for Sara to find. He studied the files, hoping for something sufficiently incriminating that he could nudge Sara into seeing past the man's amazing cock. The credit and purchase check was vaguely suggestive, but certainly wouldn't convince someone willing to overlook minor theft in the pursuit of a good fuck. Toreth flicked up and down the screen, giving the matter long consideration. Eventually he decided that Daedra had covered most of the important points in her outlined plan. All except the bridge, but that wasn't Daedra's fault. There just wasn't one close enough to qualify as handy.

That simply left the question of finding out when Rick would be alone at Sara's flat. A c&p watch on his taxi use took care of that. The most difficult part of it was arranging the whole thing without Sara finding out.

Toreth let himself into the flat as quietly as he could and closed the door silently behind him. The place smelled distinctly less catty than usual, and no evil black shadow lurked in a corner ready to scratch.

A quick glance into the living room showed it was empty. Toreth eased open the bedroom door and peered through. Rick was rifling through the chest of drawers. He was out of luck, because Toreth knew that that particular drawer held nothing but makeup. Treading carefully, Toreth crossed the floor until he was an arm's length from Rick. Then he coughed quietly.

Rick jumped, lipsticks clattering from his hand back into the jumble. He slammed the drawer and turned. He really was awfully pretty, Toreth thought. Fine, perfectly symmetrical features, untidy blond curls, and deep blue eyes stretched wide with surprise. He looked like he ought to be carved in marble and cluttering up a corporate HQ foyer.

Rick's eyebrows went up. "Para-investigator Toreth?"

"Good memory," Toreth said, and punched him in the face.

Shock and pain sent him crumpling to the floor without even crying out. Toreth followed him down, and before Rick recovered enough to struggle, had him face down and with his arms behind his back. The cuffs closed with a satisfying snick. He'd barely started to kick before Toreth rolled him over again and pressed one knee firmly onto his chest.

Blood from his nose had smeared over his face, where he'd been pressed against the carpet. Rick blinked up at Toreth, squinting, trying to see past the tears in his eyes. "What—?"

Toreth took hold of his jaw, pushing his head back, and leaned over him. Rick grunted as the added weight pushed air out of his lungs. "I broke your nose already. If you keep thrashing around, I'll break something else. We can keep that up until you cooperate, or I kill you by accident. Your choice." Rick stopped moving. "Good boy."

Toreth hauled Rick to his feet, and dragged him, stumbling, into the living room and over to the window. He slammed him face-first against the wall hard enough to wind him and draw out a scream as his nose thumped into the wall. Fuck. Sara wouldn't be happy about blood all over her nice yellow paint.

By the time Rick recovered his breath and started making noises again, Toreth had the window open wide. He caught Rick, flipped him around, and grabbed his throat in one hand. The window ledge, at a most helpful height, fitted snugly across Rick's backside. It made a perfect lever as Toreth pushed, bending him backwards out of the window. Rick managed to resist for a few seconds as he kept a grip on the window, then the hard edge of the cuffs must have dug into his wrists because his hands slipped and he went back in a rush.

Rick yelled, high and panicked, and Toreth heard the faint scrabbling as his bound hands clawed at the wall. He tried to kick out, remarkably stupid given that if Toreth let go there was every chance Rick would fall.

Toreth wedged his leg across Rick's and pinned them there. Toreth had his other hand hooked firmly around Rick's waistband, but he wouldn't be anywhere nearly as aware of that as he would be of the long, long drop to the pavement below. Rick twisted his head around, getting an excellent view of the fall, and he squeaked again. "What the hell—what are you doing?!"

"You know, you wouldn't believe how many people die while resisting arrest," Toreth said. Rick went very still. "They panic. One minute you've got them in cuffs, and the next they're trying to climb out of the window. A slip, a fall... You wouldn't believe the number of forms I'd have to fill in, either."

Rick choked out an indecipherable swear word, his throat working against Toreth's hand. Toreth shifted his grip, letting Rick breathe more easily. "Now pay attention," Toreth said. "And listen to this very, very carefully, because having to repeat myself pisses me off."

"Please! Fuck! Whatever you want."

"I want you to stop fucking up my casework," Toreth said.

Rick squinted down at him, confused into stillness. "What?"

93

"You've been stealing from Sara, haven't you?"

"No, I swear! I wouldn't—" He squealed again as Toreth pressed down harder. "Yes! Okay. Yes."

"How much?"

"I'm not...I don't know."

"Fine. Then we'll call it three thousand euros."

"Three...? Fuck, no, it wasn't that—" He stopped dead as Toreth shifted his leg as though to release the pressure holding him. "Three! Three thousand! Yes!"

"Good boy. What I want to hear next is that you've got that kind of money available in your account. Or that you can get it on credit. If I don't hear one of those, I'm going to be very, very unhappy."

He nodded frantically. "I can get it right now. Right this second, I promise."

"Yeah? A minute ago you swore you'd never taken anything from Sara."

"No, I mean it, I sw—I, fuck. I can get the money. Please."

"See? Now we're making progress." Toreth hauled him back into the room and let go. Rick slid down the wall, his eyes wide, breathing quickly. He looked about ready to crap himself. "Don't bleed on the fucking carpet," Toreth said.

Quickly, Rick pressed his sleeve to his face and yelped. "You really broke my nose," he said plaintively after a moment.

Vain little fucker. "And that's just for starters, if I don't see money moving very soon."

"I'll have to borrow it from someone. He charges me twenty percent a—I can do it!" Rick said quickly. "I can. I just. Yeah, okay, I'll do it right away."

"Too fucking right you will. I don't give a fuck how much it's going to cost you. By the way," Toreth added conversationally, "do you give blowjobs for money, as well as steal it?"

"What?" He dropped his arm quickly. "No!"

"Oh, pity. Because beating up arrogant little shits like you gives me a hard-on, and if you get on your knees right now, then I'll knock a thousand euros off your debt."

"A thousand?" Rick's gaze flicked down to Toreth's fly and then up again. He licked his lips. "Really? I, uh—all right. Yes."

While Rick struggled up onto his knees, Toreth unzipped his trousers and freed his cock. He felt ninety-nine percent sure that Rick didn't have the spine to try to bite, but that one percent could lead to some nasty and embarrassing graft surgery. "I don't want your blood all over me," Toreth said. "So open your mouth, and keep it open. Move one muscle until I say so, and the deal's off."

Toreth stepped closer and buried his free hand in Rick's curls, twisting tightly to hold him still. Rick whimpered, mouth wide open, and his tongue moved convulsively. He kept Rick's head tilted back, but not so far that he couldn't see Toreth's hand moving on his cock. Toreth smiled, watching the disgust and sick anticipation in Rick's eyes. But still the little fucker didn't try to back out. Maybe he didn't think Toreth would let him, or maybe he just thought this would be worth a thousand euros. After a minute or so, he tried to swallow, his mouth half closing, and Toreth twisted his hair. "Uh-uh. Just stay right where you are."

Toreth stroked himself faster. Luckily the games with Warrick had given him plenty of practice in knowing exactly how to hold himself to make sure that when he came he filled Rick's mouth, not wasting a drop. The calculation blunted the edge of his orgasm, but provided a completely different kind of satisfaction as Rick gagged and jerked away, managing nothing more than to hurt himself in Toreth's grip.

Changing tactic, Rick tried to lean forwards, mouth still open. Toreth wrenched his head further back. "Close your mouth. I want to see you swallow. *Swallow*," Toreth repeated, as Rick half retched. "Throw up, and I'll make sure you fucking choke on it."

Rick squeezed his eyes shut, and obeyed. Finally, the shudders eased. When Toreth let go of his hair, Rick opened his eyes and looked up at Toreth, tear-streaked and defeated. Not so fucking pretty now. He stepped back, zipping up. "What do you want, a round of fucking applause? Move the two thousand euros, now."

Toreth watched while he opened his hand screen and made the transfer. Rick didn't even try to fake it, or to contact someone for help. Probably he didn't know anyone who'd cross the road to piss on him if he were on fire. A hazard of the trade for junkie thieves, even good-looking ones.

"It's done," Rick said, voice hoarse. He stood up and wiped his mouth. "All two thousand, in her account."

Toreth eyed him, weighing up the next step. Rick had a certain underlying resilience to him, which suggested that despite the fright he'd experienced, he'd be back again. No doubt he'd be able to convince himself that Sara would welcome him with open legs. He might even be right, at least until Sara had worked him out of her system and found herself a new boyfriend.

Time to move on to the next phase. Toreth had pocketed the drug scanner before he left work. He fitted a fresh sterile mouthpiece to it, before he offered the business end to Rick. "I'm sure you know how these work. Blow steadily, until you hear the beep. Here—come on."

Rick balked, turning his head away.

"Just fucking do it. You didn't have any trouble opening your mouth for me earlier."

Eyes dark with resentment, Rick took a deep breath and blew.

The analysis took only a few minutes. Toreth had dosed himself up with suitable metabolites recommended and supplied by Daedra, but spiking the witness probably hadn't been necessary. The trace readings suggested the little shit must be supporting a wide circle of illegal dealers with the proceeds of his larceny. His additions, though, would tip the scales over into a much longer stretch of re-education. Pity Toreth wasn't a Justice officer. He'd probably be jumping for joy.

He'd set the scanner to automatically take a DNA sample. Combined with reading Rick's ID, it gave him a foolproof identification, good enough for legal purposes. "You know what this is telling me, don't you?" Toreth said. He gave Rick a glimpse of the length of the list.

"I'm clean." The unconvincing protest came automatically.

Toreth snorted. "If by 'clean' you mean, 'too broke to buy all the illegal drugs I want,' then maybe. But the crap you're taking lingers."

"So? Why do you care? That party Sara took me to—"

Yes, definitely the kind who got over a fright much too quickly. Toreth took hold of a patch of Rick's shirt that wasn't too bloodied, and walked him backwards against the wall. He saw Rick's eyes flicker to the window.

"I care because I don't want to see your newly ugly face again. If I hear anything which makes me think that you've contacted Sara, I'm going to call someone in Justice, send her this little file, and have her pull you in. No chances to make deals, no bribes, no help from your friends, if you have any. I'll be watching, and I'll make sure you get a nice long stretch of re-education. High-grade."

Finally, the threat seemed to penetrate. At the words 'high-grade,' Rick shrank back, stopped by the wall.

"They use a lot of drugs in there, or so I hear. But not the kind you like. The kind that make you forget your own name, and shit yourself, and see all kinds of nasty things while you're lying alone in the dark waiting for them to remember they're supposed to be teaching you how to be a good citizen. Understand?"

He nodded, and dropped his gaze.

"Now, before you fuck off forever, you're going to leave a voice message for Sara. You're going to say that you've had a sudden attack of conscience, because Sara is such a very nice woman. And because you feel so incredibly guilty about taking her stuff, you've given all the money back, and you've packed up and gone and you won't bother her again. I know you can make it sound good, because that's the kind of slimy little fucker you are." He looked up sullenly, and Toreth smiled. "Go on, Ricky. You have no idea how much I'd like you to try something. And I told you before," he added, as Rick moved over to the flat comm. "Stop dripping blood everywhere."

After Rick had stumbled off down the corridor away from Sara's flat, his sleeve covering his face again, Toreth went into the kitchen. He hunted around until he found a bucket, a scrubbing brush, and a couple of bottles that looked like cleaning fluids. He filled the bucket with cold water—having heard enough bitching from the interrogation level cleaning staff to know not to use hot—and went to track down the blood stains.

The things he did to keep his admin happy, Toreth thought as he started on the bedroom carpet. He could've had Rick clean up, but that would've meant having an unrestrained prisoner loose near a bottle of bleach. It would take considerably more than a mediocre wank to relax him enough to make that risk attractive. Still, it wasn't all bad. Toreth pictured the priceless expression of panic on Rick's face as he'd hung out of the window, and laughed.

Wine, Women, and Cushions

❖

R efill," Dillian said, waving her glass.

"Sorry, gorgeous, that was the last of the bottle."

"Oh." Dillian thought about tomorrow, then decided there was nothing she had to do that she couldn't cope with hung over. "Open another one."

"Another?" Cele's voice rose in mock surprise. "A second bottle? On a weeknight? Where will this decadence end?" She finished her own glass, then patted the arm of the deep sofa. "You'll have to get it. I have comfort-induced paralysis of the legs."

Dillian fought her way off the sofa and picked a rather circuitous route over to the kitchen area. Opening the wine cupboard, she looked over the selection; Cele's collection of wine was as eclectic as the rest of the contents of her flat-cum-studio. "I never asked," Dillian called over, "but why is the floor covered in cushions?"

"Present from an admirer. I met a man in a bar, and we finished up talking about soft furnishings. I had to flee the scene before the domesticity killed me. Pity, because he had stupendous legs, and hands to die for."

"And instead of roses he sent you three dozen cushions?" Dillian asked as she returned with a bottle of Zinfandel.

"Yep. Except that it was six dozen cushions. The rest are upstairs. When they were all heaped together they frightened me." Cele held out her glass as Dillian opened the wine. "A million single men in that place, and I homed right in on the fabric fetishist. I have an unerring instinct for the honest-to-Christ weirdos."

Looking up at the bedroom balcony, Dillian could see edges and corners, plain, lacy, and tasseled, poking out between the posts of the balustrade. She poured the wine, then sat down beside Cele. "What are you going to do with them?" Dillian asked.

"Well, they were a gift, so I'll pass 'em on. From now on, no one leaves here without one. Mind you, Lord only knows who'll take the pink cowhide prints." She gestured with her glass to the corner of the room, where the offending cushions lurked. "And there are four of those. You're lucky, though—you get an early pick. In fact, you can take one for Keir as well."

Dillian surveyed the plentiful choice. "I'll give him that huge fluffy zebra pattern one with the orange fringe. It'll clash with everything he's got. And everything he's ever likely to buy, come to that."

Cele chuckled. "You're evil. I like you." She drank a couple of mouthfuls of wine and sighed happily. "Well done you, for thinking of a new bottle. So, now that we've finished examining the house of horrors that is my love life, what's new on the Dillian front? Or back."

She'd been dreading this. "Nothing."

"You said that last time. And the time before. And—"

Dillian hit her with a green-spotted yellow cushion. "I know, I know."

"So who was the last one?" Cele asked, unabashed. "The blond love god? What was his name again?"

"Thorulf." Dillian sighed. "Yes, he's the current last. He wanted a relationship with someone who spends more time on Earth than off it. Not that unreasonable."

"No stamina, that was his problem. Wasn't there anyone on Mars?"

"No. Or maybe. There were a couple of vaguely-interesteds but they never came to anything in the end."

"'Vaguely'? What's wrong with these men? Are they blind?"

"I just—" She shrugged. "I haven't been in the mood."

"For almost two years? Come on, sweetheart, this is getting desperate. Sex is one of the great joys of life. Even Mr. Joined-at-the-hip-to-his-corporation has finally noticed that."

"I know." Dillian sank lower into the sofa. "Don't remind me."

Cele raised her eyes. "Lord, don't start that again. You should be pleased. The last time I saw Keir he looked like a dog with two tails."

"The last time *you* saw him, maybe."

"Oh? But I saw him only . . . " Cele paused. "Well, not more than a few weeks ago, I'm sure. I thought he looked grand."

"On the surface, maybe. But—well, I usually ask about them when I see him. I want to be sure that Keir's okay, that's all. And lately he just says everything's fine, then changes the subject. It's like he doesn't want to talk about it. That isn't right, surely?"

"Mmm . . . I hate to say it, but perhaps it's the reception he gets?" Cele held her hand up. "No, don't. It's just that, to be honest, you do glower a little when one of the forbidden names comes up."

"Why are you always so fair to them?" Petulance crept unbidden into her voice. "First it was the Bitch Queen, and now it's *him.*"

Reaching over, Cele tapped her arm. "There's nothing wrong with Seven Inches," she said seriously.

Dillian felt her mouth twist into a grimace, but couldn't stop it. "Of course not. I mean, he's probably clinically disturbed, he beats Keir up, and he kills people for a living. Oh, and he screws around like a tomcat on testosterone. Just what *I* look for in *my* boyfriends."

Cele frowned. "If you know that he beats him up, then you know more than I do. Are you serious?"

"Well—" Dillian struggled with the truth and then sighed. "Okay, hits him, then." She caught up with the conversation through the slight fog of alcohol, and realized Cele might well have no idea why that was different. Not that Dillian was sure it was. "Sorry. Do you know about that?"

Cele nodded. "I talked to Keir about it last year, before you came back from Mars."

"Oh, okay." The slight delay again, before her brain worked through the information. "You—" This time the shock of betrayal left her momentarily speechless. "You *knew*? You knew all about it and you didn't tell me?"

"Keir asked me not to. I promise that I did my in loco Dillientis thing for you. I made sure he was okay and there wasn't anything out of control going on. But I've got no business discussing his sexual kinks with anyone. Not even you."

"Oh, God. Cele. I can't believe it." True. Really true. And, in some illogical way she couldn't articulate, yet another thing to blame *him* for. "I was so worried about Keir. I didn't know it was . . . well, that it was like that."

"Hey, I'm sorry. I had no idea you were in a flap over it."

"I didn't know what to say to him. It's so stupid, but if it had been a woman instead—if Keir had been, I mean—it would've been so much easier. I wanted to talk to you and I didn't dare because I had no idea what you'd do."

Cele set her wine down and moved across the sofa, then eased her arm around Dillian's shoulders, pulling gently until Dillian surrendered and leaned into her. "I'm really, really sorry, sweetheart," Cele said. "If I'd known, I'd have said something, I promise, whatever I told Keir. Oh, no. Don't look at me like that."

"Like what?"

"Like some hapless little forest creature that's about to be shot and eaten. All big dewy eyes and twitching nose." Cele's eyes widened mournfully, in imitation of a miserable baby deer.

Despite herself, Dillian laughed. "I look like nothing of the kind."

"Yes, you do. Well, maybe not the nose, but your bottom lip was quivering." Cele grinned and put her finger on Dillian's mouth.

Dillian hadn't thought anything at all about the embrace, or at least nothing more than familiar, tactile Cele, wanting to take away any pain no matter how accidentally inflicted. The touch was something else. It brought an acute awareness of her own mouth, lips, and tongue, and that all she had to do was part those lips a little and everything would shift.

She spent too long thinking about the could bes, and Cele took her hand away. "Sorry," she said. "My mistake."

They moved apart, taking mirror image sips of wine as the tension eased.

"Everything's okay now, isn't it?" Cele said after a moment. "With Keir, I mean. Now you know it's all good clean consensual fun?"

Good clean consensual *what*? "Not really. I know Keir says he wants it, but I don't...I find it hard to believe. Blindfolds or furry handcuffs or whatever is one thing, but this is—it's not healthy. It's certainly not normal."

"I never thought you were so narrow-minded."

"Narrow-minded!" Dillian sat up. "I'm nothing of the kind! Keir's got *bruises*, Cele. It's *not* healthy. God only knows what he sees in the man."

Cele winked. "Well, I can't speak for God, but *I* know."

"That's right, so you do." Sober, she wouldn't ask, but wine and curiosity combined irresistibly. "Go on, then. What was he like?"

"I never kiss and tell," Cele said with absolute seriousness.

All she needed, of course, was encouragement. "First of all, that's an outrageous lie. And secondly, I'm only asking out of concern for Keir."

Cele pretended to choke on her wine. Dillian waited until the performance finished, then said, "Well?"

"Well—" she held up her hand, "—purely out of concern for your beloved brother, obviously, I shall reveal all. To start with, aesthetically, he was mmmmmh." She kissed her fingertips. "Heaven. Sculpture in motion. And although he's been wearing a lot more clothes when I've seen him recently, everything looks to be as I left it. He must spend a truly insane amount of time working out." She cocked her head. "That's a sign of insecurity, mind you."

"And he really is...? Dimensionally speaking."

Cele snorted with laughter. "I might be a millimeter or two out, but he's thereabouts." She leaned back and stared up at the balcony above. "Why do you suppose that everything else has been metricated since forever but we still measure penis length in inches? Mind you, it wouldn't sound half as snappy as—what would it be in centimeters?"

"Easy. Multiply by two point five four." The wine meant Dillian had to close her eyes briefly, concentrating. "Twenty-eight—seven—carry three. Seventeen point seven eight."

When Dillian opened her eyes, Cele was staring. "How do you remember that stuff? It's so archaic. I have to look it up every time I'm reading old designs."

"Easy. Easier than a photographic memory for body parts. You know, I don't believe you can really remember," Dillian added, only half teasing.

"I could draw you every cock I've ever touched. And I had a damn close look at that one. Several times, over a very satisfactory evening." She smiled, catlike. "It was ten years ago, and we were both several sheets to the wind, but I distinctly remember that he was a great lay."

Despite herself, Dillian laughed. Then the memory of the conversation in

Keir's room at New Year surfaced. She stared into the depths of her wine, hearing their voices.

Then why are you still with him?

He's an incredibly good fuck?

He'd been trying to shut her up when he said it, but he'd meant it, too. Sex. Obviously one of the great joys of Keir's life right now, as Cele had said. *Was that all it was?* God, she hoped so. Just an infatuation—although thirty-three-year-old men weren't supposed to have infatuations—which would pass. Soon. The sooner the better. Perhaps his recent reticence was a good sign after all.

When she looked up, Cele was watching her. "That's a very serious face," she said.

"I was just wondering when Keir's going to come to his senses. That man—" Cele rolled her eyes, but Dillian decided she'd be damned if she'd give him the dignity of a name. "That man doesn't care about him, not at all. Keir's going to get hurt, a lot more than bruises."

"I really don't think you're being...okay." Cele sat up straighter. "You think Toreth doesn't care. Forget fair—think evidence. You could tell that the poor bastard was floundering way out of his depth with the whole family thing at New Year, right? Right?"

Reluctantly, she nodded. She couldn't deny it, since she'd said exactly the same thing.

"In fact, half the time I was there he looked like someone had his nuts in a vise. But he turned up anyway. Why? He did it for Keir. Putting yourself through something like that, just because your squeeze invites you—doesn't that count for anything?"

"He made a pass at me." She hadn't meant to say that, but annoyance goaded the words out.

Cele's eyebrows rose, then she laughed. "Really? What did you do?"

Dillian felt her cheeks heat. "I slapped him."

"Good Lord. Must've been some pass. I guess I've been lucky." For a moment her gaze was openly appraising. "I've done the same and I didn't get slapped."

"That's because you're you." Why was Cele always so damn fair? "How come I'm the only one who can see that the man is a menace? What about what's best for Keir?"

Cele let out a short breath, sounding almost annoyed. "Any minute now you're going to say, why can't he find a nice girl and settle down?"

"I am not." Dillian frowned. "Although I'd prefer it if he did. I'd prefer it if he found a nice man and settled down. I don't know why he doesn't."

"Well, why don't you?"

The question stumped her. "We're not talking about me," she said finally.

"Actually, we are." Cele topped up both their glasses. "Or had you forgotten why this started?"

"Um." Damn. Dillian sipped her wine, thinking it over. "I suppose, when it comes down to it, right now I'm too busy doing other things. Things I'd rather do, and which make it hard to start a relationship, never mind keep one going. I don't want a man, nice or otherwise."

"How about a woman?"

Dillian smiled; she couldn't help it. "They're no easier to find."

Cele shook her head, returning the smile. "For you, there's always at least one available."

No reply, serious or joking, seemed right; after a few seconds' silence Cele added, "Which reminds me, I've got something to show you. Wait here."

Apparently unparalyzed, Cele handed over her glass and rose. She disappeared behind a tall cabinet, and drawers opened and closed out of sight. "I found something while I was making room for the unwanted guests. I shut the ugliest ones in the closet—I hope they're not breeding in there—and while I was tidying, I came across . . . this."

She came back to the living area with a large, flat folder. Before she said anything, Dillian knew what it must hold.

"Studies for the great masterpiece I never painted," Cele said. Settling down on a giant purple cushion on the floor at Dillian's feet, she opened the portfolio. Dillian found herself looking into a pencil mirror reflection of herself, a dozen years younger and . . .

"I look so happy," Dillian said. Like a dog with two tails.

"You were, sweetheart. Or I thought you were, so that's what I saw."

"I was. Why didn't you paint it? I wouldn't have minded."

Cele turned over another drawing, and shook her head. "I started, but I couldn't see it any more. I needed to paint a lover, and after we were back to being friends, I couldn't do that. It wouldn't have been healthy, sitting in the studio thinking about you like that when . . ." She waved the drawing vaguely.

That was something Dillian had never known before. Of course, she'd never asked before. "I'm sorry."

"Hey, no need. I wasn't complaining." Cele glanced at her sideways. "Much. Seriously, though, those are six months I don't regret at all."

"Nor do I." Thinking back, looking down at the sketch of her glowing smile, nostalgia twinged for something she'd thought of for years as an aberration, although she didn't like that word. A brief phase, rather, long over.

"And the reason I don't regret it," Cele said, "is that we stayed friends. Mind-meltingly great as you were, it wouldn't have been worth losing you over it."

"Never." Dillian set down one glass and took Cele's hand—strong fingers, square nails darkened around the edges with charcoal—wanting to touch her, to add the reassurance of contact. "We're first bestest friends, remember?"

"Forever." Cele smiled at the reminder of the promise, first given so long ago

103

at school. She ran her thumb over Dillian's palm, then said, "Model for me?"

"What? Now?"

"Yes, now." She withdrew her hand and wagged her forefinger. "I should warn you up front that it's mostly a feeble excuse to get you naked, but I do actually have something I want to try. And it does even have to be tonight."

Dillian counted down the diminishing protests. You don't want to do this. You shouldn't want to do this. This isn't a good idea. This isn't fair to Cele when you don't have any intention of—

Placing her wine on the floor beside Cele's, she stood up. "All right. Here?" When Cele nodded, she stripped, trying to make it as casual as she could. She was folding her clothes when Cele raised the blinds. Dillian snatched up her shirt again. "Cele! People can see in!"

"Not for long." Cele switched out the lights and came back along the length of the window. "There."

Dillian stood still, letting her eyes become accustomed to the darkness, finding that it wasn't so dark after all. With the lights on, the moon had seemed like a white disk in the sky. Now it shone brilliantly enough to cast shadows from the thin uprights between the huge floor-to-ceiling panes. Beyond the window, it overlaid the nighttime glow of the city with a net of sharply delimited silver and black.

She turned to find Cele a little way away. She wasn't looking at the moon. After a moment, Cele sighed and shook her head slowly. "God in heaven, woman. You are beautiful."

Dillian laughed, abruptly self-conscious. "I'm afraid I can't match up to those old pictures."

"You're aging like good wine. More body, and all the better for it. Didn't I say back then that you were too skinny? If you can count a woman's ribs at a glance, there's something wrong with her."

An old argument, and Dillian shied away from the memory of what Cele had been doing when she'd first made that observation. "Where do you want me?"

"Oh, Lord, don't tempt me." She began piling cushions close to the window. "Let's make these monstrous things work for their keep. Right, sit there. Look out of the window. No...a little more towards me. Knees up and together. Now, straighten your left arm. Lean back and—no, too far. Just—" Cele sighed. "Can I touch?"

It's not fair to do this when you don't— "Go ahead."

"Maybe I should sculpt you," Cele said as she posed her, fingers carefully neutral. "Abstract bronze. Something designed to be handled. I could call it 'Irresistibly Tactile.' There." She stood up and disappeared into the deeper shadows at the back of the room. "It's too dark to sketch. I'll take some pictures and work out how to recreate the light in the morning. Where the heck did I put...ah! Got you, you little bastard."

104

Dillian heard the first quiet click as Cele moved back into the main area, but didn't look around. She held still, enjoying the well-remembered novelty of posing, as Cele circled. From time to time Cele suggested a change in position, or simply rearranged her model. If some of the touches lingered longer as time passed, neither of them commented. "The moon's lovely," Dillian said eventually.

There was a silence, then Cele lowered the camera and said, "Oops! Missed my cue, didn't I?"

"Sorry?"

"I should have said, 'But it's shining on something lovelier still.' And then, oh, done something like kiss you."

It's not fair—"You aren't too late," Dillian said.

A heartbeat of silence, then Cele said, "Don't tease, sweetheart."

"I'm not. Not at all."

By the time she'd finished speaking, the camera had landed on a cushion with a soft thump, and Cele was kneeling before her in the moonlight, her hands extended, palms up. Supplication, and uncharacteristic uncertainly. A shadow hid her face, but Dillian didn't need to see it.

"Someone should take our picture," Dillian said softly, then moved from her pose, opening her arms, but Cele still hesitated.

"No expectations, I promise," Cele said. "No strings attached. Just like before."

"I remember." Then, trying to lighten the tension, she asked, "What were you saying about one of the great joys of life?"

"I don't want it to fuck things up, that's all."

"It won't. It can't." Dillian took her hands, drawing her gently forwards.

The moon lit Cele's face now, allowing Dillian to see her smile. "First bestest friends?" Cele asked.

"Forever."

The great thing about sex with another woman, Dillian mused—the best thing, in fact, the thing she'd forgotten—was that there was no natural endpoint. Sex, conversation, more sex, a pause for wine and ice cream cake, back to bed for more lazy, giggly, fun sex . . . And there was no need to feel selfish for deciding that three orgasms weren't enough after all, and that four made a much better number. Keeping the score even was unnecessary, but fun.

They'd reached another pause, this one feeling as if it might be the final one for the night. The one that would slide gently into sleep. Leading, if one looked far enough ahead, to the morning after. Not something she was worried about, not really, because it was Cele, not an awkward first morning after with a stranger. A bit of a hangover, that would undoubtedly be the worst part, and there wouldn't even be much of that because most of the second bottle still sat by the sofa downstairs where it had all—

"I love you," Cele whispered against her neck. It didn't sound at all strange. Nor at all worrying, or uncomfortable, that Cele should say this while they were lying together, with Cele's hand cupping her breast, sensual and comforting at the same time.

Dillian felt Cele tense up; clearly, she'd misinterpreted the silence. "Sorry, sweetheart. I meant—"

"No." Dillian squirmed around, and silenced her with a kiss. "I love you, too. I always will."

Cele nodded. "I know. But I also know we're not going to be shopping for a rose-covered cottage and a pair of hers-and-hers Labradors tomorrow, so chill out."

She couldn't help laughing. "I am chilled. Never chillier. Absolutely arctic. I was just thinking how nice it felt, lying here."

"Oh." Cele, rendered speechless. Dillian knew it couldn't last long, and it didn't. "Well, there you go. All *my* insecurities laid out in the open. Enjoy 'em while they're hot."

"I'd rather enjoy you." Dillian stroked her hand along Cele's thigh and up over her hip, pressing her hipbone with her thumb, then touching her stomach lightly enough that Cele drew in a breath and squirmed. The muscles tightened under Dillian's fingers, and she laughed. "What was it you said about the significance of spending too much time at the gym?"

"What can I say? It keeps me out of bars, and away from the fabric fetishists and the guys who just want to tell me about their mothers. Or their fish. God, did I ever tell you about the guy with the koi carp?"

"Yes, you did. I thought we didn't talk about him?"

Cele's stomach rippled as she laughed. "Did I say that? Well, it's probably for the best. Mmm." She squirmed, trying to urge Dillian's hand lower. "Especially when we could be doing something much more fun. And much less traumatic."

"We should go to sleep. I have work in the morning."

"Call in sick?" Cele suggested, then sighed. "You and your damn work ethic. If I look sufficiently pitiful and exploited, is there any chance you'll feel so guilty you'll—"

"Shut up," Dillian said, and kissed her.

So maybe it wasn't the last pause after all.

When Dillian came back upstairs from the bathroom, Cele was sitting on the rumpled bed in a dressing gown that shimmered with every color Dillian could imagine, and some she rather wished she couldn't. Thank goodness her hangover was hardly noticeable, even with the bright morning sunshine pouring into the flat through the huge windows. Fortunately, Dillian had remembered to hang her clothes up neatly, so they were respectable enough for a morning at work. She could go home to change at lunchtime. Except...

"Damn," Dillian said. "No clean knickers. I'm out of practice at this unexpected sleepover thing. I should've remembered to wash them in the sink last night."

"We were busy. Borrow a pair of mine." When Dillian hesitated, Cele climbed off the bed and opened the dresser drawer. "Go on. Pick whatever you like. It'll give me an obscenely enjoyable thrill all day, thinking of you in them."

Dillian laughed. "Okay." She sorted through the selection, finally holding up a pair of staunchly sensible cotton briefs, obviously designed for exercising. "How about these?"

Pouting, Cele plunged her hands into the drawer and rummaged. "How about... these?"

"From an admirer?" Dillian asked.

Cele held the scant confection of vivid red satin and lace up to the light. "Actually, no. I bought them for myself, as a treat."

"Well...okay."

Knickers donned, she put her hands on her hips and pirouetted slowly, posing. "What do you think?"

Cele wiped imaginary drool from her chin. "I think you should get dressed before something *bad* happens. Or after something bad happens, which would be better for me."

"I don't think I have time." Cele's flat didn't have any clocks, so Dillian had to hunt for her watch among the lurking cushions. When she found it, the time surprised her. "Good grief!"

"No time for breakfast?"

"No, lots of time. Why did we wake up so early?"

"Why did *you* wake up so early, you mean. I was fast asleep until someone stuck her nose in my ear and pretended to be a cat." Cele waved towards the windows. "I never closed the blinds last night. Most people wake up early here. Everyone's so used to pitch-dark bedrooms. But I always think it's a waste when the bed faces the sunrise."

Before Dillian could reply, the flat comm chimed.

"Aha!" Cele headed for the stairs down. "It's a good job you said you could stay, because while you were in the shower I ordered breakfast, and I'd hate to have to eat all this on my own."

While Cele negotiated the arrival of breakfast, Dillian looked at her clothes and wondered how much to put on and whether to go down. She was still standing there when Cele called, "Up or down?"

"Up, please." Dillian shook out the duvet and pillows and climbed into bed.

"Apple and raspberry juice," Cele announced as she made her way back across the room below. "Coffee, fresh toasted bagels, the fullest-fat cream cheese on the menu and smoked—fuck!"

The cry was followed by a crash and more swearing as colorful as Cele's dressing gown. Dillian leaped out of bed and slithered down the stairs.

"They tried to kill me!" Cele was sitting in the center of a heap of cushions and a spreading pool of fruit juice and coffee. "I swear to God, they ambushed me." She kicked a cushion, which squelched.

"I'll get a cloth."

Cele attempted to reconstruct the breakfast tray while Dillian mopped up juice and squeezed cushions into a bucket. "At least you'll be able to throw those ones away," Dillian said.

"No. I'll get them cleaned. My mother would kill me if she caught me throwing out something perfectly good, if repulsive."

"Send some to her, then. Is she retired yet?"

"Supposed to be, soon. But then she was supposed to be last year, too. She's hanging on grimly to the Intelligence training post. God only knows what classes full of eighteen-year-old Service cadets think of her. Dad thinks she's mad."

"If it's what makes her happy..."

"Oh, I know, I know. Now, I have juice in a box in the fridge, but as for the rest..." Cele poked a bagel. "What should I do with the damp ones?"

"Put them on the plate. We can put extra cheese on them. Rinse the coffee off the salmon, though."

"These are delicious," Dillian said after she'd swallowed the first mouthful of bagel.

"And only slightly fruity."

"Well, as Aunt Jen always used to say, it all goes down the same hole."

Cele licked cream cheese from her lips. "Oh, Lord, yes, I remember. And how often she said it when—do you remember Keir going through his phase of not letting any different foods touch on his plate?"

"Of course. And then afterwards, he went completely the other way, with the savory baking." After more than two decades, the memory could still make Dillian shudder. "I don't think I'll ever forget the bacon muffins."

"It was the brown-sauce icing," Cele said. "That's where it really went tragically wrong. But then, he's always had funny tastes. And he's never put off just by people telling him something can't possibly work."

Dillian had a reply ready, when she recognized the expression on Cele's face.

She was teasing, but half seriously. Pushing to gauge a reaction because she thought Dillian was worrying unnecessarily about Toreth. Instead, Dillian said, "Clearly, funny tastes run in the family."

"Oh, ouch!"

Dillian smiled to herself, and concentrated on breakfast. Eating in Cele's flat, the city spread out in front of them in the bright sunlight like some amazing art installation, was definitely an experience.

"Are you going to want to do this again?" Cele asked suddenly. "Or, I mean, are you going to have time to swing by in the next few weeks so we can..." She trailed off. "We are cool with this, aren't we?" she asked, suddenly serious.

Dillian put down her glass of orange juice. "I don't know. *I'm* cool with it. But are you?"

Slowly, Cele set her plate down on the floor, then lay down on the bed, resting her chin on her hands. "I don't know. I thought I was."

"Oh, Cele." Dillian debated for a moment, then moved up to lean against the headboard. She tugged Cele's ankle gently and said, "Come here."

Without a word, Cele turned and came to lie beside her, head pillowed on Dillian's stomach and arms around her waist. Then she sighed. "God, I'm sorry to start going back and forth on this. I thought I was Ms. Modern Relationship, now I feel like I'm turning into the limpet from hell."

"What, for wanting to know if I'm going to bolt or if I'm planning on borrowing more pairs of knickers in the future?"

Cele gently twanged the elastic on the red thong. "I'm overreacting?"

"More like underreacting. I think you're allowed to ask if I'm planning to take advantage of you again without me assuming there's an engagement ring in your pocket."

Cele patted her dressing gown pocket. "Forget-me-not notes, elastic bands, and a box of charcoals. No rings."

Dillian wriggled down to lie beside Cele, and then pulled back a little—far enough to focus on Cele's face, not so far that she lost the heat of her body. "This isn't second best, Cele. I'm not here because I don't have time to find a boyfriend or because I felt sorry for you, or I got washed away on a wave of drunken nostalgia or—"

Cele wrinkled her nose, half smile, half grimace. "I get the point."

"Good. I wanted you. Want you. I can't make any promises about the long term and I don't want to lie to you about that, not even for one night. Because I love you."

"I know, gorgeous. And I love you. Like I said before, this has no strings attached. Just like it was when you were at university. Free to start dating other people whenever, taking turns with the restaurant bills, calling before we show up at each other's flats. All the bells and whistles."

Dillian raised a skeptical eyebrow. "You don't always call before you come round *now*."

"Well, no. There's no point, is there? Not with you trying for the world record for longest celibate period for an insanely attractive woman."

Dillian snorted. "I've blown that one."

"And then some. So—" Cele grinned. "Until Mr. Right tips up, I'll take you for all I can get while I have the chance."

Dillian smiled back. "Thanks."

"My pleasure. For what?"

"For not telling me that I'm living a life of denial, or anything like that."

"Dilly, one thing about you is that you've always known what you wanted. When you were eleven, you told me you were going to be an engineer and go to Mars."

"When I was eleven?"

"Yes. Ask Jen, she'll tell you. It was New Year, the first one I spent at your house. And I said I was going to be...well, actually I think that was my mime phase."

Dillian smiled. "And Jen asked us every year. And every year you said something different."

"And Kate always said I'd be an artist. But the point is that I know you always know what you want, and if it turns out not to be me—"

"It's not that. Never."

"Okay. If it turns out not to be women-in-the-generic, then whatever else those lips have been doing recently, I know they'll be telling the truth."

Dillian snuggled closer, enjoying the familiar-unfamiliar feel of Cele's body. "I don't deserve you."

Cele wrapped her arms around her and kissed her hair. "I know, sweetheart. I know. But I'm afraid you've still got me. Now, how about finishing that breakfast?"

Playing with Fire

❖

"Congratulations," Toreth said again, as the junior left the office. Doyle paused in the doorway. "Thanks, Para. I owe you a lot. I won't forget it."

Toreth watched him go, thinking the news made a perfect bloody end to a long, hard week. A minute later Sara appeared, uninvited but expected. "Well," she said, "he got it, then."

Toreth nodded. Belqola's replacement had managed a longer stint than his predecessor, but still a short stay by the standards of Toreth's team. "I'm getting sick of this," Toreth said. "Either they're useless, like Belqola, or they fuck off ten minutes after they arrive and leave you a pile of unfinished work. No loyalty."

"Eighteen months, not ten minutes. And he's here for another six weeks, so he'll have time to wrap up his cases."

She'd always liked the bastard. "Less than a month after Stephen Lambrick left. Why doesn't Political just take my whole team?"

"Morehen's a good replacement. Better than Lambrick." She sat on the edge of the desk. "Or I think so."

The reminder of his reciprocal poaching of a very good investigator from Political Crimes managed to cheer him slightly. "What, he's more your type?"

"Andy?" She smiled. "Not rich enough for me."

He raised his eyebrows. "*Andy?*"

"Andrew. Investigator Morehen." She was blushing, and trying very hard not to, which only made it worse. "We went out for a drink and we spent a while talking. Not just the two of us—it was with a few more investigators and admins, at lunchtime. Just a drink. Nothing more than that."

Not entirely convinced, Toreth considered the idea. Morehen was good-looking enough, although he'd be more attractive if he grew his medium brown hair out of the close crop, and he was a little shorter and lighter built, and a lot poorer, than Sara usually liked them. He also had the uncompromising, hard-eyed directness that Political Crimes staff wore like a special uniform. Maybe he loosened up after a few drinks. "Well, whatever the two of you are doing, keep it out of the office."

"Toreth! You *know* I don't—"

"Yeah, yeah, I know." He fended off her indignation with an irritated wave. The brief lifting of his good mood had vanished. "Lambrick *and* Doyle. I don't know why they're going. Either of them. Lambrick's going up a grade, but it's just another junior job for Doyle."

"Political Crimes is a good career move, though," Sara said. "And they keep expanding the section so there's lots of opportunities. Promotions."

"What the hell's wrong with General Criminal?" he demanded. She wisely kept silent. "*I* like it here. And I was the one who took Doyle out of the pool. Discipline problems after qualification—you saw his file. I was the one who gave him the chance to show me he'd grown out of it." Which the man had. At the time Doyle had seemed suitably grateful for the permanent position and he had proved ambitious, hardworking, and as disciplined as a para ever was. Too ambitious, unfortunately.

"You were dead right about him," Sara said. "He was good. And *you're* good at picking juniors. You'll find someone else even better." She grinned suddenly. "Like Morehen."

He knew it was flattery, but he couldn't help being cheered. "Yeah, I expect so. September's only a couple of months away, and then it's the cattle market."

She nodded. "Get a fresh one. They always last longer. D'you want a coffee?"

"Thanks."

Sara had barely closed the door when the comm chimed. Toreth was delighted to hear Warrick's voice. They hadn't seen much of each other over the last few weeks. Warrick had been away to a conference; it had only been for a few days, but after he came back their free evenings had never seemed to coincide. "I've been trying to get hold of you," Warrick said, with an edge to his voice that Toreth identified straight away as suspicion.

"Yeah? Work's been a bastard all week, so I've been switching my comm off most evenings." Sara could always get hold of him, of course, but Toreth didn't generally advertise the fact.

"I called you at home last night and you weren't there," Warrick continued.

No question was added to the statement of fact, but Toreth answered it anyway. "I was with someone."

"Oh?" Politely inquiring.

"Yes." Sometimes he could be bothered to lie to Warrick, sometimes he couldn't. Today, after Doyle's irritating news, was a "couldn't" day. "I met someone at the gym, we went out for a drink. We ended up making a night of it."

Over the comm he heard the sound of the office door being firmly closed. "Did you fuck him or her?" This was now Warrick's chilly "quest for knowledge" voice, which suggested he was going to get wound up about this one. It happened more often these days than it used to.

"Yes, I fucked him." Toreth waited with mild anticipation for the next question. If Warrick was really irritated, he'd want to know the man's name, although Toreth never understood why he asked.

"What was...never mind. That's not why I called."

Toreth felt a twinge of disappointment. He liked these arguments because the make-up sex was usually incredibly good. It made a difference when Warrick felt he possibly had something to prove. "What can I do for you, then?" Toreth asked.

"I'm going away to a meeting next week, as you know, and I wondered—God knows why—if you'd like to accompany me. Assuming you can get away."

"You mean on Monday?"

"Yes. Sorry for the short notice. Call it a sudden impulse."

"A tech conference?" Toreth asked dubiously.

"Yes. But it shouldn't be too dull. The conference center looks excellent, even by corporate standards, and it's in the Alps. Skiing, if you're interested."

"I've never tried it."

"Dangerous, potentially painful, pointless physical activity. Just your sort of thing."

"It sounds more like yours."

Warrick laughed. "Yes or no? I need to make arrangements."

Toreth thought about it. He had an investigation running, with prisoners due to be brought in today, and they had to broken quickly before their associates could catch wind of the arrests and run. Still, some of it he could leave to his team. He could supervise at a distance if he needed to, once he'd conducted the first round of interrogations. Doyle could earn his keep for his last days on the team. Some weekend overtime would do him good. He always lied about work details, and the translation was smooth and almost unconscious. "I have a case finishing. It's just paperwork, but it all needs to be tied up before I can get away. I could meet you there a day later."

"Very well. I'll send you the information."

The next four days at work were a nightmare. It took longer to get away than he'd hoped and he didn't arrive at the conference center until late Tuesday evening. Warrick hadn't exaggerated when he said it was corporate standard. Toreth preferred cities, in his limited experience of the alternatives, but the journey up to the Alpine center impressed him. Outdoor summer snow sports were a purely corporate luxury, and the complex was visible from miles away, the brilliant lights glittering on the artificial snow. It would take more than ten minutes' chatting up an admin to get a place like this past accounts at I&I, but in this case the expenses were Warrick's problem. Easier to sort out, Toreth supposed, when you owned the corporation.

113

By the time he'd got the room details from reception and made his way through the miles of thickly carpeted corridor, Toreth had almost shed the lingering tension of his long day at work. He deserved a holiday.

He swiped the card and the door opened smoothly with a gentle nudge. The room beyond was dark, although the lights came up automatically as he stepped through. "It's me!" he called, wondering if Warrick was already asleep.

Water splashed somewhere off to his left. "I'm in the bath. I'll be out in a minute."

"Nice room," Toreth said, looking around.

"I suggested something more modest," Warrick said, his voice echoing in what must be a large bathroom. "But Asher decided she wanted us to impress potential customers and rivals. I have to say, though, it's worth every euro SimTech's paying for it."

It was. The door opened into a spacious living area with armchairs, thick rugs, and a large hearth with a real wood fire laid in the grate. Toreth wondered whether it worked. It was completely unnecessary, of course, as the room was comfortably warm already. It might be fun to try, though. Solid fuel heating was a rarity outside the sim.

Warrick appeared, wrapped in a dressing gown and drying his hair. Toreth went over, but Warrick stepped away from him slightly—not far, but far enough to make his message clear. Toreth let him go and gave a mental shrug. Whatever it was would sort itself out. He went off to put his bags in the bedroom.

When he came back into the main room he found Warrick kneeling in front of the fireplace, fiddling with the control for the hearth. "Playing with fire?" Toreth inquired.

Warrick smiled, still oddly distant. "No more than usual. Ah, here we go." With a crackle, flames started to lick up between the logs carefully arranged in the large grate. "Join me?" Warrick offered, lying down on the rug.

Toreth sat cross-legged beside him, watching the flames starting to catch on the wood. The smoke disappeared smoothly up the chimney, leaving only a pleasant, resinous scent to escape into the room.

Warrick stared into the fire. "This man you were with," he said without preamble.

"What?"

"When I called you at I&I on Friday. You'd been with someone."

"Yes?" Toreth prompted after a couple of seconds' silence, not particularly wanting to have this argument, but not particularly caring either. Although it seemed a long way to come for something they could've done over the comm.

"What was he like?" Warrick asked.

"About my height, brown hair—"

"Not what he looked like. What you did." That was a departure from the normal line of questioning. "What you did when you fucked," Warrick elaborated.

114

"Yes, I worked that bit out by myself. I was just wondering why the fuck you would want to hear about it."

"Because I want to know."

"Very clever." Toreth scrutinized him carefully, but Warrick was letting nothing escape from behind his corporate mask. "*Why* do you want to know?"

"Curiosity?"

"Killed the fucking cat. Try again."

"Well..." Warrick lay very still, staring intently at the flames. "You'll sleep around whatever I say, and I'm not asking you to stop. Because I know you won't, or possibly can't, and normally, it doesn't bother me. Recently, though... I've tried ignoring it and that doesn't seem to be as effective as it used to be. So I thought I'd try something else."

"You really want to hear about it?"

"To be perfectly honest, I'm not sure. But it can't hurt to hear it through once. Perhaps that'll stop me from thinking about it."

Toreth considered it for a few more seconds, ignoring a premonition that this was a bad idea. "Okay." He lay down next to Warrick, not quite touching. "We went to his house—"

Warrick shook his head slightly. "No. Start earlier."

"When?"

"When you first saw him."

"At the gym, like I said. I saw him watching me, and then again later. So I smiled at him and then, after a while he came over to talk to me. I noticed he had a ring on."

"And?"

"We had a bit of a chat, and he was interested-but-wanting-not-to-be. Then he said he had to go, so I went back into the changing rooms with him." Toreth twined bits of the rug between his fingers, vaguely wondering if he was going to wake up still in the car on the way to the conference center and find this whole conversation had been a bizarre dream. "We had a shower—I could see he was looking at me again— and he was attractive enough, so I asked if he'd like to go for a drink. I knew—"

He had been going to say, "I knew you were busy, so I thought I'd settle for the next best thing." The confessional atmosphere was obviously getting to him. "I didn't have anything else planned," he finished, instead.

"Where did you go?"

"Bar in the gym, first of all. Then somewhere he suggested. Not bad."

"What did you talk about?"

"I don't remember. Does it matter?"

"I'd like to know."

Toreth shrugged. "Just general conversation. He was interesting enough, but I wasn't really listening, not to the extent of remembering any of it now."

115

"About your job?"

"Yes. Some people are curious, you know. He wasn't all that curious, but it didn't put him off."

"And then you asked him...what?"

"He asked me. Actually, I thought he wasn't going to do it. But then he asked if I'd like to go back to his house." Toreth smiled. "Only took him two hours to get round to it." He shifted against the rug, getting hard at the memory of the moment of victory and trying to get more comfortable with some degree of discretion.

Beside him Warrick frowned, thoughtful rather than annoyed. "Didn't you say he was married?"

"Yes, I did. She was visiting her sister or something—that's where they usually seem to be. I didn't bother to ask."

"Did you kiss him?" Warrick asked, throwing him slightly.

Toreth had to think about it. "No."

"Do you ever?"

"Yes, sometimes."

"Ah. Women more often than men?"

"Yes."

"Makes sense. Did you touch his mouth?"

"Warrick..."

"You don't have to tell me, if you don't want to," Warrick said mildly. "Or we can stop altogether if you like. Just say so."

"I don't...never mind." He did want to stop, but he didn't want to admit it. "Yes, I did. Or rather, he sucked me, so if that counts as touching his mouth then I did."

"Actually, I don't think it does. But since we're there, did you come in his mouth?"

"No. He didn't want me to." Forestalling the next question he said, "With his hand."

Warrick nodded. "On the bed?"

"What?"

"Were you on the bed? Lying down? Kneeling? Where?"

This was too fucking weird. "Uh, I was sitting on the edge of the bed, he was kneeling."

Warrick nodded again. "His wife's bed. Their bed."

"I suppose so. I didn't think about it."

"No?" He sounded slightly surprised. "So why do you like the married ones so much?"

"More of a challenge? I don't know."

"Liar." Warrick's expression didn't change, nor his even, calm tone of voice, but something in the atmosphere altered subtly.

116

Toreth hesitated, smoothing the rug in front of him. "All right. How about, I get a kick out of seeing people do things they don't like to think they want to do?"

"Better. Does that include me?" The question had a dangerous edge, and Toreth kept quiet, wondering where this was leading. "For example," Warrick continued precisely, "I've never seen the attraction in casual sex. Maybe I should take it up."

Toreth bit back his instinctive reply, but it didn't matter, because Warrick had turned his head slightly and was looking at him sidelong. "You wouldn't like that, though, would you?" Warrick asked, his voice soft.

No, you bastard, Toreth thought, I fucking wouldn't. But he could hardly say that now. "I'm in no position to object," Toreth said carefully.

Warrick snorted. "No, you most definitely aren't. But you'd hate it. Knowing I was with someone else." His eyes closed as he turned his face back towards the heat of the fire, and his voice continued in a low litany, strangely dispassionate. "Fucking someone else. Being fucked. Telling them I want more, harder, deeper. Someone else coming inside me. Someone else saying my name."

The words flowed over him, sickening and arousing at the same time. Toreth found his hands clenching on empty air. "Don't," he said quietly.

Warrick tilted his head back, firelight flickering over his throat. "Or letting them fuck my mouth. Kneeling in front of them. Doing all the things I do for you. Ah . . . " He opened his eyes again. "Do you know why I invited you here?" he said, in a more normal voice.

A cold chill poured down Toreth's spine. "No."

"Because the last time I was away, the last time I was at a conference, I did."

"What?"

"You know what. But if you insist: I fucked one of the other delegates." Now Warrick turned to watch him again, measuring the effect of his cool, deliberate words. "Not just once. Four or five times, over the conference. On the last morning we had breakfast and then went back to the room and I nearly missed my car to the airport. He asked me to call him when I got home."

The chill had collected itself into a ball and settled in his stomach. Toreth listened to his own voice, unable to believe he was asking the questions. "He lives in New London? Who is he?"

"I don't think I'm going to tell you that."

"Did you call him?" All those missing evenings over the past weeks.

He looked away again. "No, I didn't." Long pause. "He called me, though."

Then Warrick waited, until Toreth had to ask. "And?"

"I told him I was flattered, but that I wasn't interested. Which was a lie, incidentally."

Which part? Was this all leading up to "it's over, goodbye"? Toreth couldn't force himself to ask directly. "Why did you want me to come here?"

117

There was a long silence. "Because...he's here," Warrick said at length. "And I didn't think it would be a good thing to end up doing it again."

"Did you want to?" he asked, finally appreciating the strange compulsion Warrick had about the details of his own one-night stands. Better to know than to imagine.

"Yes."

Anger flared up, and it took him a few seconds to corral it, to keep it away from his voice and hands. "It's weeks since you were away before. Why tell me now? Why the fuck are you telling me any of this?"

"Because I wanted to hurt you." A slight, sour smile in profile. "I wanted you to know how it feels."

A revenge fuck, God only knew why after all this time. But it was a better— or more bearable—reason than the ones he'd been afraid of hearing. Because he was a better fuck than you. Because I'm bored with you. Because I want him more than I want you.

"Well?" Warrick asked. "Did it work?"

Toreth took a breath, as deep as he could with the tight ache in his chest. "Yes." He couldn't imagine—and didn't want to find out—what a "no" might provoke.

"Good." Warrick knelt up, still watching the fire. "Not that I think for a moment it will stop you from doing it next time you feel the need to scratch an itch. But I wanted you to know—that's what it feels like." He rose to his feet in one jerky movement, controlled anger evident in every line, and went off into the bedroom.

For a minute that felt like ten, Toreth lay still, feeling the heat of the fire on his face. Then he stood up and poured himself a large drink.

Knowing I was with someone else.

Out of the corner of his eye, he could see the bedroom door, ajar. Warrick wanted him to follow him, or at least he was leaving the possibility open. Or maybe he'd just forgotten to close it. But Toreth didn't follow, because now that the ice of the shock was melting into anger he didn't think it would be a good idea.

In fact it would be a very bad idea indeed, because he knew that, among all the things Warrick would tolerate from him, physical violence wasn't on the list. Not for real. Not outside the game. That would make him walk, and Toreth wasn't—quite—upset enough to forget that and he wasn't—quite—angry enough not to care. A part of him *didn't* care, though. The part that hated how much he wanted Warrick. Hated knowing that, if Warrick walked out of the bedroom right now and knelt in front of the fire, and breathed, "Fuck me," that he'd do it, and that it would be wonderful, even better for the anger.

Taste of Warrick's name in his mouth, past the whiskey, and he drank again, trying to blot it out.

He hated most of all this loss of control, this feeling of someone—anyone— having power over him again. Even if Warrick didn't choose to exercise it, even if he claimed that he didn't want it, it was still there. Warrick was different to every

118

other fuck in his life, and when he was forced to acknowledge it, the rage brimmed up. Feeling it, he wanted to hit Warrick, hurt him, make him oh-so-fucking sorry for what he'd done. To wring out an apology and a promise never, ever to do it again. Never even to think about it. Yet all that was nothing compared to what he wanted to do to this other, nameless man. He tried to banish the images created by Warrick's vivid word-picture.

Someone else saying my name.

With a sharp crack the glass shattered in his grip. For a moment he thought he'd got away with it, then he saw the blood and gasped at the sharp sting of spirits in the cuts. Trying not to drip blood onto the carpet, he went into the bathroom and ran icy water over his hand until the bleeding slowed and it started to go numb. Then he was able to pull out the shards, swearing through gritted teeth at the slide of glass through flesh. Once they were all out, he flexed his hand, watching the tendons stretch, checking his fingertips for feeling. No serious damage done, he decided.

Luckily there was a first-aid kit in the cupboard under the basin, so he could patch his hand up with no worse of a mess than blood on himself and one of the towels. When he'd finished he looked at himself in bathroom mirror and thought: hypocrite. You've got no rights over him. You don't own him. Isn't that what you wanted? Isn't that what you asked him for? You can't even remember how many people you've had since you met him. He does it once, and you're breaking fucking glasses over it. Half of the General Criminal coffee room would probably choke to death laughing if they could see you now. Pathetic fucking hypocrite.

All true, but it didn't change the way he felt—hurt and angry. A bad combination. He took deep breaths, trying and failing to find even a pretense of calm. His clothes were stained with blood and alcohol and he felt dirty, so he stripped and stepped into the shower. Holding his bandaged hand out of the spray, he ran the water hot and cold until his skin burned, but it couldn't clear his mind, or stop Warrick's voice from running through it.

Doing all the things I do for you.

Eventually, when it had become a simple choice between walking out or going into the bedroom after Warrick, he got out of the shower, half dried himself, pulled on the filthy clothes, and left. On the way across the room he dropped his keycard on the floor, so there was no chance he could change his mind and go back.

Then there was a taxi to the airport, and a late flight, and another taxi, and he was back home. And still he felt the same.

Warrick lay in the dark, listening to the sounds punctuating the background of his own unsteady breathing. Breaking glass, a door opening, the shower running for a long time, then finally the outer door of the room slamming. After that he rolled onto his side and watched the minutes passing on the clock by the bed. It took an hour before he allowed himself be sure Toreth wasn't coming back, and the sick fear started to let go of him.

He'd meant to tell Toreth. Or he'd meant to tell him something. Not the way he had, though—he'd been carried away by the moment. When he'd told Toreth that he wanted to hurt him, he'd been as surprised by the truth of it as Toreth possibly could have been. Then even more surprised by how guilty he'd felt as soon as he'd walked away from the fire.

He had nothing to feel guilty about...by Toreth's standards. By his own, plenty. He had no right to punish Toreth for doing no more than he'd done for as long as they'd known each other. Warrick had been the one who had set the terms for their relationship, and Toreth hadn't broken them. Technically, perhaps, neither had he, because there was no commitment to fidelity on his part either. That, however, was semantic quibbling. He'd known perfectly well that Toreth would see it as a gross violation of his trust.

Kissing and telling. Fucking and telling. Why the hell had he thought that doing what Toreth did would be any kind of solution? In fact, now that everything was over and the adrenaline had cleared his mind, he wondered if he'd thought *anything* intelligent over the last couple of months. Not as far as he could tell, with the clarity of hindsight. He'd let himself become obsessed with the idea of what Toreth was doing with people that neither of them cared about. Then he'd done something unforgivably selfish and stupid (and he wouldn't even think about how much he'd enjoyed the illicit liaison, because that only made it worse). *Then* he'd compounded the idiocy by trying to pass the guilt along to someone who didn't have a perceptible conscience, but who had previously demonstrated a nice line in possessive jealousy.

What a wonderfully mature response to the situation.

He wasn't even sure what he'd wanted in return. An acknowledgement that he meant more than the others, maybe. An apology and a vow of fidelity would have been nice. Or not, because any promise would have been a lie and he had enough self-respect left not to want that.

The final realization, unfortunately coming about two hours too late to be of any use, was that he did care about Toreth's infidelity, but not as much as he'd thought. Not enough to want to lose him. Not even enough to enjoy hurting him, once the flush of anger had faded. Definitely not enough to have done it in such a stupidly dangerous fashion. In fact, stupid was an utterly inadequate description. Suicidal might be better, and that thought brought the fear back in a stomach-turning rush.

He'd forgotten his promise to Dilly to be careful. Somehow he'd forgotten what Toreth was and why he'd needed to make the promise in the first place. Dilly would kill him. If she got the chance. The best he could realistically hope for was that

120

he'd never see Toreth again. And, God, even after everything, he still didn't want that.

The next morning, Toreth arrived at the office early. God only knew what he looked like, because Sara didn't even ask why he was back so soon. She just brought him a coffee without being asked, and kept resolutely out of his way.

For almost an hour he resisted the temptation. Then he called up the attendee lists for the current conference and the previous one and cross-referenced the male delegates. That produced a substantial overlap, so he went with his first guess and selected those resident in New London. That left him with only a dozen names. He looked at the list and toyed with other selection criteria. Marital status would be a potential one. Whoever he was, he wouldn't be married—Toreth couldn't see Warrick taking his revenge fuck similarities that far. And age. Probably around Warrick's age or a little older. There would be no graduate student desperate to secure a good corporate job—Warrick wouldn't want to feel that he was taking advantage of someone. Even though he had been. A picture of the man formed gradually in his mind as he played with the ideas, refining the criteria. No face yet, but he was confident now he could fill in that detail. If he wanted to know. If the image wasn't clear enough already.

Kneeling in front of them.

Better to know than to imagine. Maybe.

He didn't actually run the searches, although it was a safe enough game to play. Even if he wanted to, he couldn't do anything to any of them. They weren't within reach. They were all…at the conference. With Warrick.

Abandoning the list of names, Toreth went to lean against the window, glass cool against his forehead. Nice, smooth move, he thought. Storm out in a sulk, don't even leave a message, and leave Warrick a few hundred miles away and in the same hotel as the man he'd fucked before. Very fucking clever.

If he does it again, he thought, I'll kill him. No. I'll kill both of them.

The calm certainly of the idea disturbed him. Suddenly, he badly wanted a drink, which at the same time he recognized was not a good sign at ten in the morning.

Get a fucking grip, he told himself.

He deleted the names—although he could always do the search again later—and decided that, since he'd booked the holiday, he wasn't going to spend the day hurting prisoners. For one thing, it would have been enjoyably therapeutic, and that was too unprofessional to tolerate.

"I don't know if I'm going to be in tomorrow," he told Sara on the way past. "I'll call first thing." She nodded, and watched him leave without comment.

He was heading for the stairs down, tunnel vision in full operation, when someone called his name from close by. When he swung around, he found Morehen, who offered a hand screen. "What is it?" Toreth asked.

"Since you were in the office, Para, I wondered if you could spare a minute to look at this report. I followed the General Criminal protocols, of course, but it's not quite the way I do—did—things over in Political. I—"

"Do you know what your last assessment grading said?" Toreth asked.

The investigator stared for a moment, mouth still open, and then his hand fell. "No, Para. They're all confidential."

"It said you have outstanding initiative and independence. And a lot of seniors don't like that. I do—it's why I wanted you. So if you want to keep your high grading and your nice little housing allowance bonus—"

The lift doors opened and Toreth managed to stop, aware of the other people suddenly near them. Professionalism, that was why he was on his way out of the building. And gratuitously bollocking staff in public was the way that Mike Belkin and wankers like him managed to hit record team turnovers. Wherever Warrick was sticking his cock, that was no reason for Toreth to fuck up the rest of his life.

Thinking about Warrick didn't help his concentration, though. Toreth sorted though possible conversation closers, trying to find one that would retrieve things without an apology, while Morehen slowly paled and began to fidget. "If you have any questions about report formats, that's Sara's area. You don't need to prove to me that you're trying to do your job the way I want it done. Do the work well, which I know you can, and it'll prove itself." He dropped his hand onto Morehen's shoulder. "And right now, I'm on holiday."

Morehen nodded. "Sorry, Para. I'll go talk to Sara right away."

Toreth left him there and he went down to the I&I medical center to have his hand checked out and the cuts bonded closed by someone not using his off hand. Then he spent the afternoon at the gym, winding down from murderous to merely angry. Afterwards he went home, showered and changed, and thought about going out. In the end, he decided he didn't want to.

Someone else coming inside me.

He just didn't want to. Maybe all the travel had worn him out, but he'd rather spend the evening drinking alone.

Sara stood on the doorstep of Toreth's block of flats, her finger hovering over the comm screen, and had second thoughts. Actually, they amounted to about two-hundredth thoughts. Maybe turning up unannounced hadn't been a good idea. When Toreth had left that morning, she'd decided to let him go, then changed her mind after a minute and gone after him. She hadn't found Toreth, but she had run into Andy standing by the fifth-floor lifts, staring towards the stairs and looking as though someone had punched him between the eyes. A quick recap of their conversation had convinced her that Toreth needed space.

But she couldn't leave him alone forever, and if she'd called he would have told her not to come around. He might be out anyway. She could always deliver her offering and leave. Anyway, she wasn't the one he was furious with. Suitably reassured, she called his flat. Just when she'd decided that he wasn't going to answer, the screen lit up. He looked briefly disappointed, then questioning. "What do you want?"

Sara lifted the bag she'd brought, and shook it so that it clinked.

Toreth smiled slightly. "Come up."

When he opened the door to the flat, she thought he looked less dangerous than he had at I&I, but more unhappy.

Sometimes Warrick irritated her intensely, because life had been so much easier before he came along. That said, she had to admit that there was more variety these days, between Toreth's regular coffee-break recountings of exotic sim fucks and his occasional panics over the whole concept of repeatedly screwing someone he also spoke to. Anyway, Toreth had sat through enough of her broken hearts that she ought not to begrudge returning the favor. To Sara's practiced eye, this latest episode looked something like a broken heart, even if she'd never seen the look on him before. Or even imagined it happening. She wondered if he'd noticed yet.

It took her a couple of hours and some carefully paced drinking to talk him around to the subject of Warrick. Luckily, he'd had a head start, so by the time he started talking she was still sober enough to listen and make the right encouraging noises. After that it took another hour to coax out the full story of the previous night. Or rather, a partial story that was good enough to be getting on with. At least it included an explanation of what had happened to his hand.

Her first thought was, good for Warrick. She wouldn't have put up with Toreth's screwing around for this long. Not that she let a hint of that show. Instead, she said, "Do you think he really did it? It doesn't sound like him."

"Yes, he—" Toreth stopped and stared at her for a moment. "Christ. I never thought...no, he did it. He definitely did it."

"Weird."

"*Weird*? Is that the best you can fucking do?"

She heard the anger and resolved to ignore it. "What do you want me to say? It is weird, for him. I wonder why he did it?" Then she shut up and watched him.

He filled his glass again. "How the hell should I know?"

Because *you're* the one screwing him, and because it's obvious to anyone with a functioning brain. It still surprised her sometimes that he could be so perceptive about everything but this. She bit her tongue and waited.

"He said—" Toreth stopped, looking down at his bandaged hand. "He said he wanted to hurt me. A revenge fuck, I suppose. Not that I care."

Sara hastily swallowed a mouthful of her drink, coughing a bit, and even he had the grace to look slightly embarrassed by how bad the lie was. "I thought he didn't care about all that either," she said, unable to resist prodding just a little.

"He doesn't. Didn't." Toreth blinked, as though thinking too hard was pushing the world out of focus. "He wants it to stop. That's why he asked me about the... and told me about... yeah. He wants me to stop."

Halle-fucking-lujah, Sara very nearly said, but didn't. "Yeah, maybe."

He put his glass down on the arm of the sofa and ran his hand through his hair. "I could tell him I wouldn't do it any more. Fuck other people. I could tell him that."

To her amazement, she realized he was actually considering it, despite its obvious drawbacks. Specifically, that it would be a monstrously unconvincing lie. Maybe she'd overdone it with the liquid consolation, for both of them. The small living room suddenly felt hot and stuffy. She hauled herself off the sofa and opened a window. "So, you want him back, then?" she asked as she sat down again.

"Back?" He looked baffled.

"Yeah, when you walked out you meant that as a goodbye, right? It sounded like a 'goodbye' to me. He said, 'stop screwing around,' or words to that effect. And you walked. I suppose he must have known it was a risk when he did it."

Toreth closed his eyes for a moment. "Fuck," he said expressively.

"Didn't you want it to be goodbye?"

"No, I... " He frowned, the anger surfacing again. "Fuck knows."

"What *did* you want?"

There was a pause as he picked up his glass and downed the contents. "I wanted to kill him," he said with intense, drunken conviction. "I wanted to kill both of them. Bastards. And I wanted to make him—them—fucking suffer first. I wanted him to be sorry. *That's* what I wanted."

She wished he sounded rather less literal about it. "You aren't *going* to, are you?" she asked, almost involuntarily.

Toreth peered meditatively into his empty glass for a long moment, then shook his head. "'Course not," he said. "What do you think I am? He's a fucking corporate director."

Sara shook her head as well. "Have another drink," she suggested.

The room smelled like the interrogation rooms at I&I would if they weren't kept so religiously scrubbed and disinfected. Of blood and fear and pain. And death.

In a corner behind him, out of sight but marginally in his awareness, lay the body of Warrick's faceless revenge fuck. Very faceless, now. If Justice ever got hold of the corpse, they'd need to run a DNA check to find his name. Not that they would find the body. And not that Toreth cared if they did. All he cared about was Warrick.

He inspected Warrick as he hung from the chains that disappeared into the gloom above, his feet just touching the ground. He faced the rough wall, only a few inches away but too far to provide any support or rest. Cuts, weals, and bruises made a patchwork of his pale skin. Rivulets of blood, dried and fresh, ran down from where the manacles had cut his wrists. His hair was matted with sweat, his head resting at an angle against his arm.

Toreth stepped up behind him and placed his hands lightly on his shoulders. "I'm back," he said softly.

However bad the pain is, it's possible to sleep. Toreth knew this. Even chained and beaten and gagged, it's possible to sleep, if you're exhausted enough. Warrick's head jerked upright, and he moaned deep in his throat. Toreth dragged his nails down Warrick's back, bringing fresh blood welling from old welts, and a choked scream from the body under his hands, muffled by the gag. He jerked against the chains. That should have woken him up nicely.

Carefully, Toreth loosened the gag and removed it. He wanted to hear him talk now—wanted it very much. He twined his fingers tightly in Warrick's hair, turning his head so he could see his bruised face in profile, and ran his other hand down his back again, gently, almost caressingly. This time Warrick didn't move. Toreth put his mouth against Warrick's ear, in a cruel imitation of their game. "Say it," he whispered.

With a sharp tug, pulling hair through Toreth's fingers, Warrick turned his head away. With measured deliberation, Toreth smashed his face into the wall. That got a reaction, a gasp of pain, so he did it again. Fresh red splashes decorated the bricks. "Say it."

Warrick spat blood, closed his eyes, and set his jaw defiantly.

Toreth didn't know from where he found the strength. Warrick had to know he wasn't going to let him go. He couldn't afford to, and he didn't want to. Warrick was going to die here. Maybe that was why he was still fighting. Because in the end it wouldn't matter what he did, except to himself.

He pressed up closer, so that Warrick could feel that he was hard, that he was going to rape him again whatever he said or didn't say. He didn't need to hear it, but, oh, he wanted to. "Say it."

Silence. No more than he'd expected.

Letting go of his hair, he crouched down, set his hand in the small of Warrick's back and, after a moment's pause, slammed him hard against the wall. Chained as he was, Warrick had no leverage to resist him. But he didn't fight. He hung against the wall, passive, accepting. Defying him by refusing to acknowledge the pain and denying him the reaction he wanted.

No one can resist forever.

Toreth's other hand stroked up the backs of Warrick's thighs, wandered up over his buttocks, and into the crack. Did he feel the muscles tensing, resisting him? Starting to fight back finally? He forced his fingers inside Warrick, then his whole hand, then clenched his fist and twisted, pushing hard. Warrick hissed and struggled, only for few seconds, then stopped.

"I can kill you like this, you know," Toreth said conversationally. "Not quickly, but quite easily. Blood poisoning. Internal bleeding. I've seen people die like that—it's not pleasant."

He rested his head against Warrick's hip, the skin cool against his cheek. "Is that really how you want to die? All you have to do is say it, and it won't be like that. Say it, and then it'll all be over quickly, I promise." Closing his eyes, Toreth turned his head. "Say it," he whispered against Warrick's soft skin. He could hear Warrick breathing, shallow and rasping. That was the only answer he gave.

Bastard.

Toreth pulled his fist out, still clenched, and the whimper of pain was a victory even if it wasn't what he really needed to hear. Standing up, he pulled Warrick away from the wall, into a parody of an embrace. "I'm going to fuck you," he said, feeling blood slick against his chest. "I'm going to fuck you and you...you are going to fucking well say it. Say it now."

Warrick moved against him, before forcing himself back to stillness. He drew a breath in to speak. "Plastic duck," he whispered.

Thwarted again, Toreth laughed. "I'm not going to stop because you ask nicely. There's no safe word here. I want to hear you say it."

He wrapped both arms around Warrick's waist, holding him immobile as he thrust in as hard as he could. And even though all he wanted to do was hurt him, he had to stop to get his breath back because it felt so fucking good and he could smell Warrick's hair through the stink of blood. Dizzy with wanting him, still, and this was all Warrick's fault. He'd started it. "Say it."

No response. No fucking response.

He pulled out and slammed in again, harder. Again and again, and he started to lose control, losing himself in the memory of doing this before. Warrick's shoulders tensing under his hands, sharp gasps of pain and nothing more than that. No words.

Mine, you bastard. Mine. So say it. *Say it.*

A shiver wracked him, running down his back. Then another. He couldn't stop himself from shaking. He clung to Warrick's shoulders, crushing him against the wall, his face against his neck. Despite the shivers, he felt hot, fever hot, and hottest of all where his cock was still buried deep inside Warrick. "I'm sorry," Toreth whispered nonsensically. "I'm sorry. I'm sorry. I'm sorry." Meaningless sounds, repeated on each heaving breath. "I'm—"

"Shh. Just...shh." Warrick's voice, at last. Warrick's hands cupping his face, lifting it to look into his eyes. Then, before Toreth could focus clearly, Warrick kissed him, torn lips gentle against his own. Desperately grateful, Toreth opened his mouth, coppery blood flowing onto his tongue. It tasted sweetly familiar, but he couldn't remember why because at that moment a sound began behind him, distracting him.

Warrick must have heard it too, because he broke off the kiss. As he pulled away, Toreth tried to reach out to stop him, but the chains on his wrists held him back. Under the mask of blood Warrick's expression was cold. "You can fuck me as often as you want," he said with icy precision. "That won't make me love you."

All Toreth could do was stare at him, as the noises in the room behind him grew louder. Someone was banging on the door. Someone had found them.

The curtains slapped against the back of the sofa, flapping in the draft from the open window. His neck ached from the cold air. Sara lay on the sofa beside him, fast asleep, with her head in his lap. At some point she had rolled over so that her mouth was pressed into his crotch. Well, that explained a few things.

Sara muttered in her sleep, her mouth moving against his erection, accentuating the already arousing caress of warm breath through fabric. Very nice, but she wouldn't be happy to wake up and find he'd let her stay like that. Still, he couldn't resist leaving her there until he worked out what she was saying. After listening to the disjointed fragments for a while, he realized that she was talking about m-f booking forms. He smiled faintly; he'd have to remember to tell her about that later. Sara always maintained that dreaming about work was as sad as it was possible to get. He carefully eased her head off his lap and onto the sofa.

The room felt cold, so he closed the window and found a coat with which to cover her. He didn't want her to wake up and start asking more questions. She murmured something about timetabling clashes, before she sighed and curled up. Sad it may be, but on balance he'd rather have had her dream.

In the bathroom, he rinsed his mouth out, spat into the sink, and then splashed water onto his face. Catching sight of his reflection in the mirror he was surprised by how blurred the lines of his face looked. Still drunk, he decided, but sobering rapidly towards the beginning of the hangover. He watched himself drying his hands while he considered the dream. The details were fading, but even so, loaded didn't do it justice. He'd never put any faith in the concept of symbolism in dreams. On the other hand . . .

"What *did* you want?" Sara had asked him. Whatever he wanted, he sure as hell didn't want to be here, drunk, on his own, with nothing but a day at work to look forward to. He checked his watch. Half past two in the morning. There wouldn't be a flight for a few hours, so he might as well try to get some sleep.

❖ ❖ ❖

When he left the flat before dawn, Sara still slept peacefully on the sofa. He left her a note explaining where he was going, but not why. Why was more difficult.

It felt strange, and slightly silly, to be retracing the journey to the hotel so soon. Before he got on the flight he had a cowardly urge to call Warrick instead. He had no clear idea what he was going to say, though, or even what he wanted to say, other than it would have to be the truth or he might as well not bother going at all. Nothing else would work on Warrick. So he took the easier route of the flight. It put things off for another couple of hours.

He found Warrick in the conference center, eating a late breakfast. Alone. This was as far as the planning had gone, so he simply went over to the table and sat down without saying anything. It seemed impossible that he'd last seen Warrick only the day before yesterday.

"Would you like some coffee?" Warrick said, after a moment.

"Yeah. Thanks."

Warrick called the waitress over and ordered a fresh pot. After she left, Warrick said, "I'm sorry."

Toreth blinked, thrown off balance by the echo of his dream.

"I didn't think I'd get a chance to say it," he continued. "I'm sorry I did what I did and I'm sorry I said what I said. It was...tacky. Unnecessary. Unkind. Unbelievably stupid. And several other things." He paused. "I don't suppose you could forget it?"

"No. No, I don't think so." The resolution of honesty had a novelty to it that Toreth suspected would wear off quite quickly. But for now it seemed to be doing very well.

Warrick nodded slowly, then began one of his breakfast rituals, spreading butter over a slice of toast with such exactitude that it would probably require electronic measuring equipment to detect a variation in the thickness. "How's your hand?" he asked.

"What? Oh, fine." Toreth rubbed his bandaged palm. "Nothing serious—a couple of cuts."

Warrick nodded again. "Good. That's what I hoped. I saw the broken glass in the bathroom, and the blood. I asked at reception and they said you hadn't called a medic, so—" He shrugged. "That's what I assumed—that it wasn't serious."

Toreth felt unexpectedly pleased that he'd checked. "I'm fine," he repeated, with more emphasis than it really merited.

Warrick looked at the toast for a moment, as if noticing it for the first time, then put it down on the plate. Toreth realized his hand was shaking. "What's wrong?"

"What's...Christ." Almost a laugh. "Sometimes..." He suddenly seemed to be having trouble finishing sentences. Toreth waited as patiently as he could until

128

finally, Warrick said, "Guilt—for fucking someone else and enjoying it and then for telling you about it and enjoying that, too. And fear, in case you didn't come back or you'd be angry when you did, which is relief now that you have and you aren't. I think that just about covers it." He looked up. "Why aren't you angry, by the way?"

"Honestly?" Honestly, he didn't know—he wasn't even sure it was true. But resolution or not, he could hardly say that. Toreth shrugged. "It just seems too hypocritical, I suppose."

"If it means anything at all, I won't be doing it again." Warrick smiled wryly. "Not my field."

Toreth thought about his conversation with Sara. Tell the lie, or not? All that stopped him in that end was the simple fact that it would never work. "I won't promise anything in return," he said. "I could, but—" He shrugged. "You know me."

"Well," Warrick said carefully, "I'd rather have you on those terms than not at all."

Toreth suddenly realized that he was starving. He reached over and took the slice of toast. "That's settled, then."

Sara was awakened by the fine-tuned sense that, even through the worst hangovers, always got her up in time for work. Almost in time, anyway. Looking at the debris of the night before, she made a rough calculation of the amount they'd got through, and winced. She hoped Toreth felt better than she did.

That thought made her register the silence in the flat. Curiosity got her off the sofa and to his bedroom. The door was open and there was no one there. Had he gone to work without her? She looked at her watch. If he was in the same bloody awful mood he'd been in yesterday he might decide to make a fuss about her being late. She'd make it, but she was cutting it fine.

Anyway, he wouldn't mind if she borrowed some headache tablets before she set off. Or rather, he could mind as much as he liked, but she was doing it. The very thought of going outside into the sunshine like this was enough to start her eyes watering. Trying not to make any loud noises, she opened the bathroom cabinet and started hunting for something—anything—to get rid of the pounding in her head. Searching through the precariously balanced contents without precipitating a landslide would have been difficult enough without the hangover.

For God's sake, didn't the man have *anything* in there which didn't cleanse, moisturize, or exfoliate? She knocked a stack of jars off a shelf, made a wild grab, missed them, and swore vividly as the largest landed on her bare foot. Finally, it occurred to her that she was looking in the wrong place. She opened a drawer by the basin and there, thank God, were assorted bottles and strips of pills. Been at the pharmacy again, clearly.

In the kitchen she found a mostly clean glass, filled it with water, and took the tablets. Then she downed the rest of the water, even though she felt horribly queasy. She considered looking for something to eat to settle her stomach, but then remembered whose flat she was in. She refilled the glass and went back into the living room. There, at last, she noticed the paper rolled up and stuck into the neck of an empty bottle. She flopped down onto the sofa, moaning quietly as the water she'd drunk sloshed around her stomach, and read the short note over a few times.

Great. Now she felt worried, on top of everything else.

Was it a good thing that he'd gone back to the hotel? He'd seemed fairly pissed off last night. Much as he might've deserved what Warrick had done, it had hurt him in a way which, sober, she found hard to believe. Warrick had really got to him. She didn't actually think Toreth would...do anything. On the other hand, she'd never seen him like that before. It made for a compelling spectator sport, but it also had the potential to get messy.

She lay back on the sofa and put her arm over her eyes. If he *was* going to kill Warrick, the least he could have done was to kill her first on his way out.

When it came down to it, she didn't want to think he'd do anything, but he might. Especially if Warrick's mystery fuck turned up again. She imagined Toreth finding Warrick with someone else and her stomach knotted in a way that had nothing to do with her hangover. She'd seen him angry and, if she were being honest with herself, it had scared her. But she'd never seen him genuinely lose his temper. She didn't know anyone who had. Maybe there were no survivors.

Ha, ha. Very not funny.

Right, she told herself. Calm down. Don't flap—*think.*

All she could do was get hold of Warrick and warn him that Toreth was on his way. And, maybe, that he was in a less than sparkling mood. Then, at the very least, Warrick could get rid of any evidence he might need to, including any live bodies. While they still were.

Was there a time on the note? No. Toreth might be there already, but it all depended on the flights. She had the contact details Toreth had given her in her head, so it took only a few seconds to reach the conference center. Then she won a brief duel of comm manners in order to convince the receptionist that the call was sufficiently urgent and confidential that he ought to track Warrick down for her. Not bad going, the way she felt.

Time ticked past and Sara fingered the note nervously. On the positive side, the fact that the receptionist was looking at all meant that he hadn't heard about any corpses. Maybe they just hadn't been found yet.

Then the call went through, and she realized she still hadn't decided what to say. "Warrick? It's Sara."

"What can I do for you?" Still alive at any rate.

"I, um, just wanted to let you know—" that my boss might be on his way to break your legs, "—that I've seen Toreth. I thought you, er, might be a bit worried about him."

"I never worry about him." Standard issue unreadable Warrick.

"And he's on his way back to the hotel." So you'll want to throw out anyone you happen to be screwing *before* he gets there.

"He's—" There was a brief silence, then faintly, "For God's sake, stop that. It's Sara."

Familiar laughter sounded in the background. "Tell her she's late for work."

Suddenly she felt like an absolute idiot. But a terribly relieved absolute idiot.

Warrick's voice came back, polite but strained. "Sorry about that. Yes. He's, mmh...he's here already."

"Oh. Good."

"Was there anything...else?"

"No." She grinned. "Have fun." She cut the comm before he could reply. Then she sat back on the sofa, methodically tearing the note into small pieces. No need to rush in to work now. She could go home and shower and change first. Have something to eat.

And her hangover had gone completely.

Warrick handed him a drink and looked around the reception room. Toreth looked too, tracking his gaze, trying to see if it lingered anywhere. To his annoyance, he found himself fighting an urge to touch Warrick, to stand too close.

Toreth had spent the afternoon learning how to ski, or at least how to fall over slightly less frequently. Not that he was particularly bad at it, and the instructor had complimented him on his balance, although he expected that she complimented everyone on something. It was something he'd never done before, though, and the early stages of anything new frustrated him. He liked to excel. Besides, it was infuriating and embarrassing to watch kids who barely came up to his waist skimming carelessly past him as if they'd been doing it all their lives. Which, presumably, the spoiled little fuckers had. All afternoon, as he untangled his skis yet again, he'd wondered where Warrick was. That wasn't strictly true—he'd known where he was. What he wondered was who else was there with him. The faceless fuck, somewhere in the conference center. At the same talk as Warrick? In the same workshop? Sharing a coffee, maybe.

Somewhere here, right now, anonymous in the crowd at the formal evening reception, supposedly the highlight of the conference. A sea of dinner jackets and colorful dresses moved around him, but Toreth looked only at the men. He had what he acknowledged to be a quite irrational conviction that he ought to recognize someone whom Warrick would want to fuck.

Earlier, it had been okay. When he'd found Warrick at breakfast, it had been okay. Talking had been bad, but not unbearable, and he'd got what he'd wanted—an apology and a promise never to do it again. When they'd gone back to the room, it had been more than okay, even though they'd had time to do nothing more than mess around for fifteen minutes before Warrick had to be somewhere. When Sara called, it had been funny, although the reason she'd done it wasn't.

It was a guess, but he knew her well enough to be confident about it. She'd been worried in case he'd carried out his threat from last night. In case when he did get back, Warrick hadn't been alone. Toreth didn't want to think about that. To imagine opening the door to the room and seeing them...

He's here, and I didn't think it would be a good thing to end up doing it again.

He's here, now. That was what made the difference, why it wasn't okay any more. Despite the good food and the skiing and the break from work, Toreth felt happy that the conference lasted only one more day. Turning back from his scrutiny of the room, he found Warrick watching him. "What is it?" Toreth asked.

Warrick sipped his drink, then said, "Do you realize that, for the entire evening, you've looked as if you want to punch every man I've spoken to between the ages of twenty-five and fifty?"

Of course I fucking *realize.* Toreth shrugged. "Have I?"

"Yes. I'd be grateful if you could stop it."

Toreth stared at him. Some fucking cheek after he was the one who'd...well, the one who'd done it this time. Make too much of it and he'd end up looking like an idiot. "Look," he said, striving to sound reasonable. "Tell me who he is and then there won't be a problem." Or it'd be a different kind of problem, anyway, when they stretchered the bastard out of there.

"No." The same idea looked to have occurred to Warrick.

Toreth shrugged again.

After a moment, Warrick said, "I'd like to ask you to promise me something."

He tried to remember if Warrick had ever said that before, and drew a blank. "What?"

"That if I tell you who he is, you won't do anything." It wasn't necessary to say what Warrick didn't want him to do.

"All right. I promise." As if Warrick's preferences made any difference. He wouldn't do anything because it would be pathetic—immature and stupid. He told himself to keep thinking about that.

After a long pause, Warrick said, "The man at the right-hand end of the bar. Sitting on the bar stool, talking to the woman in blue and green."

Toreth looked for a long time, assessing him carefully. Warrick's height, or a little taller. He'd been right that the man would be older, his dark hair graying at

132

the temples. Not a bad figure, although suits could hide a lot. Toreth couldn't see his face clearly from here, only a suggestion of a reflection in the mirror behind the bar. Not competition, though, he told himself. Not really. Hell, Warrick had told him that. He'd also said he wanted to fuck the man again.

Was he good? Toreth wanted to ask. No, he knew the answer to that. How good? was what he wanted to know. Or, ultimately, was he better than me?

Then the man stood up and said something to his companion, who laughed and touched his arm in farewell. Turning, he looked straight across the room and saw them. The briefest pause, then he lifted his hand to Warrick, and began to make his way across the room. Fucking hell. Glancing around, he saw that Warrick had gone slightly pale. Yes, that was right—Warrick was the one who had things to worry about here.

Toreth smiled. "Relax. I promised, remember?"

Before Warrick could reply, the man reached them. Quite good-looking, Toreth had to admit. He had a short, neatly trimmed beard, peppered with silver, which suited him. Well-defined bones, looking to Toreth like an open invitation for a well-placed punch. He smiled warmly at Warrick, and Toreth's fist clenched before he could stop it, the cuts protesting painfully.

"Doctor Warrick. Nice to see you again. I noticed your name in the program, so I knew you were here." He looked inquiringly at Toreth. "But I don't think we've met...?"

Warrick collected himself with a visible effort. "Val Toreth. Toreth, this is Doctor Frederick Girardin."

Middle name Felix—his name had been on the list, back in the office at I&I. Toreth even remembered the corporation he'd worked for: L-Sander Technologies. Now he knew. He nodded, and murmured something he hoped sounded friendly.

"Do you work at SimTech?" Girardin inquired.

"No. I'm a para-investigator." No reaction to that, which was unusual. "I'm here for the skiing. Enjoying the corporate expenses." Then, trying to ignore the bruising to his self-esteem, he placed his hand in the small of Warrick's back. A brief contact with a clear message. Mine.

He had no idea how Warrick reacted, because he was watching Girardin. The man looked between them, and a flicker of understanding—and maybe disappointment—crossed his face. Then Girardin smiled again. "I don't ski myself. But one of my party has missed a few sessions and I understand from her that the snow is very good."

That was it. There were a few comments about the program so far and which events the next day looked most interesting. A promise by Girardin that he would certainly attend Warrick's seminar and an invitation to both of them to join him for lunch, although he seemed to expect Warrick's polite refusal. Just a slight tension lingered in the air, probably unnoticeable to someone who wasn't looking for it.

"What did you tell him about me?" Toreth asked, when Girardin had excused himself.

Warrick looked bemused. "Nothing."

"You must have said something. Or he'd have been surprised to see me."

"Very well. I mentioned your existence. Not your name, or anything about you. Generalities."

"What generalities?"

"I told him I had a nonexclusive relationship." Warrick looked at him steadily. "And unless you have some news for me, that is precisely what I do have."

Toreth stared at him, speechless.

"I told you I'm sorry, and I am. I told you I won't do it again, and I won't. I said neither of those things for form's sake, nor to make you feel better. I meant them." Warrick's voice was low but emphatic. "However, I will not apologize for the rest of my life for doing *once* something that you do with monotonous regularity."

The shock made him spill out the question. "Was he good?"

After a moment, Warrick said, "I have no intention of discussing this."

With the first words out, he had to go on. "Was he better than me?"

"And I am certainly not doing so here, surrounded by people whose professional opinions I value." Overarticulating, cold and angry, and Toreth didn't care.

"You said you wanted him again. Was he a better fuck than me?"

"Is there any point in my saying no?" Probably not. Girardin had touched Warrick. He'd fucked Warrick.

Someone else coming inside me.

"Did he kiss you?"

"Toreth, I will not—"

"Did he fucking kiss you? Tell me."

Warrick looked away for a moment, then back. "Yes, he did."

White-hot, blinding anger burned through him. When it cleared, he found, almost to his surprise, that he had taken a step away from Warrick. He wanted to shout. He wanted to go after Girardin and— "Come on," he said, keeping his voice under tight control.

"Where?"

Anywhere that wasn't here. Taking hold of Warrick's elbow, he dug his fingers in. "Come on."

Slightly to his surprise, Warrick nodded. Probably glad to get away from his precious fucking peers before Toreth made a scene. The knowledge that that was exactly what he was doing—making a scene, like some pathetic fucking jealous *boyfriend*—only made Toreth more furious. Opening the first door they reached, he found a small room, half filled with stacked dining chairs.

"This'll do," Toreth said. Once through the door, Toreth closed it behind them, not letting go of Warrick. "What else did you do with him?" Images flicked through

134

his mind, so clear. Warrick on his hands and knees in front of the fire, flushed and panting, with Girardin behind him, fucking him hard. Or his hands in Warrick's hair as . . .

Letting them fuck my mouth. Kneeling in front of them.

Toreth focused on Warrick's lips, seeing them molded around someone else's cock. No, not "someone." Girardin. Name and face. Easy to imagine the smooth voice, urging Warrick to take him deeper. "Did he come in your mouth? Tell me what you did."

"I will tell you nothing of the kind. Toreth, you cannot—"

Toreth pulled Warrick forwards and kissed his unresponsive lips, bearing down hard until Warrick jerked his head away and stepped back.

Hatred surged again, the same rage he'd felt in front of the fire—the impulse to lash out, to hurt. To punish Warrick for cheating, for betraying him, for everything he could make Toreth feel. This time, with Warrick there, he couldn't contain it. He tightened his grip on Warrick's arm, his other hand lifting, curling into a fist again without conscious direction, before he saw the flash of real fear in Warrick's eyes, quickly overtaken by anger.

He released Warrick immediately, letting his hand drop. All the times he'd hit Warrick, relishing the anticipation on his face before the blow landed, not once had Warrick been afraid of him, because it was always and only in the game. One thing Warrick wouldn't tolerate; one thing that would make him walk. Gone for good. The shock of a line so nearly crossed felt like hitting a snowbank, winding him and smothering the anger.

"Fuck, I'm sorry," Toreth said automatically, and for a moment he tasted blood.

"Are you really." The expressionless voice matched Warrick's face.

"Yes. I—" I didn't mean to hurt you. He kept the lie back by sheer force of will. "Are you okay?" He knew the answer, his hand remembering exactly how much pressure it had applied, but he also knew it was the necessary thing to ask.

Warrick rubbed his arm, then flexed it. "I think so. No harm done." His voice was still unyielding. "Do I have to spell out the consequences if you ever do that again?"

So fucking close to disaster. "No. And I won't. Warrick, please—I'm sorry."

Pause, then Warrick inclined his head, once. "Apology accepted."

Relief dizzied him briefly, and he found his hand on Warrick's shoulder, very nearly for support. Warrick tensed, then moved a step closer. This time, when Toreth repeated the kiss, it was something shared, not something imposed. Warrick responded, lips parting, hands drawing him closer. Despite, or maybe because of, the fear of what had almost happened, Toreth felt the usual aftermath of an argument start to heat him, and he saw an answering lick of fire in Warrick's eyes.

"Shall we go?" Warrick asked.

He thought about it. Going back to the bedroom where Warrick had told him about...and the cuts in his hand twinged. Not there—not yet. "Against the wall," Toreth told him.

The fire flared brighter. "We have a *room*, which—"

"Against the wall," he repeated and, unfair advantage, he took hold of Warrick and turned him, feeling his automatic, helpless response to the restraint. A game, this time, their game, but with a more dangerous edge. He pressed Warrick against the wall, using his whole body, whispering threats and promises. He caught Warrick's wrist, twisting his arm up behind his back—remembering in time to check that it wasn't the arm he'd hurt.

Warrick struggled, helpless in the professional grip. "Don't. Not here."

"You want to."

"No. Toreth, that hurts. Please."

"Tell me what you want." Tell me you want me, not him.

"I—I want to go back to the room before—ah, *Christ*."

"You're a liar. Tell me you want it." He raised his voice, wondering how sound-proof the door was, and whether anyone was standing close enough to hear. "*Tell* me." Tell me you're mine.

"No. I don't—"

"Fucking liar." He reached around, rubbing his palm against Warrick's erection. "God, look at you. Look how hard you are, and I've barely fucking touched you yet. Now tell me what you want. Say it."

A few more seconds of struggling, then Warrick went still, breathing heavily. "Yes," he whispered.

"Yes, what?"

"Yes. Here."

"Tell me what."

"I want you to fuck me."

"Again."

"I want...I want you to fuck me. Please."

Please, again. Begging for it—wanting *him*. "Yes."

Yes. He brought his hand up to Warrick's mouth, brushing the lips he must have bruised. "Lick them. Do it."

Warrick whimpered, breathless, and obeyed.

Yes. His, and no one fucking else's.

Unfastening Warrick's trousers, he slipped his hand down, squeezing his buttocks, reaching further. Fingering him, opening him, then more spit for himself before he replaced his hand with his cock. Warrick cried out as Toreth thrust into him and Toreth put his hand over his mouth, pressing him against the wall. He waited for a few seconds, dreading footsteps outside and a knock on the door. Wondering if Girardin had seen them go in here, and almost wishing he had—wishing the bastard could see this.

136

A muffled protest.

Automatically, he looked for Warrick's free hand, finding it clenched against the wall, thumb extended—carry on.

"Keep still and shut the fuck up."

He twisted Warrick's wrist, hearing him moan at the pain. A flash of his dream returned, of Warrick in front of him against the rough wall. This felt so much better than even the best dream. For once, he stopped thinking about the game, and what ought to happen next, and concentrated purely on himself, doing what he wanted— long, fast thrusts, Warrick deliciously tight around him.

Not that Warrick seemed to feel neglected. Over his own breathing, Toreth heard him, moaning in his throat. He had his arm braced against the wall above his head, pushing back onto Toreth, his body asking for more, harder, deeper— wanting it. Wanting him. Toreth closed his eyes, the pleasure spiking and then building, building, until he came, choking back a cry.

He clung to Warrick, breathing deeply, face buried in his jacket. A shame he couldn't stay here forever, and he almost wished they had gone back to the room because he felt like collapsing onto a bed and passing out for a while.

It wasn't finished yet, though. Keeping his hand over Warrick's mouth, he released his wrist and turned him, pressing him back against the wall. "Open your eyes."

Warrick's breath felt hot on his hand as he shook his head.

"Open your fucking eyes. *Look* at me."

Another shake of his head—asking for it, and Toreth hesitated only a second. Taking his hand away from Warrick's mouth, he hit him across the face. Just hard enough to be what he wanted, not hard enough to mark. He saw Warrick's hands clench, saw the eager response in his body and cock. Another blow across the other cheek and, finally, Warrick's eyes opened.

And that was all right. He'd done it, and it was all right. Nothing had changed. Toreth leaned forwards, touching his lips to his ear. "Do you want me to touch you? Let you come?" He ran his hand down Warrick's chest, moving it across at the last moment to sweep down his hip and thigh.

"Mmh...yes."

"Say it." He brought his hand back up to cup Warrick's balls, squeezing gently.

Warrick moaned harshly through gritted teeth. "Please. Please...let me come."

"Then keep your eyes open."

After a moment's consideration, he put his hand back over Warrick's mouth. No one had disturbed them yet, but that didn't mean no one would notice an undamped Warrick. The precaution was justified almost as soon as Toreth took hold of him, stroking too gently—teasing. Muffled whimpers and pleas from Warrick, and he started twisting again, trying to thrust forwards into Toreth's hand. Toreth shook his head, and tightened the hand over Warrick's mouth. "Don't move. You come when I let you. When I tell you to. Do you understand that?"

Warrick nodded at once, stilled himself against the wall except for shivers running through him as Toreth's thumb circled slowly. "When I allow it." Another nod. Satisfied, Toreth settled in, keeping a slow rhythm. Watching Warrick's eyes, fascinated by the dark, glazed surrender. Wondering if Warrick could still see him and, if not, what he saw instead. It didn't really matter, as long as Warrick was here and this was better than whatever he'd done with Girardin.

His. Wanting him and needing *him.*

Warrick was growing loud now, making a noise Toreth always loved—harsh, sobbing breaths, begging without words. So very ready for it. "Now," Toreth whispered. Speeding up, giving Warrick, finally, what he needed. A moan that was almost a scream, and again, much louder, as Warrick's wide-open eyes went wider and his fingers dug hard into Toreth's arms as he shuddered and came.

After the reception—after too long spent trailing around listening to technical conversations he didn't understand—after having to swallow laughter as Warrick sat down a little too hard—after all that, when everything was over, they went back to the room.

Toreth lit the fire while Warrick disappeared into the bathroom. Then he switched off the light, kicked off his shoes and socks, loosened his bow tie, and sat in front of hearth, watching the flames licking at the dry wood. By the time Warrick re-emerged, in a dressing gown once more, it blazed brightly.

Warrick stopped, surveying the scene. Silence, then he spoke as if he hadn't paused. "Would you like a drink?"

"Please." Toreth had made an effort to stay sober at the reception because, fuck or not, he didn't fancy meeting Girardin except when in full control.

Warrick poured drinks and handed one to him without comment. He stayed standing, behind Toreth, staring into the fire.

Toreth patted the rug and said, "Join me?"

Warrick looked down at him, eyes dark and unreadable, then nodded and sat. Toreth moved around so that his bare feet were next to Warrick's, sunk deep into the thick fur. They sat in silence, watching the fire eat its way through the wood. After a while Warrick said, "That was very good, wasn't it?"

"Yes." Real fear and real danger were so much sharper than the play versions. But Warrick's question hadn't been just a compliment.

"Yes. But—" Warrick looked at him. "—it's never going to be good in quite that way again, is it?"

That wasn't regret. "Never."

Warrick nodded, and returned his attention to the fire.

It was, Toreth thought, unnecessary and somewhat annoying, because he'd already said that. He'd already promised never again, outside the game. Maybe, in view of how good it *had* been, it wasn't entirely surprising that Warrick wanted to emphasize the point when they were both...calmer. Still, he wouldn't need to promise anything at all if Warrick hadn't fucked—

Toreth took a deep breath. Forget it. He lay down on the rug and after a moment Warrick followed suit, lying in front of him, also facing the fire. He blocked most of the heat from it, but Toreth didn't mind. He was quite warm enough in the dinner jacket.

Sipping his drink, Toreth watched the embers beginning to fall through the grate. With the reds and pinks rippling over their surface, they made a pretty novelty, but he found he couldn't concentrate on them. The earlier part of the evening had returned, nagging at him. He resisted for as long as he could, then reached over Warrick to deposit his glass on the hearth. He rested his hand on Warrick's waist, feeling the heat of the fire on the back of his hand and in the warm cloth. "Girardin," Toreth said.

He felt Warrick tense. "What about him?"

"You said you kissed him."

He nodded, guardedly.

Toreth slid his fingers through the belt of the dressing gown and pulled, turning Warrick over onto his back. Then, moving very slowly, he leaned down and kissed him. Warm, sweet mouth, tasting of toothpaste and alcohol and Warrick, and as beautifully responsive as the rest of the body pressed against him. Toreth did a careful, thorough job, and when he pulled back he said, "Was it like that?"

"No." Warrick smiled, then smoothed the expression away as if he wasn't sure it would be welcome. "No, it was nothing at all like that."

"Was he—"

Warrick put his hand up, touching the lapel of his jacket. "Toreth, leave it. Please."

"No. Tell me—was he a better fuck than me?"

Warrick sighed. "No, he was not." He looked up at Toreth, his eyes clear and only a hint of exasperation in his voice. "If there is anyone out there who is a better fuck than you, then I can only pray that I never meet them, because I sincerely doubt that my nervous system would stand the strain."

Do you mean it? Do you really mean it? Tell me again. He suppressed the words, the hunger for reassurance, and said, "Good."

After a short silence, Warrick said, "Finished?"

When he nodded, Warrick turned his head away a little, towards the fire, eyes closing again. "Tired?" Toreth asked.

"Somewhat. It's been a long day."

"Want to go to bed?"

"Not especially, no—but as you prefer." After a moment, Warrick added. "I wondered whether, since the conference finishes tomorrow, you might like to stay on for a couple of days after that. Over the weekend."

No distractions taking up Warrick's time. No Girardin. "Yeah, that'd be good."

"I'll speak to the hotel in the morning."

Since Warrick didn't seem to be in any hurry, Toreth stayed where he was, watching the fire burning slowly down. After a while, he leaned over Warrick again to throw on a few more pieces of wood. Warrick didn't react, either to the crackle of new flames or the brightening of the firelight.

Toreth shifted on the rug, suddenly noticing the aches in his legs. A satisfying, postexercise feeling, from skiing and the fuck. The nice thing about this place was that he'd be able to eat as much as he wanted of the very classy food, without worrying or resorting to anything pharmaceutical to balance the calories. More skiing tomorrow. More fucking in the evening, if he was in luck. And so on, for the next three days. An attractive idea, bringing a subdued, lazy arousal with it.

"Do you want to fuck?" Toreth asked, more to find out if Warrick was still awake than as a serious offer.

"Mm?"

"I said, would you like to fuck?"

"Mm, yes." Warrick smiled, without opening his eyes. "In theory, at least. But I'm afraid that, practically speaking, I have to say 'not a chance.'"

Toreth nodded, then added, "Okay."

It wasn't a bad summary of his own feelings, but it unfortunately curtailed the evening. The closeness was pleasant, but it had begun to stir unease. It wasn't that he needed an excuse to hold Warrick, as such, it was just that he always had one. Fuck-in-progress, postcoital coma, moving together while they slept—they were acceptable. Other situations were not. Why, he had no idea; he never questioned it, he simply knew it was true.

On the other hand, they weren't precisely lying together with no purpose. They were watching the fire. He looked down at Warrick, whose long lashes and straight nose cast shadows in the firelight, and amended it to enjoying the fire. Making the most of the luxury on corporate expenses. Now that they'd lit it, it would be a shame to waste it. He stretched out, resting his head on his arm, and closed his eyes.

Wood smoke. Warm spirits from the glasses on the hearth. Smell of Warrick's hair, newly washed. The embers crackling musically as they slowly consumed themselves. Soft fabric under his hand, shifting in time to Warrick's breathing.

Tomorrow. Skiing and fucking. The bed had sturdy enough posts, so he could come back early and set things up for the game. Have everything ready and perfect for when the seminars finished. Warrick would appreciate that. There were soft

140

straps in Toreth's luggage—he had packed the ones that could be left tied for hours without leaving marks, because Warrick wouldn't want visible bruises at a conference. Not that it mattered now.

Anticipation stirred, mixing agreeably with the warmth and relaxation; he loved planning. It was attention to detail that made it work. He would order room service for dinner, and feed it to Warrick piece by piece while he was blindfolded. Finger food—lots of different flavors and textures. Some good wine, or maybe even champagne. That would do very nicely to start the evening. And then...

He pictured Warrick's body, naked in the firelight, dark hair and pale skin lit red.

Bound and on his knees. Blindfolded. Breathing quick and shallow, waiting for instructions.

Ready to be taken—completely his.

Toreth smiled, imagining voices.

"Say it."

"I'm yours."

All Work and No Play

❖

Part One: Cattle Market

Of all the evenings Sara could choose to be late, Toreth thought as he waited in her hall, it would be this one. The irony of his complaining about someone else being late didn't escape him, but the idea of what might be happening in his absence still made him grit his teeth.

"I'm really, really sorry," Sara called as she flew across the hall from bathroom to bedroom in a blur of gold-tone skin and blue towel.

He'd have preferred it if she'd sounded at all repentant. He crossed the hall to stand closer to her bedroom door, from where he could see her reflection in the window. "So you should be. You know we need to be there in plenty of time."

"Bastard got hurt and I had to take him to the vet. Poor little baby. I couldn't leave him there all on his own until I knew he was going to be okay."

The absence of a skulking, psychotic shadow hadn't yet registered with Toreth. Not surprising, because the place still smelled the same.

"I had loads of trouble getting a taxi," Sara continued, her voice briefly muffled, "and then I had to stay there while she looked at him and decided what to do. She wanted to put him under first so she wouldn't hurt him when she examined him."

Thereby suggesting Sara's hapless vet wasn't a complete idiot. Actually, anesthetizing the cat before approaching would be a good idea when it was perfectly healthy. "What happened to it?" he asked.

"He lost a fight."

"Jesus, what with? A freight transporter?"

She was facing away from the window, giving him a nice rear view, but he heard the exasperated sigh and imagined the rolled eyes that would go with it. "A fox, the vet thought. Or maybe even a small dog."

Or possibly an escaped lion. "Much damage?" he asked hopefully.

142

"Not as much as I thought when he crawled home. His tail's broken in a couple of places and he's got bites all over his back, but he's going to be fine. The vet thinks his tail might end up with another kink in it." Sara turned for the door and he took a tactical step back. She came out of the room, brushing her still-damp hair while shrugging into a dress. "Another 'nother kink, I mean. Can you get my zip?"

He zipped her up and asked, "Ready?"

"One minute. Not even thirty seconds." She dived back into the bathroom, and glass and plastic began to rattle. He was about to start a protest when she reappeared clutching a black bag. "I'll do my makeup in the car."

All very well, he thought as they left the flat, but that wouldn't get him back the time he'd already lost.

The place was packed when they arrived and Toreth handed his jacket to Sara as soon as they got inside. It was her fault they were so bloody late, so she could brave the chaos at the temporary cloakroom. Toreth always liked to arrive early, to scope out both the prey and the competition. Most of the other seniors did the same, so every year the group estimate of "early" crept back slightly. Now an event that nominally started at eight o'clock was always busy by seven.

The end of year training parties at I&I took place in the largest canteen there, spilling over into surrounding rooms. Organized by the Human Capital and Training Department, they were slightly more civilized than the drunken bash Toreth remembered from his own interrogator training at Justice, although the food and drink were just as bad. Attending were this year's final classes of interrogators, investigators, and para-investigators, plus the training staff and any of the senior staff looking to fill vacancies in their teams. Official applications and appointments to posts would take place over the next few weeks, but tonight was the important night—the September graduate cattle market.

The evenings always reminded Toreth pleasantly of picking teams for sports at school. Then he'd been one of the popular ones, always chosen early. Rarely, though, as he was now at I&I, had he been one of the choosers. He'd been too much of a troublemaker at school to be placed in charge of anything.

He enjoyed the air of competition, of winning his own choices—which he usually did, if there was anyone he wanted—and watching others lose theirs. This year Toreth had only one vacant spot on his team, which was how he liked it. A settled, reliable team made his life infinitely easier than running a changing stable. Doyle and Lambrick's departures earlier in the year had been aberrations. Lately, generous raises and accommodation provisions had helped his team's permanence. Since the SimTech case, he'd had a brittler relationship with Tillotson, but the section head had definitely been warier about refusing Toreth's budget requests.

Toreth had never felt like pushing the advantage, but Warrick's intervention and blackmail threat had obviously left a deep impression.

Toreth spotted the other General Criminal seniors in a loose group at the far end of the room near the bar, and began to work his way over to them. Most would be accompanied by their personal admins, although few of those were in the group. They'd be in the crowd, picking out the graduates their bosses wanted to talk to. From that he concluded that he wasn't as late as he'd feared. Senior para-investigators weren't the only ones looking for fresh blood. As Toreth crossed the room, he noticed Elizabeth Carey. Phil Verstraeten was still a professional and personal fixture in her team, and it wasn't long before Toreth spotted the anemic sidekick, talking to a man Toreth guessed to be a newly qualified investigator.

For the fresh investigators and interrogators, the evening wasn't so vital. It was expected that they would start their careers in the pool of staff available to be assigned to cases as required. Being chosen by a senior specialist or para for their personal team was prestigious, but not essential. Not so for the new junior para-investigators. The best could afford to be choosy. For those lower down the pecking order, the market meant an agonizing evening of watching their numbers whittled slowly down to the rejects. Marked by their failure to find a senior who wanted them, they became pool juniors, a position from which promotion to senior was unlikely. Their growing air of desperation always left Toreth hungry for a fuck by the end of the evening.

To Toreth's delight, when he reached the bar, Chevril was just ordering himself a drink. No doubt he'd waited until everyone else had got one before joining the group. Chevril owed so many drinks to so many people that his reluctance to stand a round had gone beyond a section joke and attained the status of legend. "I'll have a whiskey and soda, thanks, Chev," Toreth said.

"Got your ticket?" Chevril asked.

"Sara's got it."

Chevril took his glass from the admin tending the bar, pulling it protectively towards him. "This is my included-in-the-entry drink."

"Doesn't stop you buying one for me, does it?"

Chevril struggled with the logic for as long as possible, then finally gave up and turned to the admin. "Whatever it was he wanted," he said sourly.

"And a white wine for Sara," Toreth added to Chevril's evident disgust.

Two drinks out of Chevril in one go was something of a record. Cheered by the minor victory, Toreth joined the other seniors. In the short time he'd been at the bar, most had dispersed, which confirmed his guess that he wasn't too much of a latecomer. Looking around, he picked them out in the crowd, now surrounded by varyingly sized groups of newly qualified personnel.

Chevril would have a list of places to fill. Every year at least one of his team would've managed to piss him off irreversibly, and another two or three might decide to move on. Toreth caught a glimpse of Kel, shepherding a group towards them. Chevril muttered excuses and went to meet his admin, no doubt wanting to keep his choices away from the competition. Toreth didn't care. None of the men or women with Kel were on his own list.

That left him alone with Mike Belkin, one of the older General Criminal seniors, who usually had an even longer list than Chev. Notoriously difficult to work for, his high-profile cases and success rates still attracted willing newcomers. He didn't bring his admin to the cattle markets, nor any of the rest of his team—to avoid having their haggard faces scare away potential recruits, according to Sara. This year Belkin looked relaxed, surveying the room with a casual, detached interest.

"Not shopping?" Toreth asked him.

Belkin drained half his glass, then shook his head. "Maylor's retiring," he said, then sat back, watching Toreth with a faint smile. Waiting for a reaction.

Which Toreth couldn't help giving him. "Richie Maylor? Political Crimes?"

"Mm-hm. He's still having problems with his back after the bombing and they've decided to ditch him on a medical early retirement instead of putting up with all that fucking around on and off sick leave. He's not happy about it."

Sara had picked up a vague rumor to that end, but nothing concrete. "And you've got first pick of his team? You lucky bastard."

Belkin grinned smugly. "Favors owed; you know how it is. I only marked half of them, so there's some left if you don't get lucky tonight."

"I think I've got some good candidates lined up." And Toreth would rather choke than swallow Belkin's rejected leftovers, good as they probably were if they'd belonged to Maylor. "And I've got better things to do with my time than break juniors out of other people's bad habits."

"So that's what you're looking for?" Belkin asked.

"Yeah, one junior."

"That all?"

"I'm happy with what I've got."

"Right. And of course they would all be happy with you."

Generally Toreth didn't mind his reputation as an easy senior to work for, but Belkin managed to make it sound like an unpleasant and probably communicable disease. "I take the right ones to start with, and I got decent raises for them in the last couple of assessments so they've got no reason to go anywhere." Except Doyle and Lambrick, the ungrateful bastards.

"Hey, if I went as far as you do with Tillotson to get good cases assigned, I'd expect a nice budget, too. And flowers."

Jesus, some rumors never died. "Chev started that story, did you know that? He was fucked off 'cause he tried to chat me up and I turned him down."

Belkin's eyes crinkled in a near-smile. "You do talk shite."

"Yeah?" Toreth held up his glass. "Why would he buy me drinks if he didn't want my arse?" Belkin snorted with laughter, but before he could reply Toreth spotted Sara in the crowd, with a group of four juniors. Toreth picked up his glass and Sara's. "Got to go. Duty calls."

He watched Sara's hand as she introduced the group to him. He knew the names already, of course, but the hand signals gave her most up-to-date count of how many other seniors were serious about the new juniors.

"Jasric Ouellette." Three fingers—three seniors interested in him, as far as Sara had been able to determine.

"Andrew Rust." Four.

"Niall Custer." Another three.

"And Joielin Nagra." Five, and then a twitch of her fingers that meant "more than."

Must be good, although he'd have to ask who was interested because her pure Afro-Caribbean good looks might have something to do with it: beautiful bone structure, smooth skin like polished chocolate, full lips glossed dark red, and close-cut hair. Lovely visuals for fucking in any position, and there were certainly five-plus seniors in I&I who'd pick her out just for that.

"She was with Hepburn when I found her," Sara said in an undertone as they made their way to the bar. "But I pried her away while he was busy with someone else."

Drinks arranged, Toreth cleared a table of a group of new investigators, who seemed to be testing the limits of human ethanol tolerance. He arranged his haul to his satisfaction, two talking to him, two being tested out by Sara. While he listened to Ouellette describe his experience in his Computer Crimes investigation placement, Toreth kept half an ear on Sara's conversation with Rust and Custer.

"Are you a junior?" Rust asked her.

Sara laughed. "God, no. I'm the Para's admin."

"Oh." A pause, as Rust clearly tried to think of something suitable to say to such an inferior creature.

"If you look, there are plenty of admins here," Custer commented, quiet and neutral.

"Well, yes. Someone has to carry the screens and get the drinks." Rust laughed, stopping when the other two failed to join in.

Toreth smiled to himself, then noticed that Ouellette's account had come to an end. Nothing in it had caught his attention, so he turned to Nagra. "You took the intermediate pediatric interrogation option." A specialty his team currently lacked. "What did you think of it?"

"I enjoyed the challenge of working with a restricted set of tools. I took the impaired reasoning and medically vulnerable courses for the same reason."

"Light touch?" Ouellette said, with a subtly insulting inflection that reminded Toreth of Belkin.

"I took all the basic courses." Her tone had a touch of both anger and defensiveness; Toreth suspected she'd heard this accusation before. "There are only so many specialist options."

"I don't remember seeing you in any of the high-waiver ones, though," Ouellette said.

Her eyes narrowed. "Anyone can get a confession with a neural induction probe."

"But can anyone get the right confession?" Toreth asked. The confrontation broke off as they both belatedly remembered his presence, and the rivalry shifted into more subtle areas. Competitive anecdotes, accounts of extra work experience assignments taken, jockeying to mention who had bested whom in various exams—Toreth listened more than he talked, letting the two of them fight it out. In the end, he'd take the best of these two, and the best of Sara's pair, and set them against each other again.

"What do you think of Rust?" he asked Sara after the first half hour, when they returned to the bar.

"Reminds me of Tillotson," she said without hesitating. "And he's an arrogant wanker. If you're seriously thinking about him, I'm resigning right now."

"He had good scores, but you know how much that means. Okay. Tell him and Ouellette to fuck off while I get drinks for the other two." She'd enjoy the chance to do that.

Who to take? Custer had the better training grades, but Toreth had had his fingers burned before by Belqola and his ninety-fifth-percentile scores. One evening's conversation wasn't much of a basis for selection either, but both juniors seemed willing to sit out the interview, rather than chase off after another offer—a good sign from both of them, given that they should have no problem finding some kind of place. Especially promising since General Criminal was far from the highest-status section in the division.

After an hour or so he found himself leaning towards choosing Custer. Rather quiet, but disciplined, which made for a good junior if rarely a spectacular one. Nagra had a sharper edge, which might mean she'd be effective and independent, or might mean she'd spend her time undercutting him in an attempt to curry favor higher up the I&I food chain. His mind almost made up, he found himself looking at Nagra again from a distinctly nonprofessional perspective. With no need to apply his rule of not fucking inside the team, he decided see how far Nagra would go to impress a potential boss. She was tempting enough, even without the added spice of coercion.

Dispatching Custer for more drinks, he shifted a little closer to her. Sara looked studiously away. "What do you think of the evening?" he asked. "As a way of recruiting juniors?"

"I suppose it's better than picking names out of a hat. But it's rather loud, Para."

Nice of her to leave him an opening. "You're right—it's no way to really get to know people. We could go somewhere quieter, if you'd prefer. A bar. Or somewhere closer. Do the trainee juniors still rate single rooms in their last year?"

Nagra smiled easily. "Is that a pickup?"

The directness caught him by surprise. "Would you like it to be?"

"Well..." The smile again, and still no sign of nervousness. "No. I'm not usually a lesbian, Para, but for you I'll make an exception."

Which got her the job there and then.

Toreth was mildly flattered that when he told her, she didn't hesitate to accept. "I'd be honored," she said. "You've been top of my list since I did the General Criminal placement. And even before—how could I do better than working for the man who cracked the Selman kidnapping?"

He wondered whether she'd ever get to hear the real story. "I'll make it official tomorrow." He waved into the crowd. "Go enjoy yourself—you don't have to hang around with me."

He'd expected at least a polite half hour out of her, but instead she stood. "Thanks, Para. I look forward to starting work."

He watched her go, then turned to Sara, who'd been snickering quietly into her drink.

"Did you warn her?"

"About what?" Sara asked, so innocently that she might as well have said yes.

Nevertheless, he clarified the question. "Did you warn Nagra what it meant if I tried to pick her up?"

"Maybe." Sara examined his face searchingly, then grinned, obviously reassured by his smile. "Yeah, I did."

"Good. I couldn't tell—she's very smooth. I think she'll work out well."

"Me too. And she's friendly. For a para, I mean."

Toreth nodded, not taking offense. Custer reappeared, holding the drinks. Nagra's absence clearly registered at once, and his expression was a perfect blend of optimism and expectation of disappointment. "You can leave the drink," Toreth said. "Thanks for giving me the chance to talk to you."

"No, thank you for *your* time, sir," the junior said with immaculate politeness, before he headed away.

Settling back with the fresh drink, Toreth surveyed the crowd. Successes and failures were beginning to settle out, with some faces circulating between groups, moving down the hierarchy of rejection. Some had given up, and clusters of new juniors collected on the fringes, trying unsuccessfully to convince themselves that the pool wasn't such a bad place to start.

The evening's pervasive undercurrent of desperation and the fear of failure had given him a buzz of arousal, sharpening now that the serious business of the night was over. Maybe he should have tried Custer, since he'd changed his mind

148

about Nagra. Too late to go try now, because the man was already talking to another senior, looking as cool and collected as he had done with Toreth. He'd certainly bear watching in future, Toreth thought. Still, it wasn't so late that Warrick would be tiresome about being woken up—in fact, he'd probably be awake.

"I thought you were busy for the weekend?" Warrick said as he closed the door.

"I was. I am. I was practically passing the door, though, so I thought I'd drop in." A lie, but an easy one.

"I made some coffee not long ago, if you'd like a cup," Warrick said. "I was planning to work late and—"

"Afterwards." Toreth caught him by the arm and steered him into the bedroom, already unfastening his own shirt. "Afterwards, coffee would be great. Now, I want you in here. Strip."

"What the hell brought this on?" Warrick didn't resist, though.

"I'll tell you later." Toreth kicked his way free of his trousers, underwear, and socks in one go. "You're still dressed." He took Warrick's shirt off, to give him a kick in the right direction. Then he banged the bedside drawer open and shut without finding what he was looking for.

"In the bathroom," Warrick said as he finished undressing. "We emptied the last tube and I didn't—"

Toreth was already leaving. "Don't go anywhere except in bed."

The urgency had damped down now that he was here and naked. With the prospect of a fuck soon—very soon—his body seemed content to treat this small delay as a pleasant sharpening of anticipation rather than an infuriating stumbling block. He rifled through the bathroom cabinet, whistling happily and making a mess that would annoy the hell out of Warrick when he found it in the morning. There—got it.

Back in the bedroom, he found Warrick sitting on the bed, with a somewhat wary half smile. In an excess of happy enthusiasm, Toreth bounced onto the bed beside him, making it creak alarmingly.

Warrick laughed. "For God's sake, be careful!"

Toreth contemplated the tube of lubricant, then threw it to him. "Fuck me."

"Don't I get any say in the format of the proceedings?" Warrick asked, although his eyes and his smile and his stirring cock rather took the edge off the question.

"No." Toreth lay down, spine tingling. "Just do what you're told, for once in your life."

"Don't I always?" Warrick asked with an unconvincing sigh, then immediately spoiled the effect by adding, "Turn over."

Toreth had to admit the prospect of easy access to Warrick's mouth appealed, so he obeyed with the absolute minimum of grumbling. Only enough, in fact, to persuade Warrick to shut him up with a kiss which proved what a good idea it had been.

A sigh turned into a hiss of pleasure as slick fingers pressed into him. Arousal peaked again, and it was all he could do to stop himself from pulling Warrick down on top of him, just to get the hard contact against his cock.

Despite the urgency, he could wait for a while. Only fair to give Warrick a chance to catch up since—mmm, yeah, just like that—since he was starting from cold. Completely unselfish reason, nothing to do with the fact that Warrick was melting his spine from the inside with every flex of his fingers.

Then, somehow, it was all wrong. The changes were so subtle he would never have been able to put them into words, but when Toreth opened his eyes, Warrick was staring across the room over his head, frowning slightly. Still fingerfucking Toreth, but only his body was on the job. His mind was...

"What the hell are you thinking about?" Toreth snapped, meaning: *who* the hell are you thinking about?

"What?" Warrick damn near jumped, then smiled sheepishly. "Still got work on my mind, I'm afraid." His thumb stroked apologetically over the skin behind Toreth's balls. "It's not easy to switch focus midstride."

Great. Second place to the bloody sim. If it *was* the sim, and not Girardin or some other... Toreth pulled away. He propped himself up on his elbows and looked down at his wilting cock. "Thanks a fucking bunch."

"I'm sorry." Warrick knelt up, then sat back on his heels. "What can I do to remedy the situation?"

"Forget it. I might as well go home and leave you to it."

"Mm." Warrick climbed off the bed and started collecting his scattered clothes. For a moment, Toreth thought Warrick was simply going to take him at his word and leave him there in bed. Then Warrick added, "Come on."

"Where?"

"Just get dressed and come on."

Toreth lay in bed and watched Warrick dress. Warrick didn't say anything else. Apparently "come on" was supposed to be enough after ruining a previously great evening. Talk about taking someone for granted. Which, okay, was technically no more than Toreth had done when he'd dragged Warrick into the bedroom in the first place, but if Warrick hadn't wanted to fuck he should have said something. Bastard.

When Warrick had gone, Toreth smacked the bed with both palms, swore aloud, then threw himself out of bed and started hunting for clothes.

150

He tracked Warrick down in the kitchen, leaning against the worktop and finishing a sandwich.

"Hope you washed your hands," Toreth said.

Warrick snorted. "Of course. Do you want one?" He offered a plate, which held another sandwich.

It took Toreth a moment to identify the smell—banana. "God, no. Those things are disgusting." Putting fruit in sandwiches wasn't natural to start with, and the fact that Warrick then put *pepper* on them only added another level of unsavory weirdness.

"I made them before you showed up, so it seemed a shame to waste them," Warrick said through the last mouthful of bread. He put the uneaten sandwich down and brushed his hands together. "I want to show you something."

"What? And where?"

"Not far. It won't take long, if you have plans to be somewhere else."

Toreth had meant to leave and head on to a bar and find someone willing to fuck with more than ten percent of their attention. That wasn't really a plan as such, though, and a few minutes wouldn't make any difference. "What about that coffee?"

Warrick held up a thermos flask. "Reheated, but I put something in to hide that."

"Okay. Lead the way."

They took the lift up to the top floor, and strolled in silence along a deserted corridor until they reached a door. It opened to Warrick's iris scan, revealing a narrow flight of stairs. The sign at the foot of them said, *Roof Garden.*

"I didn't know this place had one," Toreth said as they started to climb.

"Of a kind. It was in the plans—rather elaborate in fact—but it caused too many problems. The weight of wet soil, problems with leaking water and so on. So they closed the thing down. And then...well, you'll see."

Another secure access door at the top of the stairs allowed them out onto the roof space. "There are some lights," Warrick said, "but it's better without."

Once Toreth's eyes adjusted, the moon provided enough light to navigate across the open space—a waxing harvest moon, yellow and heavy in the sky. The footing proved to be smooth and firm. They picked their way between chairs and tables set out in groups around the entrance. Pots and low troughs held plants, and Toreth could smell flowers. Across the other side of the roof stood a collection of objects he couldn't make out. Most of them were still, showing different shades and textures in the cool moonlight. A few moved in the wind, which was stronger up here than it had felt at street level. "What's over there?" Toreth asked.

"The sculpture garden. Residents donate a new one from time to time, and they're rearranged as people see fit. I bought something from Cele for it; I'll have

151

to show it to you when it's light. In fact, we should come up to enjoy the sun one afternoon. I don't know why I've never thought of if before. Come over to the side."

Heights didn't bother Toreth and never had, so he followed Warrick without hesitation. A wall ran around the roof at waist height and they walked slowly along beside it. The moonlight couldn't compete with the brilliant artificial lights, which spread out below them from a higher vantage than he'd expected. The cool September breeze cut through Toreth's shirt, and he wished he'd picked up his jacket. "Fuck, you can see for miles."

"Yes. This area is on a slight hill. You don't notice it on the ground, but it's obvious if you look at a topographical map. That's the university, over there. The grounds aren't well lit, but you can just see the edge of the AERC atrium. I think it's all rather beautiful."

"Yeah. It's not a bad place, is it, New London? From a distance. The lights go on for fucking miles. Far as you can see." Toreth stopped, looking out over the city, judging distances before he pointed to a brighter glow away and to the left. "That must be I&I. Or the closest part of Int-Sec, anyway. Those white buildings. I was over there earlier tonight—the lights don't seem that strong on the ground."

Warrick joined him, slipping between Toreth and the wall. He set the thermos on the wide, flat top of the wall, and poured coffee into the single cup. He passed it back and Toreth drank, the coffee deliciously hot, and with a hefty dose of brandy to make up for the reheated flavor.

"You were at I&I? This late?" Warrick asked.

"Yeah."

"New case? You didn't mention anything important in progress."

"No." Toreth wrapped his hands around the cup. "I was at the cattle market— recruiting bash for this year's trainees."

"I see." Warrick's tone didn't change. "And does that always make you chronically horny?"

Toreth choked on a mouthful of coffee, then said, "Actually, yeah. The juniors are all so fucking desperate. I&I recruits them competitive to start with and there are always too many of them and not enough seniors looking. Half of them would do *anything* to get a place. They all want it so much, even the good ones who're bound to find someone." Just talking about it was turning him on again. Maybe the fresh air would clear SimTech from Warrick's mind. "You can taste it. If you're a senior with an empty slot, it's a fantastic place to get laid."

Warrick leaned on the wall, peering downwards, which gave Toreth some interesting ideas that would have to wait for a warmer night.

"I'm deeply grateful I never had to go through anything of that kind," Warrick said in a cool, distant voice. A reaction to the mention of I&I, was Toreth's first guess, until he reviewed what he'd said.

Fantastic place to get laid.

Since the skiing trip—since Girardin—Toreth had made an effort to keep his casual fucks beneath Warrick's radar. Previously he'd enjoyed winding Warrick up with them, but the fantastic make-up sex wasn't fantastic enough to risk another evening like the one at the conference. Discretion made for an easier life all around. But, for God's sake, it wasn't as if he *had* fucked anyone at I&I tonight. Maybe he hadn't said so, but the state he'd arrived in should've been a clue. He might have a highish sex drive, but he wasn't superhuman. He was wondering whether to say something when Warrick surprised him with a question.

"I assume you found a senior without any difficulty when you qualified?"

"No. Or rather, it wasn't like that in my year. They were still setting the division up, so it hadn't been running long enough to develop traditions like the market. Pity, really. It's a fun evening if you get picked early by a good senior. Plus, I was already an interrogator when I did the conversion course. That's not the same as being a fresh trainee."

Warrick didn't comment again. No doubt the mention of interrogation had been too much. Toreth looked out over the city towards I&I. The hard-core drinkers and those drowning their sorrows would still be there. He lifted the cup to his lips again, letting the steam warm his face, and the lights of Int-Sec starred and swam as the brandy vapor stung his eyes. "They really light the place up, don't they?" he said.

"Yes. And it's on a hill." Warrick straightened. "Quite deliberate, I'm sure."

"Huh?"

Warrick took the cup, refilled it, and drank. "A deliberate part of its placement when they built it, no doubt. As a constant reminder of the presence of our guardians. Or oppressors, as some people would say."

"That's sedition."

Warrick leaned back against him, the scent of coffee and brandy drifting back with him. "No one's listening."

Toreth rested his hands on Warrick's shoulders, feeling a hint of warmth through Warrick's jumper. "I am."

"And are you going to turn me in?" Warrick sounded amused.

"For fuck's sake..." He didn't give a shit about the sentiment. What bothered him was the faintly sickening thought of Warrick saying something like that when there was some bored idiot nearby who'd report him. Corporate or not, some things weren't sensible. But he couldn't think of how to say it in a way Warrick would take seriously.

The tension must have communicated itself through his hands, because Warrick said, "Rest assured I wouldn't dream of saying any such thing anywhere I might be overheard."

"You never know who's listening. It's bad enough that your bloody brother doesn't know how to keep his mouth shut, without you starting the same fucking thing."

153

"Tarin's opinionated, yes. But he—"

"He's a moron. If he's got any friends who think like him—and I don't want to know if he does—then I hope they don't tell him anything important, because he's a fucking liability. No. Anyone who can't manage not to criticize the Administration when there's a para-investigator sitting six places down the table isn't bright enough to qualify for liability."

"But you had no intention of reporting him." Brief pause. "Did you?"

No disagreement with Toreth's characterization of Tarin, then. "Of course not. But he didn't know that. The point is that it doesn't take much to raise suspicion, whether it's you or Tarin. SimTech might not be big enough to keep you safe if someone heavy went for you."

"If I were arrested, I wouldn't have to rely on one of your despised Justice representatives." Warrick still didn't sound to be taking it seriously enough for Toreth's liking. "SimTech's lawyers would begin proceedings and then I&I would have to—"

"Political criminals have no automatic right to independent representation. And then I&I starts pulling in contacts and I end up on level C and someone asks me if I've ever heard you say such-and-such, and I have to say yes."

Warrick turned his head. "Would you?" Inquiry, not condemnation or surprise.

"Yes. Or—" It was a shock to discover that what he wanted to say was, no, I'd deny it for as long as I possibly could. He'd have to try, even though he knew the resistance would be pointless and stupid. The realization disoriented him, putting a touch of vertigo into the panorama spread before them. Unconsciously, he tightened his grip on Warrick's shoulders.

He thought of Warrick at I&I, in a holding cell, waiting for an interrogator to send for him. The image morphed seamlessly into the memory of his own hour spent pacing the detention cell, after Marian Tanit's death, waiting for Psychoprogramming to take him away. The sharpness of the memory surprised him—the only time Toreth had seen I&I from the other side, and it had been an hour too long.

"It's not a question of what I'd want to say. If things got serious it wouldn't be one of those bloody juniors from tonight asking me. It'd be a specialist interrogator, or even Internal fucking Investigations." A stronger gust of wind curled over the parapet, and he shivered. "I'd be pumped full of drugs, I'd be . . . I know how it works. Don't even fucking joke about it."

Warrick set the cup down on the wall and turned, kissing him, then brushing Toreth's mouth lightly with his finger. "I'm sorry. No levity intended. Topic closed?"

"Yes. Yeah, sure."

Warrick touched him again with his fingertip, the soft pad running over his lower lip, smooth edge of his nail tickling slightly along the upper. Toreth flicked the tip of his tongue out quickly, and Warrick gasped at the contact, surprised. Then Warrick laughed. "Will you stay?"

Toreth thought it over. Warrick looked interested now, and focused, as far as Toreth could tell in the dim light. He certainly sounded it. For a brief moment, Toreth considered leaving anyway, just to show that he could. He didn't bother coming up with a reason to drop the idea. "Okay. Let's go back down, though—I'm freezing my bollocks off."

From Warrick's flat they wouldn't be able to see I&I. Toreth had had quite enough of work for one evening.

Part Two: Doubles

"What's wrong?" Sara asked as they took their seats in the coffee room. Then, when Toreth didn't reply, she added, "Not *still?*"

Toreth nodded, staring into his mug, wishing he'd never told her about it. Maybe if he didn't say anything she'd drop it.

The problem was that Warrick was too tired to fuck. Persistently so. It was SimTech's fault, and it had been going on for nearly two weeks. Toreth hadn't minded, much. At first. He'd turned up to Warrick's flat on a Friday, unannounced, having spent most of the day thinking, on and off, that he wouldn't mind a fuck. In fact, by the time he'd been out for a drink with the team to celebrate Nagra's official arrival, it had turned into more than "wouldn't mind." He hadn't seen Warrick for a few days and Toreth had been feeling...edgy. Wondering, being honest with himself, what Warrick might be up to. He'd made his excuses and left the bar early, to the accompaniment of some very unsubtle sniggering from Sara. He wondered what she'd told the others.

As soon as Warrick opened the door, looking exhausted and preoccupied, Toreth had known it was a bust. When Toreth asked what was wrong, Warrick had shrugged and said, "Work," in a tone of voice that had discouraged curiosity. After that, Warrick had made coffee and they'd talked for a while, and then gone to bed. Toreth had tried not to make his demands *too* demanding, but he hadn't been able to pretend he'd come around for coffee. In return, to be fair—not that he felt like being anything of the kind right now—Warrick had made an effort and sucked him off before he fell asleep. At least he'd fallen asleep afterwards and not during. Toreth didn't like sex to be "making an effort." He liked to think he was worth more than that. He needed to know he was.

By the time he'd woken up in the morning, Warrick had already gone off to SimTech, leaving an apologetic note and a very nice breakfast keeping warm. That only, somehow, made things worse. Toreth had spent the rest of the day wondering what he'd done with his Saturdays before he'd known Warrick. Nothing very fun, apparently.

Then, on Monday, he'd made his biggest mistake and spent ten minutes bitching to Sara about what a lousy weekend he'd had. That had been the start of her predictable but irritating interest in the situation. Since then Toreth had spent an inordinate amount of time in the gym, and done so much paperwork that he'd eventually run out, for the first time in years. And now... now it was Friday again, and he was at work again, fancying a fuck again. Not that he'd been living in celibate misery for the last fourteen days, but it was the difference between having what he could have (strangers in bars and a new trainee down in the Pediatric Interrogation Section) and what he couldn't.

Was Warrick finally growing bored of the regular fucking? Toreth searched his memory, going back over their recent encounters—or not so recent, now. The last time had been after the cattle market. They'd had a bad start, and Warrick had put that down to work, too. After the trip up to the roof Warrick had shaken off whatever it was and it had been great. Or it had seemed great at the time. Had Warrick wanted it as much as before? Toreth realized he had his teeth clenched hard enough to make his jaw ache. He forced himself to relax. Why the hell was he so wound up? Warrick had been busy with SimTech before. This was no different. Except that it was. Girardin made it different. Could he be cause or effect?

Toreth tapped the edge of his mug, watching the ripples run into the center. *Was* that it? A couple of years of kink, and now a retreat back to the corporate world. Greener grass, he thought sourly. No more I&I, and a safe, social peer. If not Girardin, then someone like him. Carnac, maybe—he'd make a prestigious partner for an up-and-coming corporate. Dillian would be so fucking happy. No, Toreth told himself. It was work. SimTech temporarily demanding more of Warrick's time, nothing more sinister than that. It had to be.

Forcing the thoughts away, he dragged his attention back to the present, only to find Sara regaling him with details of her latest boyfriend, which was frankly taking things too far. Especially since it was early stages and the new acquisition was still a paragon of incredibly annoying virtue.

"I don't know why you're bothering," he said when she paused for breath. "He sounds just like the last one. And the one before that. Why the fuck is Tim—"

"Tom."

"Fine. Whatever the hell he's called, he's still not going to be any different. If you're lucky, you'll get another ring out of it before you ditch him or he ditches you. Jesus, spot a fucking pattern, Sara. Why don't you just do what Belkin does with his admins and call them all 'hey, you'?"

Her lips tightened, and then she asked, "Why don't you call him?"

"There's no point. He's called me." Which meant Warrick couldn't be bored, didn't it?

"So you have spoken to him?"

"Not really. After the first couple of times I set the comm to take messages."

156

"And?"

"And he always says the same thing—he's very sorry, but he's still too fucking busy to see me. Work."

"If it was me, I'd call him. Let him know you're still alive. If you're not saying anything he probably thinks you don't mind." She stood up. "Not that you ought to take *my* advice, considering the state of *my* love life."

Toreth watched as she rinsed her mug and flounced out of the coffee room, head high. Oh, Christ. Flowers on Monday, if he wanted any coffee in his office over the next few weeks.

Back at his desk, he gave in and called Warrick's personal comm. The answering "Yes?" was sharp, so he limited himself to asking if Warrick would be available tonight. Trying not to sound desperate, or bitter, or anything else humiliating. Whether he succeeded or not, it had no effect on Warrick. "I'm sorry, but I can't say yes or no. I'm in a meeting right now—I ought to be able to let you know once it finishes."

Toreth cut off the comm without answering, and buried himself in work for the rest of the day. At first he hoped that Warrick would call. As the day wore on, though, the feeling of hanging around, of being ready (and eager) to accept whatever scraps of attention Warrick might be willing to throw to him, finally became too much. As he returned to his office from afternoon coffee without Sara, he made his mind up. If Warrick couldn't be bothered to make the time, then he couldn't either. Warrick could play with his precious bloody corporation and welcome. Even if he *did* call back wanting to fuck tonight, he could fucking whistle for it.

Infuriatingly, about half an hour after this satisfying resolution, the comm chimed.

"I'm sorry I didn't call earlier," Warrick began. "But I've been in the same damn meeting since nine o'clock."

"And?" Why the hell do you think I care?

"Could you make it over to SimTech this evening?"

Opening his mouth to refuse, Toreth heard himself say, "Sure, what time?"

When the conversation finished, Toreth found that his black mood had lifted, which annoyed him all over again. It was a strange feeling—happy and irritated at the same time.

It had better be a *bloody* good fuck.

Arriving at SimTech, twenty minutes late, he found Warrick already in the sim. He lay absolutely still in the couch, his face hidden by the visor. If Toreth hadn't recognized his clothes, it could have been any man of Warrick's build.

Ignoring the sim technician busy preparing the next couch, he crouched beside Warrick, close enough to catch his scent and so be quite sure. And his hands, of course—he knew those. He touched Warrick's right wrist lightly, fingers automatically sliding around to find the pulse. It tapped slow and even against his fingertips, chipping away the last of the anger.

First contact in two weeks. Toreth ran his hand slowly along Warrick's arm, over the restraining strap, knowing Warrick wouldn't be able to feel it. That, for once, he couldn't disapprove of Toreth touching in public—in front of the employees, no less.

The technician coughed.

"What?"

"Doctor Warrick wanted you to join him right away."

Feeling oddly reluctant, Toreth settled into the couch beside Warrick, watching him until he had to turn his head away for the technician to fit the visor.

When the small, white entry room appeared around him, he found Warrick sitting at the table, reading a book, his feet resting comfortably in midair on nothing visible. He didn't look tired now, but then he wouldn't—he never did in the sim.

Warrick closed the book, which vanished. "Glad you could make it."

Being late had seemed like a good idea at work. Now, with Warrick so clearly unfazed, Toreth regretted it. "Stuff came up, sorry."

"No problem at all. Actually, I appreciated a little time just to sit and relax. Shall we get started?" Without waiting for an answer, Warrick touched the controls and a very familiar room appeared around them. Heavy furniture, dark wood, a fire in the grate, and the warm, buttery light of the candles that filled the air with the sweet scent of beeswax. When he turned around, he saw the ridiculously oversized four-poster bed.

He'd already registered the squeak of wood and the quick, heavy breathing, so he wasn't surprised to see bodies on the bed. He was surprised to see who.

Warrick, kneeling astride another man, leaning forwards over him, and being enthusiastically fucked from below. His partner's hands gripped Warrick's hips, pulling down and pushing up. Toreth looked around, but Warrick was still beside him. Also still beside him. "It's a recording," Warrick said.

The sim had never made him feel sick before, and it wasn't the sim that sickened him now, or stirred anger to chase the feeling away. Warrick fucking someone else, and even if it was supposed to be work, nothing fucking personal, he certainly looked to be enjoying himself. Overly sensitive, perhaps, after Girardin, but he couldn't help it.

"I don't want to—" And then he stopped dead, his mouth open, as the Warrick on the bed leaned back, thrusting down hard, giving Toreth a clearer view of his partner.

It's the sim, isn't it, said the part of his brain not numbed by the sight. You can do anything in the sim. That's the whole point of it.

158

Dark hair disordered and damp with virtual sweat. Head thrown back to high-light the delicious sweep of his throat. Lips parted as he breathed encouragement. Warrick.

Or—another thought he didn't like—someone else in Warrick's body?

"Who's that?" Toreth asked.

"In a way, they're both me. One of them is me, the other one is a shell—a copy of my sim body, programmed to have sex in the same way I do. To have the same responses and so on. Or approximately so. It's rather more complex than that."

"So which one's you?"

Warrick studied the entwined bodies for a moment. "The one on top."

"Jesus." It was, Toreth thought, an unfairly juicy secret to have kept. He moved around the bed, to improve the view, absorbing the implications of the situation as he watched the recording. It wasn't conducive to calm thought. The Warrick on his back had his hands clenched in the sheets, his back arching in a way that was so familiar it sizzled down Toreth's spine and straight to his groin.

"Stop." The voice came from the bed, the first words spoken by either of them, and it took Toreth a moment to work out it was the supine Warrick who had spoken.

"What?" the other replied.

"I'd like you to fuck me."

Kneeling Warrick reached down and touched his mirrored lips. "Are you sure?"

"Yes."

"Good." He nodded, with a detached, assessing satisfaction at variance with his obvious arousal. "Then turn over."

Sim-easy fucking—no preparation, no lubricant, no tedious messing around. Only a few seconds before Warrick thrust deep, once, and then stopped, with an expression Toreth also knew well—Warrick on the edge, perilously close to coming. He clicked his fingers, and the control panel appeared beside him. A few adjustments and he recommenced fucking. Fucking himself. There was an insult that would never sound the same again.

If it had occurred to Toreth to try to look away, he wouldn't have been able to. The compelling weirdness of the sight before him absorbed him utterly, arousing and yet at the same time rather unsettling. He knew Warrick, knew how he responded, what he wanted, and the picture before him didn't quite match up with what he knew.

Eventually Toreth said, "You're very quiet."

"Who?" Warrick asked from beside the fire.

"The fucking you. Both of you."

"Am I?" Warrick tilted his head, listening, considering. "I suppose I am. That's the difference between professional and personal sex. Also, it requires a certain amount of concentration."

159

"Yeah? I would've thought doing yourself would be easy."

Warrick smiled. "In a way, yes. Certainly by that stage, when the shell has a significant measure of autonomy. This is one of the later training sessions. At first I had to split my attention between both bodies simultaneously, until the program learned my responses."

Toreth tried to imagine that, and gave up. "You're feeling with both bodies?"

"To begin with, yes."

"Fuck." That on its own opened a whole range of possibilities. On the bed, Warrick's hands slid down his partner's back as he thrust harder. Toreth knew how that felt, both to do it and to have it done to him. Feeling them at the same time, though... "Could we do that? Could I feel what you feel when I fuck you?"

"No. Or rather, theoretically, yes, if I set the system up to do it. However, there are no protocols or safety assessments in place yet. We do have it penciled in for later development."

Something to persuade Warrick to do later. For now, he returned his attention to the recording. Warrick fucking and being fucked, two familiar pictures joined impossibly together. Warrick on his hands and knees, and Warrick kneeling upright. Bodies moving together, so perfectly attuned. Was this what Warrick had been doing for the last three weeks? It made him feel... it was Warrick fucking someone else and even if the someone wasn't real, it stirred feelings he didn't like to acknowledge. How could he possibly be jealous of a computer program?

"What did you say it was called?" Toreth asked.

"The body is a shell. The program directing it is called an ee-ee-es. Evolved Expert System. Usually pronounced 'Yes.'"

"How come I've never seen it before?"

"Commercial confidentiality, among other reasons. The tests aren't open to nonstaff volunteers."

"So why now?"

"We're suspending the project. I thought you might like to see it working, before everything is switched off and uninstalled from the system."

A noise from the bed distracted Toreth, as the Warrick being fucked—the copy, wasn't it?—gasped. "Yes. Suck...mmh, yes." The words changed into a moan as he curled down onto the bed, hands clenching in the rumpled bedspread as he came.

Of course—in the sim, distance was no guarantee of safety from Warrick's mouth.

Before long, the copy-Warrick lifted his head, and then knelt up, revealing an already-restored erection. Inhumanly fast, even for the sim, which had added benefits for male users. Toreth glanced at Warrick. "Bit of an improvement on the original."

Warrick shook his head, but before he could reply, the copy-Warrick said, "Change places?"

160

That earned him a proprietorial pat on the shoulder from his creator. "I'd be delighted."

Watching them swap around, Toreth made up his mind. "Turn it on." It was the thing Warrick wanted him to ask, the reason he'd brought him here. "The live version. Go on."

Warrick smiled. "All right."

The pair of Warricks vanished, or at least reduced in number to a single figure seated on the edge of the vast bed. Naked, hands folded in his lap, expression blank. Counting the Warrick at the controls there were still two of them. Possibilities and permutations raced through Toreth's mind so quickly that he couldn't pin any one of them down. "Has anyone else had it?" Toreth asked.

"Yes, I'm afraid so. Although not always in that shell—in my body. A trained Yes can be used in different shells, although they work best in a limited set. The self-shells are used primarily for training and for—" He stopped.

"For what?"

"Comparison trials."

"For...you mean, for people to fuck that, then fuck you and see which was better?" Jealousy stirred again, rippling quickly through him.

"Not quite. Rather to see if the experiences are comparable. It's a little more technical than that, but that's the gist. The object of the exercise isn't to create exact replicas, but to produce behaviorally autonomous objects to interact with sim users. Within their area of competence, they have to be convincing. You might have noticed that one thing we don't have in general use in the sim is true virtual people. There are humanlike objects but their range of behavior is predefined and so limited."

Computer legislation was something Toreth had only a basic grounding in, but there was one fact he remembered. "Autonomous? Like an AI? Isn't that illegal?"

"Yes. Or rather, sentient AIs are. We're trying to create something that will be suitably interactive, without it being legally sentient. We have all the appropriate permissions, of course. However, the legislation is sadly unclear, as is almost inevitable. Defining sentience, what constitutes a sentient AI, and how to delineate any one example and separate the AI from the systems around it, and so on."

Despite a genuine effort to stay interested, Toreth could feel his eyes glazing over. It never stopped surprising him how Warrick could talk any situation to death once he found a technical angle that interested him.

Warrick shrugged. "A very difficult area to even attempt to set in concrete terms. The Yes is one of our most promising approaches. They become convincing simulacra in a single area, but profoundly limited in others, or at least that is the idea. Stopping them learning isn't easy. We had hoped it would find us a way around the law, in that they could be classified as merely unusually flexible expert systems. However, as soon as you add a humanlike physical—or virtual—body, people make assumptions. And by definition, the things have to act human."

A computer creation, not a person. Impossible to think of it as such, though, despite the eerie stillness. It was too exactly like Warrick to be a thing. "So they've forced you to cancel the project?"

"Not as such, no. The permission for the projects requires periodic revision, with an Administration-appointed committee from the Communications Systems Assessment Division being responsible for that."

"They're part of the Data Division," Toreth said with surprise. "They have a building in the Int-Sec complex."

"Yes. The sim is classified as a means of information transfer, so they're responsible for monitoring our compliance with the relevant legislation. They delivered a report on the Yeses three weeks ago, and we were given a month to respond to their concerns. That's why I've been at SimTech all hours of the day since." Warrick sighed. "Unfortunately, our own assessment is that the burden of proving that what we're doing falls within the terms of the licenses has become too great for SimTech to bear. Answering all the points they raised will divert too many euros and people from the rest of the sim, and we have a tight schedule to deliver the first production run. So we've called a halt ourselves."

"Christ. What a waste."

"Not really. The work has been done, we've assessed a number of methods and had considerable success." The attempt to highlight the positive couldn't hide Warrick's disappointment. "It's a delay, not a cancellation. All the code will be archived until we have time to activate the project again."

"Including him? It." "It" sounded better.

"Yes."

Toreth contemplated the autonomous object on the bed. "Wake it up."

Warrick touched the controls, and turned around, abruptly naked in the firelight. Toreth felt the unreal heat of the fire on his own suddenly bare skin. "KA-forty-one, initiate interactive mode," Warrick said.

A number, not a name, Toreth noted. Probably Warrick wouldn't be interested in hearing about prisoner depersonalization theory.

The Warrick on the bed looked up at them, then over to the clock and back. "Good evening."

"Good evening," real-Warrick said. He extended his hand, and the Yes took it, rising smoothly to its feet and then standing beside...beside himself. They turned to Toreth.

"Go on. If you want to, of course," said real-Warrick.

Except neither of them were real. The *real* Warrick—warm flesh and blood— was elsewhere, still and unresponsive in the couch. The whole sim felt suddenly fragile around him. Feeling strangely self-conscious, Toreth moved over to the copy. He hesitated for a moment, wondering what to do, then settled for kissing it. Like kissing Warrick, and not like. Physically perfect, but something a little off in the response. Exactly what, he couldn't say. Disappointing in a way, but at the same time oddly reassuring to know that he could tell the difference.

He deepened the kiss, beginning to explore with his hands, and the body leaned into him, responding to his touch and touching in return. Then, with no perceptible transition, he *was* kissing Warrick, unmistakably so. He pulled back at once, looking between the man he still held, and the figure standing beside him, and for a moment, he wasn't sure. He didn't *know*. Then the explanation occurred, and he released his hold.

"You swapped," he said accusingly to the Warrick he'd kissed.

"Yes." Warrick had the same satisfied expression he'd worn when the Yes asked to change places. "You spotted it very quickly."

"Of course I did." Reflexively, Toreth wiped his mouth.

"No 'of course' about it—some people can't tell, or don't notice for a while."

"Don't do it again."

"No?"

"No. It's—" He wasn't sure what it was, other than extremely unnerving. He hadn't known. For that one small moment, mouths together, virtual breath mingling, he hadn't been sure whether Warrick was real or not. Normally he enjoyed the weirdness of the sim, but the idea of fucking Warrick and not knowing who—or what—he was touching almost frightened him. He shivered.

"Would you like to go out?" Warrick asked. "Now that you've seen it."

"No. It's just...fucking strange."

Professional curiosity sparked in Warrick's eyes. "Because it's not a real person? Or because it's me?"

"The second one. If it didn't look like you, I think it would be okay."

The copy spread its hands. "I can change my shell, if that would make you more comfortable."

Toreth looked sharply at Warrick, who shook his head. "That's the Yes talking." He smiled. "It's rather more agreeable than I am."

The Yes—or what he thought was the Yes—smiled too, an eerie mirror. "Somewhat. All part of my function. What are your preferences? I'm a far more accomplished male, but I can try female if that's what you'd like."

Had it been listening to everything, then? "Don't you know what I like?"

"How should I? We've never met before and Doctor Warrick left me no instructions. But I always enjoy expanding my knowledge."

"But if you're—" Not sure he believed Warrick wasn't playing games, Toreth looked between them again.

Warrick laughed. "I give you my word, it's not me. And it doesn't have my memories, except of shared time in the sim."

Too unnerving to think about for long. "You have no idea who I am?" he asked the Yes.

163

"None at all."

Feeling rather ridiculous, he said, "My name's Val Toreth."

"Ah!" Eyebrows rose, and the Yes glanced at Warrick. "I have heard the name before. Once or twice. It's a pleasure to meet you." It tilted its head, inquiring. "So, should I change?"

"No." Toreth took a deep breath. "No, you're fine as you are."

"Good. There's nothing to worry about, I promise. I don't bite—except on request." It took a step towards the bed, and offered its hand. "Come on."

Reaching out, Toreth clasped the warm, imaginary flesh. Creepy it may be, but not so creepy that the idea of the fuck didn't appeal more.

They made a gentle start, slow and sensuous. The pace made it easy to keep track of which body was where, to be sure who was what. He still caught himself pausing every so often to think, am I sure? But the intervals between the checks grew longer as he allowed the physical pleasure to overcome the unease.

Fucking two men wasn't something he did very often. With threesomes he liked there to be at least one person involved who didn't quite want to do it, and that often meant a couple with a reluctant husband or wife. So two men had a certain novelty in itself, albeit entirely overwhelmed by who they were. Lying on his back, a Warrick on each side pressed against him full length, his arms around them, was something he had never dreamed about, never fantasized, never imagined. Freeing an arm, he offered his wrist to real-Warrick. "Check my pulse, would you? I have a feeling I've died and gone to heaven."

Warrick grinned, and complied. "Present if a little fast, flatterer."

Toreth accepted a kiss, and then turned to the other side. "Do you play the game?" he asked the copy.

An inquiring frown creased its brows. "Game? Why don't you explain the rules to me, and I'll see?"

Warrick ran a distracting hand down his side. "That's not part of the training."

"No?" Toreth didn't look around—he was watching the Yes, which was listening to the conversation with apparent interest. "Why not?"

"Some things I prefer to keep private. Or at least not to make available for others' use."

Toreth looked around at him and smiled, not bothering to hide his satisfaction. "Good."

He rolled Warrick over, moving to lie on top of him, taking hold of his wrists and pinning him, thrusting against him. A moment of stillness, and Warrick conjured something oil-slippery between them, turning the sensation from pleasant to exquisite as their cocks rubbed together. Very, very nice. And, wonderfully, not all they could do. "Fuck me," he said, looking at Warrick beneath him, but addressing the Yes.

If it didn't understand him, Warrick passed the message along, because he felt hands holding him, stilling him, and then a cock sliding into him, smooth and infinitely satisfying.

"Ah, *God,* that feels good," copy-Warrick breathed in his ear, and Toreth couldn't disagree. He stopped moving, letting the copy's thrusts shift him against the solid body beneath him. He didn't need to ask Warrick if he was comfortable, because he would be—everything sim perfect.

Perfection indeed, or at least nothing obviously missing sprang to mind.

Surrounded by warm skin, by Warrick's maddeningly arousing smell, he shivered at the copy's mouth on the back of his neck, a touch of teeth only adding to the stimulation. At the same time Warrick's mouth pressed against his, Warrick's hands pulling him down and sliding along his sides to grip his hips and urge him to move faster.

Whether because of Toreth's response, or because of a direct instruction sent by the original, the Yes shifted above him, bracing its arms and thrusting into him deeper and harder, making him moan, and Warrick in turn buck beneath him, hands releasing him to reach further towards the Yes. "More," Warrick gasped, as Toreth sucked his throat hard—no need to worry about marks here. "Yes, that's ... that's it. That's—*ah.* I want you—"

He felt the peculiar, liquid twist of reality reordering itself in obedient response to Warrick's thoughts, and then Toreth found himself inside Warrick, cock already buried deep at the instant he became aware of it. He groaned, overwhelmed by the sudden sensations; fucked and fucking, bringing the earlier recording vividly to mind. They came together with sim-tuned perfection, Warrick's cry covered by his own, and a soft echo of them both from the lips pressed into his shoulder.

When he opened his eyes, they were still in the bedroom. There was only one Warrick present, though, lying beneath him and holding him. As Toreth lifted his head, Warrick released him. "What do you think of it?" Warrick asked.

Toreth rolled off him and settled into the feather mattress. "Pretty good," he said. "But ... "

Warrick frowned. "But?"

"But it isn't you, is it?" Then he winced inwardly, because that sounded far more ... meaningful than he'd intended. Luckily, Warrick didn't seem to notice.

"No, it isn't. However, as I said, it's not supposed to be an exact replica of me. It shares some of my sexual responses and preferences, that's all. What I meant was: how did you rate it as a convincing sexual partner?"

"I, um ... " Toreth sat up and rested his elbows on his knees, trying to come up with something useful and, unusually, failing. With the physical distraction of the fuck over, the unease had returned, and that was rapidly overwhelming the memory of how much fun it had been. He stared at the flickering candles, hoping for inspiration. "It wasn't bad, I suppose. It knew what it was doing. It was good at it. It was a bit...passive. Or something. I don't know—maybe I wouldn't think that if it didn't look like you. But...there was something missing. It felt like—"

Then, finally, he put his finger on it. It felt like strangers in bars and temps at work. It felt like all the fucks he'd had over the last fortnight and every single fuck in his life before he'd met Warrick. It threw the distinction into sharp and disturbing relief.

Nothing sounded in the room except the low crackle of flames, until Warrick said, "Are you hungry? I haven't eaten anything since breakfast."

Toreth took the diversion gratefully. "Yeah. Yeah, I am. Want to go out and get something?"

He heard a snap of fingers behind him as Warrick called up the console, and for once Toreth was glad to see the sim fade about them and to find himself back in the couch and the real world.

As the lift opened into the reception area, Warrick said, "Needless to say, everything I've told you is still highly confidential."

"Sure. Not a word to anyone." This time he meant it. Not even Sara, who had heard all his other virtual fuck stories. This one would pass a coffee time nicely, but he didn't feel like telling it.

"Would you sell it?" he asked as they stepped out of the building into the cool evening. "If you can get around the legislation?"

"Yes, of course. It's only a question of time and resources. Truly humanlike objects are an important feature of the sim as it was originally envisaged and we desperately want to keep them."

"No, I mean, will you sell that one. You."

"Ah. No. A modified version of the Yes might be commercialized, but not in that shell. No real people will be used."

"Good."

"Well, I say none. One business proposal is to license shells from well-known porn actors. That would come into its own in the longer term, when the per-unit cost of the sim is down to a level that private ownership becomes widespread. Although before that, it would be viable in leisure centers..."

Toreth lost track of the details, enjoying the walk, and the sound of Warrick's voice, whatever he was talking about. Enjoying the solidity of the real world, noticing all the things he wouldn't normally give a second thought to: the smell of the evening city, voices in the distance, lighted windows, and the thin crescent sliver of the new moon.

The thought intruded that the sim could be this real. They had models of the campus, or at least of this part of it. Of the SimTech building, too. He could so easily be walking through an illusion, with the Yes beside him. "Look at the moon," he said, cutting into Warrick's flow. Saying it only so that when Warrick stopped and looked up, he made an easier target to grab hold of and kiss. For once, public as it was, Warrick made no move to pull away and Toreth didn't release him until he was absolutely sure.

"Well?" Warrick raised an eyebrow. "Am I real?"

Toreth stared, his hands still on Warrick's shoulders. How the hell had he *known*?

Warrick laughed. "Everyone suffers from that from time to time."

"Even you?"

"Mm. Actually, no. I can always tell. But then I've worked with it for a long time, and I know where the flaws are. A few of the small, simple rooms are close to indistinguishable from the originals, but nowhere this complex. I keep hoping, though." He gazed up at the moon again, his voice soft. "The world is so beautiful, when you look at it. So detailed. So sharp. Everything's just *there*—so much more than we need. Light we can't see, sounds we can't hear. Sometimes I wonder if that's what it takes to make it real. But one day, I'll go into the sim, into a world like this, full of other users mixing with people who are no more real than the scenery, and I won't know. The illusion will be perfect. Then it'll be finished. Not commercially finished, but complete as I conceived it. I'm sure it can be done. Will be done, in the end."

If Warrick expected a response, Toreth had no idea what to say. This was Warrick's world, not his, and the passion in Warrick's voice was as disconcerting as the Yes. After a moment, Warrick shook his head and smiled, a little ruefully. "That's what it's about, after all, at least according to Asher."

"What?"

"SimTech. The Yeses. Asher says it's all about proving that I was right and the people who said it would never work were wrong. Back before SimTech, when they closed the project."

Which sounded like a convincing theory to Toreth. "I wonder where she'd get an idea like that."

"I've always suspected Dilly." Warrick glanced at the moon again, and then laughed. "It doesn't hurt to dream, does it? Come on. Before I faint from very real hunger."

They started walking again. It had been a once-in-a-lifetime evening, Toreth thought, at least if SimTech didn't start the Yes program again. That would be fine with him. One Warrick had to be enough for anyone.

167

Gee

❖

Taking an extra-long Friday lunch always felt slightly naughty to Sara, even when, as today, Toreth had suggested it. Two cases had finished and no replacements had yet arrived, so he'd said they deserved a celebration.

Unfortunately, they were late setting off, and by the time they reached the commercial buildings on the periphery of the Int-Sec complex, most places were full. Even with the bright sunshine, the blustery October wind had obviously discouraged people from venturing too far. So for once they made it a little further—off the Int-Sec grounds altogether, and to an Italian cafe-bar neither of them had visited before. They found a table in a quiet corner, and Toreth offered to buy. Sara glanced at the menu, then said, "Surprise me."

"Okay, but don't blame me if you hate it. Juice?"

"Pineapple, please."

The surprise would be steak and chips, because it always was. She watched Toreth threading his way between the tables, idly appreciating the rear view, and the way his hips moved as he squeezed between two chairs. Not something she ought to be looking at, she reminded herself sternly (and unsuccessfully). When he reached the bar, Sara shook her head and fished out her hand screen. She was supposed to be making arrangements for tonight, for a double date with her sister, and Fee would kill her if she forgot.

After a minute or two, a quiet male voice said, "Excuse me?"

Sara looked around to find an elderly man standing a couple of meters away. Once he must have been handsome and powerfully built. Now age had begun to melt muscle away, leaving a stooped frame. But his thinning hair was neatly cut and combed and he was smartly dressed, although the style was almost old-fashioned enough to look like a costume: a blue blazer and striped tie, and shoes so highly polished it was hard to see the color. "I'm sorry?" Sara said.

The man smiled, a hesitant expression at odds with his appearance. "Ah—the man you were talking to—his name wouldn't by any chance be Valantin Toreth, would it?"

168

"*Valantin?*" Not even his despised parents called him that.

The man clearly mistook her surprise for a negative. "No, of course not; I apologize for troubling you."

"No, sorry—I mean, yes, that's him."

"Ah." He hesitated again, obviously torn between staying and going. "I wondered if—"

"Jesus fucking Christ!" Toreth's voice was loud enough to attract attention from tables right across the bar. "*Gee?*"

The man took a small step back. "Yes."

Toreth slammed the glasses down on the table, slopping juice over the rims. It took Sara a moment to read it as surprise, not anger. "What the hell are you doing in here?"

"I, ah—I was passing by when I saw you come in, and I thought I recognized you. I wanted to say hello, that's all. I won't disturb your lunch."

"Yeah, well, hello." The pause slowly slid into a silence, and Sara took the opportunity to cough quietly. "Sorry," Toreth said. "Gee, this is Sara Lovelady, my admin. Sara, this is, uh, Gerald Evans."

No job description given for Evans, she noted, as she stood up to shake his hand.

The man nodded at Sara, only briefly, before his eyes went back to Toreth. His gaze was intense now, almost hungry, as though he could pull something out of Toreth just by looking at him. "You're doing well?"

"Fine. I moved to I&I from Justice with the Interrogation Division. I made senior para-investigator."

"Youngest ever," Sara said impulsively.

"Really?" Evans beamed. "A senior para-investigator. I should have recognized your uniform, of course. Well, that's wonderful. Didn't I always say you had it in you?"

"Uh, yeah." A short, awkward pause followed, before Toreth said, "How about you?"

"I'm retired. I have been for years. Ah, yes. Tempora mutantur..."

"And we change with them," Toreth said.

That drew another delighted smile. "Yes, indeed." He took Toreth's hand in both of his and shook it warmly. "A pleasure to see you again, my boy. Really it is. A pleasure. But I must be going. I, ah—"

"Yes?"

"We parted on bad terms, I know. I wanted to let you know I quite forgave you for your little prank." He squeezed Toreth's hand. "Well...goodbye, and good luck—not that you seem to need it." Evans released Toreth's hand, and nodded to Sara. "Goodbye, Ms. Lovelady." Then he turned and strode smartly away.

Toreth sat down and pulled a glass towards him. "Would you fucking believe it?" he said, apparently to the juice. "Gee Evans."

169

Sara lasted for an agonized thirty seconds before she said, "Who was that?"

"Someone I haven't seen for a fuck of a long time."

"Oh, come *on*."

He took a sip of juice and made a face. "This is yours. Or they fucked up the order." He tried the other glass. "No, my mistake; this is the grapefruit."

"*Toreth.*"

A silence, then Toreth nodded. "Okay. But first—" He swirled his glass, spreading the spilled juice in a circle on the table. "First you've got to promise not to laugh."

Sara stared at him. "Laugh?"

"Some of it's . . . soppy, Chev would call it. Although where the hell he got that from, I don't know."

"Kel, I expect. And of course I won't laugh." More seemed to be required. "I promise."

"Okay. Right. I don't know if I ever mentioned, but when I was thirteen, I was sent to a Retraining Center." Toreth looked up. "Heard of them?"

Sara shook her head. "No more than the name."

"Before your time. They were a bit like the Assessment Centers are now. Administration-run, one step down from a juvenile re-education facility. Except that back then they weren't just somewhere to send you to keep you out of trouble while they found out what the problem was and whether it could be fixed. Kids mostly stayed there until they got old enough to be passed on to one of the adult places."

He paused again, so she asked, "Why were you there?"

"I stabbed someone at school." He smiled—the one that always made her shiver, which she duly did. "The little tosser was so fucking scared of me that when he got out of the ICU he wouldn't say I'd done it, not even on a witness interrogation. He was underage, of course, so they couldn't really interrogate him. But everyone knew it was me, so they whipped up some poxy psych report and bundled me off to this RC place." He shrugged. "It was okay, actually. I mean, it was a prison: all the doors locked on the outside, there was a fuck-off huge fence, and the guards were six foot six, and that's across the shoulders. Ready to kick the shit out of you at the first sign of trouble. But it was okay. You know—relatively."

Relative to being at home was what he meant.

"And because it was supposed to be educational, they did have lessons. Gee was a teacher. Pretty good teacher, too—he taught me how to read. Or, well . . . I *could* read, I just didn't want to." He shook his head. "Hard to explain, now. But Gee actually liked teaching. We spoiled it for him, of course. Jesus, he loathed most of the kids in there."

"I bet."

"What did he used to say when we got a new one sent in? Fuck, I can't remember. Oh, God, that was it—'another one down from the trees in search of the secret

170

of fire.' Real knuckledraggers. Most of them were doped all the time, or so fucking fried on smuggled-in stuff that they couldn't remember their own names."

"And you weren't?"

He grinned. "Even back then I drew the line at filling myself full of that kind of crap. So I ended up listening, for a change. I was bored, I suppose. There wasn't anything better to do, and I was Gee's star pupil, just 'cause I was one of the few kids in there who *could* think without moving my lips or drooling. He used to call me—" He paused, looking down, circling the glass again.

"What?" Sara asked.

"Ah, shit. He used to say I looked like an angel." Toreth actually flushed. "My hair was a lot longer then, and lighter and—" He raised his eyes, frowning. "I knew you'd laugh."

Sara cleared her throat. "I wasn't!" Or not much. She decided to try flattery. "In fact, I can kind of see his point."

The frown darkened. "Don't take the piss. I was telling you about Gee. Do you want to hear it or not?"

"Please." She picked up her glass and settled back.

"Okay. What he *really* wanted was to be a teacher in an olde-worlde boys' school. Kind of place that only ever existed in books anyway. Of course, nowhere respectable would've let him within a hundred kilometers. He was cracked—completely fucked in the head. Still is, I should think. But the RCs would take anyone mad enough to work there, so he got to make his own little fantasy world. He had a study, a bit like the club room in the sim: wood panels, carpet, two leather chairs, huge wooden desk, all the props. He'd decorated it himself; everywhere else was plastic-coated walls and steel furniture screwed to the floor." Toreth stared across the bar, eyes distant. "I remember how it smelled. Nice, actually, compared to the rest of the place. Him, and boot polish, and paper and burning dust. He had a fake coal fire, which must've been a hundred years old. Amazing it never set fire to the building. One whole wall was paper books. Old, a lot of them. All school stories or spanking stories, or books about—" He frowned. "What's the word? Ah, yeah—corporal punishment. Anyway, he used to make me stand there, in front of the fire, and read them to him."

The abrupt turn in the conversation, coupled with Toreth's matter-of-fact tone, left Sara wondering if she was hearing it correctly. She couldn't help asking, "Make?"

"In a way. He called it private tuition. He pulled me out of lessons to do it, and when the alternatives were standing there reading out regulations for the flogging of ratings in the eighteenth-century British Navy or sitting through the brain-numbing crap the rest of them got, it wasn't much of a choice." He frowned thoughtfully. "You know, I bet some of that was restricted historical material. I've never thought of that before. He was lucky no one reported it." Toreth took a sip of his grapefruit

171

juice. "Anyway, Gee liked boys—blond boys—and he had a spanking kink like you would not believe. No, not a kink. A real fetish. He genuinely couldn't get it up without it."

"He used to spank you?" Sara was amazed by how calm she sounded. Not to mention how calm *he* was.

"*Oh* yes. With a slipper, mostly." His eyes crinkled, halfway between a smile and a grimace. "He had a cane as well, though. Kept it hanging on the wall—a meter, meter and a half long, about as thick as your finger. When he got it down he used to say, 'This is going to hurt me a lot more than it hurts you.' I used to tell him to fucking try it himself."

Toreth wasn't always the most truthful storyteller, and she suddenly and very badly wanted this to be a lie, although she knew it wasn't.

"He didn't use it very often, thank God. It was for when I actually did something wrong, which was less often than you'd think, because *fuck* that thing hurt. It was always multiples of six." He shifted, hunching down in the chair. "Thirty, that was the most. Just once, when I deliberately screwed up an external test he'd arranged 'specially for me. Christ, he was furious. Enough that I don't think he even got off on it at the time. Bet he enjoyed remembering it afterwards, though. It was supposed to be thirty-six, I think, but he stopped when the—God, it was..." He stopped, wincing at the memory, then shook his head. "I was sick afterwards, in his wastepaper bin. He wasn't very pleased about that, either."

Her outrage escaped in a squeak, and he straightened up and smiled. "I suppose it all worked out in the end, 'cause I never threw another fucking test, I can tell you that."

"But that's barbaric!" She couldn't keep quiet any longer. "*And* illegal. *We* couldn't do that. You weren't old enough for a waiver, even if he was allowed to do it."

"I suppose so." He sounded vaguely surprised by her outburst. "Legal wasn't a big thing in the RC. No one who lets their kids get sent somewhere like that gives a fuck about them, and who else is going to care? Anyway, it was usually a slipper, which was okay. Bend down, hands on your knees, keep still. Take it like a man." Toreth snorted with laughter. "Can you believe he really said that?"

Sara still couldn't believe the bastard had done it at all, but there didn't seem to be much point in saying so.

"It was supposedly for getting the reading wrong," Toreth continued, "which is why the lessons worked. I used to concentrate so hard, getting it word perfect, making him wait. An hour or so and he'd be squirming in the chair, desperate for it. Then I'd start fucking it up, on purpose, and eventually he'd tell me to take my trousers down. It never did much for me, but I've had a lot worse."

Grossly unfair as it was, she had the urge to ask Toreth how he could've let Evans do it to him. "Did he ever—?" Abuse you. Rape you.

172

"Fuck me?" Toreth nodded. "Not often, though. Wasn't what he wanted. Mostly he'd come while he was smacking me, if he came at all. He was getting on a bit, even then. But if I'd been behaving, he'd make an exception. Considering that he didn't actually like touching, he wasn't a bad lay. He gave a decent handjob, anyway, although he used to wrap his hand in a white hankie first. Completely fucking cracked, like I said. He'd do other stuff as well, when I could sweet-talk him into it. First man—adult—I ever fucked, which was about as much his thing as the spanking was mine."

The tone was as unmistakable as it was unbelievable. Affection. "You *liked* him?"

Toreth blinked. "Never really thought about it like that, but I—yeah, I suppose so. Okay, I was fifteen, so I thought Gee was about a hundred and fifty, but he was fit enough that it wasn't completely disgusting. He was the one who started me on my exercise kick. Something else to pass the time that I ended up enjoying."

Sara struggled for a response, finding nothing. This wasn't supposed to be the kind of thing you simply told someone over lunch, never mind worry that they'd *laugh* about it. She knew she was staring, and couldn't help it. Toreth didn't seem to care, though. If anything, he looked faintly amused by her reaction. It just wasn't—

She thought back to a conversation with Warrick, when Carnac had been at I&I. Toreth *wasn't* normal. Most of the time he could pass well enough, and then something like this happened, almost as if to underline how profoundly not normal he was. "What happened in the end?" she asked.

"Nothing very exciting. After a couple of years, when I'd stopped fucking around with the reading and learned some stuff from him apart from pervy school stories, Gee swung me a resit for my level threes, and another psych test. He sent the results to the Interrogation Division, and I got a promise of sponsorship for training there if my level fours were okay. And then the RC kicked me out and sent me home. I suppose I counted as a success for them. You should've seen that fucking bitch's face when I told her I was—" He stopped dead. "Anyway, that's it," he said after a moment.

That fucking bitch—Toreth's mother. They'd need to be late into an alcohol-fueled night before he would manage a whole sentence about *her*. "So he's the reason you ended up at Interrogation?"

"Yeah, I suppose so. I was getting a bit old for him by then, so he wanted me out of the way."

There was a tight edge in his voice, and Sara decided to drop the subject. "What did he mean about the little prank?" she asked.

"Oh, yeah." Toreth ran his hand through his hair. "The little prank. Fuck. Last few weeks I was there, Gee started breaking in my replacement. Younger model. He looked like a pig. Really, he did—pink and shiny, with a fat, scrunched-up little face and tiny eyes. A pig in a blond wig. Bastard."

Clear anger showed now, for the first time, and Sara wasn't sure where it was directed.

His smile had turned shivery again. "A fortnight before I went home, I planted a camera in his study, and got some lovely stuff: spanking, a couple of canings, lots of Gee with his hand on his cock through his trousers and that expression on his face—disgusted with himself and loving it. Pig-boy crying and begging him to stop." He shrugged. "Pig-boy was a lot better at that bit than I was. Gee never got much out of me beyond screaming at him to fuck off and screw himself when he was laying into me with that bloody cane. He didn't mind, though—as long as you were still bending over and you were making *some* kind of a noise, he was well away. Anyway, last day there, I broke into one of the computer rooms, made about a hundred copies of the recordings and passed them out round the place. Kids, guards, whoever wanted one. Fucking hysterical. I bet there's still people out there with them."

All she could come up with was, "Did they arrest him?"

"Oh, fuck, no. Gee was fine. Didn't even sack him. It's hard enough to find people to work in those places without giving them the boot over a little thing like that."

A little thing like that. Sara simply stared, all attempts at a sensible reaction abandoned.

Toreth shook his head. "Funny how it's all so clear. I haven't seen him since that last day at the RC, and he was pretty fucking pissed off, I can tell you. Dragged me into his office, and—". He shrugged. "I broke his cane. And maybe his jaw; I didn't hang around to find out for sure. If I did, he never told anyone because nothing happened about it. Although he wrote to me later."

"What?"

"Gee wrote to me, after I left the RC. Pen and ink. He's got the most amazing handwriting, all loops. He knew my address, of course, from my file."

Could this, actually, get any stranger? "What did he *say*?"

Toreth shrugged. "No idea. Didn't open them."

Apparently, it could. "Toreth—"

"Couldn't really see the point, since I was never going to see him again."

"Toreth—"

It must have been her tone of voice that made Toreth lean back, instantly wary. "What?"

"I—" Sara stopped, considering. There was nothing she could say that Toreth would want to hear. Pity or sympathy would only anger him, questions about how he'd felt back then would do the same. Anything that tied what had been done to him to the present, and especially to his kinky thing with Warrick would meet with...what? Blank incomprehension, at best. It wasn't a path she had any business following, either. They were his issues, and his relationship, and if she tried to say something, she'd be doing it for herself, not for him. "Have you ever told Warrick about him?" she asked.

Now Toreth stared. "Jesus, no, of course not. You know what he's like about that kind of thing—I&I sets him off badly enough and that's all legal. He'd blow a fuse, and then he'd go on and on about it. I don't need that kind of hassle."

Well, there was one sign of a basic grounding in reality, even if some of the reasoning was rather skewed. "Of course not, no, you're quite right."

"Anyway, I haven't thought about Gee in years. Weird, meeting him like that. He hasn't changed that much, except for being older. Still wearing the same fucking shoes, too. All that time I spent staring at them." There was an uncharacteristically uncomfortable silence, then Toreth drained his glass and said, "Do you want some wine? There's nothing important on this afternoon, is there?"

"No. I mean, no, there's nothing on. Red, please."

"I'll give them a kick about the food, as well. It ought to be here by now." Toreth rose, but didn't leave right away. He stood, staring at the door, lips pursed. Then he shook his head, and set off for the bar.

Watching him cross the room had temporarily lost its appeal, so Sara went to the ladies instead, in search of some soap and very hot water. She could still feel the print on her hand where Evans had shaken it.

Shopping & Fucking

❖

Part One: Shopping

While Toreth talked on the comm he kept an eye on Warrick, who lay beside him on the bed. He looked composed on the surface, if flushed and slightly bitten, but Toreth knew him well enough to see the irritation beneath. Warrick was pissed off because the call was from I&I. Toreth's job had intruded into Warrick's flat. Worse, it had done so right in the middle of a nice Saturday post-gym fuck.

Saturday routine, interrupted. Especially annoying when Toreth had made a special point of wrapping things up yesterday to spend a whole day with Warrick. Trust some selfish bastard to want to confess today. He felt tempted to tell Parsons, or even a pool interrogator on duty, to handle the interrogation for him, but the case was too important not to be personally present. "I'll be three-quarters of an hour," he told the detention officer, regretting it even as he said it. There was no point delaying, though. If he and Warrick fucked now the summons would loom over the whole thing and spoil it.

He finished the call. Warrick rolled over onto his back and pillowed his head on Toreth's stomach. "You have to go?" Warrick asked.

"Yeah. Work." Toreth didn't move, though. He lay watching the clock, determined to wring every second out of it. Sometimes he really felt like resigning, and then... Unfortunately, there was never an "and then" that he could come up with. I&I had always been his life. I&I and now Warrick, and he hated it when the two got in each other's way. "Sorry about this," he said. "I can't guarantee when I'll be finished, either. We can pick it up tomorrow, if you like."

Warrick sighed. "Much as I'd love to, I'm afraid I can't tomorrow. I've arranged to see Dilly."

Clearly, Toreth wasn't invited. A shame in a way, because he always liked to see her, even though she didn't like to see him. "Can't you cancel?"

"No, it's too late. We have plans. And we're both so busy that if we don't make plans and stick to them, then we never get together."

176

In a general sense he knew Warrick did lots of things without him. Work, family, friends. But he rarely considered them in any depth, or in a way that made them feel real. The idea made him mildly curious (and maybe a touch jealous). "Where are you going?"

"Out for brunch. Then there's a lunchtime concert and afterwards we're probably going shopping. I'm making dinner for some of her university people in the evening."

"Shopping for what?"

"Supposedly furniture. She's finally decided she hates the things in the flat too much to live with them, now that she's going to be on Earth for a while. But I expect we'll end up with the usual things."

As if he ought to know what they were. "The usual things?"

"She buys clothes to wear twice and leave behind next time she goes off-world. I buy things for the kitchen." After a moment he added, "You'd find it very boring."

"Oh, I don't know."

"What, *shopping*?"

"I could give it a go." For one thing, watching Dillian trying on clothes wouldn't rate very high on his hardship scale.

Warrick twisted around to look at him. "That wasn't a serious suggestion, was it?"

"Yeah, why not?" He ran a finger along the line of Warrick's jaw, enjoying the slight roughness. "We'd have to go to the right kind of shops, that's all." An idea was forming. Even without Dillian, it could still be fun.

There was a short silence. "Toreth, if this is leading where I think it's leading, I'm not sure—"

"I am." He hadn't been, but Warrick's voice held that particular touch of real reluctance that made it irresistible.

"Not in public."

So that was the problem. "It wouldn't be in public, it'd be in a shop."

"Not with other people there, then. I wouldn't be able to . . . get into the mood."

"Yes, you would. Think about it." He twined his fingers through Warrick's hair. "Think about racks and shelves and drawers of gear. All the fuck toys you can imagine. It'll be so much better than virtual shopping. You'll be able to touch things, see how they feel. Try them, maybe. Choose exactly what you want; pick exactly what you want me to do to you. I'll buy it for you—whatever you want. And then we can get it wrapped and bring it straight home. No waiting. It can be a birthday present."

"It's not my birthday, and I don't want to do it."

Toreth couldn't recall a prisoner who'd ever made a less convincing denial. "Call it an early New Year present, then. Come on, you love the idea."

"No, I don't," Warrick said, despite some fairly solid evidence to the contrary. He laughed. "I'll sort something out."

After that, getting up and going to work didn't seem so bad.

The reason Warrick hadn't protested more when it was first mentioned, weeks ago, was that he was fairly sure "I'll sort something out" had meant it would never happen. After a while, when Toreth had failed to raise the idea again, he'd decided that he'd been right. So when Toreth had left a message one Friday, saying he'd be around to collect him on Saturday afternoon, Warrick hadn't connected it with the previous conversation. It was a little odd that Toreth didn't say why, but not strange enough to merit serious thought.

The first twinge of concern came when Toreth was not merely on time, but ten minutes early. The concern grew when he wasn't even upset that Warrick wasn't ready. He merely waited in the hallway, whistling in the particularly irritating way that meant he was in a tremendously good mood.

"Where are we going?" Warrick asked as the taxi set off.

"It's a surprise." That *was* worrying, and for some reason shopping was the first idea that came into his head.

"I said I didn't want to do that." He knew he'd guessed right when Toreth smiled and looked out of the window, without saying a word.

He'd said he didn't want to, and he'd meant it. The fact that Toreth could turn him on by talking about the idea didn't mean a thing. When he used the right tone of voice, content wasn't very important. What he did with Toreth was private. A few people knew, mostly people who'd noticed bruises and been concerned to one degree or another. Beyond that, at work, there were rumors and stories that he occasionally caught the tail end of. Inevitable, he supposed. And Sara had to know, of course. She went to Toreth's flat, for one thing, and the chains on the wall were hardly subtle. In fact, he didn't mind her knowing. He had at first, but he'd grown used to the idea, because she so obviously didn't care.

What they *did,* though, the process, the detail, the mechanics—they were secrets. His feelings about it were another level of secret again. Nobody needed to know about it and he certainly wasn't voluntarily putting himself on display. Toreth loved it, of course. Making him react in public, setting up situations where he could turn him on, leaving him desperate and *wanting*. Watching him struggling through social events, sometimes having trouble remembering his own name. Warrick let him do it, because God, it was good in the end. From time to time Toreth went too far, and they'd argue and then, of course, the fuck afterwards was even better. Hopeless situation, really.

As hopeless as this one.

He was mildly surprised when the taxi stopped on the edge of one of the more upmarket shopping complexes. He'd been expecting somewhere seedy, somewhere dark and dangerous. "Here we are," Toreth said.

Toreth opened the door of the taxi and waited for him, not saying anything else. This was, Warrick realized with surprise, a chance for him to back out, although it wasn't spelled out as such. He could tell the taxi to go home and Toreth wouldn't mention the thing again. Warrick didn't, though. He climbed out, watched as the taxi pulled away, and then followed Toreth into the building.

He didn't want to disappoint Toreth, or reject the care and planning, which were gifts in themselves. And, yes, he could feel the first faint stirring of excitement at the idea of what might be ahead of him. What harm could it do to satisfy his curiosity about what Toreth had arranged? He could always change his mind later.

The shop was tucked in a quiet corner of the ground floor of the complex, away from the bright shop fronts. There wasn't even a sign, only a numbered door with a security scan, which opened for Toreth's ID. Beyond was a small, square room with a desk, half a dozen low upholstered seats and two doors leading from it. The walls and ceiling were painted a rich dark blue, with silver flecks on the upper half, suggesting stars.

The woman at the desk put down a hand screen as they entered, then stood up and came out from behind the desk. Her short hair was dyed black, with a green-blue sheen to it like a beetle's wing case. Short, plump, and dressed in multilayered blue and silver that matched the walls, she seemed an unlikely person to be working in . . . whatever this place was. She looked between them, assessingly, then turned to Toreth with a warm, welcoming smile. " Welcome to the Shop. Can I help you?"

"My name's Val Toreth."

"Oh, yes, of course. You called last week and spoke to Shel—I should have recognized the picture from the credit check. I'm Fran." Toreth nodded. "This is your first time here, isn't it? I can run through how it all works here, or downstairs, as you prefer."

"We'll go down."

"Fine. Let me just lock the door." She reached over the desk briefly. "We're a bit short-staffed today. There. Follow me."

"Wait." Toreth turned to him. "Shut your eyes." Game voice. He hadn't meant to play in public, he thought, as his eyes closed obediently. Toreth led him across the room and he heard the door open. "Steps down."

Toreth held his arm tightly as they descended, fingers digging into his biceps. The last noise of the city above faded out. Putting out his free hand, he touched a brick wall—painted, but he didn't open his eyes to see what color. "End of the steps . . . now. Corridor. Curtain ahead. No!"

179

The sharp voice snapped his eyes shut as he started to open them. Despite his resolve, here he was, stuck fast in the role, with every moment of acquiescence giving Toreth permission to do more. Still, he could always change his mind later. How many times had he thought that in the past? And of course, he always could. It was just that he never did.

The curtain brushed across his face and the light through his eyelids dimmed, then brightened in the space of a few steps. He heard a low, surprised whistle from Toreth. They had entered a larger space, their footsteps echoing on what felt like a stone floor. The dry, warm air carried a musky, complicated scent of age and leather, with hints of a multitude of other things—dust, oil, metal, paper. Sex—definitely sex. Where the hell were they?

Hands on his shoulders turned him. He wondered what Fran thought about it. Probably nothing. She must see it all the time.

"Okay, you can open them now," Toreth said.

In the car and on the way downstairs he'd imagined...well, he'd tried not to imagine anything. When he hadn't been able to avoid it, he'd steered himself towards thinking about glass cabinets and white walls. Packaging and price labels. Everything a little distant, a little untouchable. Clinical. He'd be able to walk around and pick something out without feeling...just without feeling. Without humiliating himself in public under Toreth's appreciative gaze.

The cellar which housed the Shop was nothing at all like that. It was made up of small, interconnected rooms, linked by low brick arches. This part of the building must be considerably older than the rest above, or it had been very skillfully designed to look it. The lighting was low, but where they stood the lights above had brightened, forming a pool of relative clarity in the gloom. Fran moved around, leaving him with a clear view into the Shop, and the light moved with her. Sensors, he thought, trying not to look at the contents of the room—better to break his mind in gently to what was all around them. Sensors to pick up movement, to illuminate the immediate merchandise and keep everything else as shape and suggestion. When they started to browse, the light would seem to follow them around, if the controls were smooth enough. It was a nice effect, and he'd have to remember it for the sim.

He let his attention slip gradually onto what the lighting showed. Had Toreth already seen it when he'd said, "all the fuck toys you can imagine"? Presumably not, if he'd contacted the place for the first time the week before. Still, he'd certainly met, or exceeded, his promise. The room was full, and so were the rooms on either side, for as far as he could see.

New and obviously secondhand items were jumbled together, displayed on tables and shelves. Not a price label in sight. Tall, wooden cabinets, with dozens of drawers in different sizes, stood against the dark-painted walls. Where there were gaps between the cabinets, the walls were covered in things hanging from hooks.

Or hooks hanging from things. He stared at a complicated frame nearby, something hung with neatly coiled whips, knowing he recognized the shape, until his mind produced the answer. A rack. A real, functioning rack. Heavy, polished wood, and a faint gleam of oil on the metalwork. The straps were worn, dark around the edges with old sweat, obviously well used. Who had owned it? Who had, finally, brought it to this place?

From one of the further rooms beyond he caught a gleam of light and a moving figure. They weren't alone down here. In the next room to the left he could make out more large pieces of equipment, although it wasn't possible to discern function from here, only vague form. Through the arch ahead, the walls were painted white and lined with tall bookcases filled with paper books. Off to the right were racks of clothes—costumes in a myriad of materials. Beyond those rooms were more, filled with shadows. The layout drew the eye onward to new areas, hinting at discoveries to be made.

Treasure trove. Aladdin's cave. A king's ransom in leather and steel.

No packaging and no glass cabinets. He could touch anything and everything, and that was what the woman who'd followed them downstairs was saying, when he managed to focus on her words. "And if you need any help, or if you want anything specific, just ask. Take your time. When you find something, let me know and we can talk about prices then. Don't forget—everything's negotiable."

All the words made sense, but he couldn't hold on to the meaning. God, he was losing it already, with the darkness and the strange, exciting smell. It didn't matter—Toreth would remember it all. Now he was talking to Fran, but watching Warrick. The light from above sharpened the planes of his face, drew attention to the hard lines around his mouth and eyes. Cruel. It made him look cruel, and predatory. Dangerous. Compelling.

He noticed a change in the room and realized that the conversation was over. Good job he hadn't been required to say anything. Fran looked between them, smiled, and disappeared back up the stairs.

Toreth walked a little way off, and the light divided, amoeba-like, to follow him. "Well." He gestured around the room. "Go on, then."

Where to go first? Warrick hesitated in the face of the bounty. "It's like Aladdin's cave."

"Huh?"

He caught Toreth's frown, but he didn't feel capable of an explanation. "It doesn't matter. How about this way?"

As Fran had recommended, Warrick took his time. There was so much to see, it overwhelmed him at first. How the staff would ever find a specific item, he couldn't imagine.

It was, oddly, no different from shopping for anything else, except that virtually everything he touched, everything he picked up, was a turn-on. After an indeterminate length of time, he found he had reached a plateau of arousal. Surprisingly, it wasn't uncomfortable, just something that was there. Like in the sim, he could work around it, almost ignoring the feelings as he opened drawers, examining the chains, masks, gags, and dildos (these latter two items plastic wrapped and in drawers labeled with neat handwritten notices politely reminding customers to "speak to the staff" if they "wished to test" them).

After a while he began to see that the rooms were themed, items collected together, however haphazardly. There were plenty of things he liked, but nothing that really called out to him. He spent time sorting through racks of elaborate, intricate costumes of leather and studs, appreciating the beautiful craftsmanship more than anything else.

At first, Toreth shadowed him, making suggestions, fastening things and distracting him with bruising kisses. By the time he looped back to the book-lined room, though, Toreth had wandered off on his own somewhere. Not surprising, given his usual attention span and the toys all around. In the first bookcase Warrick looked at, the books mostly appeared old, and he was surprised that even these were freely available for examination. Taking a volume down from the shelf, he was about to open it when he realized he wasn't alone.

In a dark corner, out of the ambit of the attentive lights, a black-clad man leaned with his arms braced against the wall. For a moment Warrick wondered if he was ill, until he caught sight of the woman crouching in front of him. Also dressed in black, and shadowed by his body, she was almost invisible. However, she was also quite clearly, and not in the least subtly, fellating him. Her head moved rhythmically, long dark-blonde hair swinging in the gloom. As he watched, the man threw his head back and sucked air in through his teeth, letting it out on a long, shuddering breath. Warrick stood, book in hand, until the man turned and caught sight of him. He smiled, quite unselfconscious, refastening his trousers. Then he reached down and lifted the woman to her feet by the leash around her neck. "Would you like to borrow her for ten minutes?" he asked. "She's very good."

The woman showed no reaction to the offer, positive or negative. It must have been the surreal atmosphere of the cellar, combined with a couple of hours' shopping, but Warrick seriously considered it. Then he imagined Toreth walking through the archway and seeing the scene he had just witnessed, but with himself starring. It would be a shame to get blood all over the books. "No, thanks."

The man merely nodded, and it was only then that Warrick noticed he also wore a leash. The woman took hold of it and wrapped the thin leather around her hand, still without saying a word, and they departed towards the stairs. How the hell, he wondered, had Toreth *found* this place?

Leaving the library by a different archway, he eventually found his way to a smaller room, towards what might be considered the back, if the stairs were the front. There, in a corner, he saw something.

182

It looked like a wardrobe, broad and tall, but not deep. What attracted him was the color of the wood. It exactly matched the wood of his bed and the rest of the bedroom furniture. In fact, it might almost have been from the same set, except that he'd had the furniture made for the room when he'd moved into the flat, and this was much older. He studied it from a little way away. Unlike most items in the Shop, its purpose wasn't obvious. Just a cupboard? For no particular reason he felt certain not, but even if it was it would make a nice addition to the bedroom. Not that he'd ask Toreth to buy it. After he'd found this incredible place and arranged the visit it would be ungrateful to ask him for an armoire.

There was a lock, but no key in it, and no obvious handles. A few moments' examination found the catches, and the double doors folded back smoothly in sections to lie flat against the sides. The interior was also wooden, but tapping it showed it to be a shell covering what, from the weight of the thing, must be a metal frame. Four chains with padded metal manacles were bolted into the top and bottom. Stepping inside, he reached up and took hold of them. Too long at the moment, but they looked designed to be adjustable. At the right length, they would hold him with his feet barely touching the floor. Stretched. Helpless. Open.

He closed his eyes, spread his legs a little, imagining the cabinet in his bedroom. Imagining the manacles, hidden and secret, and ready for him. Almost too much to think about. Almost. He leaned forwards, putting a little of his weight onto the chains, wary of tilting the frame, and rested his forehead on the smooth wood. It smelled of fresh wax and polish. Perfect. It was perfect. It felt somehow familiar, as if it had been waiting for him, his already.

Toreth spoke from behind him. "For your flat."

He let go of the chains. "Yes." He moved aside to let Toreth examine the cabinet. "It matches the bedroom suite."

"Does it?" Toreth ran his hands over the wood, testing the seams and the fit with unexpected professionalism. Bracing his hand on the frame he took one of the chains and pulled, eventually putting most of his weight on it. Then he let go and stepped back. "It's very nice."

Warrick shook his head. "It will be far too expensive. I'll—"

"I can afford it."

"You don't even know—"

"I said, I can afford it. If you want it. Do you?"

"Yes." An honest answer, because that was the rule. "Yes, I want it."

"Then try the manacles." They proved to be far too small, although Warrick had to bite his lip to hold back a moan at the tight press of cold steel. "I'll get her to change them."

Warrick nodded. "They don't look like they're original to it anyway."

"Does it matter?"

"Well, it would be a shame to spoil it, if it *was* all original."

Toreth laughed. "I just want to fuck you in it—I don't care whether it's original or not." He stepped back, looking it over. "There's only one problem with it."

"What?"

"We can't wrap it and take it home. But that doesn't matter—I like a little anticipation."

"I don't."

Toreth could move so quickly, so skillfully, when he wanted to. Before Warrick could react he was pinned face first against the wood inside the frame, his hands spread above him and pressing against the chains. "It doesn't matter what *you* want," Toreth breathed into his ear. "All that matters is what *I* want. Say it."

"It doesn't matter what I want."

Toreth's hands pressed down over his, driving the links into his palms. "Say it."

Suddenly, he couldn't breathe. "It doesn't...it doesn't matter what I want. It only matters what you want."

"Close enough." The pressure on his hands lifted briefly, then Toreth caught one arm by the wrist and twisted it up behind him. His other hand slid slowly down Warrick's arm, down his side, around his hip...

No. Not in public. Not in public. Somehow he couldn't manage the words.

Toreth's hand molded gently around his cock, not moving at first, just holding him, then pressing him back slightly against him. Warrick fought to keep still. "You really *do* want it, don't you?" Toreth whispered. "I should make you ask me for it on your knees. I should make you beg me for it, while I fuck you in front of it. But how long would it take before you came? Twenty seconds? Ten?" His hands tightened and Warrick's breath caught on a whimper. "Five? Probably not even long enough for me to get my cock inside you."

Desperately, he tried not to listen. He wouldn't let Toreth do it. He was going to stop this soon. Very soon. He *wouldn't* let him—

Then Toreth released him and stepped back, leaving him leaning against the wood, shaking. "I'll go find her," Toreth said, in a matter-of-fact voice. "Wait here."

There wasn't much chance of him going anywhere else, at least not until he got himself back under control. He sat where he couldn't see the cabinet, on the edge of a table with heavy staples set at the corners, and concentrated very hard on being somewhere else. By the time Toreth returned, he had regained a tenuous hold on calm.

"Ah," Fran said. "Yes. It's beautiful, isn't it? We've had it for a while now. I'll be sorry to see it go."

Toreth smiled. "It's going to a good home."

"His place? I thought so. Let me show you something." Fran reached into the cabinet and he heard a click. The back panel slid out in two pieces, revealing metal cross braces and the edge of the frame, with sturdy brackets to secure it to

184

the wall. "All fairly self-explanatory, I think. Do bolt it in place, though, into a solid wall, or you might not be coming back to buy anything else. It's been professionally restored, and the frame has been tested to—" She glanced at Warrick, then at Toreth. "—more than adequate weight limits."

Toreth nodded. "It'll need new cuffs."

"I'll find some pairs for him to try."

"Hang on. Do they have to be padded?" Toreth asked.

"Up to you, of course. But I'd normally recommend it, if you're planning to take his weight off the ground with them."

It was strange, standing there while being discussed in the third person. Strange, and strangely relaxing—another way to surrender. He'd chosen the gift, and now Toreth was filling in the details, the fine planning that Warrick knew always turned him on.

"Okay. Padded."

"Suspension cuffs...suspension cuffs..." Fran turned slowly, surveying the room. "I think...over here." She opened a large unlabeled drawer, revealing a tangle of metal with glimpses of leather, satin, and silk.

Toreth picked out half a dozen pairs, sizing them by eye. "Give me your hands."

It wasn't until the second pair had been tried and discarded that he even remembered Fran was there, watching, and that he hadn't been going to do this in public. Too late, now. The feel of the bonds around his wrists was too intimately connected with the game to be anything other than intensely arousing. By the time the best-fitting pair had been chosen he felt lightheaded from the on-off sensation and the heavy click of the locks. He could hear his own breathing, quick and shallow, but couldn't steady it.

"Do the ankle cuffs fit him?" Fran asked.

"I don't know. Try them."

Fortunately, they did. He didn't think he could bear another fitting session.

"Now," Fran said, "I'm afraid we get to the painful part."

It took him a few seconds to realize what she meant. She was talking to Toreth, of course, not to him. "Including the new cuffs and delivery—"

"Hang on," Toreth said, and then turned to him. "Go away."

"What? Why?"

"It's a present—you're not supposed to know how much it costs." He smiled slightly. "Sara explained that to me once."

Warrick had wondered. He wanted to hear at least the starting price, though, because he had a feeling that Toreth was going to buy it even if it was a ridiculous amount of money, even if he couldn't really afford it. The damn thing—the lovely thing—was clearly an antique as well as being beautifully made. "I just want to know how much."

185

"Well, you can't always have what you want. Remember?" Toreth's voice hardened into the tones that these days he had to fight to disobey. "Go away. Play somewhere else until we're done."

"No, I—"

Toreth hit him, backhanded, not very hard, but the surprise made him gasp. Fran didn't even blink. "I said, go away." He smiled again, a cold shark smile. "And, as I know you're not fucking deaf, if you don't go right now you're going to regret it."

God, he doubted that. He still went anyway, though, while he could still stand, and because he didn't want to find out how far Toreth was willing to go in this strange kind of public. As far as Warrick would let him, he suspected.

It was Toreth's money, after all, and he could spend it how he liked. It wasn't as if he'd get nothing out of it.

Warrick wandered through the jumble, feeling strangely disconnected from it now that the choice had been made. Eventually, he stopped in the central room with the bookcases. He picked a book out at random and sat on the set of library steps. He'd spent ten minutes trying and failing to read the book—mostly illustrations anyway—before painfully out-of-key whistling heralded Toreth's reappearance. Fran seemed to have gone another way, because he was alone. "All done. Are you done?"

The image flashed into his mind of the couple he'd seen earlier, with himself kneeling. Toreth would certainly appreciate it. But... "Yes." He stood up and replaced the book. "Let's go." That could wait for another time, because he knew that they'd be back.

Part Two: Fucking

It was late, but not too late, by the time Toreth got to the flat. Late enough that Warrick would have begun to wonder if he was coming around this evening or not. When he pressed the comm for the flat, Warrick answered more quickly than he'd ever done. He must have been sitting, waiting for it—all evening, probably. "Can I come up?" Toreth asked.

"The door's open." Despite the hair-trigger answer, he looked calm enough.

Let's see how long that lasts, Toreth thought.

As it turned out, it didn't even last as long as it took for Toreth to go up in the lift. Warrick stood in the open doorway, waiting for him, pale and only a whisker away from shaking. "When did you do it?" he asked.

"Yesterday afternoon." Toreth came in past him, closed the door and locked it, while Warrick watched him. "I took the time off work and had them bring it straight here. They fitted it, too, so you don't have to worry about my dubious D-I-Y nonskills."

He walked down the hallway to the bedroom, and after a moment Warrick followed him. The cabinet had been bolted to the wall opposite the windows. He'd had it put there because the late afternoon sun hit the wall in that spot. He liked the idea of Warrick chained in the sunlight. Toreth brushed his hand over the closed doors, admiring. Out of the gloom of the Shop, the grain of the dark wood was even more beautiful. "Is it all right here?" he asked.

Warrick was still standing in the hallway outside. "It's exactly where I would have put it."

"Good." He sharpened his voice. "Come here."

They stood in silence, looking at the cabinet. Warrick waited beside him, not asking the question he so obviously and desperately wanted to. Toreth waited, too, letting the tension build, then said, "Is there something you want?"

"Yes."

"Then ask."

"I want to try it tonight. Please." Struggling to keep his voice level. "I've been thinking about it all day. All the very unproductive day."

He ignored the request. "When did you find it?"

"As soon as I came home. The flight didn't get in until quite late and I came in here to sort out my luggage. I tried to call you, to . . . to say thank you. But you weren't answering."

"No. Did you have a good night?"

Warrick smiled, lopsided. "I had to sleep in the spare room in the end. And I didn't do that very well."

Toreth had brought a bag with everything he might possibly need. Warrick would have the things anyway, but it was safer this way, just in case. Planning was important, because it was attention to the details that made something like this perfect. And he'd loved packing the bag, taking his time, thinking about what it meant.

While Warrick watched, he emptied the bag and arranged everything by the right-hand side of the cabinet, so that he wouldn't have to move away. A side pocket of the bag held the key to the cabinet. He'd taken it home with him yesterday to make sure this was the first time Warrick would see it open in place. He thought about the doors, and then decided Warrick would want to do it. "Open it up."

Warrick did, fumbling with the key. The doors swung back, revealing the new manacles and adjusted chains. Everything perfectly prepared. Everything just right.

"I tried the cuffs yesterday," Toreth said. Warrick stared at him, eyes wide. "Only the wrist ones. I got the second one closed against the edge of the cabinet.

187

They're a bit tight on me." He looked at Warrick consideringly. "That turns you on, doesn't it? The idea of me in chains."

Warrick nodded sharply. "Just the idea. The times we tried it, it didn't feel right."

"Good. Bores me rigid. Okay, strip." He leaned against the edge of the cabinet and watched. "I fucked up the timers. I meant to set them for a minute and it was ten. I thought they were broken and I'd still be chained up there when you got back from wherever it was."

Warrick laughed unsteadily, folding his clothes. "New York. That would have been a nice surprise."

"For you. I'd have felt like a complete fucking idiot. I spent nine minutes planning how to kill Fran next time we go shopping, and then they opened." Toreth stood up. "All right." There was a silence before he added, slowly and deliberately, "I can't chain you up and listen to you beg me to hurt you, and then hurt you and listen to you to beg me to fuck you, and then fuck you and listen to you scream, if you don't *stand in the fucking frame.*"

He was rather surprised when Warrick actually managed to move. "Reach up. Stretch." He fitted Warrick's wrists into the manacles, feeling him shiver against him as the locks clicked closed. "Spread your legs. Further. No, do what you're fucking well told to do."

Balance is an instinct. He'd known it would be hard for Warrick to trust the chains, to take the bite of the steel and let himself hang free. He'd hoped he wouldn't be able to do it. Kneeling, he pulled Warrick's ankle to the side, fitted the cuff quickly, and repeated the action with the other leg. He stayed where he was, his hands resting on Warrick's heels. "This is just because it's the first time. Next time, you'll do it properly. You'll do what you're told, when you're told to do it. Understand?"

"Yes." Breathless, from a combination of excitement and the strain of having his arms stretched. "Yes. I'm sorry."

"Sorry is no fucking good to me." He stood up again, picking up the belt from the pile of Warrick's clothes as he did so. "There. All done. Now there's nothing you can do. No way out. No way you can stop me doing anything I damn well want to you, is there?"

Warrick swallowed. "No."

"Can you move?"

"No."

"Try."

The frame didn't even creak. He watched Warrick writhing against the chains, feeling their solid strength. It was an easy and reliable way to get him going. Eventually he gave up and hung in the chains, not saying anything. Waiting for Toreth to decide what to do to him. When the rush from that idea had died down, Toreth stepped up right behind him and said, "Do you know why I had my comm turned off? What I did last night, after I put this in here?"

Warrick's head came up. He didn't say anything, but he was so clearly listening that he didn't need to. "I went out to a bar. I don't think you've ever been there. You wouldn't like it—some of the I&I people drink there after work." He moved the belt to his left hand, and began stroking Warrick with his right, long slow sweeps down his back, over his buttocks. "I went to a bar and I met a couple. They were looking for someone for a threesome. Did I ever mention that I do that kind of thing sometimes?"

Warrick still didn't speak, but Toreth could feel the tension in his muscles. "I'm sure I must've done. Anyway, he was all right—attractive enough but nothing special—but the interesting thing was that *she* looked like Dillian." Warrick moved under his hand, a helpless twitch of his shoulders. It made Toreth want to bite him and so he did. Warrick moaned through gritted teeth, responding and very obviously hating that he had.

It took a few seconds before Toreth could carry on. "Not exactly like her, but enough that I noticed right away. Her eyes. Something about her mouth. And dark hair, in the same sort of general style. Interesting, as I said. And, come to think of it, it means she must have looked a bit like you. I didn't notice that, at the time." He reached over Warrick's shoulder, brushed his fingertips across the smooth wood. "There should be a mirror, just there. So I can see you." He stroked Warrick's cheek, then said, "Turn your head. Do it."

Slowly, Warrick obeyed. His eyes were closed, and his lips pressed tight together. "It's not that important, I suppose—what she looked like. Or who. All cats look the same in the dark, as the saying goes. I didn't talk to her much in any case. He was the one who came up to me and it must've been his idea in the first place. I could tell she wasn't sure about it. She was only going along with it because he wanted her to. He wanted to watch me fuck her."

Toreth slid his hands up Warrick's arms, letting the belt trail across him. He'd love the touch of the leather, even as he hated listening to this. Toreth leaned closer, adding a little of his own weight and coincidentally bringing his mouth close against Warrick's ear. "So, tell me what happened in the end."

Out of the corner of his eye he caught the flick of lashes as Warrick's eyes opened. Good—that had surprised him. He pushed harder, stretching Warrick against the chains. "Tell me what happened. I want to know you're paying attention to me."

Silence, nothing but Warrick moving against him as he struggled reflexively to brace his feet, finding no purchase in his light contact with the smooth wood.

"You'll have to do it, eventually. So tell me."

"No. I—ah!"

"Tell me."

"You fucked her. While he watched you." His voice was cold, edged with pain.

Toreth laughed, and released the pressure. "No, I didn't. They bought me a drink, and we talked for a while, and then I said I wasn't interested." Warrick craned his neck around further, trying to see his face. "They gave me a number, in case I changed my mind, but I deleted it after they'd gone off to talk to someone else. And after that I went home and spent the whole night thinking about this evening. In fact, I woke up once and nearly came round here, but it was some godforsaken hour of the night and you don't like those, do you?"

"I wouldn't...have minded."

"I'll remember you said that, next time. Tell me how it feels."

"It's hard to breathe properly. And it hurts. They hurt." He tugged at the chains on his wrists and gasped softly. "I didn't think they'd hurt so much."

"Too much?"

"No. God, no."

"Enough?"

"No."

Toreth coiled the belt around his hand, getting the strap to precisely the right length. "And?"

Warrick hung his head, the chains twisting as his shoulders tensed in anticipation, his breathing rapid. God, but he looked incredible like this.

"You know you have to ask for it. Don't make me remind you about things like that."

"Hit me."

"How hard?"

Warrick didn't reply for a moment. Then he said, "As hard...as you want to."

"Good. Very, very *good*." And he brought the strap down.

Toreth had dreamed about this, about having Warrick like this, hanging in chains. Except he remembered that in the dream he'd hurt him, genuinely hurt him, beyond the game. Now, here, it would be as perfect as he could make it.

In his pile of essentials—towels, gel, straps, gag, hip flask—he'd forgotten a clock. He could just see the one by the bed, although he found himself begrudging looking away from Warrick long enough to read it. He'd set himself a goal of half an hour and an absolute maximum limit of an hour, because this was something new, and he didn't want it to end up with another trip to Accident and Emergency. A very boring way to spend the evening, unless someone from Justice took an interest in the injuries, in which case it would be an awkward evening.

He left himself plenty of time for the wrap-up.

Stepping away, he undressed. Looking at Warrick, listening to him, trying to shut out everything else in the room. It didn't take much effort. It had become a ritual part of the game—a pause before he finished it. There was a thought that went with it. Mine. He's mine. He'll never walk away—not as long as he wants this. Not as long as he needs it this badly. I can make him stay. He'll never leave me. It was the only time he could think it. The only time he could almost believe it.

Then it was over, and he stepped up close. Hands on Warrick's shoulders, back where they'd started. The touch was also part of it, and it pulled Warrick back from wherever he'd been. "Yes," Warrick said. "Please."

"Please, what? Tell me what you want."

"Fuck me. Please. I want—" A fine shiver ran through him. "I need you to fuck me."

Not yet. Not quite yet.

He put his hand to Warrick's mouth, fingers pressing against his lips. "Lick them."

Warrick opened his mouth eagerly, taking him in, and his other hand tightened on Warrick's shoulder. God, he loved that. Wet mouth around him, sucking. Tongue against his fingertips. It was an effort to take his hand away.

Just spit wasn't going to be enough, but it was fun to start with. Making Warrick do it to himself, although they'd gone beyond any pretense of force today. He knelt behind him and licked him a few times, enough to cause a sharp gasp, then slid a finger into him.

He'd thought that the chains might make it more difficult, but they didn't. Warrick was already relaxed, open to him, enough not to need this. But he didn't stop. As he kept working, he could hear Warrick starting to whimper. It gave him a dizzying feeling of power: trust, vulnerability, the heat of Warrick's body in the tightness around his fingers, and the sweat-damp skin against his mouth. Kisses interspersed with hard bites, each drawing out another soft, pleading sound of surrender.

Mine. He's mine.

All his fingers and finally his whole hand buried inside. Being careful how he touched him, he slid his other hand slowly up Warrick's thigh. Warrick tried to squirm away, desperate movements, desperately constrained. "Please, no. Not like that. I don't...I want you to...I want—"

Toreth dropped his hand away, even though "Not like that" didn't last long, as he'd known it wouldn't. He moved his arm, fucking him slowly and deeply, listening to Warrick falling apart above him. He could hear the sob in his voice now, between heaving breaths. "More. Yes, more. Please. Please, Toreth. Please."

A few more thrusts, then he pulled his hand out, wiped it on the towel and stood up. Warrick panted, twisting weakly in the chains, still whispering, "Please."

He twined his fingers in Warrick's hair and turned his head, kissing salty tears from his cheek and eyelashes. "Now," he whispered, although Warrick probably couldn't hear him. "I'm going to do it now."

Wrapping his arm around Warrick's waist, he slid in, all the way in one smooth movement. He always promised himself he was going to go slowly, to make it last

191

at least for a little while, but he usually waited too long. So that it was usually like this, struggling for control for a while before letting go and just fucking him, too hard and too fast because it felt so fucking good he couldn't bear it.

Now, Warrick was relatively quiet, only moaning deep in his throat as his hips jerked helplessly against him. A few more thrusts and Toreth was nearly there, pulling back just enough from the edge to reach down with perfect, practiced precision for Warrick's cock.

Warrick screamed. Contained and reflected back by the cabinet, it was deafening. His head went back, fast and far enough to have broken Toreth's nose if he hadn't been expecting it, and he screamed again, and came, every muscle tightening against the chains.

Muscles tightening around him, and often that was enough to tip him over. Not this time, not even with Warrick shuddering in his arms, and the smell of fresh sweat from his neck. Toreth counted strokes, unable to believe it wasn't yet, wasn't quite yet. He knew that he often cried out as he came, but afterwards he rarely remembered exactly what he'd said. Warrick's name, other things. He didn't care. Nothing mattered except that he was going to—

"Mine. Oh, God, yes, Warrick. *Mine.*"

He had no idea how long it was before he opened his eyes, but it surely couldn't have been more than a couple of minutes. When he did, he realized that he had almost his full weight on Warrick, and that his ears were still ringing faintly. He stood up on the second try. Warrick hung limp in the chains, and his fingers were taking on a distinct and alarming bluish tinge. When Toreth knelt and unfastened the ankle restraints, he didn't react. "Warrick?" He stood up and shook him gently.

"Mm." He stirred and lifted his head a fraction. "Mm?"

"Can you take some weight on your feet, please?"

"Mm. I . . . yes. Can try."

He did try, although the efforts didn't seem likely to have much immediate effect. In the end, Toreth supported him with an arm around his waist and undid the manacles one-handed. Nice easy design, he thought vaguely.

By the time he'd done it, Warrick was sufficiently with it to make it as far as the bed without actually needing to be carried. He collapsed onto it bonelessly and went out like a light. He was smiling. Toreth shoved him into something approximating a comfortable position, then sat on the edge of the bed. The sight of Warrick sprawled there had a muted version of the kick he'd got earlier. He'd done this to Warrick—he came like that for and because of him. No one else would ever be able to make it that good. No one but him.

Nice for his ego, anyway, although the thought didn't have the same certainty now. The feeling was slipping away, as it always did, try as he might to hold on to it. So after a few minutes he decided on a shower to help wash the last of it away quickly. He thought about waking Warrick, then decided that nothing short of a shock stick would do the job. Warrick could have a shower later. It wasn't Toreth's sheets that were going to suffer this time.

By the time Toreth had had his shower, he felt surprisingly awake—far too awake to even think about going back to bed. He cleaned up the cabinet, with Warrick still unmoving on the bed. Then he raided the fridge for juice and went into the sitting room. He sprawled on the sofa, feeling generally extremely pleased with his life—high, almost. So much so that it took nearly three minutes for boredom to set in. After that, it took him another couple of minutes to find the remote for the large screen. Warrick rarely watched the thing and sometimes Toreth wondered why he bothered to have one at all.

"Housekeeping—screen on." With the sound turned low (not that Warrick would wake up if he turned it to full volume), he found the porn feeds and flicked through them, pausing from time to time to heckle. Watching other people fucking bored him, even live. It was a turn-on, in a reflexive way, from the sounds more than anything else. Overall it was too plastic and unreal, though. Nothing at all to do with him. Still, it beat watching the news.

He thought back to the couple he'd met last night, both of them calm on the surface, but him so keen underneath, her so reluctant. Weird. He'd have done it with them anyway, and enjoyed it, but even so it was weird. He couldn't begin to imagine wanting to watch anyone else fucking Warrick. He could hardly bear to think of it happening at all.

That line of thought led somewhere he didn't want to go. Warrick had fucked away from home once, that was all. Once since they'd...known each other. Once outside work in the sim. But he'd never do it again. Warrick had said so himself and Toreth believed him. He didn't have to think about it any more. About Warrick wanting someone else, about what they might have done.

Wanting a distraction from the unwelcome thought, he flicked back and forth through channels until the image went away, buried under other people, other bodies. Dull, most of it. A recording of himself and Warrick, though, that would be a different question. Warrick would never let him do it, unfortunately. He'd be terrified that the tape would escape, which was weird in itself when you thought about how much there must be from the sim of him doing God knows what with God knows who. Warrick would still say flat no, though.

On the other hand, there was no law saying that he had to tell Warrick he was going to do it. What he didn't know couldn't hurt him. It would be easier to set it up in Toreth's own flat. He could have a word with the surveillance techs at work. They'd be able to come up with something nice and discreet. How long would it take to watch Warrick come, a frame at a time?

"Oh, you found it. Well done. I haven't seen it for weeks." Warrick's voice came from right above him. Toreth craned his neck back to look up at him, his cheek brushing Warrick's silk dressing gown. He hadn't noticed the shower running, but Warrick's hair was tousled and he smelled warm and clean.

"I didn't think you'd wake up," Toreth said.

"I . . . noticed you weren't there." Warrick held his arms out, turning his wrists around for inspection. "Look."

The skin was red, which would fade by tomorrow, but there was an interrupted ring of bruising coming up around each wrist that wouldn't. Toreth took his hands and examined them with professional attention. Just bruises as far as he could tell like this, and the skin over the distal heads of the ulna and radius had been abraded. "Can you feel your fingers?"

"They were a little numb when I woke up. The hot shower seems to have sorted them out."

"Clench your fists. Hm. Looks okay. It's the edge of the cuffs. They'll do it every time, unless you put more padding on. Or I could get them changed. Fran said it was no problem."

"Mm." Warrick took his hands away and came around to sit on the sofa. "I'll see how it looks in the morning."

Which probably translated as "no." He remembered Warrick's voice, twisted with pain. "Felt good?"

"Yes. Or rather, it hurt. It was very clear and very specific. I could feel it until quite near the end."

"And then?"

"Then I lost it." Warrick sounded almost as analytical and cool as he did in the sim. "When you fucked me—when you had your hand inside me—I lost everything, except you. I always do when it's that good."

Toreth imagined Bastard, sitting in Sara's lap and purring like a road drill. If Toreth had the vocal cords for it himself, he'd sound exactly the same right now.

Warrick looked at the screen and frowned. "Isn't that illegal?"

With an effort, Toreth managed to tear his eyes away from Warrick and check. "Yeah. But only doing it, not showing it. They do it all with computers, you should know that. It's hardly going to be a real dog, is it?"

"No, I suppose not. I'm not thinking straight yet." He smiled. "You may have irreversibly melted some synapses. Is she real, do you think?"

Toreth paid more attention to the screen. "Hard to tell. She could be. The CGI ones are usually a less convincing shape."

"Yes, she looks real to me." Warrick shook his head. "What a very peculiar job."

"You can talk. Don't you have fuckable animals in the sim yet?"

"Not as such. Not that were made specifically for that, but it would only need the behavior programming and I don't keep too close a restriction on what the programmers get up to—it stifles innovation. There's obviously a demand. But market research isn't my job."

Taking that as a request, Toreth changed channels until he found something with less fur and more leather. Warrick lay down on the sofa next to him and put his head in his lap. To begin with, it felt deeply strange. Only Sara did that and never, of course, when he was naked (and only occasionally when he was hard, if she hadn't noticed). After the first minute or two it stopped being strange and started to be interesting. More interesting than whatever was happening on the screen, anyway. Warrick shifted position and his still-damp hair moved, soft and tickling. "You'll get your hair sticky," Toreth said.

Warrick turned his head, rubbing his cheek along the length of his cock, then said, "I like a problem with an easy solution." Then he rolled over onto his stomach and replaced his cheek with his tongue—long, slow licks from the base upwards, then sucking gently at the tip.

Toreth leaned his head against the back of the sofa, a fraction of his attention still on the screen, luxuriating in being able to sit and take it, without having to plan what to do next. Not that he normally minded, but it made a very pleasant change. As Warrick's mouth slid down around him he moaned softly, echoing the muted sounds from the screen. That triggered a random thought, something he felt curious enough about to ask. "Do you mind?"

"Mmh?"

"Doing that while I'm watching—" And he had to look across to check. "—Women fucking each other with, um, champagne bottles?"

Warrick lifted his head and glanced at the screen. "Not really." He leaned on his elbow and looked up. "Why should I? After all, I have no idea what you're thinking about while I'm doing it at any other time."

"Well, I'm—" Always thinking about you. Except when I'm thinking about fucking your sister at the same time. Or occasionally you and Sara, and God knows where *that* one comes from. "No, I suppose not. But I can tell you it's never champagne bottles." For a few seconds he considered asking Warrick if he ever thought about other people when they were fucking. The pleasure of a no wasn't worth the potential pain of a yes, though. Besides, how could he believe it anyway?

"Did you want me to carry on?" Warrick asked.

"What? Oh, yes. Please."

Warrick smiled, and carried on, slowly and very thoroughly. By the time Toreth came he'd had his eyes closed for a quarter of an hour and he'd forgotten the screen was even on. He only remembered when the sound cut out as Warrick switched it off a minute later. "We should go to bed," Warrick said.

"In a bit." Meaning never.

Warrick stood up, dragged Toreth to his feet, and prodded him back into the bedroom. It seemed like miles, but it had been the right idea because the bed felt wonderful.

About fifteen seconds later he was on the verge of falling asleep, when Warrick spoke. "Toreth?"

"Uh?"

"Was that all true?"

It took him a few seconds to get the context, then he nodded drowsily. "Yeah, 'course it was."

"Everything?"

"Uh huh. All of it." Well, everything except that he hadn't deleted their number—he still had that safe. "She looked like Dillian. I didn't fuck her."

"Why?"

What a time for bloody questions, especially ones to which he didn't know the answer. "'Cause I was coming round here today, I suppose. Didn't want to waste my energy fucking strangers when I knew I'd need it for fucking you."

"That doesn't usually stop you."

They hadn't had one of these conversations for months (because he'd managed to keep his mouth shut about things for most of that time) and he didn't want one now. Then again, he'd started it, so he ought to make some kind of an effort to smooth things over. "No. But...this was special."

"Yes. Yes, it was. Thank you."

Sounded very formal. "For what?"

"For buying the cabinet. For fucking me and making it so good that I almost hoped I'd die when it finished. For not...well, just thank you."

No argument after all, thank God. "Pleasure," he mumbled. "Any time."

Warrick moved up against him and laid his arm over his hip. Toreth was too nearly asleep to protest, even if he'd remembered that he ought to. "I'll remember you said that," Warrick said.

Part Three: Icing on the Cake

The bruises had turned out worse than they'd looked last night. They weren't wide, but they were very black and very obviously from manacles. Pleading delayed jet lag, Warrick took the day off work. There were advantages to being the boss, but he would have to go in tomorrow. To sit through meetings, talk to people, and possibly meet sponsors in the afternoon. A long-sleeved pullover would cover things, as long as he remembered not to tug the sleeves back. Someone would see them, even so, and the story would fly around the building.

Before he started breakfast, he spread his hands flat on the kitchen table and looked at them. The bruises bound his wrists, enchanting reminders of the night before, and he found himself hypnotized by them, losing time. After a while he could nearly feel the manacles against his skin. By the time he tore his attention away, the toast was cold and he didn't feel hungry anyway.

Going through to the bedroom, he stood and looked at the cabinet. It had been left open and the chains hung free, unlocked. He could do it now, just for a little while. Toreth had said he'd been able to close the manacle against the side. Of course, Toreth was taller than he was, but he could stand on something.

It was a stupid idea. He needed Toreth there, to make it work. He needed his voice, his hands, and his pure presence. If he did it on his own it would simply hurt like hell and make the bruises worse. So he closed and locked the cabinet and put the key safely away, in a box on the bedside table where he kept small things he didn't want to lose. Then he sat on the bed and looked at his wrists until he couldn't bear it any longer.

He undressed slowly, making it last for as long as he reasonably could, then went over to the cabinet. He reached up, stretching, and touched his fingertips to the silky wood, breathing in the scent of the restorer's polish. That was going to add a new dimension to antique shop visits.

Then he lay on the bed, closed his eyes, and began to work through the previous evening in as much detail as he could recall. He didn't touch himself anywhere to start with, because if he did, this wouldn't last long. Thinking about it, that was all. That was enough. He lingered so long over "stand in the fucking frame" that he was already breathing heavily by the time Toreth locked the chains around his ankles.

He soaked himself in the memory of the first moments, when it was finally complete. Pain. Pain in his wrists. Muscles constricted around his chest, making each breath distinct and precious. Better than any of that, the feeling of total surrender, exactly as he'd imagined it in the Shop. Toreth behind him, possessing him without even touching him. Stretched and helpless and absolutely vulnerable. Losing himself almost before it started, long before Toreth fucked him.

Toreth, fucking him. His mind jumped track to the end, forgetting his resolve to take his time. Putting his hands flat on his hipbones, he pressed down, holding himself still. But he wanted it *now,* and Toreth wasn't there to make him wait. Slowly, he slid his hands across, brushing his cock. A gentle touch to start with, which wouldn't last long. Discipline. He backtracked to the place at which he'd left the narrative. What were the words? "There is nothing you can do. No way out."

After a few minutes, when he had almost reached the point of imagining the bite of the strap across his shoulders, he quite suddenly thought about calling Toreth, and telling him what he was doing. Why he was doing it.

I couldn't stop myself. I needed it. This is what you do to me.

Toreth would love to hear it. Automatically, he dismissed the impulse, as he had when the idea had occurred before. Then he thought, why the hell not? Toreth always said that I&I didn't monitor personal comms, and all past evidence had borne that out. They'd risked far more serious things than a little dirty talk. Finding the comm earpiece, he rearranged himself on the bed and called through, not giving himself time for second thoughts. Before Toreth answered, he suddenly thought, "What if he's—" and then the call connected.

"Val Toreth."

What if he's in an interrogation? "It's me. Are you too busy to talk?"

"Not at all." Toreth must still be in an extremely good mood if he didn't sound wary at the request for a conversation. "I'm just having a coffee in my office, in fact."

He took a deep breath, feeling suddenly self-conscious. Ridiculous, when he thought of all the explicit conversations he'd had in the sim. Still, if he could've thought of a halfway plausible excuse for calling, he might have used it, but his mind went blank. He settled for "Guess what I'm doing," hearing his voice catch on the last word.

There was a pause, and Toreth said, "Are you really?"

"Yes."

"Where?"

"On the bed. Looking at the cabinet and thinking about last night. About you fucking me." He closed his eyes, and for some reason that made it less peculiar. "About how much I wanted you. How much I needed it. How much I want it again."

"Okay, then, how much?"

He smiled, because even as he'd been speaking he'd guessed Toreth would ask that. He never seemed to get tired of hearing about it. "Enough that I called you so I can hear your voice while I fuck my own hand and pretend it's yours."

There was a brief pause, and he wondered if he'd actually managed to surprise Toreth. In fact, he seemed to have been checking his schedule because eventually he said, "I can't get away. I'm really sorry." For once, he sounded as though he meant it. "Not even for lunch. I've got things all day that I can't cancel."

"I don't want you to come round." That wasn't true, but it sounded good. The tiny hint of independence laced into the conversation would sting Toreth. "I just wanted you to know...that I couldn't stop myself. Thinking about last night—"

"No. Don't think about last night. Think about tonight."

Less than a dozen words, and the idea of doing it again, the idea that they *would* do it again, over and over, that the cabinet would be there forever and— He somehow managed to stop himself from moving and lay gasping for breath, waiting to get himself under control because insofar as he'd *had* a plan, he'd wanted to drag it out a little longer than this. Now that he'd actually made the call. "Not tonight," Warrick said when he could speak. "My wrists—"

"Don't worry about that. You can come round to my flat." Toreth's voice changed, sliding subtly into something hard-edged but seductive. "I don't need chains to make you do what I want. I don't need anything. I can take whatever I want from you, however I want it, and you can't stop me. Are you listening?"

"Mmh. Yes." One hand on his cock, one holding the bedpost—not really what he wanted, but at least he could tense his arm against it, pain flaring down from his wrist. "Don't stop."

"Or I can chain you to the bed, by your neck, so you don't have to worry about your precious wrists, and fuck you. Not like last night. Slowly. Slow and hard, until you don't know what you're saying, and then until you *can't* say anything."

Toreth speaking right against his ear was always exquisite and here, when it was all the contact he had, it was nearly unbearable. He desperately wanted to hear it right to the end, but he couldn't hold back, thrusting up into his fist, tighter and faster.

"I'm going to come deep inside you and leave you there, aching for more. You won't be able to lay a single finger on yourself then, however much you want it, because I'll be watching you to make sure you don't. And eventually, when I'm ready—"

Then he lost the words as the orgasm ripped through him—nothing like last night, of course, but still good. Far better than it would have been without Toreth's voice. He came considerably more quietly on his own than he did in company, although he never heard himself when Toreth had really worked him over. This was somewhere in between and so for once he was aware of how loud it was. He didn't have a hand spare to put over his mouth, so he bit his lip instead and the small, sharp pain made it worse.

When he'd subsided back to panting, he heard Toreth laugh quietly. "See you later," he said, and cut the call off before Warrick could reply.

He opened his eyes and let his muscles relax. Mm. Well. That had been novel. On reflection, he should have tried it before. A pity he hadn't heard what came after "when I'm ready," but he would find out tonight.

There was a long silence in the office afterwards. Toreth lined pencils up on the desk and listened to the blood humming in his ears. Could he wait until this evening, or was he going to have to add another ten minutes to an already overlong coffee break?

"I would have left, you know," Sara said after a while. "If you'd asked."

He swept the pencils up and dropped them into the holder. "Did you want to?"

"Not really, no. That's a great voice you've got for that."

"I can use it for leaving messages for you, if you like."

"Um. Does he do it often?"

"First time." It was oddly disturbing. Exciting to think of Warrick doing it, but so unexpected that he felt unbalanced. He hated unpredictability.

"I thought so. I mean, I can't imagine him doing it at all. I'd never have believed you, if you'd told me. So what brought it on now?"

"Do you remember the address you found for me? The sex gear shop?"

She nodded. "You went, then? What's it like?"

"It's an amazing place. You should go, just to have a look. I'll take you there sometime. I bought him...well, it's like a wardrobe, with chains. Wrists and ankles. It's antique, as well. Cost a fucking fortune. I remembered your rule, though, about presents."

"You didn't tell me about it before." She sounded surprised and almost offended.

He thought about it for a minute. Why hadn't he told her? Since she'd found the place she'd have liked to hear about it. He shrugged, at her and at himself. "Nothing *to* tell before. They only delivered it the day before yesterday. That's why I took the afternoon off."

"Does he like it?"

He laughed. "Just a bit. We tried it out last night and he went into orbit." And so did I. "He's never done it before."

"But I thought you had chains already? I mean, I've seen them."

"Not quite like this. It holds him just off the ground, away from the wall. He's got no support at all, unless I take his weight."

She winced.

"Yeah, I think so, too. I prefer the comfortable part. You should see the bruises on his wrists."

"Didn't sound to be hampering him much. Did he even want to know if you were on your own?"

"No. He just asked if I had time to talk."

Sara shook her head. "Jesus, it's a good job you like him."

He blinked at her, nonplussed. "*Like* him?"

"You'd never get rid of him, if you didn't. I wouldn't let go of anyone if they could get me so worked up just thinking about the night before that I had to call them at work and masturbate over the comm. If they tried to finish it, I'd be round with a tranquilizer gun and all the chains I had." Sara stood up and picked up his mug. "I've got work to do." She grinned at him. "And so have you. Are you going to be busy?"

"Am I...no. No, I don't think so." He grinned back—no, probably more of a smirk. "I'd hate to make any promises I couldn't keep."

After she'd left, he sat back and thought for a while about what she'd said. Half of him liked the sound of it, wished he could believe it was true, and the other half, in the cold light of day, wanted to run from the idea that it might be. That they could be so, so... Tranquilizer gun and chains.

So he opened a case file, and didn't think about it again.

200

❖ ❖ ❖

After the second shower of the morning—he was going to end up wrinkled—Warrick went out to shop for baking ingredients. There wasn't any reason for a mass baking, other than that it was something relaxing, time-consuming, and didn't require too much concentration. The jet lag wasn't entirely a cover story. He could take some of the savory things around to Toreth's tonight, to save them the distraction of a takeaway, and the rest he could take in to work tomorrow. They always received a flatteringly warm reception. Maybe he'd drop in on Dilly on campus. He added a lemon cake to the list, because she liked them.

Back at the flat he set to work. Mixing things by hand proved to be a little painful, but the electric hand mixer hurt, too, so he gave up and took a couple of painkillers. He hadn't wanted to, because he liked to feel the aftermath of a good night, but it wasn't usually this bad. Maybe he'd have to pad the manacles more after all. It would be a shame, but he couldn't end up looking like this every time.

With the cushion of the painkillers, the project proceeded smoothly, and he managed to reduce the number of times he thought about last night to about ten an hour. How long would it take to reach the status of just another session? He was torn between wanting it to stay special, and the irresistible idea that it could be like that again. He wasn't optimistic enough to aim for "often," still less "always," but "again" he could just about manage to believe.

Still, he did get the memory under control to the extent that when he heard the door to the flat open, he was mildly annoyed that Toreth had changed his mind about being able to get away. He was unlikely to accept a desire to make gingerbread as a legitimate excuse for not wanting sex. So it was a relief as well as a disappointment when Dillian called, "It's me!" And then, "Do I smell lemon cake?"

"I'm in here, and yes, you do."

He heard the door close, and her voice coming down the hall. "God, you're a mind reader. I called at SimTech and they said you were jet-lagged, so I thought I'd come round." She came into the kitchen, stopped in the doorway, and inhaled deeply. "Mmm. And on the way over I remembered the last time you were lagged you made me a lemon cake and I was really hoping you'd do it again."

"It's on the rack—don't touch it."

"I know, I know." She came and looked over his shoulder. "Oh, not gingerbread as well. With real crystal stem ginger?"

"Naturally. What else?" He glared at her, mock affronted.

"I feel spoiled. Are you going to ice the cake? Can I lick the bowl out?"

He laughed, thinking about all the times when they were children. "Yes, of course. Do you remember 'helping' Jen, when she made them?"

"Yes, I do! We always used to fight over the bowl."

"So she'd make us sit on opposite sides of the table and take turns until it was gone." He floured the board and started rolling out the gingerbread.

"And *you* used to kick me when she wasn't watching so I'd jump and not get a proper fingerful."

"I don't remember that."

"Well, you did. I used to have bruises. You could be so mean. I bet you don't even remember that you pulled my hair once, trying to get the first go, and she was so cross she rinsed the bowl out, right in front of us, and we didn't get anything."

"Actually, yes, I do." He offered her a piece of dough. "Sorry."

"Good. So you should be." She leaned on the countertop, nibbling the dough, and watched him pressing the gingerbread into the tin. "You know, it's grossly unfair that you got *all* the cooking genes. You'd think there'd be enough left over to let me boil an egg without—"

She stopped so abruptly that he looked around. "What's the matter?" he asked.

"Keir, what happened to your hands?"

He should have thought, because the problem had occupied him in one way or another almost all morning, but the flour was hiding the worst of it. Shaking his sleeves down had no effect, as he'd rolled them up tight to keep them clean. "It's nothing."

"The hell it is. Wash your hands."

"Dilly—"

"Wash your hands. Show me." Reluctantly he did it, and her eyes widened as she saw the bruises emerging. "Was it him?"

"Yes. Or rather, it was *us*."

She took his wet hands gently, turning them over, studying the damage as carefully as Toreth had done the night before. Then she released him. "I want to know how it happened."

He picked up a tea towel and dried his hands. "I very much doubt that. It's just a few bruises, nothing to get excited about."

"Don't try that tone with me—I'm not one of your employees. I want to know *exactly* how it happened."

"Trust me, you don't."

"Why? Because of what I'll think of him? What did he do?"

"Drop it, Dilly. Please."

"No. Not this time. I'm not giving up, so you might as well tell me now."

He briefly considered telling her that sometimes she sounded exactly like Jen. Except that he knew that, once she'd made her mind up, she could be even more stubborn. "All right. I'll show you." He raised his hand at her expression. "It's really much easier. In the bedroom."

She followed him, close behind, as if she was afraid he might try to run. That was more Toreth's trick, although in this situation he could see the appeal.

She looked around, frowning when she saw the cabinet. "Is that new?"

202

"Yes."

He took the key out of the box and put it in the lock. He glanced at her, tempted to ask if she was sure, but he knew an implacable Dilly when he saw one. Maybe this would even reassure her, in a strange way. It was furniture, and you couldn't get much more safe and respectable than nice antique furniture. Besides which, short of throwing her out of the flat, he didn't see an alternative. So he turned the key, opened the doors, stepped aside. She stared for a long moment, then put her hand up to her mouth, her face ashen. She stepped back, away from the open door until she bumped into the edge of the bed. "Oh, my God."

"Dilly, it's just—"

"I know what it is. I can see what it *is*." Her color returned as she continued, anger creeping into her voice. "I've got some imagination—not that it takes much. I know what chains look like, and I know what those things are for." She looked between him and the cabinet. "That's how you got the bruises. You wouldn't be able to reach the floor. You'd have all your weight on your wrists."

"Yes." She'd always had excellent spatial perception. A natural structural engineer.

"Oh, God. Keir, it—it must hurt. It must be—" She shook her head.

Well, he was tempted to say, that is rather the point. "You already know what we do. I told you at Mother's house."

"No. You didn't make it sound like this. *He* didn't, although God knows I should expect *him* to lie."

"Toreth? When the hell did you talk to Toreth about it?"

"It was...it doesn't matter. He said it was a game."

"It is."

"No. This isn't what games are. You don't hurt people you're supposed to love. It's—it's *wrong*." She sounded furious now. "And I don't believe that you want this. I won't. It's—" She bit back the words, whatever they were going to be. "Close the doors!"

"Dilly—"

"Close the fucking doors! I don't want to see it any more." She'd gone pale again, her hands clenched, and the brief, treacherous thought crossed his mind that Toreth would love to see her like this. It appalled and amused him in equal amounts. He closed the cabinet up, put the key away, and went across to her. She had her arms folded across her chest, and she was still staring at the cabinet.

"Dilly?" He touched her shoulder and was immeasurably relieved when she didn't flinch. "Dilly, I'm sorry you're upset. And I'm very sorry if knowing about it changes how you think of me. If it makes you—"

"No!" She looked around. "Don't be silly. I'm *worried*. No, not worried. Worried was before. I'm afraid for you."

"There's no need to be." The assurance felt useless, even as he said it. Showing her the cabinet had been a terrible mistake.

"No need?" She stared at him. "You know what he is. You told me you were being careful with him. You told me it was safe. You promised it was." Unspoken: you lied to me. There wasn't much he could say to any of that, but clearly she could see that her words weren't making any impression.

"Keir, listen to me. He could do whatever he wanted to you." She sounded like an adult speaking to a child who deliberately refused to understand something terribly obvious. "When you're...like that. He could *kill* you and you couldn't stop him. You couldn't do *anything* to stop him."

The words carried a terrible, illicit thrill. "If he wanted to kill me, I couldn't stop him anyway." He was amazed by how calm he sounded. "Any time I'm alone with him is just as dangerous. He's stronger than I am, and he's been trained how to do it. But it's not going to happen."

She swallowed, looking ill. "How can you stand there and say that?"

"It's true. Look, it's been nearly three years and—"

"I meant what he does—his job. How can you say 'he's been trained' and not *care*? How can you even let him touch you?"

"You sound like Tar."

She didn't smile. "I owe him an apology."

"Dilly, I fuck Toreth, not his job."

"I bet you wouldn't say that if you'd seen what he does to people."

And, for that, he couldn't answer her. He couldn't tell the truth and he couldn't bear to lie. So he stood next to her until the silence answered her for him and she sat down abruptly on the bed. She said something, too quietly for him to hear.

"I'm sorry?"

"I said, did you enjoy it?"

"No. It made me sick." That he could be truthful about.

"Good. I'm glad." She looked up, questioning. "But you had to know what it was like?"

He nodded, hoping she wouldn't want to know any more. "We're getting off the topic."

"No, we're not. He is the topic. This is all him. You're different since you met him. We didn't used to have secrets. We were—" She thumped the bed angrily. "We were close. We were always close. And now we're just friends, and God, I *hate* him." She sounded on the verge of tears and he desperately wanted to hug her and tell her everything was going to be all right. All that held him back was the fear that she wouldn't let him. That she would push him away because of what he'd shown her.

"I'm going to make some tea." Maybe if he left her alone for a while, she'd be able to get some equilibrium back.

He'd poured the water into the pot and was wondering whether to set things out here or go through to the living room, when Dillian appeared in the doorway. "If you won't listen to me, I'm going to tell Mother," she said. "Maybe she can talk some sense into—"

It was a shame about the teapot. It had been a wedding present, but he'd always liked it and any connection with Lissa was long gone. It smashed impressively at his feet, and the fountain of tea and subsequent cloud of steam only added to the effect. He pulled off his trousers and socks before the heat could do anything worse than redden his shins. Dilly stood on the other edge of the steaming pool, their differences temporarily forgotten.

"Oh, God, I'm sorry. Are you all right? That was so stupid of me. I didn't think, I didn't—" She stopped, staring at his feet.

It took him a moment to register the bruises on his ankles. He hadn't even noticed them before. Before she could say anything beyond the apologies, he left the room.

He took his time changing, and by the time he got back Dillian had cleared up the broken china and mopped up the tea. The water was boiling again. In the bedroom he'd tried to think of something, some clever argument, but he couldn't. He sat down at the table, and spoke before she could. "Please don't tell her, Dilly. It's got nothing to do with her, it will only upset her, and threatening to tell her won't stop me doing it, if that's what you were hoping."

"I didn't—" She took out another pot and measured out the tea before turning around to face him. "All right, yes, I was. I won't really tell her."

He daren't let her see the extent of his relief. "Thank you."

"I'm sorry about the teapot. Are you sure you're not scalded?"

"Quite sure. No damage done. Do you feel better now?"

She frowned. "No. I'm still worried to death about you, you've still got bruises all over and a wardrobe full of chains, and you're still sleeping with a psychopath. So, no, I'd say not."

He had to admit that, as a rather melodramatic summary of the situation, it wasn't bad. "That's not . . . I can only say that you don't understand, and I appreciate that hearing that probably doesn't help."

"Then explain it to me."

"I can't," he said, without even letting himself consider whether it might be possible.

"You mean you won't."

In that, she was probably right. He tried a different approach. "You don't want to hear about it."

"No, maybe not. But I need to understand." Her voice sharpened. "I'm not a child. I'm not going to faint with horror if you tell me that he hurts you. I know he does. What I want to know is why it's all right."

"Very well. Sit down and I'll try." As he said it, he had the feeling that it could only make things worse. He couldn't let her leave like this, though. "Would you like some lemon cake? It'll be cool now."

After a couple of seconds she nodded. When he brought the slice over she licked her finger and dabbed up a few crumbs. "Lovely." Then she waited.

He sat down, poured the tea, and pushed her cup across. "The most important thing is that it's not about Toreth. It's me. I want it. I need it. I think I always have. I used to do it with Lissa. Oh, not like this. Just scarves, that kind of thing. She only did it to humor me. I could always tell when she wanted something because she'd offer to blindfold me."

She made a face, the one specially reserved for mentions of the woman he wasn't supposed to know she referred to as the Bitch Queen. "I bet she did."

"I wondered—or at least I wonder now—if that was one of the reasons it didn't last."

Dillian snorted. "It didn't last because she didn't deserve you. Oh, and you can stop looking at me like that, because it's absolutely true. She didn't, and he doesn't either."

He'd thought that she wouldn't be able to resist the follow on. The simplest way to deal with it seemed to be to ignore it. "Nothing's changed at all except that now I know what I need and I've met someone who's compatible."

"You're just putting up with him because he likes to hurt you?"

Now she was willfully misunderstanding him. "Dilly, if you aren't going to listen, what the hell is the point of my saying anything?"

To his surprise, she subsided. "You're right. I'm sorry. Go on."

He found he'd lost track of what he'd meant to say. "What do you want to know?"

"I don't know. You keep saying you need it—what's 'it'? Tell me . . . tell me what it's like."

"Like?" He looked down at the table. "I'm not sure if I can, to be honest. I can tell you what we *do* easily enough, but I'm afraid it wouldn't be very reassuring. Or it would sound ridiculous. God knows, it must look strange enough. You know some of it, although the cabinet was new, yesterday. Toreth bought it for me, as a present." He risked an upward glance. She sat, picking at the cake, watching him assessingly. "But what it's like . . ." He hesitated, searching for an approach to the question. "One thing about it is that I don't particularly enjoy pain. Not from cold." He took hold of his wrist, pressed his thumb against the bruise, and winced, because even though it was supposed to be a demonstration of exactly that, the pain was surprisingly unpleasant. "That hurts. Just hurts, nothing else. But after half

206

an hour, an hour, I'd barely even feel that. He's incredibly good at that part of it. Building it up so I can take more, and then more again, until I *want* him to do things that the rest of the time would be...unbearable."

"You're right," she said after a moment. "That isn't very reassuring."

He shook his head. "That's not what it's really about. The essence of it is... is losing myself, my *self*, and belonging to him completely. Being taken, and not just physically. Everything else is what I need to get me there."

She opened her mouth to say something, so he went on quickly. If he stopped now, he might never be able to do this again. "When he hurts me—eventually, when it goes far enough—there's a point when I finally lose control." He looked down at his cup, talking to it, not to her. "Or rather, I give it up, although that may be a distinction without a difference by then. It's more profound, more fundamental, than simply permitting him to tie me up in the first place. Often I don't even remember afterwards what I did, what I said. Just how it *felt*."

He could feel himself getting caught up in it, right in front of her. Half of him wanted to stop right now, because she would be horrified. Half of him hoped that if she could *see* it, she might somehow understand.

"I expect there's a lot of complex brain biochemistry involved. It feels...I can't explain it, not in a way that does it justice. It's not that the pain isn't there any more, but it changes, although I can't say how. It goes on, and on, and it keeps getting better, more intense. When I'm chained, when I can't do anything, can't move, can't...I've cried, I mean really cried—tears—begging him to finish it, to let me come, and I've still loved every second of it. And then...then, when he does it, when he...finally...fucks me, or when he—"

"Keir," she said sharply.

He had, for a moment, forgotten that she was there. He looked up, startled, then smiled apologetically. "Sorry. Mm. Yes. Right. Well, you did ask."

Her cheeks were pink, but all she said was, "I did ask."

"And?"

"And you're right about that, too—I don't understand."

No more than he'd expected. "I can't imagine being able to explain it well enough that you could. But did it help at all?"

She thought about it for a long time, finishing the last bits of the slice of cake. "Well...I'm willing to believe that you really enjoy it. And, I suppose, to believe that he doesn't make you do it."

"That's an improvement, then."

"But I can't...Keir, he still *does* it. He hurts you. He *wants* to hurt you. He's dangerous."

That he indisputably was. "It's not so much that he wants to hurt me. He does it because...no, it's not right to say that he only does it because I want it, either. It's not that simple."

207

"So what is it, then?"

He looked at her, still worried for him, still uncertain, and made a decision. "If I tell you this, you must promise not to repeat it to anyone. Everything else is about me, but this is about Toreth and I have no right to tell you things like this about him."

She hesitated, then said, "All right. I promise."

"Toreth is...he finds it almost impossible to trust people. I can't explain how much the idea of risking caring, of dependency, frightens him." Angers him, he almost added, but a little self-censorship, in the interests of reassurance, couldn't be wrong. "But he trusts me, partly because of what we do. I'm not saying that he doesn't enjoy it for its own sake. I assume he does. But it's also because of what he can do to me. What he can make me do. Making me prove to him, over and over again, how much I need it. And then he can allow himself to reciprocate, just a little. To...well, do you remember Carnac? The socioanalyst?"

She nodded, looking surprised.

"He was at I&I at the beginning of the year—the hows and whys don't matter. He told me that Toreth loves me. I don't know if it's true. I don't know if he's even capable of it, in the way that a—that someone else might be. But I need him, and he lets himself need me in return. Does that make any sense at all?"

She didn't answer.

"Dilly, I know he's dangerous, and—" he took a deep breath, "—to be honest, I want that. But I'm as safe with him as anyone could be. He's never hurt me, not outside the game. Never, in three years. If he did—if he did it even once—then I would leave him."

"Truly?"

He didn't know which part she meant, but the answer was the same. "I promise."

"Do you think he'd let you go?"

That was something he'd occasionally considered before. Not often, because Toreth tended to give the impression that he was perpetually on the verge of walking—or running—away himself. It was a real question, though, and one he couldn't answer. In place of an answer, he said, "You said once that the important thing was that I was happy. Do you still believe that?"

There was a long silence, before she sighed. "Yes, of course. But it's not a fair question. I have to say yes, don't I?"

"No, not if something else is more important to you, especially if it's a good reason. Not, for example, if you still think I'm in real danger from him."

She shook her head, nearly smiling. "You're so...so *reasonable* sometimes. It's absolutely the most annoying thing about you."

"I'll take that to mean that you don't." He gave her a space to argue, but although she frowned, she didn't say anything. Maybe she'd simply decided it was a lost cause. He hoped not. "To get back to the point: I *am* happy." And that surprised him a little, as it always did. "Very happy, in fact. I'm not pretending that Toreth doesn't have an extensive collection of faults, or that he isn't difficult to be with sometimes, or that what I have with him is anything like an average relationship. But it is what I want."

She sat, staring down at the table, biting her lip, then looked up. "Should I ask again?"

It took him a moment to understand her. Then he said, "I still think it would be an incredibly stupid thing to do."

"As stupid as letting someone hang you up by your wrists until they're black and blue?"

"Almost exactly that stupid, yes."

"Oh, dear." She sighed again. "And that's it, I suppose, isn't it? Keir, I'm sorry about what I said, when we were in the bedroom. I'm—"

"No, don't apologize." For whatever it had been. He could feel things beginning, slowly, to return to normal, although they could never be quite the same. Whether the change was for better or worse he'd have to wait and see. "It was my fault for showing you the damn thing in the first place. I should just have explained."

"I don't think it would have mattered much. I'd have freaked out either way. Maybe this was better. At least we talked."

"At least that, yes." He reached out and laid his hand on hers. "And you were right about some things, too. It used to be SimTech that ate up all my time, and now it's SimTech and Toreth, and I haven't been paying as much attention as I should to other things which are just as important."

"Keir, I didn't mean—"

"No." He tightened his grip as she started to pull away. "I'm glad you said it. And we'll do more things together, I promise. Not just shopping—real time alone, to talk."

"That would be nice." She closed her other hand over his, fingertips gently stroking the bruises. "I hate feeling like you're disappearing."

"I'm not, I promise."

"Good." She sat in silence for a while, then shook her head, dismissing a thought unvoiced. "Can I have some more cake?"

"Wouldn't you like me to ice it first?" He smiled, and pulled his hand back gently. "You can have first lick of the bowl."

Pool School

❖

"I should've gone to the canteen earlier," Sara said as she dumped her burden on the coffee-room table and sat down beside him. "All they had left were the really cheap baps, so that's what we've got. The donut's for me, the crisps are yours if you want them."

"Yeah. And I'll have the corned beef," Toreth said. Not too bad if you ate it quickly and didn't concentrate on the flavor. "And the cheese and onion."

"Tough." Sara took possession of the disputed sandwich. "Cheese and onion's mine. You got first pick. That one's cheese and beetroot, have that."

Toreth hated beetroot, as she well knew. "I thought you had a date tonight?" He breathed on his palm and sniffed it suggestively.

She shrugged. "I've got mints in my desk. He'll have to cope. And he'll have to do a lot better than he did on the first date if he's expecting to get close enough for it to matter. Now, where was I?"

Sara unwrapped her sandwich, which Toreth knew was destined to remain untouched for at least five minutes while she finished the story. As usual, Sara continued their previous conversation as if there hadn't been a fifteen-minute break.

"So then Dillian said she'd never even *been* to a strip club. Can you imagine? She's thirty-whatever and never—anyway. So Cele said she had to, just for the aesthetic experience, and I said I'd organize it. Dillian said I'd better not tell Warrick what we were planning, but she was only joking because she called later to say he's free that evening and he's coming, too." Sara picked up half a sandwich, gesturing with it for emphasis rather than eating it. "You know, it's funny but the first time I met Dillian way back when—at the theater, you remember—I thought she was going to turn out to be a bit of a stuck-up rich bitch. But she's okay. Not as friendly as Cele, but okay."

"Don't you want to know what I think about her?" Toreth asked through a mouthful of corned beef.

"No need. I already do. You want to screw her."

210

"She's Warrick's sister," he said, aiming to sound disapproving and very nearly managing it.

"Yeah, and that's why you want to screw her. Because they have that weird identical twin thing going on, even though they aren't." Her eyes narrowed. "In fact, I bet you've thought about doing both of them at the same time. Side-by-side comparison. Or top-and-bottom comparison."

"That's disgusting," Toreth said, grinning hugely.

"I *knew* it!" Sara shrieked with delight, shedding grated cheese liberally. "You are *sick*."

"Maybe." He swallowed the last mouthful. "But I have fucking fantastic dreams."

Sara examined her sandwich, wrapped it up again, and picked up the donut. "So, are you coming on Saturday?"

Toreth hesitated, not entirely sure why. He thought it over while he extracted the limp beetroot from the second sandwich and piled crisps over the lurid pink stains on the synthetic cheese. Warrick was a truly spectacular fuck and utterly shameless in private. In public, though, he still liked to keep a distance and what he called "a minimum standard of civilized behavior." His presence would put a major limit on the amount of fun Toreth could have, especially if Dillian was there, too.

On the other hand, it would be a pity to let Warrick have all the fun—alcohol, great bodies to at least look at, and three lovely women for the evening. It would also make a change. In the weeks since he'd bought the cabinet for Warrick, most of the evenings they'd spent together had been at Warrick's flat, using the cabinet, or fucking in front of it if Warrick didn't want the bruises. They were certainly getting their money's worth out of the gift, but variety would be nice. He squashed the sandwich down, scattering crisp shrapnel over the table and floor. More memos from the cleaners, no doubt. Fuck them. "Yeah, okay. Count me in."

There was no reason for Toreth to worry about the evening, he told himself in the taxi. Sara had organized it, she was responsible for any disasters ensuing. Just so long as nothing happened to Dillian. Like SimTech, Dillian brought out Warrick's worst overprotective streak.

When they reached the club, he assessed it while Sara handed her coat into the cloakroom. Toreth classified these places primarily on how strongly they smelled of stale sweat and whether his feet stuck to the floor. This one had a clean carpet and an air conditioning system that filled the air with a faint, musky perfume. Newly decorated, excellent sound system, lighting low but not dingy. One of Sara's more tasteful venue choices.

There were mixed strippers and an equally mixed crowd. He spotted six or seven groups made up of lower-ranking corporates enjoying an evening entertaining clients on expenses; other groups were probably on early pre-New Year office outings. Single men and couples of various kinds made up the remainder of the crowd. Respectable, insofar as a strip club could be—the sort of place where dancer meant dancer, not anything more available. Toreth relaxed a little.

When Warrick arrived with Cele and Dillian, he wore a smart-casual jacket and tie that screamed corporate. He still attracted a few looks, but probably for the two women with him. His first comment to Sara and Toreth was, "So is this what you two do for fun when I'm not around?"

At this relatively early hour the larger stage was still curtained off, waiting for performances later. They spent a while wandering between the smaller platforms clustered in the middle—spotlit and with and without central poles—watching the dancers. Pairs and singles, in varying gender combinations and degrees of undress, worked the crowd and almost looked to be having fun doing it.

Cele, of course, was in her element, but her cheerfulness didn't have any positive influence on Dillian, who was less friendly than Toreth had seen her for months. Or rather, perfectly friendly with everyone except himself. Maybe it was the time of year stirring bad memories. In recent months she'd seemed to have at least partially forgiven him for the pass over the washing up at the family gathering last New Year. Well, she didn't need to worry. He fully intended to spend this New Year getting pissed with Sara and an assortment of I&I staff Warrick wouldn't want to meet. Fuck families—his own and everyone else's.

Dillian and Sara concentrated on the men. Toreth and Cele had an edge in being able to appreciate all the bodies on display, although Toreth remembered belatedly that was technically also true for Warrick. Warrick was quiet, watching more than talking, but smiling as well. Real smiles, too, not his half-smile mask. Good start to the evening.

"She's nice, don't you think?"

He looked around, but this time Cele was talking to Dillian. Cele nudged her, and pointed out a dark-haired woman, pale-skinned and somehow aloof.

"Just my type," Cele continued. It was hard to tell in the club lighting, but Toreth could have sworn Dillian blushed.

Oh ho. *Interesting.* Toreth circled around to the other side of the group, where he could watch the two women more easily. Dillian had always struck him as what Kel would call "straight, but not narrow." There was something there, definitely. Not an entirely new thing, either, because nothing had fundamentally changed in the way they related to each other.

Cele slipped her arm around Dillian's shoulders, laughed, and pointed. Following her gesture, Toreth spotted Warrick, leaning on one of the stages, looking up at a male dancer. Talking, by the look of it, although Toreth couldn't be sure from this angle.

212

The man was blond, nicely built, and young—very early twenties. After a moment, he crouched down, balancing easily on the balls of his feet. The light caught his hair as he shook his head. Toreth watched, gritting his teeth, resisting the urge to go over. What the hell were they talking about? Much too long for a simple compliment. Finally Warrick reached up and handed over a folded note, a piece of the brightly colored faux-currency for sale behind the bar. At least he hadn't followed the traditional route of tucking the tip into the man's G-string.

The dancer grinned and straightened. Warrick strolled back, smiling to himself. "Well?" Toreth asked, trying to keep the edginess out of his voice.

"Believe it or not, he's a university student at SimTech." Warrick turned to look at the man. "Rather more rhythm than your average computer scientist, I think you'll agree. It's against the university rules for first-year postgrads to have evening jobs, so I thought I'd better reassure him that I have no intention of reporting his extracurricular employment." Warrick looked back, one eyebrow arching slightly. "Was that a satisfactory explanation? Or would you have preferred that I took a camera over to record the interview?"

When Warrick made the effort, he could be insanely annoying. "Jesus, all I said was 'well.'"

"There was a certain . . . never mind. Look but don't touch, I think was the general rule of the establishment?"

"Yes." Don't fucking forget it.

"And that is all I intend to do." Warrick looked around. "Where are Dilly and the others?"

After a few minutes' searching, they found them by an oddly incongruous pool table, tucked away to one side of the room. Sara and Cele were playing—Cele rather well, Sara terribly badly—while Dillian watched. "What the hell's this?" Toreth asked.

Distracted, Sara hit the cue ball harder than was wise, and it took flight. Warrick caught it one-handed and tossed it back to Sara, who dropped it.

"Pool school, until the main show starts," Cele said cheerfully as Sara scrabbled under a chair for the lost ball. "I thought I could teach anyone but I think I might've finally found a hopeless case. Your round, sweetheart," she added to Dillian.

"I'll give you a hand to carry the drinks," Toreth said, starting for the bar before she could refuse the offer.

As they waited at the bar, Toreth said, "I haven't forgotten New Year, by the way."

Dillian's expression frosted over. "What about it?"

"Never again. I promised, and I keep my promises."

"Oh." She looked startled but at least a little pleased, which was just the effect Toreth had hoped for. The fascination Sara had spotted surfaced again, unquenchable. Maybe if he could put her in a positive mood, he'd get somewhere with her—not tonight, but eventually. He could wait.

"I saw the present you bought him," she said suddenly.

Toreth blinked. "What present?" Not that any of them were good things for Dillian to see, but the worst would be—

"The cabinet."

—the cabinet. "He likes antique furniture."

"He showed me inside it."

"Really." Nice of Warrick to warn him. At least it explained the resumption of hostilities.

She looked up at him, her expression fierce and intent. "I'm keeping an eye on him, and I'm watching *you*. I don't care what he says—if it goes too far, don't think I won't call Justice."

He managed to keep his voice level. "He wouldn't thank you for it. Quite the opposite."

Her determination didn't waver. "I know, but I'll do it anyway—because I love him."

"Fine." Only the fact that Warrick would be unbearably tedious about it stopped him from returning the slap from last year and telling her to mind her own business. "Do you know what? I don't care, because there won't be any need. It's all under control. It's just a fucking game."

She frowned, looking as though she were trying to strip the skin and bone away and see right into his mind. Then she nodded. "I hope so."

He glanced away, down the bar, but there was still no one free to serve them. "Nice to see Cele again," he said. "Did you know she was after me to model?"

She visibly adjusted to the change of topic, then said, "She mentioned something like that, yes."

"Keeps passing messages through Sara, and Warrick when she sees him at SimTech. Sounds a bit boring, though. I don't sit still well. Do you ever get naked for her?"

"Do I...?" Her voice shot up in pitch and volume. "Do I *what*?"

Toreth checked the open neck of her shirt—definite blush starting. "Do you ever model for her?" he asked slowly. A misunderstanding, clearly, and all Dillian's fault.

"Oh. Um." The flush deepened, creeping up her throat. "Sometimes."

"What's it like? Do you have fun with her?"

Her mouth opened and closed. Just then, the barman finished serving someone else. Dillian waved to catch his attention. "Drinks over here, please," she called and Toreth smiled.

When they returned to the table with the drinks, the game was still in progress. Cele was obviously doing her best to let Sara down gently, but it was a one-sided affair. Toreth sat beside Warrick, dividing his attention between the pool and the SimTech postgrad, who was dancing on a platform not too far away. Lots of rhythm indeed, and plenty of other assets as well. But Toreth's occasional glances in Warrick's direction revealed no hint of an untoward interest. The blond's G-string was fringed with the scrip notes, and Toreth wondered vaguely what cut the place charged to change them back into real cash. As he watched, the music paused, and the shift changed, replacing the student with a generically blonde girl less to Toreth's taste. Hopefully less to Warrick's taste, too. On the other hand, he couldn't help remembering that Melissa had been blonde when Warrick married her. It was gradually dawning on Toreth that there were less stressful places to spend an evening with Warrick.

Determined to ignore the irrational edginess, he nudged Warrick's elbow. "Warrick?"

"Yes?"

Toreth pointed over to the woman, and Warrick followed his hand. After a moment, Warrick asked, "What about her?"

"What do you think of her?"

His mouth quirked. "Do you want a formal assessment? Very well." Warrick studied her carefully, for what seemed to Toreth to be an unnecessary length of time. "She's very attractive," he said finally. "But—for my personal tastes—a little too feminine. Too soft. I prefer a more athletic look, in women as well as men. More sculpted." He looked back to the pool table, where Cele was reaching for a shot, one knee on the edge of the table. "Speaking of athletic, Cele used to work part-time in a gym. A long time ago, now—even before you met her the first time, I think. I've always thought she has an extremely attractive physique, but back then she was irresistible."

Cele? She and Warrick had always both said they'd never fucked, and what the hell did he mean by irresist—and then he caught Warrick's half smile. *Bastard.* Toreth closed his mouth and returned his full attention to the pool table. "Ever played?" Toreth asked Warrick as the game drew to its inevitable conclusion.

"Oh, yes. Sign of a misspent youth." Warrick sipped his drink. "I played for my college—won a few intercollege matches, too."

Toreth bet that Warrick's youth hadn't been anywhere near as misspent as his own. Played for his fucking *college*, indeed. "Want a game now?"

"Love to."

It's near-impossible to fake never having held a cue before, but not so difficult to play less well than you can. Toreth held back, missing the odd easy pot, assessing Warrick's game. He obviously knew what he was doing, but he was nowhere near up to Toreth's standard. Toreth dropped his game a notch, letting Warrick pull level, before he deliberately fluffed an easy shot to let Warrick win.

Warrick laid his cue down on the side of the table. "Thanks. That was fun." His nostalgic smile stirred evilly entertaining ideas in Toreth's mind.

"Another game?" Toreth offered. "We could make it a bit more serious, if you like?"

"You mean betting?"

"Something like that. How about strip pool? One item of clothing per game."

"Oh, good idea!" Cele exclaimed.

"Strip..." Warrick looked around the club. Nothing to worry about there, as Toreth had already decided. This was the kind of place that would treat all-male strip pool as a spectator sport, not a reason for violence.

"Oh, go on," Sara said.

Dillian looked neutral about the idea, but then she disliked him and the other competitor was her brother. Toreth was fairly sure any incestuous yearnings between her and Warrick took place only in Toreth's own fantasies.

"Well now, why not?" Warrick picked the cue up again and smiled. "For one thing, if all the games take that long, we'll both still be fully dressed when the place closes."

"I'll get some more drinks," Sara said. "Same again for everyone?"

"See if they sell popcorn," Cele called after her as she left.

Not wanting to scare his opponent, Toreth kept his play down for the next game. He didn't let it drag on too long, though. At the end, Warrick removed his jacket, hanging it neatly over the back of a chair. Toreth watched, sipping his drink and nibbling a handful of the popcorn that Sara had managed to procure from somewhere. Salted, just as he preferred it. "Wrists hurting?" he asked Warrick in an undertone as they set the table up again.

Warrick looked at him blankly for a moment, then smiled. "Not at all." He tugged one sleeve back. "See?"

Toreth only noticed the faint marks because he knew they must be there. They hadn't used the cabinet since last weekend, but even with the healing accelerator cream from the I&I pharmacy, the bruises should look worse. He took Warrick's hand and ran his thumb over the skin of his wrist. A barely perceptible oiliness hinted at some kind of concealer. Warrick planning ahead, as usual. Well, thank God for that. Dillian had been enough of a pain in the neck already tonight without seeing her brother bruised to fuck.

Toreth put losing the next game down to sheer carelessness and distracting thoughts about Warrick in the cabinet. He played as he'd played in the last game, giving Warrick chances, keeping him hoping. The result should have been the same. Warrick, though, performed notably better. Maybe he hadn't been kidding about being a whiz back at university. Toreth had left him too big a lead, and at the end he watched Warrick sink the black, then exchange the cue for his glass with a very satisfied smile. "Fuck. You're a lot better at this than you let on." Toreth added his jacket to Warrick's—the last piece of clothing he intended to lose for the evening.

216

"It's a long time since I played. Although we have a setup in the sim—have done for years." Warrick racked the balls with millimeter precision, then lifted the triangle away without moving a single ball. "Nicely limited physical problem with broad user familiarity. Your break."

The next game went quickly and decisively. Warrick slowly removed his tie, rolled it up and slipped it into the pocket of his jacket, looking distinctly less happy. "Want to change your mind?" Toreth asked as he set the table up. "Last chance."

Warrick smiled. "Oh, I don't think so. I'm just getting my game back. I think you'll be in trouble soon. In fact, I should offer *you* a chance to back out."

Obviously bluffing—Toreth knew false confidence when he saw it. "Oh yeah? Want to up the stakes? Loser pays a forfeit?"

"Which is?"

Toreth savored a delicious image of Warrick, naked, on his knees, sucking Toreth off in the middle of the crowded club. He would never do it, of course. And Dillian would...well, the English language didn't possess the adjectives to describe the fit she would throw at the mere suggestion. It would be worth it just for that. "Oh, we can decide that at the end of the game," Toreth said.

Warrick tilted his head, staring at the tip of his cue as he chalked it, weighing the suggestion up.

"That's okay," Toreth said. "Since you're obviously going to lose, I don't blame you for being scared to—"

Warrick's head snapped up. "Scared? Nothing of the sort. I was merely trying to come up with an appropriate idea, that's all." Warrick set the chalk down decisively on the edge of the table. "I'm sure I'll be able to think of something when the time comes."

"You heard that, didn't you?" Toreth asked their three spectators.

Sara, Cele, and Dillian all nodded. For a moment, the conspiratorial expression of barely suppressed amusement shared by Dillian and Cele stirred unease, then Warrick tapped him on the shoulder, and he forgot about it. "My break, I think," Warrick said.

This time, with Warrick irrevocably committed, Toreth stopped fucking about and played seriously. Time to show off exactly what he could do and to let Warrick know how thoroughly he'd been had.

Warrick trounced him. Maybe, Toreth thought as the black went down while Toreth still had half a dozen balls on the table, he didn't know false confidence when he saw it after all. Quite a crowd had gathered, and when Toreth pulled off his shirt, there were appreciative whistles, from male and female onlookers. Cele and Sara led it, of course.

In the next game, Toreth played his hardest, and also not far below his absolute best. It wasn't enough. Warrick played safe for a few minutes, giving him no chances, until the balls were beautifully set up, then he cleaned up the table in one visit with remorseless efficiency. "Shoes count as one item," Warrick said.

"No way. Two."

Warrick turned to the crowd, obviously appealing to them for a ruling. Which was unanimous. Toreth removed both shoes, watching Warrick, who leaned against the edge of the table with a faint smile curving his lips. God, he was *enjoying* this. All his protestations about keeping things quiet in public and here he was, center of attention, watching his regular fuck stripping in front of his sister and one of his oldest friends—and smirking like he'd planned it all along.

Toreth racked the balls. Over the music and voices, he could just hear Sara behind him. "I hope he's got smart underwear on," she said.

"What if he ended up being taken to hospital?" Cele chimed in.

Sara choked on her drink. "Oh my God! Does your mother say that, too?"

"All the time. And 'but what if you get hit by a bus?' Even though everything's been autoguided since before I was born. I always thought it was a Service thing."

"No. Must be a mother thing," Sara said. "Give me some more popcorn. Dillian, does Kate . . . "

Toreth shut them out and concentrated on his game. Winning outright was no longer a realistic option, but if he could get Warrick out of his shirt at least, then he'd be able to say he hadn't been comprehensively thrashed when the story went around the section next week. No way would Sara keep quiet about *this,* no matter what threats he issued.

Losing that game wouldn't have been quite so bad if Warrick hadn't finished the frame by potting the black off three cushions. The crowd clapped, the noise transmuting into whistles as Toreth stripped off his jeans.

"Oh, yes!" Cele crowed as Toreth revealed his white briefs. "Timeless classic! Now, girls, you see what I was going on about before." Cele gestured expansively, taking him in from head to foot. "My dream model, if he'd only agree to stand still long enough."

Dillian and Sara were laughing too much to say anything at all.

Cele turned to Warrick. "Any chance of making the forfeit . . . ?"

"Oh, no." Warrick smiled as he lifted the rack away, showing a feral glint of teeth. "I don't think so. Nothing that easy."

"Maybe I'll do it anyway," Toreth said. It didn't sound quite so boring now that he had an incentive. A few hours alone with Cele would be plenty of time to find out more about her and Dillian.

Cele brightened. "Really? I don't suppose you'd like to put that in writing, would you?"

"Are you still playing, Toreth?" Warrick asked silkily. "Or do you want to concede the game? It's a foregone conclusion, really." Toreth downed his drink and picked up his cue. "Keeping the socks?" Warrick asked in a low voice as Toreth passed him.

"I thought I'd try a bit of distraction."

Whether the distraction worked or not, Warrick wasn't quite on his previous form. Or maybe he was sandbagging again to spend longer watching Toreth bend over the table. Either way, Toreth held him to a closer game, and was even briefly ahead, before Warrick took the first of his last three balls with an admittedly impressive double, leaving himself an easy cleanup. Warrick watched the black trickle into the pocket, then turned, eyebrow arching. "Well?"

No way was he playing the last game in socks and nothing else. He rolled the socks together, then batted them over to Sara with his hand. She caught them and called, "Good luck."

"You'll need it," Cele added.

Actually what he needed was a miracle. Warrick grinned, twirled his cue around in his hand and said, "I'll make it quick."

Which he did—fast, but brutal. No showing off in this game. Toreth grimly played his best, but it took only a few minutes before the last hopes of avoiding embarrassment vanished with the black ball. Applause changed into a slow clap, and Toreth sighed, waved his hands to indicate surrender, and reached for the waistband of his briefs. Warrick grabbed his wrist and stopped him. "Wait," Warrick said, then disappeared into the crowd.

Toreth sat on the edge of the table and tried to maintain an air of dignity in the face of the forfeit suggestions being offered around him. Most of them were illegal, physically impossible, or both. Some of the spectators drifted away back to the stage, or to the bar. Most didn't, as there was so obviously still more to come. Eventually, Warrick excuse-me'd his way back through the crowd, wearing an expression of gleeful anticipation that made Toreth's heart sink. "Where the hell have you been?" Toreth asked.

"Arranging your forfeit." Warrick offered his hand. "Come on."

Bemused, Toreth let Warrick lead him across the bar, crowd parting for them and closing in behind. He counted a dozen grabs on various parts of his anatomy—although at least two were Cele—before . . .

"Oh, no, no, no. No fucking way!"

"If I recall correctly, you were the one who suggested the idea of forfeits in the first place. Five minutes up there, then the briefs come off."

"Now just hang on one fucking minute—"

"I could make it ten," Warrick said blandly. "Or twenty even. All evening, in fact, since we didn't set terms before we started." Toreth stared, unable to think of a reply. "Or naked from the beginning, if you'd rather, but then how would the audience show their appreciation?"

"You are dead." Toreth climbed onto the platform. "So fucking dead, you have no idea."

Warrick smiled, tapped his watch, and sat down at a table with the other three.

The spotlights came up and Toreth stepped into them, blinking at little at the brightness. The music was already playing, of course. He stood still for a moment, catching the beat, until a piece of popcorn hit his midsection and he heard Sara exclaim, "Good shot!"

Traitor.

He'd been to enough of these places to have a general idea of the principles, and dancing was a critical club pick-up skill. Listening to the music, he let the rhythm slide down his spine and into his hips. He heard laughter from the crowd, catcalls and whistles, and more or less encouraging comments from the dancers nearby.

The spotlights left him feeling oddly isolated. The audience was visible but shadowed, forcing him to squint a little to see faces. Amateurs were clearly excluded from the no touching rule, though, because hands reached in from beyond the circle of light, tucking in money but also groping before they withdrew. He kept moving around the platform, using the music to slip away from the most insistent hands. By the time the five minutes were up, he felt thoroughly mauled.

Good job, Toreth thought, that he'd kept an eye on his own watch because Warrick, the bastard, kept quiet as the time ticked past the mark. He paused, looking over to the expectant table. Cele lifted her hand to her mouth and whistled piercingly. "Off!" she called, and the rest of the onlookers picked up the chant.

Toreth grinned, and bowed. Notes scattered onto the stage like confetti as he pulled down the briefs and threw them in the general direction of Sara. Then he stayed in place, one hand holding on to the pole, leaning away from it, listening to the shadowy crowd applauding until the spotlights went out. As his eyes adjusted back to the lower lights, he knelt and scooped up the paper money. Might as well take his earnings.

"Yes, maybe, but I'm talking *useful* length," Cele was saying as Toreth approached the table. "That's what counts, isn't it? Come on, Keir—back me up on this one. My artistic reputation's at stake here."

"Ahem," Warrick said pointedly, and the conversation stopped.

Cele looked up at Toreth, a question forming, and he shook his head as he dropped the notes on the table. "Nope. I don't have a tape measure and anyway, you've seen all you're seeing for the evening."

"I'm afraid the underwear is missing in action," Warrick said, holding out Toreth's clothes in a neatly folded stack. Then he lowered his voice and added, "Not that I have a problem with that."

Once dressed, Toreth sat down and drained Warrick's drink, then made a grab for Sara's. She snatched it out of his reach. "Jesus, that pays well." Toreth looked at the colorful notes on the table in front of Warrick, separated into piles by denomination. Another stack seemed to be comm numbers written on scraps of paper and torn edges of scrip money. "I'm in the wrong fucking job."

Warrick gathered the cash up. "I promised to distribute it among the dancers, in return for letting you use the facilities without a licence."

"What, now you're pimping for me as well? Nice one."

"Good God, if only. I could probably afford to retire." Warrick leaned down and kissed his neck. "Or at least to drop a sponsor or two at SimTech."

Speechless again, Toreth watched him go. When he turned back to the table, Cele was grinning. Even Dillian was smirking, trying unsuccessfully to wipe the expression away when she caught his gaze.

So, now that you've seen the goods, can I interest you in a fuck? "Is he often like this when he's out with you two?" he asked Dillian.

Dillian shook her head, still smiling. "Not very often, no. And hardly ever since—"

"Before SimTech," Cele said.

Dillian frowned. "Before Melissa."

Toreth wondered whether it was the thought of Melissa that annoyed her, or the idea that he might have had a positive influence on Warrick.

"Coincidence of timing," Cele said briskly. "We've all got to grow up sometime." Then she grinned. "Well, you hard-working professional types do. *I* plan to stay wild and reckless until I get to be old and crabby enough to shout at the young 'uns and hit people with my walking stick."

Sara raised her glass. "I'll drink to that."

Lacking a glass of his own to toast with, Toreth took advantage of the distraction to pocket the comm numbers that Warrick had left on the table. The money might be gone, but he was quite happy to take remuneration in kind. He'd paid a lot worse forfeits in his time.

Without the Game

❖

It had started the previous night, as Toreth had stood over the bed in Warrick's flat. Warrick lay asleep, or maybe passed out, damp with sweat, his wrists bruised by the manacles. Quite suddenly, Toreth had been angry. Inexplicably, irrationally, bewilderingly furious. He'd left before Warrick woke, walking home through slushy city snow in the hope that the cold February air would clear his mind. By the time he reached his flat all he'd achieved was wet feet and a headache. He'd slept fitfully and spent the whole of the day in a tired, bad-tempered haze, with the anger spiking every time he thought about the night before.

Then Warrick had called him just before he left work and asked him—no, told him—to come around tonight. Not a mention of the fact that he'd not been there that morning. Shortly afterwards, Sara had asked him what on earth was wrong with him, wasn't he getting enough? and his reply had been...well, flowers were at the top of his to-do list for tomorrow.

He almost hadn't made it to Warrick's. In the taxi over, watching the wintery night passing, he'd had the very strong feeling that he didn't want to see Warrick. He still didn't understand why he hadn't changed his mind right then and gone home. Or why he hadn't done so a little later, when Warrick had opened to door to the flat, looked right through him, and said, "You're late."

The argument had started approximately ten seconds after that, in the hallway, and they were still at it now, fifteen minutes later, in the bedroom, with no end in sight. A serious argument, eroding his self-control with every word. Any moment now, he was going to lose his temper, or at least his ability to put up with Warrick's "*I'm* being *perfectly* reasonable" tone of voice, which drove him mad at the best of times. This was rapidly heading towards being one of the worst times ever.

"So how often would you say we've done it in the last month?" Toreth asked.

"I have no idea. But it's hardly 'every time' you've been here."

You liar. You fucking *liar.* He made another, futile effort. "I'm not saying we can't do it ever again, I'm just saying you need to give your wrists a chance to heal up first."

222

"I'd like to do it tonight," Warrick said, "and I still fail to see the problem."

Finally, his temper slipped away from him and he shouted, "That's because you don't bloody well want to see it!" Grabbing Warrick's hands, he held them up in front of his face. "Look at them! No, don't fucking glaze over at me, *look* at them."

Warrick tugged sharply, trying to pull away, but Toreth held him fast. Probably wouldn't do much for Warrick's concentration, but he didn't want him turning away, which would make it that much easier for him not to hear what he didn't want to.

"Pretend they're mine," Toreth said. "Pretend they're Dillian's and I did it to her."

That suggestion finally had the desired effect. Warrick blinked, focusing, hopefully seeing the livid bruises with some degree of objectivity. For a moment, Toreth thought that might be enough, but then Warrick shook his head. "They're only bruises. If we do it again tonight, they'll be slightly worse bruises tomorrow, that's all."

He should go. He should turn around and walk out right now before he did something unforgivable. He tried bleeding off a little of the anger into an exasperated sigh. "Okay. Were your fingers numb this morning?"

"Toreth, I don't need a medical lecture." Warrick had stopped resisting his hold, apparently deciding to try ignoring the situation instead.

"I think you do. Now answer the fucking question."

That phrase drew a sharp look. "Yes. A little. They're perfectly all right now."

"Warrick, I do this for a living. No, keep looking at me. You don't want to hear it the rest of the time, fine. But you're going to hear it now. I do this for a living. If you keep overdoing this, the repeated pressure from the cuffs and the chronic inflammation are going to damage the nerves. *Permanently.*"

"I took the anti-inflammatories as soon as I got up."

"It makes no fucking difference in the long run. If we do it tonight, you might be okay tomorrow, but that's not the point. I know it's going to happen in the end, because I've seen it before. There's only so much that can be done with nerve regeneration to repair that kind of damage. At worst you could lose the use of your hands, and at best you'll be in pain for the rest of your life. Even if they regraft the whole fucking arm, it might not cure it. Do you know what phantom nerve pain is?"

"Of course," Warrick said. "It's come up in several sim projects. But in any case, they are my hands. Not that I'm not touched by your concern."

"Christ, are you even fucking listening to me?" The idea of hitting Warrick was becoming so damn tempting. Not to hurt him, but to make him *see* past this infuriating, uncharacteristic fixation. "Right. Fine. You want another reason? When I interrogate a prisoner—before I start—I get something called a damage waiver. It tells me exactly what I can do to them, how much they can be injured. Whether they can die."

223

"Toreth—"

"Shut up and *listen*. If I exceed the terms of the waiver, I'm breaking the law. I could be dismissed from I&I. If I went far enough I could get re-education, or restrictive detention. Do you have any idea of the life expectancy of paras in prison? Let's just say I wouldn't need to bother packing a fucking toothbrush." He shook Warrick's hands sharply. "This doesn't *have* a waiver. It's assault with intent to occasion actual bodily harm. It doesn't matter whether you consented or not, or even if you got on your knees and begged me to do it. The bastards at Justice wouldn't give a shit about any of that, if some officious medic reported it. They'd just get all wet and sticky about the chance to screw over someone from I&I."

Warrick seemed to be listening now, at least if he wasn't simply waiting until Toreth ran out of things to say.

"The time when we broke your wrist, pratting about with that chair, do you know what I was thinking in Casualty? 'If anyone calls this in, if Justice finds out, I'm fucked.' You were there in fucking *handcuffs*, Warrick—handcuffs that I took from work. It was a miracle nothing happened. Okay, in the end I might not have gone to prison, or even been sacked, but it would've done my career no fucking good at all. I easily could've been bounced back down to junior for something like that. Bringing the division into disrepute, or whatever the hell they call it. Do you at least understand *that*?"

Warrick nodded, his expression closed.

Was he finally getting somewhere? Already knowing the answer, Toreth asked, "Did you go home for New Year?"

Warrick stayed silent for a moment, then said, "No."

"And why not?"

"Because..."

"*Say* it."

"Because I didn't want Dilly to see the bruises."

"And I was fucking glad you didn't go, because if she had she would've been down at Justice in five fucking seconds flat and I'd have got an arrest warrant for New Year. I still might, because you know damn well you can't hide from her forever. And if it isn't Dillian, it'll be someone else. It's going to happen." Toreth stopped and took a deep breath; he was almost scaring himself now. "I'm only going to say this once more. Pull yourself together and get a grip on it, or I'm taking that fucking cabinet back to the Shop and getting a credit note that'll keep you supplied with gags and belts for the rest of your life. You can fuck up your hands if you want to. Do you know what?—I don't care. But I'm not going to risk screwing up my life because you're so obsessed with suspension fucks that you don't even notice that—" He stopped dead, understanding sweeping over him like vertigo and leaving him dumb with the shock of revelation.

You don't even notice any more that it's *me* there with you.

224

Eventually, he realized that he'd tightened his grip on Warrick's hands—he must be hurting him. Letting go, he stepped back. Warrick lowered his hands slowly, and rubbed them together, kneading his palms with his thumbs. His expression hadn't changed, and Toreth couldn't tell whether he was thinking about what he'd said, or had noticed the sudden halt, or was still being stubborn. Again, he wanted to hit him, shake him, anything to get a reaction from him, but now the impulse was distant and easily ignored.

He finally found his voice. "Warrick, you know it's not that I don't want to do it. Just the opposite. But give it a rest. A month. Six weeks would be better. And then we can do it again. Think how good it'll be when we do, when it's been so long since the last time." That was beginning to sound dangerously like pleading, so he shut up.

Warrick looked at him for a moment, still unreadable, then walked away to the window and stood staring out at the falling snow, his reflection hidden. The snowflakes framed him, each one briefly picked out by the light from the window. Toreth sat down on the bed, wondering if anything he'd said had actually made an impression. He hated the idea of issuing an ultimatum. In fact, he'd never done it before, because it meant acknowledging that either of them might have the right. This time it mattered enough that he didn't care.

A minute passed, then two, and he tried to decide what he was going to do if Warrick still insisted on going on with it. Walk out if he had any sense, but he doubted it. Adrenaline from the anger and frustration still pumped through him and whatever his mind was saying, his body wanted Warrick. Wanted him desperately, even like that, if that was all he could have. Thinking with his dick, Sara would say.

"I'm sorry," Warrick said.

The last of the anger vanished, replaced by relief so intense that he felt sick, and glad that he was already sitting down. At least he could manage to sound steady. "Don't be sorry, just be sensible about it."

Warrick turned around to face him, and leaned against the window, his hands on the sill. "Yes. I will be. Or at least I'll try to be, in future. You're quite correct about the situation. Even if I haven't been obsessed, precisely, then I've certainly been thinking about it far too much. Not only with you, but at work, the rest of the time, and—" He shrugged. "All right, obsessed probably *is* the word. I should've noticed it myself. It's no different to overdoing it in the sim, and I've warned enough people about that over the years."

"And?"

"And yes, like the sim, a break is a very good idea. I need to...regain some perspective. We'll stop, for however long you think is best. I'll give you the key, if you like, and you can take it home with you."

He nodded. "Thanks."

225

"No, thank you. For…"

Toreth waited through the silence of Warrick trying to paraphrase something he thought was going to panic him. These days they both knew what the pauses meant, and sometimes he felt like telling Warrick that he might as well go ahead and say whatever it was. Not today, though.

"Thank you for making me see the situation more clearly." Christ, that was bland. It must have had started out life as something good. Well, it didn't matter, as long as Warrick meant what he'd said, and he usually did.

"No problem. Any time." He kicked off his shoes and moved further up the bed. "Now, come to bed and we can fuck. If you still want to." Then he found himself hesitating, looking for the right words. Must be contagious. In the end, all he could think of was, "Without the game. Just us."

Which sounded unbelievably stupid, said out loud. Luckily, Warrick didn't seem to think so because he smiled, warm and genuine. "I can't think of anything I'd enjoy more."

Printed in the United States
220536BV00001B/62/P

9 781934 081105